Margaret Mayhew was born in London and her earliest childhood memories were of the London Blitz. She began writing in her mid-thirties and had her first novel published in 1976. She is married to American aviation author, Philip Kaplan, and lives in Gloucestershire.

OUR YANKS

It was August 1943 — and into the quiet country village of King's Thorpe roared a Fighter Group of the American Eighth Army Air Force. The villagers had never seen anything like them before. Some, like the Brigadier, hated them on sight. They were late for this war just like they'd been for the last. They chewed gum, smoked in the street and whistled at girls. Young Sally Barnet — fifteen-going-on-eighteen — thought them gorgeous and used her large blue eyes to good advantage. The one thing you couldn't do about the Yanks was ignore them, and finally everyone — even the Brigadier — came to accept them as their own.

Books by Margaret Mayhew
Published by The House of Ulverscroft:

THE RAILWAY KING
THE FLAME AND THE FURNACE
THE MASTER OF AYSGARTH
OLD SOLDIERS NEVER DIE

MARGARET MAYHEW

OUR YANKS

Complete and Unabridged

CHARNWOOD
Leicester

First published in Great Britain by
Corgi Books
London

First Charnwood Edition
published 2001
by arrangement with
Transworld Publishers
a division of
The Random House Group Limited
London

British Library CIP Data

Mayhew, Margaret
Our Yanks.—Large print ed.—
Charnwood library series
1. World War, *1939 – 1945*—Social aspects
—England—Fiction
2. Americans—England—Fiction
3. Love stories 4. Large type books
I. Title
823.9′14 [F]

ISBN 0–7089–9292–7

Published by
F. A. Thorpe (Publishing)
Anstey, Leicestershire

Set by Words & Graphics Ltd.
Anstey, Leicestershire
Printed and bound in Great Britain by
T. J. International Ltd., Padstow, Cornwall

This book is printed on acid-free paper

For Isabella, George, Charlie and Luis

and

For all the Yanks who came Over Here —
especially those who never went home

Acknowledgements

I thank the following who told me about their memories of Northamptonshire village life under American ‘occupation’ during the Second World War: Bill Sharpe, George Sansom, Arthur and Doris Hartley, Mary Bailey, Kath Fenn, Jim Brown, Mary Broughton, Arthur Bould, Doris Price, Nora Masters, Kenneth Nelson, John Wooding and Phyllis Scotney.

I am also grateful to American Eighth Air Force veterans Merle Olmsted and Jack Ilfrey for their very generous assistance, to military aviation historians Tony Palenski and David Knight for their expert advice, to Eleanor Allen, Colin Basford, Tricia Quitmann, Andrew Vidal, Oliver and Karen O’Sullivan. And I thank Jane and John Paige for all their kind hospitality and their wonderful help with my research for this book. As ever, I thank my editor, Diane Pearson, and my husband, Philip Kaplan, who patiently answered so many questions about Yanks.

They brought colour into our lives, and when they went away it was all grey again.

An Englishwoman remembering the American forces in England in the Second World War.

I still remember the Yanks almost more than I do the war.

A Suffolk woman.

We won't do much talking until we've done more flying. We hope that when we leave, you'll be glad we came.

Brigadier General Ira C. Eaker, Commander of the United States Eighth Army Air Force in Britain, speaking at a dinner held to welcome him in 1942.

All my love,
as Always.
And, thank you, Michael.
Mary.

An anniversary remembrance note on a wreath at the American cemetery in Madingley, Cambridge, left on the grave of a young American flyer killed in 1944.

Preface

After the Fall of France in June 1940, during the Second World War, Great Britain fought on alone against Nazi Germany until the Japanese attacked the American Fleet at Pearl Harbor on 7th December 1941 and the United States entered the war.

American troops began to arrive in the United Kingdom in early 1942 and the United States Eighth Army Air Force started building their own operational air bases in East Anglia and the Midlands, as well as taking over some former RAF stations. Remote rural communities suddenly found themselves invaded and occupied, not by Germans, but by Americans.

1

The Reverend Henry Dawe, Rector of King's Thorpe in Northamptonshire, was the first to arrive for the Parochial Church Council meeting on an August evening in 1943. The meeting took place, as usual, in a lofty room that had been added onto the back of the sixteenth-century rectory in Victorian times and was used for various parish functions. The room faced west, looking out across the old croquet lawn and the area of rough grass beyond it that sloped down towards the stone boundary wall and Willow Brook. At six o'clock, and with double summer time, the sunlight was still streaming down through the high windows showing up dust motes swirling around like plankton. For some reason, in spite of all efforts with mops and brooms, the room was always full of dust. It gathered as grey fluff under tables and chairs and snowballed across the floor to hide under radiators and pipes and in dark corners. The rector dragged one of the trestle tables into the centre of the room and flapped at it with his handkerchief before starting to move the necessary number of chairs. He was on the fourth when the outside door opened and Sam Barnet, village baker and one of the two church-wardens, stood there. Rock solid, dependable, worthy. 'Get the bigwigs and the parish worthies on your side right from the start,' a bishop had once advised the rector candidly, many years ago. 'You can't do the job without them and they can make your life a hell.' Four generations of Barnets had baked bread for King's Thorpe in unbroken succession and this great-grandson was, fortunately, on the rector's side. On the whole, he thought, most people in the village *were*, but he was well aware of his shortcomings — of his failure to give a strong pastoral leadership, of his rather uninspiring sermons and his tendency to vacillate, of his advancing age. There was also all the awkwardness of having no wife and the circumstances surrounding that.

'Evening, Rector. I'll give you a hand with those.'

'Thank you so much, Mr Barnet.'

The remaining seven chairs were in place round the table in a jiffy and the rector was doing some more flicking with his handkerchief when the other Council members began to arrive. Miss Cutteridge, the PCC secretary — in an apologetic rush although she was several minutes early — Miss Skinner, deputy head teacher of the village school, with firm tread, Mr and Mrs Dakin, devout and unfailing worshippers, Mr Wells, retired bank manager and the council treasurer, Miss Hooper, the church organist, Mr Rate, the local builder and, precisely as the nearby church clock struck six, Brigadier Mapperton, the other churchwarden for nearly fifteen years, and one of the biggest wigs, who was on nobody's side but his own.

'All present, Rector?'

'Except for Lady Beauchamp, Brigadier. I'm sure she'll be here in a moment.'

'No idea of time, foreigners. Well, let's get on with it.'

'I think perhaps we should wait a few minutes . . . '

'Damned inconsiderate.'

The rector wasn't sure if the remark applied to himself or to Lady Beauchamp but, at that moment, to his relief, she arrived. Anyone from a neighbouring village or town counted as foreign to most of the King's Thorpe population, but the brigadier had probably meant it literally. A Hungarian father accounted for Lady Beauchamp's rather exotic dark looks, though it was the rector's understanding that her mother had been completely English and that she had been born in England. She certainly spoke without a trace of any accent.

'Good evening, Rector. I'm sorry to be the last.'

He smiled at her, well aware of the brigadier glowering away beside him. 'We haven't begun yet, Lady Beauchamp.' She was easily the youngest member of the council, having valiantly stepped into her late husband's shoes in the family tradition. He felt sorry for her having to sit through what he knew to be somewhat tedious meetings, but, if she was bored, she always hid it well.

They moved to their places round the table and he bowed his head in prayer. 'Heavenly Father, we ask Thy blessing on this meeting and Thy guidance in all our deliberations. Grant us understanding and tolerance of each other and help us to discern Thy Will and so fulfil Thy purpose for this ancient and beautiful church on Earth, through Jesus Christ our Lord. Amen.'

The prayer was his own composition, tailor-made for the occasion. He varied it from time to time, but the plea for understanding and tolerance was always included in one form or another: a warning shot across the bows that he sincerely hoped would take effect. It was his task, as chairman, to keep the peace.

The meeting began peaceably enough. The minutes of the last meeting were read out by Miss Cutteridge and duly approved and signed. An apology for absence from Mr Hobbs was also read out and accepted without quibble. Having the largest farm in the parish, he had a cast-iron alibi at harvest time and the rector suspected that Ronald Hobbs's general unpopularity made his absence rather welcome. Arrangements for the Harvest Festival were discussed and for a forthcoming jumble sale at the village hall in aid of the Red Cross. Visits to the sick were organized, and Miss Cutteridge and Mrs Dakin volunteered to recruit ladies in the village to carry out needlework repairs to some of the church hassocks. Lady Beauchamp kindly agreed to a coffee morning being held at the Manor in November to raise money for the church flowers at Christmas. A recent inspection for deathwatch beetle had, thankfully, proved negative.

The rector moved on to the thornier problem of the leaking roof in the north transept. At the last meeting Mr Rate had offered to carry out the work at cost price and taken considerable umbrage when Brigadier Mapperton had insisted on an estimate from another builder in Peterborough. The estimate received had been considerably more than Mr Rate's but the brigadier was not ready to let the matter rest there.

'You get what you pay for, that's the point. Prescott's will do a first-rate job.'

Miss Cutteridge's shorthand pencil faltered above her notebook and Bill Rate went as red as his bricks. 'Are you implying that my work is shoddy?'

'That chap you sent to do the leak in our conservatory was no good. Went on leaking just the same.'

'If you'd told me there was a problem, Brigadier, I'd've come round and seen to it myself.'

'No point. I telephoned Prescott's and they came at once and did the job properly.'

The rector intervened hurriedly, smoothing the builder's ruffled feathers. 'I'm sure we all have every confidence in you, Mr Rate. Your firm has carried out excellent work for us in the past.'

In the end it was put to the vote and the brigadier defeated, but far from satisfied. The next item on the agenda was to decide how best to spend a recent legacy. The late Miss Dorothy Weatherington, a spinster of the parish, had left the church one hundred pounds in her will to be spent as the Parochial Church Council saw fit. It would have been much simpler, in many ways, if she had been more specific, the rector thought wearily: a memorial tablet, fabric repairs, upkeep of the graveyard . . . As it was, the field was wide open. Leonard Dakin raised his hand. 'Since we all learned of this generous legacy, Rector, my wife and I have both prayed for guidance from the Lord in the matter.'

'Indeed, we all look to God to guide us, Mr Dakin.'

'Our prayers were answered, Rector. God spoke to us very clearly. His message was that the money be spent on creating a Lady chapel in the south side aisle. Thora and I both sincerely believe that there is a great need of a quiet corner for private prayer; for worshippers to commune without disturbance.'

'I hardly think there would be enough space available, Mr Dakin.'

'Oh, but there would, Rector. The aisle pews stop several feet short of those in the nave. There's quite sufficient room to make a small chapel. It would only require, say, a dozen chairs and kneelers and, of course, an altar — carved of wood, perhaps, by a local craftsman. The altar cloth could be embroidered by our talented needlewomen in the village. The statue of Our Lady should perhaps be commissioned from outside, but Miss Weatherington's generous legacy should be more than adequate.'

Brigadier Mapperton shifted impatiently. 'Our Lady? Statue? All sounds like a lot of damned popery to me. We've got a perfectly good altar already. No earthly need for another one and certainly not with that woman on it. We got rid of the Pope so we didn't have to have all that nonsense, Dakin. Next thing we know you'll want the rector dressed up in lace and throwing incense around.'

Miss Skinner said briskly, 'I don't think Mr Dakin intends anything as extreme as that, Brigadier. But I must say I agree with you. I can't see the need for a Lady chapel. In my view, the money would be far better spent on things we really *do* need — new hymn books, for example, new robes for the choir — some of them are almost beyond repair. There are plenty of practical possibilities.'

Miss Hooper's hand shot up. 'How about the organ, Rector? The bellows are starting to go. If we don't do something about them soon I won't be able to play at all.'

'There's a special fund for the organ,' Thora Dakin said stubbornly. 'If Miss Weatherington had intended her legacy to be spent on it, she would surely have said so. In our prayers Leonard and I clearly discerned God's will — '

'What God wants and Miss Weatherington intended may not be the same thing at all.'

'That's *blasphemous*, Miss Hooper.'

The organist shook her frizzy nest of grey hair. 'No it isn't. It's a fact. We have to decide what Miss Weatherington would have approved of and I don't think she'd have liked your Lady chapel idea. She was never one for anything High Church. She liked things kept simple. I know that for a fact. Isn't that so, Rector?'

He sidestepped adroitly: 'As a matter of fact, I was going to suggest that the legacy might be spent on repairing the cracked bell.'

Brigadier Mapperton shifted again. 'What's the point of that? We can't ring the blessed things. Not while the war's on. That's the invasion signal.'

'I realize that, of course, Brigadier, but it occurred to me that it would be very nice if, when the war ends, we were able to ring out a full peal of bells in celebration of peace.'

The treasurer shook his head dolefully. 'We won't have much to celebrate if the Germans win.'

Miss Skinner delivered a schoolmistress's sharp reprimand: 'There's no *question* of them winning, Mr Wells. None whatever. We shall go on fighting until the enemy is defeated. And, of course, now that the Americans have entered the war, things should be much easier.'

'Damned Yanks,' the Brigadier barked. 'Left it to the last moment, as usual, when we've done all the dirty work. Only came in when the Japs caught them napping. They don't know the first thing about fighting . . . no discipline, no backbone. All talk and no action. Mollycoddle their men — '

'Could we perhaps return to the item under discussion . . . '

Miss Skinner nodded. 'Of course, Rector. I'm afraid we've gone rather off-course.' She looked round the table. 'I think Miss Weatherington would have approved of the Rector's proposal about the bell.' A firm glance towards the Dakins. 'And that it would certainly have God's blessing. It's a *splendid* idea. How astute of you to think of it, Rector.'

'Thank you, Miss Skinner. It occurred to me, you see, that the sound of church bells has played a very ancient role in our country's history. It is a sound that was just as familiar to a man's ears a thousand years ago as it is to ours today. A sound that summons us to prayer, that celebrates our joys, tolls for our griefs and gives thanks for our deliverances.' He quite surprised himself with his eloquence and fervour and was even more surprised when, after only a brief discussion, everyone agreed except the Dakins, who eventually, and reluctantly, gave way. The next item on the agenda — pruning and clearing to be done around the graveyard in the autumn — went smoothly, Mr Wells volunteering to organize a working party to tackle the job by the end of October. The rector braced himself for the final item on the agenda: Any Other Business. He had another proposal to make and the brigadier's earlier remarks had warned him of the rocks that could lie ahead. He coughed and cleared his throat.

'I think we are all aware that the aerodrome outside our village, previously occupied by the RAF, is about to be handed over to a Fighter Group of the American Eighth Army Air Force. Building has already been in progress for some weeks to accommodate what, I understand, could be a large number of American airmen who are expected to arrive imminently.'

'And a confounded nuisance they'll be,' Brigadier Mapperton growled. 'We must keep them out of the village at all costs.'

'That would be rather difficult, Brigadier. The

aerodrome is only a mile away.'

'Make it out of bounds. Can't have them slouching around the place, chewing gum.'

'They have come from far across the sea to our aid.'

'Only when it suited them. Had to be kicked into the war.'

The rector cleared his throat again. 'Nonetheless, I feel that we should welcome them — make some sort of gesture to our American cousins.'

'*Cousins*! They're mostly a lot of foreigners. Far more German blood than English, I've heard. French, Italians, Poles, Swedes . . . all sorts of odds and sods mixed up together.'

Miss Hooper shook her head. 'The first settlers were English, Brigadier, and they must have plenty of direct descendants.'

'As a matter of strict historical accuracy,' Miss Skinner remarked, 'the very first settlers in North America were probably Vikings, several hundred years earlier. Not to mention the Spanish after them. Of course, that's not counting the Indians who were there long before anyone else.'

Thora Dakin had come out of her sulk about the Lady chapel. 'I think the rector is quite right. It is our Christian duty to make the Americans feel welcome. Our Lord preached tolerance towards all men, whatever their race or creed. We ought to organize a reception of some sort at the village hall for them. Tea and sandwiches, say.'

Miss Skinner said sharply, 'For all those men? Be practical.'

'Well, not perhaps *all* of them.'

'Out of the question. However, I imagine we could issue an invitation to the officer in command and suggest that a token number might like to attend. Extend the hand of friendship. That seems perfectly reasonable.'

Brigadier Mapperton banged the trestle table with the flat of his palm. 'Hand of friendship be blowed! We've got nothing to be friendly about. They sat around while we had our backs to the wall and didn't lift a finger to help us.'

Mr Wells frowned. 'They've lent us some ships and so forth?'

'Obsolete stuff they'll make us pay through our noses for.'

'Still, they're our allies now. We could surely run to a modest welcome party for them. It seems only right and proper.'

Lady Beauchamp said quietly, 'I rather agree, Mr Wells. We ought to do something. If it's any help, we could invite them to the Manor. The drawing room will hold at least fifty people, or more.'

'It wouldn't be necessary to trouble you, Lady Beauchamp.' The rector smiled at her gratefully. 'This room would do perfectly well, I'm sure. Or the village hall.'

'If we had it in the hall I could play the piano for them, if you like,' Miss Hooper offered. 'And it'd be easier for the catering there, wouldn't it?'

'Well, that's certainly a thought . . . '

Miss Cutteridge looked up from her notes. 'We could manage sandwiches and teas quite easily, Rector. There are plenty of cups. What would we put in the sandwiches, though? I wonder if they would mind paste? The salmon flavour is very nice, or perhaps the sardine and tomato.'

'I don't think they'd mind very much, Miss Cutteridge. I'm sure they'd understand about our rationing.'

Brigadier Mapperton snorted. 'They won't know the meaning of the word. Steaks and fresh eggs — that's what they'd expect. Fat of the land, they live on. Give them paste sandwiches and they'd laugh in your face. Give them *nothing*, I say. Give 'em a taste of what it's like to go without.'

Sam Barnet nodded. 'I'm rather to your way of thinking, Brigadier, but for a different reason. I don't think we should encourage these Americans to come into the village. We've our women to consider. Most of the men are away and there's not many of us left here to protect them. What about our young girls? My Sally's just turned fifteen.'

Bill Rate said, 'I dare say their officers'll keep good control of things. They'll not want trouble with us.'

'All very well for you to talk, Bill, you've no daughters, only sons.'

'And all three of them are away fighting for their country, Sam. Like this lot of Yanks will be doing. I'd like to think the locals'd treat my boys right, wherever they are.'

The baker said levelly, 'You've got work up there at the 'drome, haven't you? It's in your interest to be friendly.'

'That's got *nothing* to do with it and I'll thank

you to withdraw that insinuation.'

'I'm sure Mr Barnet didn't mean anything offensive . . . '

'Oh, yes, he did, Rector. My trade's building and there's no shame in taking on honest work where you can find it. When those Yanks come marching in let's see you refusing to sell your fancy cakes to them, Sam. Make a mint, you will. So will others in the village. We've got seven pubs, all told, and I'll wager every one'll be full every night.'

The brigadier hit the table top again. 'Drunks littering the streets! No respectable woman daring to show her face out of doors. Is *that* what you want, Rector?'

At that moment, Thora Dakin, who had been frowning to herself, lifted her head. 'We've forgotten about the sugar, Rector.'

'Sugar, Mrs Dakin?'

'For the teas. What would we do about it for the Americans? I expect they like lots of sugar.'

This provoked another outburst from the brigadier and more argument in its wake. Enthusiasm was lukewarm but it was eventually apparent that Brigadier Mapperton and Sam Barnet were the only ones flatly in opposition.

'I suggest we vote on it, Rector,' Miss Skinner said at last.

'I was about to propose that. Will all in favour of a welcome party raise their hands, please.'

The result was nine in favour to two against. 'Well, if there's no other business . . . ' He brought the meeting to a swift close, standing and bowing his head. 'We thank Thee, God, for the freedom we enjoy in this land. We pray that we may do all that lies within our power, whatever it may be, to help and support all who are engaged in the fight to liberate those who suffer under the tyranny of our enemies. Through Jesus Christ, our Lord. Amen.'

He stood by the open door as they left. Brigadier Mapperton muttered crossly at him. 'Damned stupid idea of yours, Rector. I'm surprised at you. Mark my words, it'll lead to no good.'

Miss Skinner was the last. She lingered for a moment. 'Mr Barnet had a valid point, you know. The young girls in the village will need protecting, whether we welcome these Americans or not. I still have great reservations, I must say. We will need to be on our guard. I've never met an American but from their films they appear to inhabit an entirely different world from us. Very glamorous. Very attractive to innocent eyes.'

'I appreciate that,' he told her gravely.

'Have you thought about Agnes?'

'Agnes? She's engaged to be married.'

'I somehow doubt that the Americans would let that stand in their way, especially with her fiancé safely absent. I should be on your guard, too, if I were you.'

'Surely, Miss Skinner, if we show them respect and trust then it is more likely to be reciprocated.'

She gave him a grim smile. 'You have a much greater faith in human nature than I, Rector, but I suppose that's only right in your calling. We know next to nothing about these people but they scarcely have a reputation for self-restraint, so far as I'm aware.'

'Fortunately for us, perhaps. Wars aren't won by restraint, are they?' He looked past her shoulder towards the unkempt croquet lawn where the trees were casting their shadows across the long grass. It was a beautiful English evening at the tail-end of a warm summer, with all the haziness of a dream. Early in his ministry he had spent several years in Africa, where the relentless glare of the sun had thrown everything into harsh relief. He much preferred the soft light of England where one thing melted into another, giving the whole a mysterious and magical quality. All was peaceful and serene. They'd been lucky so far in King's Thorpe. The war had passed them by. No bombs had dropped anywhere near. No guns had been fired within earshot. There had been little evidence that a world war was in desperate progress, except for the distant drone of heavy bombers going to and fro and only occasionally overflying the village. A Polish tank regiment was camped in woods five miles away and Canadian soldiers were stationed in a requisitioned stately home beyond the next village, but the Poles and the Canadians preferred to spend their free time and money in the towns. As for the King's Thorpe aerodrome, for the first year of the war it had been nothing more than a satellite landing strip for a much larger RAF station further north. A squadron had finally arrived in 1941 and had flown Spitfires on patrols out to sea but after a few months they had been moved away. A new squadron had taken its place briefly and then, in turn, had been posted elsewhere. There had been no dogfights overhead, no crashes — or none that the village had witnessed. He had visited the aerodrome once, at the invitation of the RAF chaplain, and had found it a bleak, muddy, uncomfortable place, the men living and working in huts of brick and concrete and corrugated iron. A lot of work was being done there now and in a great hurry but he wondered what the Americans would make of it.

'They will be far from their homes and their own country and some of them will be coming here to die. I don't think we should forget that, Miss Skinner.'

She nodded. 'Yes . . . you're right. We must keep that in mind. Well, goodnight, Rector.' He watched the schoolmistress striding away from him, a bulky figure in the green tweeds she wore whatever the season, her pork-pie felt hat skewered firmly to her head. He closed and locked the door and stood still for a moment, thinking. Unlike the Dakins he had never heard God's voice with any certainty. His own prayers never received such clear answers but he thought that guidance did appear in other ways — through thoughts coming into his mind that gave him the power to see things more clearly. And he saw clearly that he was right about the Americans. When strangers were willing to come miles across an ocean and lay down their lives in the struggle against evil, then they should be welcomed, even if it was only with a cup of tea and a paste sandwich.

An inner doorway connected the parish room to the back hall of the rectory. He was about to go into his study when Agnes came down the stairs.

'How did the meeting go, Father?'

He looked up at his only child, the light of his life. By some blessed quirk of nature, she had taken after his own dear mother in looks. Exactly the same eyes and hair and the same smile. The kind of true and real beauty that would last a lifetime. 'Not so badly. We managed to agree on most things.'

'Supper's ready.'

'Thank you, my dear.' He followed Agnes down the stone-flagged passageway and into the kitchen where they now took all their meals. It was far more convenient and warmer than the chilly wastes of the dining room. Once upon a time, before the war, there had been a cook and a kitchen maid, as well as a housemaid, but the cook had gone to work in a munitions factory and the maids had both joined the ATS. Mrs Halliwell now obliged on two mornings a week and did some cooking for the larder when she and her bunions felt up to it. Otherwise it was Agnes who coped. He sat down at one end of the massive pine table that had been there since the days of a far larger Victorian household when the rector had had eight children. He hoped that the supper, whatever it was, had been cooked by his daughter and not Mrs Halliwell, who had a heavy hand as well as bunions. It had. 'It's oxtail,' she told him. 'They had some at the butcher's today.' She set the plate of stew in front of him.

She was an excellent cook, creating appetizing dishes out of the most unpromising wartime ingredients — tails and tongues and trotters and all kinds of offal and animal parts that nobody would have dreamed of eating before — but he was almost too tired to eat. More and more to be done in the parish, he thought, and less and less energy to carry out all his duties now that he was getting on in years. Since Sylvia had left him, bored out of her mind, as she had put it, with the life of a country parson's wife, he had found it a constant struggle. Various village ladies had nobly stepped into the breach and, as Agnes had grown up, she had shouldered an increasing share of the burden that her mother had laid down. In addition to teaching in the school kindergarten and at Sunday school and running the Brownies, she fulfilled any number of other parish duties for him.

His daughter sat down to eat opposite him and he observed her covertly, thinking of Miss Skinner's words of warning. Agnes was engaged to be married to Clive Hobbs but, as Miss Skinner had cautioned, her fiancé was away serving in the army and likely to remain so for the rest of the war. Just to himself, he admitted that he was rather relieved about that. It put off the day when he must come to terms with marrying Agnes to a young man he did not care for. He had been dismayed when Clive had presented himself at the rectory, not so much to ask for Agnes's hand as to announce that he was taking it. He could see, though, how it had come about. Agnes and Clive had known each other since they were small children and as she had grown into a beautiful young woman, Clive had pursued her relentlessly and with all the assurance of his privileged situation. The Hobbs family with their acres and their property and their fingers in many pies were important people in King's Thorpe. Still, the rector had demurred and prevaricated. Agnes was only eighteen. She had met so few young men in her sheltered life. Was she truly in love? Had she any idea what that should feel like? Did she feel anything close to the passion he had felt, and still felt, for her mother? He had worried about these things in private, but, in the end, there had been no real reason to withhold his consent — other than the irrational dislike of his future son-in-law, which he kept to himself. People told him how fortunate his daughter was. In his view, it was Clive who was the fortunate one.

He had wondered sometimes since if Agnes was marrying to escape the wearing routine of rectory life, just as Sylvia had been desperate to escape, but when he had asked she had denied it vehemently and pointed out that she would still be living in the village and still intended to go on helping him. Her answer had made him wonder guiltily if *that*, instead, was part of the reason. She knew how much he depended on her in every way and marrying Clive meant she would stay in King's Thorpe. There was no denying that he was selfishly thankful for it. He doubted, though, whether, once married, she would find it easy to carry out many parish duties. Clive Hobbs struck him as the kind of man who would demand a wife's full attention. There had already been arguments, he knew, over her teaching at the kindergarten. Agnes had announced her intention of continuing; Clive wanted her to stop. The outcome remained to be seen.

'You're not eating, Father. Is anything the matter?'

'No, nothing, my dear.' He picked up his knife and fork. 'I'm just a bit tired.'

'Mrs Gibbons sent a message. She says Mr Gibbons has taken a turn for the worse and she'd like you to go and see him as soon as you can.'

Matthew Gibbons had been bedridden for several years, wavering uncertainly between this world and the next. There had been many false alarms about his final departure, but the rector always hurried to his bedside.

'And Mr Law rang about the magazine. I said you'd ring him back. Is the stew all right?'

'Delicious.' He ate some more to please her. 'We're going to give a welcome party at the village hall for the American airmen when they arrive. It was agreed at the meeting. Nothing elaborate, of course. Just tea and sandwiches. Your help will be appreciated, my dear, if you can manage to spare the time.'

'When are they coming?'

'During the next week or so, apparently. The proposal is to invite the commanding officer and a limited number of others. Impossible to ask them all, with the best will in the world. But I feel we should do our utmost to welcome them and show that we care.'

'They haven't cared very much about us up to now, have they?'

He was rather taken aback; he had expected her full support, as always. 'You can understand their reluctance to become involved in another European war.'

'I'm not sure I *can* understand — not very easily, anyway. *We* didn't want to get involved in one again either, but we did because we wouldn't stand by and let the Nazis tyrannize other countries. The Americans have only thought of themselves all along, haven't they? Tom thinks they're despicable.'

'Does he, indeed?'

'They wanted to keep their precious neutrality at all costs, didn't they? They refused to help us and they're only fighting now because the Japanese attacked them — not for our sake.'

He said ruefully, 'Brigadier Mapperton would certainly agree, my dear.'

'Well, it's true, isn't it?'

'Up to a point. But there must be many Americans who would have liked to join in much sooner. Indeed, some of them did. American pilots fought in the Battle of Britain, you know.'

'It doesn't excuse the rest of them.' She smiled at him. 'But don't worry, Father, I'll help with the teas.'

He smiled back, thinking how very dear she was to him, and it suddenly crossed his mind — no more than a faint stirring in his consciousness, like a soft little summer breeze passing through leaves on a tree — that he half-hoped that Miss Skinner's fears might be justified.

* * *

Sam Barnet found his wife in the sitting room, engrossed in her knitting; something for the Forces, to judge by the look of it. He'd had his evening meal earlier, before the PCC meeting, and now he fancied a cup of tea and a piece of cake and a quiet sit-down before he turned in early. He'd be up well before four, in time to stoke the oven furnace and heave an eight-stone sack of flour down the ladder from the store above the bakehouse for mixing up in the trough. There were no fat bakers. It was back-breaking, sweat-of-the-brow work and he did it all himself, now that Roger was away, except for a school-age lad who came to chop the sticks and bring the coal in. He'd noticed lately that he was getting more and more aches and pains — in his back and his hands, and sometimes trouble with his chest and eyes from the flour dust. The cakes were women's work and he left those to a hired woman, Mrs Trimwell, and Sally to do once he'd finished the bread and the oven was cooler. They couldn't make the very fancy cakes any more because of the shortages, but they'd plenty of eggs from two hundred chickens to make good, plain ones. Freda was busy counting stitches, muttering away under her breath, so he went and put the kettle on the hob himself. While he waited for it to boil he put the cups and saucers and the milk in its matching jug out on a tray with a clean white cloth underneath. He liked things done nicely in the house and sometimes wished that Freda was a bit more particular in that department. The kitchen was in a real muddle with the dirty dishes from the meal still piled in the sink. He took the Coronation cake tin off the larder shelf and cut two slices of Madeira — a thin one for Freda and a larger one for himself. It was still good and moist, he noted with his baker's eye. It'd be one of Sally's, more than likely: she was very good at the cakes. When the kettle had come to the boil he made the tea in the teapot and fitted the wool cosy over it, with a bit of a struggle. Another of Freda's knitting attempts with the hole for the spout not in quite the right place.

When he carried the tray back into the sitting room Freda was shaking her head over the knitting lying in a khaki heap on her lap.

'I've gone wrong somewhere, Sam, but I'm blessed if I can make it out. I've got too many stitches.'

He set the tray on the side table. 'What's it meant to be?'

'A pullover. The WVS are sending comfort parcels to every man from the village who's away serving in the Forces.' She held up the knitting which dangled lumpily and lopsidedly from the needles. He felt sorry for the soldier who might have to wear it. Freda was no good with her hands. No good at knitting or sewing and hopeless in the bakehouse. She had tried when they were first married, but everything she'd touched had turned to disaster. Cakes never rose or they burned, pastry turned to lead, even simple rock cakes were more rocks than cakes. But she was good with the customers and popular in the village, which was all useful for business. He was proud of the bakery and of being the fourth generation of Barnets to run it. The family had made its mark in the village, he reckoned; earned a respectable place. He was proud to serve on the Parochial Church Council, to be churchwarden, to read the lesson at Sunday matins, to serve as a school governor, to be seen to count for something in the community.

Freda had come from the next village, the daughter of a carter who ferried goods in a horsedrawn covered wagon. He'd aimed his sights higher when he'd been looking for a wife, but the minute he'd set eyes on her he'd been bowled over. She'd had beautiful long, nut-brown hair in those days and a slim figure with a tiny waist. The hair was cut short now and mostly grey and having Roger and Sally had put paid to the waist, but she was still a fine-looking woman. Sally took after her in looks, though she had gone and dyed her hair blond which he thought was not only a shame but unseemly. He'd been furiously angry about it, but powerless to stop her. She knew her own mind, did Sally, and he had a hard job keeping her in order. She was good with the customers, though, as well as at making the cakes: quick as anything with the serving and the money and all smiles.

Too much so with some of the men, for his liking. As soon as she'd left school she'd started in the bakehouse, but he didn't want her staying there for ever. He'd other things in mind for his only daughter. A respectable marriage to somebody suitable. He'd had his eye on one young man in the village who was away at the Front at present, but it might turn out to be someone from Stamford or Peterborough. Someone from a decent, prosperous family of some standing, like his own. The Barnets had come a long way since his great-grandfather had rolled up his shirtsleeves and plunged his arms into the flour.

He poured the tea. 'Where's Sally?'

'She's gone out. Round to see Doris.'

'She spends too much time with that girl. I'd sooner she kept different sort of company.'

'What's wrong with Doris?'

'She's in service,' he said, a shade uncomfortably, knowing that so had Freda's mother been as a girl.

'Other jobs are hard to find in these parts and she's too young to join up. Anyway, she's more like a daily help, so far as I can see. Doesn't have to live in and skivvy all hours of the day and night, like my mother had to. It's different these days.'

He didn't want to hear about it and wished Freda would keep quiet about her mother. She'd probably told all and sundry in the village. 'Well, Sally'll have to stop going out in the evening once the Americans get here. We can't have her doing that any longer.'

'You won't stop her, Sam. She's not a child.'

'She's only fifteen. That's too young to be out alone.'

'I used to go all over the place. No harm in it.'

He wanted to say, but didn't, that she'd gone all over the place a sight too much, in his opinion. Left to her own devices, so far as he could tell. Freda's mother had died when she was ten, leaving six children under twelve and a husband who drank more than a drop too much and was off carting more than he was ever home. He put Freda's tea and cake on the table beside her and straightened the antimacassar on the back of his armchair before he sat down. 'All well and good in those days but things have changed. We can't trust these Americans.'

'We don't know that, Sam. Give them a chance.'

'Not where Sally's concerned. I'm not having some Yank trying it on with her.'

'Bound to, aren't they? She's a pretty girl. It's nature's way.'

He said fiercely, 'I'll soon see about that. I'll tell her she's not to have anything to do with them. Not to speak a word to them.'

Freda smiled. 'You'll have to stop her serving in the bakehouse, then. They'll be down here in the village buying things and she'll have to talk to them, won't she? I can't see our Sally keeping silent when a handsome young American comes in the door. Of course she won't. I wouldn't either, not at her age.'

'I'm not talking about her serving cakes and such. She's not to have anything to do with them other than that. Nothing whatever. And I'll tell her so straight.'

'You do that, Sam, if it makes you feel better.'

'I've half a mind to ban them coming in the bakehouse.'

'Well, that wouldn't be much good for business, would it? They'll have money to burn, I dare say. Think of that. Calm down now, Sam, and drink up your tea before it gets cold.'

As he drank his eyes went to the latest letter from Roger, propped against the clock on the mantle and the sight of it comforted and soothed him. Never a moment's worry over the boy — not like with his sister. They'd be making him an officer soon, no question. A lad like that. He'd done well at Dunkirk as a corporal, bringing more than thirty men safely back across Belgium and France to the beaches when all higher rankers had been killed; they'd made him up to sergeant for it. Next it'd be Second Lieutenant Barnet. A medal perhaps, before the war was over. He'd come home and, in the course of time, he'd take over the bakery and settle down sensibly. That was the plan. He was a good boy, Roger. The fifth generation of Barnets, to be followed, with any luck, by the sixth. He didn't ever allow himself to think that Roger might not survive the war. 'What I'd like to know,' he said, 'is how long the Americans are going to be over here.' Bloody Yanks he might have called them, but he never swore in front of Freda.

'Till they win the war for us, I suppose.'

'*Them*! Win the war!' His teacup rattled with indignation. 'What've *we* been doing for the past three years, then, I'd like to know?'

She knitted two plains and two purls. 'Not losing it.'

* * *

Erika Beauchamp went into the Manor through the tradesmen's entrance round the side. She passed by the kitchen and stuck her head round the door to let the cook know she was back. Her mother-in-law was in the drawing room, seated in her chair, sherry glass in hand.

'You've been a long time, Erika.'

'It dragged on a bit.'

'Those meetings always do. Geoffrey always found them extremely tedious.'

She poured herself a sherry. 'I dare say Alex will think the same when he's grown-up and it's his turn. Did he go off to bed all right?'

'Half an hour ago. He didn't want to, of course, but I was very firm. The child's getting out of hand, in my opinion. Going to the village school can't be doing him any good.'

'It's not doing him any harm and I'm not sending him away to boarding school now. We've been through all that, Miriam.'

'Richard would have wanted him to go to his old prep school.'

'And I don't. Not yet, anyway.'

'It can be very selfish to hang onto one's children.'

'I'm not hanging onto Alex. I simply don't agree with sending small boys away so young.'

'Richard went at seven. He was perfectly

happy. And they've evacuated the school to Wales, you know. Alexander would be safe there.'

'He's safe enough here.'

'Not with all these aerodromes everywhere. The Germans could come over and drop bombs on them.'

'I doubt if they'd aim any at the village.'

'You can't be sure.' Miriam sipped at her sherry. 'He may not get into Eton, if you're not careful. Not without proper teaching. Had you thought of that?'

'They *do* teach them properly at the school here. It's a very high standard. Eton might not be right for him, in any case.'

'Beauchamps have always gone there.'

'And Alex probably will, too. We'll have to see.'

'He should be with his own kind, Erika, especially having no brothers or sisters. It's not fair on him, you know. Oil and water don't mix. It was bad enough having those dreadful evacuee children foisted on us.'

'They weren't dreadful.'

'Their habits and language were appalling.'

'They'd just never had a chance to learn anything different. And Alex enjoys it at the village school. He gets on with the others very well.'

'There will always be a gulf.'

'Don't let's discuss this any more, Miriam. Let's just agree to disagree.' She swallowed half the sherry in one go and, with it, her irritation. The two of them had never seen eye to eye from the beginning. Whatever kind of bride Miriam had had in mind for her only son, the

Beauchamp heir, it had certainly not been an exiled Hungarian musician's daughter. When Richard had first brought her to the Manor, Miriam had listened to the story of their meeting in the manner of Oscar Wilde's imperious Lady Bracknell. 'On *Waterloo Station*? How *extraordinary*!' Her eyebrows had continued to rise as Erika explained how they had bumped into each other when they were running for separate trains, and they had risen even further when Miriam, with more probing Lady Bracknell questions, had unearthed a Hungarian father who played the violin. She had obviously pictured some swarthy gypsy sawing away wildly in cafés and had only been partly mollified to learn that he was actually a soloist at concert halls. Musicians of any kind or ability were not socially acceptable. The fact that Erika had gone to a very acceptable boarding school for young English ladies had helped matters a little, but Richard's mother had not been able to conceal her disappointment when her son had announced their engagement on another visit a few weeks later.

Erika and her mother-in-law had sparred constantly from the start — a long-running skirmish that had escalated into a pitched battle by the time Richard had inherited both the Manor and the title on his father's death. Within five more months he had been sent to France with the British Expeditionary Force; within four more he had been killed. Title and Manor now belonged to his son but the last thing Erika had wanted was to go and live where her mother-in-law was still solidly in residence. She had stayed on in the London flat with Alex, all her energy devoted to caring for him, her bitter grieving for Richard kept for when she was alone at night. Then the Blitz had started and after several nights of heavy bombing and near misses she had packed the suitcases and taken Alex to King's Thorpe — for the duration of the war, she supposed, however long that was going to be. Forced under the same roof, she and Miriam had cobbled together a kind of truce: the twelfth and the thirteenth baronets' widows finally united in a fragile armistice for the sake of the fourteenth. The house was very old and very beautiful but it was also freezing cold in winter, far too big and impossible to keep up or run in the way it had been in the pre-war days. No fuel and no army of servants — only Mrs Woods, the cook-general, who was too old to do war work or join up and Doris, a village girl who was too young and came in daily to give some half-hearted help.

To change the subject she said, 'There's going to be a welcome party for the Americans coming to the aerodrome — some of them, anyway. The rector suggested it at the meeting. I offered the Manor.'

'The *Manor*! Americans! They wouldn't know how to behave. I couldn't possibly have them here.'

What a wicked old snob she was, Erika thought. And it wasn't for her to say who came to the house; not any longer. 'I'm sure their commanding officer would know perfectly well how to behave and so would the others. Anyway, you needn't worry because they're going to have it in the village hall. Of course Brigadier Mapperton was dead against the whole idea, but then he would be. And Sam Barnet's convinced they'll rampage through the village, raping and seducing all the women — Sally in particular.'

'More than likely. That girl asks for trouble with those clothes she wears and her dyed hair — at her age. No wonder her father's worried. I hope you won't let Alexander anywhere near any Americans, Erika.'

'Are you afraid he might catch something?'

'He could pick up bad language.'

'Swearing, you mean?'

'I meant Americanisms . . . the dreadful way they talk. I've heard it on the wireless. Their accent and all those peculiar words they use. It's like a foreign language.'

'Very useful for Alex to learn it, then. Perhaps they should teach it in schools.' Erika finished off her sherry. 'Mrs Woods said dinner would be ready soon so I'd better go up and say goodnight to him now.'

She went upstairs to her son's bedroom in the nursery wing. It had been Richard's room as a child, too, and very little had been changed. It had the same chipped white-painted furniture, the same bed, the same toy-soldier curtains, the same worn blue rug, the same pictures on the walls with *The Light of the World* hung above the bedhead, the same books in the glass-fronted bookcase. Richard's old teddy bear still sat in his place of honour on the window seat. He had liked the idea of keeping it that way for his son and she had agreed. Alex himself didn't much care one way or the other. He was in his striped pyjamas — jacket unbuttoned — propped on one elbow against the pillows and reading *The Just So Stories* — one of his father's books. She sat down on the end of the bed. 'Time you went to sleep.'

He looked up at her with Richard's eyes. 'Can I finish this story?'

'All right.' He'd probably go on and finish the rest of the book but what did it matter? It was the holidays. No school to think about in the morning.

'Granny made me go to bed.'

'It was time you did, darling.'

'I can't sleep when it's so light still.'

'You can if you try.'

'I do try but it doesn't work. I don't like Granny sometimes. She wants me to go away to boarding school, doesn't she? She keeps saying I ought to.'

'Only because she thinks you'd enjoy it.'

'I wouldn't. I'd hate it.'

'You might not, later on, when you're older. But you're not going away yet, so you needn't worry. I promise.'

'Granny can't make me, can she?'

'No, she can't.' She hesitated. 'You *are* happy at the school here, aren't you, Alex?'

'It's not bad. Miss Skinner is jolly strict, but she's all right. Mr Reynolds is scary, though. He's always caning people if they do something wrong.'

'How about the other boys? Do you like them?'

'They're OK. I like Alfie Hazlet — he sits next to me. And his brother Tom's nice. I like some of the others, too.'

'Why don't you ask them home?'

'They wouldn't want to come. It's too different.'

'Nobody teases you about living at the Manor?'

'Not really.'

'And you don't feel left out, or anything?'

He shrugged. 'I don't think so. I'm not in Dick and Robbie and Seth's gang, but I wouldn't want to be.'

'Do you like living here? In this house?'

'It's OK. It's a nice house. I liked it in the flat in London, as well. It was good fun with the bombs. Will we go back to London after the war, or stay here?'

'I'm not sure. It depends. The Manor will be yours properly when you're grown-up, you know.'

'It was Daddy's before, wasn't it?'

'And your grandfather's and your great-grandfather's and several more greats. The Beauchamps have been here a long time.'

'Will Granny still be living here when I'm grown-up?'

'Perhaps. It's her only home, you see.'

He pulled a face. 'Well, she wouldn't be able to tell me to go to bed or boss me around *then*, would she?'

She smiled and leaned forward to do up the

pyjama-jacket buttons before she kissed him goodnight. 'No, she wouldn't. I must go down now — dinner will be ready. Just to the end of that story, remember, then you must go to sleep.' When she looked back from the door he was engrossed in the book once more.

2

Tom Hazlet woke just before dawn when Farmer Dixon's vicious old cockerel was starting up in the distance. Alfie was lying curled up beside him and he listened to him breathing steadily for a while to make sure he was fast asleep. Very slowly and very carefully Tom slid out of his side of the bed and picked up his clothes from the floor. If Alfie woke he'd want to come too and he'd make a big to-do when he couldn't so Mum would wake up as well and there'd be another to-do. He tiptoed to the door and then out onto the narrow landing space between the two upstairs rooms where he stopped to listen again. Mum was still asleep but Nell was stirring in her cot and she'd start grizzling soon. He was down the wooden stairs, through the kitchen and out of the back door in a flash and without a sound.

He pulled on his socks and his shirt and shorts, hitching the braces up over his shoulders, tugged his jersey over his head and laced up his boots. Then he grabbed the old sack he kept at the back of the hen-house before he wriggled through the gap in the hedge into the five-acre field beyond. It was no trouble seeing his way; he could see well, even on a night without a moon, because, to him, it was never truly dark — not once his eyes had adjusted so that he could make out shapes and shadows. Now, with the dawn coming up, it was easy and he moved fast, traversing the corn stubble towards the railway line. He scrambled up the grass embankment, stepped over the dull gleam of metal rails and slithered down the other side to head on in the direction of Hollow Wood in a dip in the land beyond. His bare legs were scratched by the stubble and his boots soaked by the dew.

He'd set his copper-wire snares near the warren at the edge of the wood the evening before and he was counting on one of them having worked — if a fox or stoat hadn't got there before him. The first was empty but the second one, further on, had a dead rabbit caught by the head in the copper noose. He went on to the third where he found another rabbit snared but still alive. When he'd been smaller it had bothered him when that happened but now he'd learned how to kill it instantly. He stretched its neck quickly, just like Dad had taught him, and the rabbit stopped struggling and hung limp. He took his pen-knife out of his shorts pocket, opened up the sharp blade and gutted the two rabbits, burying the innards in the soft earth. All the while he kept a sharp ear open. Farmer Dixon was as sour-tempered as his cockerel and Hollow Wood was on his land. A miserable old skinflint, Tom called him — and worse names sometimes now that he knew them. The old bastard could well spare a rabbit or two, but he wouldn't.

When he'd finished his work he wiped the blade clean on some grass, folded the knife and put it away. It was light by now and he set off homewards with the copper snares and the dead rabbits in the sack slung over his shoulder, keeping to the shadow of hedges wherever he could. As he drew near the railway embankment he heard the whistle of an early train approaching. Tom hesitated. There was plenty of time to cross the line but he'd never quite forgotten the old tramp who had gone and got one boot stuck under the rail and been found with the foot still in the boot, his head rolled down the embankment, and the rest of him like he'd gone through the mangle. So he waited at the bottom of the slope and presently the engine came chuffing round the corner. The driver gave him a wave as he went past and Tom waved back. Then the carriages followed and he saw men in khaki-coloured uniforms crowded at all the windows, looking out. He gave them a wave too and they waved back, grinning at him. One of them let down a window, yelled and threw something out to him. It landed in the long grass at his feet and when he crouched down he saw that it was a packet of Wrigley's chewing gum.

Instead of going home, he ran along the track to the station half a mile away where he hid the sack in a thicket behind the coal dump. The train was standing at the platform and the men he'd seen in the carriages were streaming out into the yard outside the booking hall and climbing into army lorries painted with big white stars on the side. He watched them from a distance for a while. He knew they were Yanks by the chewing gum; he could see them chewing away all the time. And he wasn't the only one watching. Lots of people had come out to gawp. They were standing in huddles, staring at the Yanks like they'd come from the moon. Mostly nosy old women like Mother Becket muttering to each other. Dick and Robbie and Seth and all that lot were there too. He could have been one of them, if he'd wanted, but he didn't like going round in a stupid gang all the time; it was much better on your own. The lorries started grinding out of the yard and when Dick and the others ran after them the Yanks began throwing things for them. Tom ran too and barged Seth aside with his elbow. He was gone with his catch before they could all fall on him.

When he got back to the cottage, Mum was in the kitchen carrying Nell round on one hip. 'Take her for me for a moment, so's I can get on, will you, Tom?' She dumped the baby in his arms and he sat down with her on his lap, wrinkling his nose. She smelled of wet nappy and sick and her nose was all snotty. He didn't like her much. Not yet, anyway. There'd been two other babies before her, after Alfie, but they'd both died. One when she was six months old from measles and the other when she was born. He'd seen the midwife through a crack in the bedroom door, holding her up by the feet and slapping her. She'd looked just like a skinned rabbit.

Alfie was eating bread and dripping at the table and scowling at him. 'You left me behind. I wanted to come too.'

'Mum wouldn't let you.'

'She lets *you*.'

'I'm nine. You're only six.'

His mother was riddling the range fire. 'I don't

like you going neither, Tom.'

'Caught a couple of rabbits for you,' he told her casually. 'Left them outside.'

'You poach them from someone's land?'

'Course not.'

She didn't really believe him, he knew that, but she wouldn't say any more. Rabbits were food. Good food. And when Dad was away all the time working on the new aerodromes, helping build runways, the old Oxo tin on the kitchen shelf never had much money in it. When Mum had skinned the rabbits he'd clean the skins, stretch them and nail them out on a board, and then sell them to the rag-and-bone man for a penny each, next time he came round. He was bursting to tell the other piece of news. 'The Yanks are here. I saw them coming in on the train.'

Alfie looked up from his bread and dripping. 'What're yanks?'

'Americans, stupid. They gave me these. They were throwing them for people to catch.' He groped in his pocket and laid his two prizes on the kitchen table. Nell made a grab at them but he kept her out of reach.

'What're they?'

'Chewing gum and chocolate. Can't you see? It says Wrigley's Chewing Gum here and on this one it says Hershey's Milk Chocolate.'

Alfie looked hopeful. 'Can I have some?'

He was feeling generous. 'All right. You can try a bit of gum.' He opened up the yellow packet and unwrapped a stick. It smelled minty. 'Here you are. You have to chew it.'

Alfie stuffed it sideways into his mouth. 'Tastes funny.'

'That's with the dripping, I expect. You ought've waited.' He offered the chocolate bar to his mother, hoping she wouldn't want it.

'No, you keep it, Tom. Share it with Alfie.'

He probably would but he wasn't going to say so; you had to keep Alfie in his place. 'I might go up to the aerodrome later and take a look. See how the Yanks're getting on.'

'Can I come too?'

'No, you can't.'

Alfie started to snivel which made Nell start up as well. She smelled worse than ever. To his relief Mum took her back. 'Alfie can go with you. Long as you take care of him.'

'Do I have to, Mum? He'll be a nuisance.'

'He won't be, will you, Alfie?'

Alfie shook his head, grinning all over his face now. 'I won't, I promise.'

Tom stared at him. 'What've you done with the gum?'

'Swallowed it.'

'*Stupid*!'

* * *

'Bloater,' said Miss Cutteridge apologetically. 'I'm afraid that's the only flavour the shop has in. Mr Watts says they won't be getting any more for some time.' She was looking quite upset. 'I was hoping we'd be able to offer something nicer, like salmon, if possible. Anyway, Mr Watts is going to let us have a quantity very reasonably priced and it's Shippam's.'

The five ladies of the Welcome Party committee were gathered in Miss Cutteridge's small and neat sitting-room. Erika Beauchamp had been ushered to the most comfortable armchair, once a large ginger cat had been removed. 'I don't think we should worry too much, Miss Cutteridge. They won't expect anything special.'

'I do hope not, Lady Beauchamp. It's just that they must be accustomed to all sorts of delicious food. It may seem a little strange to them.'

'They'll jolly well have to lump it.' Mrs Vernon-Miller, stalwart of the local Women's Voluntary Service, never minced her words. Her complexion clashed with her plum-coloured twinset and, lit sideways from the window, she had a very noticeable moustache. 'If it's the best we can do. How many of them are we expecting, anyway?'

Erika said, 'The rector thinks only about fifteen or so. The group commander and some other officers. Of course we don't know how many of the village will turn up.'

'We'll have to charge an entry fee for them at the door. Can't have a free-for-all. The Americans wouldn't have to pay, of course.'

'How much do you suggest?'

'Sixpence. Enough to cover costs and to keep out the rag-tag and bobtail. We don't want any trouble.'

Miss Cutteridge frowned. '*Trouble?* Surely we don't expect anything like that.'

'You never know,' Mrs Vernon-Miller told her

darkly. 'Not everyone's keen on the idea of Americans turning up here. There's plenty in the village against it, especially the older ones. They still remember the last war. The Americans were late then as well. What about decorating the hall?'

'Perhaps we could put some bunting round — strings of Union Jacks?' Mrs Salter, the verger's wife, suggested. Mrs Vernon-Miller squashed her. 'Rather premature. We haven't won the war yet.'

'How about an American flag?' Erika said. 'They'd appreciate that.'

'Where would we get one? There won't be one in the village.'

'Perhaps in Peterborough or Stamford . . . I'll see if I can find one.'

'We could always draw one with crayons,' Mrs Salter said bravely.

Mrs Vernon-Miller gave her a withering glance. 'How many stars and how many stripes?'

'Oh. I'm afraid I don't know exactly.'

The displaced ginger cat jumped up onto Erika's lap, to Miss Cutteridge's embarrassment. When he had been prised off, in spite of her insistence that she didn't mind, they went on to discuss teacups and saucers and how many helpers would be needed, the cleaning of the lavatories and the order of events. The Americans had been invited for four o'clock and the rector was to make a speech of welcome. While they had the tea and the bloater sandwiches, Miss Hooper would play the village-hall piano up on the stage.

'It does rather need tuning,' Erika pointed out. 'Could we find someone to do it?'

'There isn't anybody,' Mrs Vernon-Miller informed her. 'Not since Mr Bodkin died. He always tuned it. You can't get anyone to do anything like that now. I can't even find anyone to repair my alarm clock. Anyway, the piano sounds quite all right to me.'

She was probably tone-deaf, Erika thought. She also thought how much she disliked this type of meeting — the wrangling, the pointless digressions, the unconscionable time it all took and, most of all, the feeling of being an outsider, only present by virtue of being Lady Beauchamp. In reality, she was just as foreign to them as the Americans. Three years spent in the village was nothing. People who had lived there for more than twenty were still considered to be newcomers. But for Alex, she would have been anywhere but in a place like King's Thorpe. She would have joined one of the women's services, gone to work in a factory, done some real war work. As it was, since the Manor evacuees had gone back home, she had had to content herself with whatever the local WVS offered. She might, perhaps, have left Alex to the tender mercies of Granny for the duration, but Alex needed her. He'd lost a beloved father and his small world had been turned upside down. Truth to tell, she needed him too. He was all that she had left of a beloved husband and so like Richard in so many ways. His son was her greatest comfort in her grief. To see him was to see Richard again.

After some more lengthy discussion the

Welcome Party meeting finally ground to a halt. Mrs Vernon-Miller walked down West Street with Erika, grumbling about the verger's wife.

'I can't think why *she's* been co-opted. Never anything sensible to say. It should have been the rector's wife, of course. It was all his idea in the first place.'

Erika said nothing. By some sort of tacit agreement in the village, Mrs Dawe's flight from King's Thorpe years ago was only alluded to obliquely, never openly discussed.

At the corner of Pig Lane, where she lived, Mrs Vernon-Miller paused. 'I expect you've heard the good news on the WVS front — about the mobile canteens we're getting?'

'No.'

'Converted charabancs, apparently. The Americans are paying for them. Coffee and buns for their bases — that's the general idea. I should have thought tea would do perfectly well, but apparently the Americans don't care for it.' Mrs Vernon-Miller squared her shoulders. 'Something else useful for us to do.'

* * *

'Damned if I'll go,' Brigadier Mapperton told his wife. 'Damned Yanks! Damned if I'll go.'

From long experience, Cicily Mapperton knew that it was best to keep silent. She turned the page of her book surreptitiously — a romantic novel that she had borrowed from the library in Peterborough. The heroine hated the hero and had just slapped his face, but she knew, also from long experience, that this state of affairs wouldn't last. Meanwhile she could picture the present scene vividly in her mind's eye — the heroine, her eyes flashing defiance, and the dark and dissolute hero who had just seized her by the wrist with a grip of steel.

Her husband had reached the far end of the Persian rug and turned on his heel to pace back again.

'We've been fighting this war for four years while they just sat on their backsides and watched us. All that big talk of theirs about freedom and liberty but when it comes down to it, the only thing they care about is their own. Don't give a damn abut anybody else. Hitler could have had the whole of Europe for all they cared. The only thing the Americans care about is their own precious skin.' He reached the other end of the rug and started off again. 'Damned if I'll go. You agree, naturally.'

Cicily Mapperton put her bookmark between the pages. 'Of course I do, Lionel.'

'Cheek of the rector even to suggest it. He knows my feelings in the matter. I made them perfectly clear at the PCC.'

'Perhaps he thought that with your position in the village it might look a bit strange if you weren't there . . . '

The brigadier stopped. 'Huh! Some truth in that, I dare say. Can't be helped, though. Principles are principles.' He walked on and came to a halt again beside the grand piano with its array of silver-framed family photographs. Himself and Cicily on their wedding day — it was like looking at two strangers — completely unrecognizable; his mother in Court dress; his father in his general's uniform; his daughter at twenty-one and a later photograph in her Wren officer's uniform; the one of his son done when he'd been promoted to captain only six months before Singapore fell and he'd been taken prisoner by the Japanese. They didn't even know if he was dead or alive. If the damned Americans had had the guts to come into the war earlier and help stop the rot with the Japs, things might have been very different. He resumed his pacing. 'They'll probably get a turn-out. People who don't give a damn about the principle of the thing.'

'I expect they will.'

'Might look a bit odd if we don't show our faces.'

'Considering your position, Lionel. Churchwarden and everything.'

'Huh . . . Wouldn't need to stay long.'

'Only a moment.'

'Make the point that I don't approve.'

'That's right, Lionel.'

The brigadier sat down in his armchair and snatched up *The Times*. His wife went back to her novel.

⋆ ⋆ ⋆

Miss Cutteridge's turn on the brass-polishing rota was for the last Sunday in each month and it was her habit to go to the church on the Friday after lunch. Elijah Kerfoot was scything the grass between the ancient and toppling gravestones as she made her way up the path and she bid him good afternoon. The old man paused at the end of a long sweep to raise his cap and she stopped for a word with him about his arthritis, which troubled him as much as her own. Inside the church it was cool and dim and utterly quiet. She always enjoyed the quiet. God's presence seemed almost palpable; she was sure that she could feel Him there, though sometimes she wondered if he would trouble Himself for just the one person. *Where two or three are gathered together in my Name there am I in the midst of them* . . . Christ hadn't said anything about only one, so far as she could remember. She really must ask the rector about that.

As usual, she knelt for short prayers before she began: for her long-dead mother and father that they might rest for ever in peace, for all the poor unfortunate people suffering under the Nazis, for little Sarah Turner who was very poorly, for Harry Wilmcott, the tiler, who'd fallen off a ladder and broken both legs, and for Matthew Gibbons who was permanently on her sick list. And, as always, for William who, unlike herself, had never grown old. When she had finished she rose, rather stiffly because of the arthritis, to her feet. There were three large brasses set in the floor in front of the altar, four wall memorials along the north aisle, a small, plain floor brass in the south aisle and another wall plaque in the chancel behind the choir stalls to Brigadier Mapperton's younger brother, John, who had been killed at the Battle of Verdun in 1916. Then there was the big altar cross, the altar candlesticks, the communion chalice, the baptismal ewer, the brass-topped churchwarden's staves and the collection plates. She always started off with all the moveable pieces which she cleaned on the table in the vestry with the dusters she kept specially for the job and a tin of Bluebell metal polish that she used very sparingly because, like everything else, it was in short supply.

When she had finished in the vestry she tackled the three brasses set in the stone chancel floor. She worked on her knees — rather painful and the stones were always cold, even in summer — beginning with the chain-mail armoured Sir Richard Beauchamp, who had gone on the Seventh Crusade before he had died at King's Thorpe in 1265. The brass image of his wife, Alice, in veiled headdress, a mantle worn over her shoulders to reveal the graceful folds of her gown, was set close beside him. The third brass, at a distance from the other two and rather larger, was a fine rendition of the next baronet, Sir Geoffrey, also in full armour, though there was no record of him fighting any battles. He had evidently neglected to arrange for an accompanying one for *his* wife. Nobody knew where she had been buried. Later Beauchamps had been laid to rest in the family mausoleum in the churchyard. Not the last baronet, though, of course, Miss Cutteridge thought regretfully as she rubbed away; he would have been buried somewhere in France. She hoped that one day he would be brought home to lie with his ancestors. Such a pleasant young man. Always so cheerful and so polite. Such a sad tragedy.

She had just started on Sir Geoffrey's right foot when she heard the heavy clunk of the south-door latch being raised and the creak as the door swung open. Mrs Dakin or Mrs Vernon-Miller, perhaps, whose turn it was to do the flowers? Except that they generally did them on the Saturday morning. Hearing nothing more, Miss Cutteridge crawled forward on her hands and knees to peer round the edge of the choir stall. Her eyes widened. *An American*!

He was standing at the far end of the nave, caught in a shaft of sunlight from one of the windows, and staring up into the barrel-vaulted roof: a dark-haired young man in a brown leather jacket, khaki shirt and tie and olive trousers, a peaked cap dangling idly from his fingers. An extraordinarily casual military uniform. Undoubtedly an American.

Miss Cutteridge withdrew her head, debating the situation. She ought to speak up and ask him to shut the door before the birds got in but she felt flustered at the thought. She had never spoken to an American before and was not certain that he would understand her, or she him. If she did nothing he might go away and no action or conversation would be necessary. She retreated on her knees to Sir Geoffrey and waited hopefully, holding her breath. After a while footsteps started slowly down the nave towards the altar. In a moment he would discover her in this foolish position, on the floor clutching her dusters and the Bluebell. There was nothing for it. She rose creakily to her feet, screwed up her courage and stepped forward from behind the choir stall to confront him.

He started violently and dropped his cap. 'Jeez . . . you scared the hell out of me, ma'am. Thought you were a ghost, or something.'

She blushed. 'I'm so sorry. I was cleaning the brass, you see.' She indicated Sir Geoffrey. 'It has to be done every week or it tarnishes.'

'Oh, sure . . . ' He bent to retrieve his cap and held out his hand with a smile. 'The name's Ed. Lieutenant Ed Mochetti, United States Eighth Army Air Force.'

She transferred the Bluebell to the dusters and put her free hand in his, babbling nervously. 'Oh really? Goodness gracious. Bless my soul. How do you do?'

He was rather swarthy with dark brown eyes and black hair. Somehow she had always thought of Americans as fair and blue-eyed. And his name had sounded odd. If one overlooked the peculiar uniform, though, he was really a very handsome young man. Very handsome indeed. Her heart fluttered a little as she looked up at him. 'I'm Miss Cutteridge. Emilia Cutteridge.'

'Of King's Thorpe, England?'

'Well, yes . . . though I was actually brought up in Oundle, near here. My family lived there.'

'I'm from New York City myself.'

'Good heavens! Imagine that.' She did so, with some difficulty. Skyscrapers soaring and glittering at night with millions of lights; Times Square and those dazzling neon advertisements flashing away; the Empire State Building; Broadway with all the theatres; Fifth Avenue with the wonderful shops; huge American cars, those yellow taxicabs . . . everything she had ever read or heard or seen about New York raced through her mind. It seemed simply unbelievable that somebody from there should be standing here in St Luke's, talking to her.

He twirled his cap round and round on his index finger. 'Just got over with my Fighter Group. We're based up the road a little ways. Thought I'd take a look at the village. All those houses must be real old. Same as this church, I guess.'

'Well, yes. St Luke's was begun in the twelfth century, though of course there have been a lot of changes and additions since then. Unfortunately, the pews are only nineteenth-century.'

He grinned. 'Where I come from that makes them pretty old.'

'Does it really? Well, yes, I suppose it would.'

'I'm Roman Catholic myself, but I guess this church isn't.'

'Oh, it was once — for several hundred years — until King Henry VIII changed everything.'

'Yeah, the one with the six wives. I know all about him. There was a great movie with Charles Laughton.'

A movie was a film, she thought. She very seldom went to the cinema herself, though, of course, she had heard of Charles Laughton. 'We're Protestant now, I'm afraid. But I'm sure there would be a Roman Catholic church in one of the towns.'

'No, that's OK. We've got an RC chapel at the

base and a visiting chaplain. They take care of us. This sure is a beautiful old place.' He walked about a bit and stopped at one of the tombs in the south aisle. He read aloud, his American accent twanging in her ears.

' 'Know reader though in dust I lie,
As you are now, so once was I.
And as I am, so must you be.
Therefore prepare to follow me.'

'Hey, this guy gives it to you straight from the shoulder. *Hic jacet*. What does that mean?'

'It's Latin for 'here lies'.'

'Well, Richard Wilbur's been lying here since 1688. That's quite a while.' He went on staring down at the tomb for a moment.

She wondered what his job was. The leather jacket hid any insignia. 'Do you fly aeroplanes?' she asked politely.

'Sure do. Except we've no planes to fly right now. Waiting for them to be delivered. Any day now and you'll be seeing us up there, and hearing us. I guess that won't be too popular with you folks. Us making a racket.'

They both turned at the sound of someone coming into the church. Agnes Dawe stood at the far end of the nave, caught, just as the young American had been before, in the shaft of sunlight. She was pink in the face and gasping for breath. 'I thought my father might be here, Miss Cutteridge. I've been looking for him everywhere. Mr Gibbons has taken a turn for the worse. I think it's really serious this time.'

'I'm afraid I haven't seen him, dear. I'm so sorry. Would you like me to help look?'

'No, it's all right, thank you. I'll try the Turners. He might have gone there.'

She hurried out again, closing the door carefully behind her, the latch clunking loudly into place.

'The birds get in, you see,' Miss Cutteridge said. 'It's best to shut it.'

'What?' The American was still standing in the aisle, staring towards the door.

'The birds get in if you don't shut the door. They can make an awful mess.'

'Oh, sure. Sorry. I'll remember another time. Who was that girl?'

'Our rector's daughter, Agnes Dawe.' Perhaps she ought to have introduced him, but she hadn't understood his rank and she'd quite forgotten his odd surname. And anyway, it had hardly been the moment. Not with poor Mr Gibbons perhaps meeting his Maker at last. 'Well, if you don't mind, I really should get on with the brass.'

'Sure. I must be getting along.'

'Are you coming to the Welcome Party?'

'Welcome party?'

'It's all arranged for next Saturday afternoon. At the village hall. Nothing very exciting, I'm afraid. Just some refreshments and a little entertainment, but we hope you'll enjoy it.'

'I hadn't heard about it,' he said.

'Your group commander is coming with a number of you.'

'I guess it depends who he picks, then.'

'Well, I hope you do come.'

'I hope so too, Miss Cutteridge. It's been good to meet you.'

She went back to Sir Geoffrey and polished him thoughtfully. The first real live American that she'd ever met. Fancy that! She'd had some difficulty understanding the way he spoke and some of the words he'd used but, all in all, she thought he had seemed perfectly civilized. Not nearly as bad as she had feared or Brigadier Mapperton had predicted. And he'd remembered *her* name while she'd forgotten his.

* * *

'Refreshments and a little entertainment, that's what the old girl said. What do you reckon that means, Ben?'

'A lot of English old maids pouring crap tea. Stuffed shirts, blimps and fossils. No floor show.'

'Yeah, that's what I figured.'

'I don't know why the hell the CO had to pick on us.'

Ed Mochetti lit a cigarette. 'I guess he wanted a couple of pilots and saw us first. She was a nice old girl.'

'Yeah, well, I'm not interested in old girls, only young ones.'

'Saw one of those, too. She came into the church.'

'I haven't seen a pretty girl over here yet.'

'This one looked kinda interesting.'

'Maybe she'll be at the party. Maybe one of us'll get lucky. I sure hope it happens soon or I'll go nuts.' Ben Feinstein shook his head. 'What a country! These guys live in the Stone Age. Nothing works. The plumbing sucks. This place is a dump. Look at it.'

Mochetti looked. The lounge of the Officers' Mess where they were sitting was housed in the old brick-and-corrugated-iron hut left behind by the RAF. It was furnished with a sorry collection of broken-down armchairs, plywood tables and some threadbare carpeting — also left behind by the British. His easy chair was missing a front castor and he had his right leg over the other arm and one foot on the floor to keep it balanced. 'OK. It stinks. So what? Our guys'll fix it. They'll fix everything the way we want it.'

'Meantime, we're living in shit.'

'Go take a look at the village down the road, though. Boy, is it beautiful! And real old. You know what, they've got seven of those bars they call pubs. I stopped by one. It was like something out of a story book.'

'Yeah, but the beer's lousy and there's no Scotch. That's what I heard.'

'There could be some at this Welcome Party.'

'Forget it, Ed. It's gonna be a real yawner.'

* * *

'If you could make some more sandwiches, Agnes dear, that would be so kind. We seem to have a long queue at the door already. Oh dear, it's going to be rather a crowd.' Miss Cutteridge was standing on tiptoe, peering out of the window.

There was hardly room to move in the small kitchen at the back of the village hall. The Welcome Party committee and several willing helpers had been hard at work for the past hour slicing bread and smearing it thinly with margarine and Shippam's Wholesome Bloater Paste. The tea urn was simmering away in its corner, cups and saucers set out ready, sugar put in the small bowls, bottles of lemonade and ginger pop lined up for the children, the finished sandwich triangles arranged neatly on china plates and covered with clean tea towels. A special plate of sandwiches with extra margarine and paste had been set aside for the Americans, with a different-coloured cloth. After some discussion, it had been decided that the guests of honour should have their tea and sandwiches taken to them, while the rest would have to queue up at the hatch. It had also been agreed that nothing should be served until the Americans had arrived.

Agnes scraped out the last of the paste from one of the jars and opened another. She had spread ten more rounds when Mrs Vernon-Miller, who had somehow taken command, stuck her head and shoulders through the hatchway. 'We're going to open the doors now. Everyone ready? Jolly good.' Her face was crimson beneath her WVS beret.

They filed into the hall — practically the whole village, so far as Agnes could tell from her view through the hatch. They stood about in clumps, talking and looking round. The black-smith's voice boomed out above the rest.

'Where's the bloody Yanks, then?' Somebody else shouted back, 'Late again.' Miss Cutteridge peered out of the kitchen window once more. 'Oh dear, I hope they come soon.' Twenty more minutes passed before a loud squeal of brakes outside announced their arrival. The waiting villagers turned, as one, towards the door and suddenly fell silent.

Agnes watched as they entered the hall — twelve or so of them in a group, dressed in well-tailored uniforms with olive jackets, light-coloured trousers, and high-crowned caps with gilt badges at the front. They removed the caps and paused uncertainly, confronted by a wall of eyes. There was a moment of silence when nobody moved or spoke and then Miss Hooper at the piano launched into 'The Star-Spangled Banner'. The Americans came to attention and saluted — an odd-looking salute with the palm downwards. When the anthem had finished the American commander in the centre of the group took a step forward towards her father, right hand extended, but with a warning rattle of the keys, Miss Hooper went straight into 'God Save the King' and the Americans all came back quickly to attention and saluted again. At Miss Hooper's final, crashing chord her father advanced firmly to shake the commander's hand.

'Good afternoon, Colonel. We welcome you and your men to King's Thorpe.'

'*Colonel*?' Mrs Salter whispered in Agnes's ear. 'But I thought they were Air Force. What funny salutes they have.'

'Thank you, Reverend. Very good of you to invite us to this gathering. We appreciate your hospitality.' The American group commander showed very white teeth as he smiled. He was tall, fair-haired, broad-shouldered and sun-tanned and his voice with its strong American accent, clearly audible to the very back of the hall, made a startling contrast to her father's soft, English tones. Agnes studied the Americans. They looked like beings from another world, totally untouched by war. Well-dressed, well-groomed, well-fed, fit and healthy . . . and well pleased with themselves. The colonel was introducing his men, in turn, to her father, who then began village introductions. Mrs Vernon-Miller's face reappeared with a hiss. 'You can start serving now.' At the clink of the teacups there was a rush for the hatchway.

'Would you take the American sandwiches out, Agnes, dear,' Miss Cutteridge asked. 'Mrs Salter and I are taking their teas.'

'Which plate is it?'

'The one with the blue cloth over it.'

As Agnes set forth with the superior sandwiches, Miss Hooper started up again at the piano on the stage, beginning with 'Keep the Home Fires Burning'. The Americans were still standing in a group with her father, the two Lady Beauchamps, Brigadier and Mrs Mapperton, Mr Reynolds, Miss Skinner, Dr and Mrs Graham and other village notables. She waited for Miss Cutteridge and Mrs Salter to finish handing out their cups of tea before she went round with her plate, starting with the colonel, whose tunic seemed covered with bits of shining brass as well as a pair of silver wings; he flashed her a smile as he took a sandwich. The next hesitated. 'What's in these?'

'It's bloater paste.'

'What the heck's that?'

'It's fish.' He pulled a face and shook his head. She moved on to the next uniform and offered the plate.

'You're Miss Dawe. The rector's daughter.' This one smiled too and had silver wings pinned on his chest as well, but not so much brass and, unlike his commanding officer, he was dark and foreign-looking. 'Saw you in the church the other day. I was talking with Miss Cutteridge when you came in.'

'I'm afraid I didn't notice you.'

'Yeah, well I was behind a pillar and you were in a big hurry. Some guy was ill and you were looking for your father. Did you find him all right?'

'Yes I did, thank you.'

'Is the guy OK? The one who was ill?'

'Yes, he's better now. Would you like a sandwich?'

'Sure.' He didn't seem interested in the filling but went on looking at her. The one standing next to him was staring too, making her feel uncomfortable. 'The name's Ed Mochetti. This guy here is Ben Feinstein. I'm from New York City. He's from Los Angeles.' It all sounded unbelievable to her. She held out the plate to the one from Los Angeles. 'Will you have a sandwich?'

He eyed them. 'I'll pass, thanks all the same.'

Miss Hooper, her bird's nest of hair disintegrating at the back, was working her way steadily through a selection from *The Maid of the Mountains*. 'Excuse me.' Agnes moved on towards the next American who turned out to be from somewhere in Texas and she had difficulty in understanding what he was saying. Another spoke behind her. 'Say, can I have one of those, or have I been a bad boy?'

'Sorry.' She offered the plate hurriedly. He smiled and told her that he was from Brentwood, Tennessee, wherever that was.

* * *

'Hands off, Ben. I saw her first.'

'Tough. There's only about three chicks here worth looking at and she's one of them. It's every guy for himself. What the hell's in that thing you're eating?'

'Who knows?'

'It's probably poisoned. I wouldn't put it past these Limeys. You see the way they keep looking at us like we're aliens or something?'

'I guess we *are* aliens to them.'

'Well, *they* sure look strange to me. I reckon some of the old ones have been around for about two hundred years. They don't smell too good either. You noticed that, Ed? I guess that's not surprising with their lousy plumbing. God almighty, that woman's playing tunes my great-grandmother knew. Can you believe it? I tell you, this country's stuck in time. And take a look at that Confederate flag they've hung up — what the hell do they think they're doing?'

'You've got to hand it to them for trying.' Mochetti swallowed the rest of his sandwich and drank some of the tea which tasted as though it had been made from old boots. A huddle of village girls aged about fourteen or fifteen were staring at him and when he winked at them they started to giggle. The rector's daughter was still going round the other guys with her plate. Not much chance that she'd be coming by again. He'd make a move soon.

Ben nudged him. 'Get a load of those kids. Kind of cute.'

'But kind of young.'

'Yeah, I guess we'd be breaking the law.'

The plate was empty and the girl heading towards the back of the hall. 'See you in a while, Ben.'

'She's got a ring on her finger, Ed, didn't you notice?'

'No, I didn't.' He shrugged. 'So what?'

He wove his way rapidly through the crowded room and caught her up just as she was about to disappear through a doorway. 'Hey, could I have another of those sandwiches?'

By the way she looked at him he had the feeling it was the wrong thing to have asked. 'I'll go and see if there are any.' He waited until she came out again empty-handed. 'I'm sorry but they've all gone.'

'That's OK.'

'There's some tea left, if you like.'

He shuddered inwardly. 'No, thanks.' Ben

hadn't been kidding. There was a ring on the third finger of her left hand: an engagement ring with a blue stone and what looked like diamonds each side. The guy must have some dough.

'I thought you Americans would get plenty of food,' she said pointedly, and he realized that she had him marked down for a class A hog.

'Yeah, we do OK. I guess we're lucky. You've had it pretty bad over here for a long time.'

'We've got used to it.'

'It's all new to us, see. So we get things wrong. Cigarette?' She shook her head and he lit one for himself, debating how to play it. He'd never met an English girl before. She was different from the girls he'd known back home. Reserved. Wary. And she didn't think a whole lot of him at the moment. She was already backing off.

'I must go and help in the kitchen.'

'Oh, sure. When will I see you again?'

She looked startled and her cheeks coloured. 'I really don't know.'

'Seems like we'll be around here for a while. What do you do — when you're not handing out sandwiches?'

'I teach at the school.'

Ben'd better believe this. The rector's daughter *and* a schoolmarm. He was about to say something else when somebody started clapping his hands and asking for silence and his CO climbed up onto the stage to speak. Get it right, Ed prayed. The guy wasn't famous for his tact and they'd be chewing on every word. He could sense the girl's distrust beside him, and in the whole room.

'On behalf of our Fighter Group, I'd like to thank all you good people for your welcome and your wonderful hospitality.' So far, so good, Ed thought, breathing easier. 'We know you've had a tough time these past years. Well, now that we're over here, your troubles are ended. You British can rest easy. You can leave it all to us. We're going to fight this war for you and we're going to win it for you, and we won't stop until the job's done. Thank you.'

There was dead silence in the hall and then the sound of someone storming out and a door banging. Ed put his hand over his eyes. 'Oh, boy.'

3

Tom lay on his stomach in the ditch at the roadside, with just his head poking out. That way the sentry at the gate couldn't see him but he could see part of the aerodrome and watch the Yanks coming and going. Six fighters had taken off earlier in the day — roaring right over him, making his heart pound in his chest with the thrill. Once or twice they'd flown low over the school during classes so nobody could hear a word the teacher was saying. When that had first happened he'd rushed to the window to look out and got thrashed afterwards by Mr Reynolds. Six stinging strokes of the cane across his hand that had left great red weals, but it'd been worth it to see the fighters zooming past. Sometimes the Yank bombers went over the school, too. Flying Fortresses with girls painted on them and the big white American star; they made the whole building shake. But it was the fighters he liked best. The bombers were elephants and the fighters were greyhounds. That was the way he thought of it. He'd watched the fighters climbing and diving and turning and he'd never seen anything so exciting in his life.

It was wet and cold in the ditch and his corduroy jacket and shorts were soaked, but he scarcely noticed. He went on watching and waiting patiently for the planes to come back. A lorry went in at the gate and then a jeep came out and roared off down the road. The jeeps were almost as good as the fighters. The only other cars in the village were Dr Graham's Morris, the district nurse's Austin 7, the policeman's Ford 8 and the old Daimler that did for a taxi and for weddings and funerals. None of them was fun like the jeeps. People kept grumbling about them going too fast and on the wrong side of the road, but he thought the way they raced around was wonderful. There'd been a whole lot of grumbling about the Yanks ever since the Welcome Party two months ago. Nobody'd liked the speech their colonel had made and then the Yanks had gone and fused all the electricity up at the aerodrome and all over the village as well. Old codgers like Brigadier Mapperton had kicked up a big fuss about that. It'd been off for three days before they got it mended. Not that it'd made any difference at home, as they didn't have any electricity anyway.

The Yanks came into the village all the time — mostly on bikes but sometimes they walked. They went into the shops and bought up everything and into the pubs and drank all the beer, so that meant more grumbling. Their bikes were parked everywhere, specially outside the Land Girls' hostel. Girls liked them all right, he'd noticed that. And not just the ones in King's Thorpe. Lots of others came in on the bus from miles away, just to try and meet the Yanks. He'd seen them all dolled up and waiting around near the pubs.

More lorries were grinding up the road; a long

convoy of them. He watched them slow and stop outside the 'drome entrance and the striped pole swing up to let them in. The guard was busy talking to the driver in the first lorry and Tom saw his chance. He was across the road in a flash, slipping between two lorries and in through the open gateway, under the raised pole. Nobody stopped him or seemed to notice and he kept on walking towards some huts. As he reached the nearest, the door opened and a Yank came out. He was wearing overalls and a cloth cap with the peak sticking straight up in the air. 'Hi, kiddo. Want somebody?'

He shook his head boldly. 'Just looking round.'

'Sure. Want to see the radio shack?' The Yank opened the door behind him again and beckoned. 'Come right on in.'

The hut was long and narrow with wooden work-benches all round the sides and electric lights with metal shades hanging low from the ceiling. More Yanks, dressed the same, looked up from valves and coils and wires and grinned at him. 'Hi there! What's your name, kid?'

'Tom,' he said. 'Tom Hazlet.'

'You from the village, Tom?'

He nodded. They let him wander round the work-benches and watch them repairing and testing things and warm himself at one of the two iron stoves that heated the hut. His wet clothes steamed as they began to dry out.

'Like some toast, kid?'

'Wouldn't mind,' he said casually. He was starving hungry.

They opened the stove doors and started

toasting thick slices of bread on the end of screwdrivers. When they were done, they spread something on them out of a jar and handed one to him. 'Peanut butter, kid. Ever tried it?'

He shook his head. It tasted sweet and nutty and kept sticking to the roof of his mouth. He unstuck it with his tongue and swallowed.

'Like it?'

'Yes, thanks.'

'Want some more?'

'Yes, please.'

He had three more slices, sitting on a crate by the stove. They'd painted pictures of girls in their underclothes on the whitewashed wall near him — skimpy, frilly things nothing like the women's underclothes he'd ever seen hanging out on clothes lines. He turned his head sideways to look at them more closely.

'Say, kid, can you bring us some bread from that bakery in the village when you're next up? We'll give you the money.'

'Course I can. Easy.' They tossed him over some coins. He counted them up quickly and stowed them in his pocket.

'How about eggs?' another said. 'Real, fresh eggs? Not that powdered garbage. We don't get none, 'cept for our pilots. A penny each if you can get us some.'

He hesitated. He could get the bread all right because it wasn't rationed, but fresh eggs were different. They were hardly ever in the shop. Mam kept a few hens but he couldn't take those eggs. Lots of other people kept them, though, including Farmer Dixon. 'I might be able to manage a few,' he said at last. 'I'll try.'

'You got a sister, Tom?' one of them drawled, chewing gum.

'Yes.'

'What's her name?'

'Nell.'

'How old's Nell?'

'She's ten months.'

They all crowed with laughter and he laughed, too, though he didn't really see the joke. He was finishing his last bit of toast when the fighters started coming back. The first one went roaring over the hut, rattling the windows. He jumped up and ran to look out.

'Know what those are, kid?'

'They're P-38s,' he said. 'Lightnings.' He knew because he'd asked the Yanks in the village.

'Want to go an' watch 'em?'

'If it's all right.'

'Sure it's OK. You ain't no spy. Come on.' One of them took him outside and called to another Yank going by on a bike. 'Hey, Chester. This is Tom. Wants to take a look at the planes. Can you take him out there with you?'

He rode in front, balanced on the crossbar, and they raced round the concrete track at the edge of the aerodrome and out to the far side where there was a hoop-shaped corrugated-iron hangar, some canvas tents pitched on the grass and several huts that looked as if they'd been made out of old wooden crates. A Lightning was taxiing along the track from the other direction and two Yanks in caps and overalls were standing watching and waiting for it.

Chester propped the bike against the nearest hut. 'Stay right here out of the way, Tom. Don't come any closer, case you get hurt.' He did as he was told. The fighter turned off the track and onto a concrete stand and the engines stopped, the propellers turning slower and slower until they were still. Chester and the other two Yanks had gone forward to put chocks in front of the wheels and Chester got up onto the wing and helped open the cockpit cover. The pilot climbed out. He stood there on the wing with his goggles pushed up onto the top of his helmet, oxygen mask dangling, a yellow life vest over his brown leather jacket, a white scarf round his neck. Tom gazed at him. He had seen lots of pictures of fighter pilots in comics but this one was really real. The pilot jumped down to the ground and stood talking to the three Yanks for a while until a jeep came fast along the track and stopped. The pilot walked over towards it, carrying his dinghy pack, and when he saw Tom standing there and staring, he grinned at him. 'Want a lift back, kid?'

He sat in the front in the space between the driver and the pilot. There were four more pilots squashed in the back with their packs and the jeep roared at top speed back round the track. His heart was pounding again with excitement. When they stopped outside a hut and all of them had spilled out his pilot said, 'You from the village, kid?'

'Yes, sir.' The pilot would be an officer and he knew that you always called them 'sir'. He pulled up his socks. 'I'm Tom Hazlet.'

The Yank lit a cigarette and snapped his lighter shut. 'Know anyone who'd do laundry there, Tom?'

He thought of the often-empty Oxo tin on the kitchen shelf. 'My mum might.'

'Where do you live?'

'Number 14, in the high street, past the bakery.'

'Great.' The pilot ruffled Tom's hair with one hand. 'I'll come by and see her.'

'What name shall I tell Mum, sir?'

'Lieutenant Mochetti.' He pronounced it Lootenant, like the Yanks always did. 'Call me Ed. Like some gum?' Tom caught the Wrigley's packet neatly.

He walked straight out of the main gate, ducking under the striped pole and past the sentry on duty, who gave him a wave. On the way down the hill towards the village, the old bus that had been converted into a WVS canteen passed him going up. He could see that bossy old trout Mrs Vernon-Miller looking out. He swaggered down the high street, chewing a piece of Wrigley's, and ran into Dick and Robbie and Seth. Dick barred his way.

'Where d'you get that gum?'

'Yank pilot.'

'You been up at the 'drome?' Seth asked suspiciously. 'You get inside?'

He knew they were always hanging about up there. 'Nah. No use trying. They won't let you in. It's Top Secret.'

He wasn't going to tell them about it, not for all the tea in China. He sidestepped Dick and sauntered on down the street, hands in pockets, chewing his gum and whistling.

* * *

Sergeant Chester Somers freewheeled down the hill towards the village. He'd bought his bike in a second-hand shop in Peterborough and it had cost him ten shillings, even though it was real beat-up. He reckoned it had been through a lot more than two owners, like the guy had told him, but he'd paid up. Soon as he'd arrived in England, he'd cottoned on that you couldn't get about without one. For a start, the base wasn't like the ones back home where everything was close together. Over here, the RAF had put buildings all over the place and kept the planes scattered round the airfield so the Germans couldn't bomb the lot together. It made good sense but it meant ground crew had a long way to go, to and fro. And off base, if you weren't taking the liberty truck into one of the towns and you hadn't got a bike and couldn't hitch a lift, you walked. He'd done some work on it — fixed the loose chain and the bent mudguard and the dud brakes and now it was pretty good. He'd taken a while getting used to the British lever brakes on the handlebars instead of coaster brakes like back home, and when he'd first hit them he'd gone clean over the handlebars. And he had to keep remembering to stay on the wrong side out on the roads. He'd got lost a couple of times riding around the countryside because the lanes twisted and turned so much he never knew where the hell he was heading, and the signposts had nearly all been taken away to fool the Germans if they invaded. He'd found out that if there *was* a signpost it had probably been turned round the wrong way, or borrowed from somewhere else. He reckoned the British needn't have bothered — the Jerries would get lost anyway.

* * *

He reached the foot of the hill and swung round to the left under the brick railroad arch and then round to the right again once he was through. Another half-mile and he rode into the village. He liked King's Thorpe. Coming from a small place himself, he felt more at home there than in one of the big towns and he'd never seen such quaint old houses; there was nothing near as old back home. Only trouble was, King's Thorpe didn't seem to like Americans. He'd found that out the first day he'd gone down with some other guys from the base and spent an evening in the Black Bull. He wasn't much of a drinking man, but he'd heard that the British pubs were friendly places. Well, the locals had been real unfriendly. They'd turned round and stared like they didn't want them there at all. Then things had got a whole lot worse when some of the guys had started shooting their mouths off and passing remarks about the beer. Hal had told the barmaid she ought to put it back in the horse, and Don had kept grumbling about how Americans were always charged more. 'The only thing cheap over here's the women,' he'd said in a loud voice. If the landlord hadn't stepped in there could have been a fist-fight.

Chester reached the first houses and slowed his speed. It wouldn't be smart to be seen tearing through the village because that was another thing the locals didn't like. Well, he could understand that. They'd got kids playing in the street and old folks crossing. It was mostly kids and old folks left as nearly all the men had gone off to fight unless they were doing something essential. Any girls he'd seen around had generally come in from other places and he didn't reckon much to the look of them.

He pedalled slowly down the street, aware of curtains twitching and unseen eyes watching him from dark windows. At the end he turned right into the street where most of the stores were — the high street, they called it. There was one halfway along that sold cigarettes and what they called sweets. He tried to learn the British words for things and use them because it seemed more polite. Sweets and biscuits, pavements and shops, petrol and lorries and torches. English cigarettes, he knew, were in short supply but he liked them a whole lot more than the American ones. He dismounted and leaned the bike against the wall outside the shop. ROBERT LAW, Tobacconist and Confectioner it said over the doorway. Whoever Robert Law was, he'd never seen him in there; it was always an old woman behind the counter. The bell on the door jangled loudly as he opened it. He had to stoop to enter because the lintel was so low and there wasn't much room inside either.

It was so dark that, at first, he didn't spot the kid. Like all the village boys, he was dressed in grey shorts and a grey jumper, woollen socks and black lace-up boots, and everything was darned or patched all over and near worn out. The old woman was halfway up a ladder, reaching down one of the glass jars from the shelves. She unscrewed the lid and shook out some kind of striped candy onto the scales and then tipped it into a paper cornet and folded the top over. The boy reached up with a big copper penny and a ration book so she could cut the coupon out. The English kids had had it tough, no question. They looked skinny and undersized to him — like they hadn't had a square meal in years. And their clothes were either too small or too big — never fitting just right. In his own family, there hadn't been the money for fancy stuff but they'd always been dressed decent — never in old cast-offs or hand-me-downs. And they'd never known such a thing as clothes rationing.

He asked very politely for a packet of Players. 'No cigarettes. Only pipe tobacco,' the woman told him curtly, pointing to the near-empty shelves behind her. Somehow he figured she *did* have some, stashed away for other customers, not Yanks, but he thanked her as he left. The little kid was starting on his candy outside and he gave him a Baby Ruth bar from his pocket. The boy's face lit up. 'Thanks, mister.'

'What's your name?'

'Alfie. Got any gum, mister?'

He searched in his pockets and found some.

‘Here you are, Alfie.’

‘Thanks.’ The kid put it carefully in his pocket, like it was treasure, and ran off.

Chester pushed the bike along the street, hoping to find another store selling cigarettes. He passed a butcher, a grocer’s and a hardware store and came to a baker’s. A green and gold HOVIS sign was fixed to the wall above the window. When he’d first seen the same sign at a railroad depot he’d thought it was the name of the place. Then when he’d kept on seeing it, he’d finally figured it out. Metal letters alongside the sign spelled out S. BARNET and underneath them, but smaller, High Class Baker. He peered in through the window and saw big wooden trays set out with loaves of bread stacked on end and different kinds of small cakes. They looked pretty good and made him feel hungry so he lifted the latch on the door and went in. Another bell jangled with a hollow sort of sound as he stepped down into the store but this time it wasn’t an old woman serving, but a young girl.

There was no counter, like in the candy store — just the wooden trays set out on two tables — the one under the window and another against a wall. And it was real warm, with a good smell of fresh baking. He stood by the door, waiting while the girl attended to a customer, and he watched as she put cakes into the woman’s shopping basket and the money into a tin in a drawer. She was quick as anything with the change, he noticed. He still couldn’t figure out the English money; all those halfpennies and pennies and shillings, never mind the sixpences and the threepenny bits and the farthings. She had quite a chat with the woman, smiling away at her, and he went on waiting patiently until they had finished talking. As the customer turned to leave he opened the door for her, making the bell jangle again on its leather strap, but she gave a loud sniff instead of thanks as she passed him on her way out. The girl smiled at him, though. She had some lipstick on — a soft pink colour — and she wore a blue and white spotted scarf tied in a bow at the top of her head with a lot of blond curls showing at the front.

'Hi there,' he said.

'Hallo.'

'That doorbell looks like a real old one.'

'It's a sheep's bell,' she told him. 'It's been there for years and years. Drives me mad.' She tilted her head to one side. 'Can I get you something?'

He realized that he'd been standing there like a dope, just staring at her. 'Some of those, I guess.' He pointed.

'The rock cakes? How many?'

'Huh . . . maybe six. And a couple of those there, please.'

'The raspberry buns?'

He nodded. 'They look real good. You make 'em here?'

'Oh, yes. Everything's baked in there.' She nodded at a big black iron door set in the brick wall at the back of the store. 'Dad does the bread, and Mrs Trimwell and me do the cakes. Do you have a bag, or anything? To put these in?'

'Gee, I'm sorry . . . '

'I'll see if I can find something for you.' She vanished through a door and returned after a moment with a brown paper bag. 'Mum hoards them. She's got a drawerful.' She put the cakes into the bag. 'Anything else?'

He wanted to delay things a little. 'What are those over there?'

'Cup cakes they're called. They're just plain sponge. We used to ice them but we can't get the sugar now.'

'I'll take six of those, then.'

She gave a giggle. 'Goodness, you must be hungry. Don't they feed you enough? I thought you Americans were supposed to have plenty — steaks and ice cream and things.'

'Not often — we don't.' He could have told her some things about the garbage they served up in the Mess: about the stink of the powdered eggs, the greasy mutton, the sweaty Spam, the chip beef that looked like vomit, or worse, the chalky dried milk, the endless Brussels sprouts . . . but he didn't want to talk about that. He wanted to find out more about her, and to know her name.

She put her head on one side again. 'What do you think of it over here, then?'

He'd been asked that question lots of times since they'd arrived in Liverpool and he was always very careful what he answered. They'd been warned about giving offence: provided with a booklet all about the British. They'd been told not to criticize or complain; not to brag or throw money around; to keep out of arguments; never to laugh at a British accent, and never ever to talk about coming over and winning the last war . . . or doing the same again this time. 'It's great,' he said. 'Everything's just great.'

She mocked him with her blue eyes. 'You're having me on. Just being polite. It's awful here — with the war on. You must hate it. It's lovely in America, isn't it?'

'You been there?'

She giggled again and he realized that she was younger than he'd thought at first; the lipstick and her hairstyle had had him fooled. Only seventeen or eighteen maybe. 'Me? Go to *America*? What a joke! But I've seen it at the pictures.'

'Pictures?'

'On the films. At the cinema.'

'Oh . . . ' He smiled. 'It's not all like that, see.'

'Are you an officer?' she asked, head on the other side now, looking him over.

He shook his head. 'I'm a sergeant.'

'You look like an officer. You all do. It's the nice uniform, I s'pose, and the shirt and tie. Our lot look quite different — the officers and the men. It's a lovely uniform, yours. So smart. Not like ours. What d'you do up at the aerodrome?'

'I'm ground crew,' he told her. 'An aircraft mechanic.' He thought she looked a bit disappointed, maybe because he wasn't a pilot?

She put the cakes into the paper bag, twisted the top at each corner and handed it over to him. 'That'll be sevenpence, please.' He pulled a bunch of change out of his pocket and sorted through it helplessly. 'Heck . . . will this do?'

'That's *much* too much. That's half a crown. Two shillings and sixpence, see.'

'How about this?'

'Still too much. That's a florin.'

That was a new one to him. 'A florin?'

'Two shillings. That's twenty-four pence. Look, I'll just take it, shall I? It'll be quicker.' He held out his hand and she stirred the coins round on his palm with one finger. Her hands were small and slender with nails the colour of seashells. 'Here we are: a sixpence and one penny.' She looked up at him, smiling. 'It's easy.'

As he put the coins away in his pocket, a middle-aged guy wearing a white overall came in through the side door she'd used. 'You can leave off now, Sally,' he told the girl. 'Your mother wants you. I'll look after things here.'

She shrugged. 'All right, Dad.' She smiled again at Chester over her shoulder as she went.

'Anything else you want?' The guy leaned both hands heavily on the counter, sleeves rolled up above muscled forearms and looking *real* unfriendly.

'No, sir. Thank you.' The sheep's bell jangled as he opened the door to go. He'd got two messages loud and clear. Her dad didn't like any Yank hanging round his daughter. And her name was Sally.

* * *

'I don't want you talking to those Americans, Sally.'

'I can't serve them if I don't talk to them, can

I, Dad? They spend good money. You ought to be glad.'

She was a sight too pert for his liking, sometimes. 'You know what I mean. Serving them's one thing, chatting to them's quite another. You were being much too friendly to that American. You don't want to encourage them.'

She rolled her eyes. 'I was helping him with the money, that's all. They can't work it out. Theirs is different. They have dollars and cents. A hundred cents to a dollar; it's much easier than our old shillings and pennies and things.'

She's been doing a lot of talking to them, he thought anxiously. Not just to that Yank today. She was putting on her coat now and tying her scarf round her head. 'Where do you think you're going, then?'

'Round to Doris, like I always do on Fridays.'

'I don't want you going out alone after dark. It's not safe. Not with those Americans about.'

'Doris is three doors away, Dad. And I'm not staying in all evening just cos you don't like the Yanks.'

She was gone before he could think of anything else to say. He sat down slowly in his armchair.

'You can't stop her, Sam,' Freda said, needles clicking placidly. 'You can't keep her prisoner. And you won't keep the Americans away from her.'

'I'll have a bloody good try,' he burst out, swearing in front of Freda for once. 'Damned if I won't.'

She came to the end of a row and turned the knitting. 'You go and put the kettle on, Sam, and make us a nice cup of tea.'

* * *

Ed Mochetti took the bend under the railroad bridge fast. It was raining hard and the jeep skidded as he hit a mud slick but he corrected easily and roared on. The rain was pelting down on the canvas tilt and gusting in through the jeep's open sides and he had to keep working the windshield wipers with his left hand so he could see where he was going. In the back there were ten bags of laundry — his own and nine from other pilots: shirts, underclothes, socks, pyjamas . . . everything they'd collected up. He slowed his speed as he entered the village, overtaking a coal merchant's horse and cart trundling along and stopping dead with a screech of brakes for an old woman who stepped straight out in front of him and tottered across the street. She was dressed in long black garments and took her time, shooting him a malevolent look. Probably put some goddam spell on him. He turned into what they called the high street. Number fourteen, the kid had said. Past the bakery. He saw the bakery with the sign over, S. BARNET, and looked for numbers outside the cottages down the street. There weren't any — or none that he could see. An old guy was standing at his doorway under a porch, smoking his pipe. Ed shifted his chewing gum to one side and yelled out to him.

'Say, number fourteen? Can you tell me which it is?'

Either the guy was stone deaf or he was faking it because he went on smoking and taking no notice. Ed cut the engine and got out of the jeep and into the rain. 'Excuse me, sir. I'm looking for number fourteen.'

The old man peered up at him with rheumy eyes. 'You a Yank?'

'Yes, sir.'

'Late again.'

'Sir?'

'Late for the last one. Late for this one. Always late.'

'You mean the war, sir?'

'What else'd I be talking about? When're you Yankee Doodles going to start doing some fighting, eh? That's what I'd like to know. Sitting around, eating your heads off. Drinking all our drink. Bothering our women. When're you going to start killing some Jerries?'

'Soon as we get the chance. Give us time.'

'Time? We've got no time. You lot yellow, or something? Our lads've been fighting and dying for four years. I fought in the Boer War myself and we wasn't yellow.'

'Would you just tell me which is number fourteen?'

'No, I'm not telling you. You can find out for yourself.'

Ed went back to the jeep, dripping wet and fuming. Crazy old fool. What did he want, for Christ's sake? Blood and guts raining down from the skies? Sure, the Group hadn't done any real combat missions yet but, hell, they had to get in some practice first. Two guys had already been killed in flying accidents and they wouldn't be the last. If they wanted dead Americans, there was no shortage with the Eighth bomber squadrons. None at all. He flicked the ignition switch, toed the floor starter and drove on slowly, peering out of the side of the jeep along a row of thatched-roof cottages until he caught sight of a rusty one and four nailed up over a doorway — the figure four hanging upside down. When he knocked, the door was opened by a thin woman in a flowered overall, carrying a baby on her hip. He smiled at her politely.

'Mrs Hazlet? Tom's mother?'

'What's he done now?'

'Nothing,' he said hurriedly. 'Did he say anything about laundry to you? We've a whole lot needs doing and I wondered if maybe . . . '

Her face cleared. 'Oh, yes, sir. He did mention it. I'd be glad to do it for you. Please come inside.'

He bent his head and stepped down from the street directly into the low-ceilinged cottage interior. The rainwater, he noticed, was running over the sill and into the room, forming a large puddle on the stone floor. It was dark inside, so dark that she'd lit the oil lamp above the table where she'd been sewing. Looking round, he felt as though he was in some kind of folk museum. There was no electricity at all, so far as he could see, and sure as hell no central heating. The old black cooking range in the open fireplace looked like something his Italian grandmother had always talked about. A kettle was simmering away on the top and there was a row of five flat irons, in diminishing sizes, standing upright at the back. A piece of cord strung above the range from one side to the other had washing pinned all along it. Clothes that looked kind of like rags.

'Will you have a cup of tea, sir?'

He shook his head quickly. 'No, thanks.' Tea, he knew, was rationed — not that he wanted any of it.

'I'll show you the washhouse, then, shall I?'

Still carrying the child, she led him through another low doorway into a small back room with a sloping corrugated-iron roof. Away from the range, it was bone-chillingly cold and damp. He noticed a tin bath hanging up on a hook and a couple of old buckets. 'We get the water from the standpipe, just down the street,' she said, pointing to the buckets. 'And I do the whites in there.' She showed him a copper cauldron in the corner, set in a brick surround. 'When the fire gets going underneath, it boils up and the clothes come nice and clean. I do the rest in the washtub. Then I rinse in the tub outside and put them through the mangle before I peg them out.' She opened a back door so that he could see onto a concrete yard with a long clothes line. There was a muddy cabbage patch beyond and a henhouse with a few bedraggled chickens scratching about behind wire netting. He noticed a small hut standing at the end of a cinder pathway and figured it had to be an outside privy. She shut the door and led him back into the kitchen. 'I iron them in here — on the table.

I think you'll find I do a good job, sir.'

The baby had started whimpering and the woman shushed it and rocked it to and fro on her hip, watching him anxiously.

'How much would you charge?' he asked. Better straighten that out first.

'Threepence a shirt,' she told him. 'They take a lot of time ironing to get them nice. Tuppence for a pair of socks. The same for underclothes.'

'Pyjamas?'

'Threepence — as there's two parts. But if you think that's too much . . . '

'No, no,' he said. 'That's OK by us. I've got some laundry with me in the jeep. OK if I leave it with you now?'

She smiled at him and he could see how glad she was. 'That'll be quite all right. I'll start on it first thing tomorrow. It'll be ready in three days. If you could collect it then.'

He schlepped in the ten canvas bags over his shoulder and set them down in the washhouse. 'I brought some wash-powder.' He handed her the packet of Oxydol. 'There's plenty of it at the base.' He wished he'd brought some chocolate to hand over as well.

'Oh, *thank* you, sir.'

'Ed's the name.' He stared uneasily at the huge pile of laundry. 'Sure it's not going to be too much for you?'

'Oh, no. I'll be glad of the money. It'll be such a help.'

'OK, then.' He chucked the baby under the chin and it chortled at him. 'What's your name, sweetheart?'

'It's Nell,' the woman told him.
'She's cute.'
She saw him to the door and he stepped over the puddle, ducking under the doorway as he went. 'Say hallo to Tom for me.'
'He'll be ever so sorry he missed seeing you. I do hope he's not a nuisance. He loves the aeroplanes, you see.'
He grinned. 'Yeah . . . me too.' He drove back along the high street. The old guy was still standing under his porch, smoking his pipe, and he gave him the finger as he went by. Further along the street he passed the entrance to the rectory. He'd called in there a couple of times but there'd been nobody home. Once, he'd gone round to the schoolhouse and tried looking in through the windows. They were all too high-silled to see in except for the kindergarten round the back. He'd taken a peek in there and seen Agnes Dawe with a bunch of little kids sitting in front of her, drawing things in chalk on a blackboard. Looked like she was teaching them to count. One of the kids had spied him and started pointing, then they'd all turned round. Agnes hadn't seemed too pleased, so he'd gone away. Now, on an impulse, he stopped the jeep, reversed back up and turned into the rectory driveway between the two stone gateposts. The gates themselves were missing, for some reason, but he could see the iron supports where they'd hung. He'd admired the house last time; it was a fine old place, built of the same stone as the rest of them with a slate roof, tall chimneys and steps going up to a white front door. Like all the doors

in the village it needed a repaint. Paint was hard to get, he guessed, like most everything else. Gas, booze, eggs, meat, coal, paper, sugar, you name it . . . these guys had been doing without for years and doing it with their ration books so it was jolly English fair play all round. He parked the jeep and his gum and walked up the steps. When he tapped with the brass knocker the rector himself opened it. Ed smiled politely, as with Mrs Hazlet; he figured you couldn't smile too much with the natives, unless they were like that old guy up the street. 'Lieutenant Mochetti, sir. I wondered if your daughter was home?'

'I'm so sorry, Lieutenant.' The guy pronounced it the English way, even though there was no such thing as an 'f' in the word. 'She's still at the school, teaching.'

'Well, thanks all the same.' He turned to go but the rector stopped him.

'But she'll be back soon for lunch. Come in and wait — if you'd like to.'

Inside it was cold as an icebox — no central heating here either, or if there was it wasn't on. There was electricity, though — real old-fashioned fittings — and a lot of dark, heavy furniture. Stuck in time, Ben would have said, but it all went with the place. He took off his cap and his leather A2 jacket — reluctantly — and followed the rector into a panelled room that was only slightly warmer than the hall. About three pieces of coal were smoking away in a small grate.

'My study,' the guy told him and removed a

pile of books from one of the two leather chairs beside the fireplace, balancing them on top of another pile on the floor. 'I'm afraid it's always a bit untidy. Do sit down, Lieutenant. Would you care for a sherry? I think there's a small amount left.'

For all he knew sherry was on the ration too. It would certainly be hard to get. 'No, thank you, sir.' He wasn't certain what else to call him other than 'sir'. Father wasn't right; maybe reverend, or plain mister? 'Is it OK if I smoke?'

'Yes, of course. I'm sorry I don't have any cigarettes to offer you. I don't smoke myself and nor does Agnes.'

He lit one of his own and sat down. The chair reminded him of the ones in the Mess; he could feel a loose spring sticking into him. The rector sat on the opposite side of the fireplace and smiled at him. Nice guy, Ed thought.

'We're all of us in the village extremely grateful to you young Americans for coming over to lend us a hand. Very grateful indeed.'

He said frankly, 'It doesn't always look quite that way to us, sir. A lot of people figure we came over too late again and that we haven't done much since we got here.'

'Oh dear. Perhaps some of the older inhabitants . . .'

'Yeah, sure.' He was sorry he'd said anything; the guy was looking upset. 'The kids are real friendly, though. But maybe that's just the candy and gum.' He refrained from adding that most of the girls were pretty friendly too.

'I don't believe it's that, Lieutenant. Perhaps

you don't quite understand. In many cases, fathers and older brothers have been away for months, even years. You're providing what many of our children — especially the boys — are missing. Men to look up to.'

He said slowly, 'I guess I've never thought of it like that.'

'Believe me, it's true.'

'Well, maybe the others'll think better of us when we start combat missions. When we start losing a lot of men, like our bomber squadrons.'

'I've heard about their losses . . . terrible. Truly *terrible*, Lieutenant. Six hundred on one raid alone last month, I believe.'

'Same number back in August when they got started on the big ones and a couple more missions in October lost thirty ships each. I guess you could say we're not doing too well so far.'

'To go in broad daylight seems a great risk.'

'That's what your RAF says. Only we think it's harder to do what they do — go at night. Maybe we'll be proved wrong in the end.'

'Perhaps you're both right — for different reasons. And with our weather I don't suppose there's much difference sometimes. In that bad fog we had recently I could hear some of your bombers going round and round, trying to find their airfields when they came back.'

'Yeah, that's a big problem when you've learned to fly somewhere like Texas.'

The rector leaned forward and prodded at the coals with a poker. A small flame flickered up and then died. 'I'm afraid the village has very little to offer you in the way of entertainment.'

'You've got seven pubs, sir.'

He smiled. 'There used to be even more, believe it or not. There are the Saturday night dances in the village hall, of course. Have you been to one?'

Mochetti had heard about them from some of the other guys. A three-piece band with that same old girl playing the piano, some old-timer squeezing the guts out of an accordion and another banging away on the drums. No liquor and more of those paste sandwiches. 'Not yet, sir.'

'They're really most enjoyable. Almost the whole village goes. It's a family occasion.'

'That so?'

'There's a modest entrance fee of one shilling — just to cover the costs and the refreshments, you know. You might enjoy it.' The clock on the mantelpiece started chiming. 'Agnes will be home any moment now.' The rector cleared his throat. 'She's engaged to be married, I expect you know that?'

'Yes, sir.' If he was being warned off it was being done real nicely.

'Clive, her fiancé, comes from one of our old farming families. He's away in the army — still in England at the moment, thank goodness. Training for the day when we invade the Continent, I imagine. Like your people. Though that day still seems a little far off at the moment. We'll just have to hope that you Americans will be able to speed things up, now that you're here. Ah, I think that's my daughter now . . . you'll stay to lunch, of course, Lieutenant?'

As she came into the room, he got to his feet. He noticed that she coloured up as soon as she saw him there.

'Lieutenant Mochetti was passing by, Agnes. I've asked him to stay to luncheon.'

'It's only bubble and squeak.'

'I'm sure he won't mind, will you?'

'Sounds find to me.' What the hell was bubble and squeak? And where was the wife? She hadn't been mentioned and he couldn't remember her at the Welcome Party either.

'That's settled then. While we're waiting, I insist that you have that sherry, Lieutenant.'

It was sweet and syrupy — like medicine — and he drank it down in two gulps — like medicine. The rector was asking something about the Group's function. No harm answering in general. 'We're here to escort the heavy bombers, sir. To see off any enemy fighters who try to bounce them. That's our job. Little friends, they call us.' He'd passed over the grim fact that if the target was beyond a certain distance the P-38s couldn't go all the way there and back with the bombers. No fighter could — not yet.

'You make it sound almost simple, Lieutenant.'

He smiled. 'Ask me the same question in a couple of months' time, sir, and maybe I'll give you a different answer.'

After a while the daughter came back to tell them that lunch was ready. He followed them down a dark passageway into a kitchen that was another museum piece. Some kind of big cooking range — though not as ancient as Mrs Hazlet's — heavy pots and pans hanging from hooks, blue and white dishes ranged along shelves, a large wooden table in the centre, scoured pale from scrubbings. They sat up one end of the table and the girl served out something from a frying pan and put it in front of him.

'It's cabbage, onions and potatoes,' the rector told him. 'My daughter grows them all here in the garden.'

He tried a forkful cautiously. He hated cabbage, even more than he hated Brussels sprouts; wouldn't ever touch it if he could help it. It wasn't bad, though. In fact, when he ate some more, he reckoned it was pretty good.

The girl sat in silence but her father seemed determined to be friendly. 'How long have you been in England, Lieutenant?'

'Since August, sir. We came over on one of the big liners from New York — close on twenty thousand on board. It was a real shock to us guys when we got to Liverpool, I can tell you. First time we'd seen what the Luftwaffe had done to your cities.'

'And where do you come from in the United States?' The guy was trying real hard to be nice — a lot harder than his daughter.

'New York City. I was born in Manhattan.'

'We've heard of Manhattan, of course, but I'm afraid we're rather ignorant about American cities. What part of New York is that exactly?'

'Well, Manhattan's where all the famous

landmarks are: the Empire State, the Rockefeller Center, Central Park . . . It's kind of an island. See, you've got the Hudson river on one side and the East on the other. To get to other parts of the city you have to cross one of the bridges.' He drew with his finger on the wooden table. 'The Bronx is up there, Queens is over there, Brooklyn's down there and Staten Island's over this side. That's the layout.'

'And you were brought up in Manhattan?'

'Yes, sir. My grandparents emigrated from Naples in the last century. My parents run an Italian restaurant on 53rd street.'

'How interesting. Do they do the cooking themselves?'

'They sure did when they first started. Now, they've got help. They're wonderful cooks, both of them — all the great Italian dishes. I guess they wouldn't know how to do this one.' He'd meant it as a compliment to the bubble and squeak but the minute he'd said it he realized it could be taken two ways and, from the look on her face, the girl had taken it the wrong one.

'Agnes makes some Italian dishes, I believe, don't you, my dear?'

He watched her colouring up again. 'Not really, Father. Only things with macaroni.'

He said easily, 'Well, I'd sure like to try one of them sometime. I haven't eaten macaroni in ages.'

She didn't answer that and the father tried some more. 'Do you speak Italian, Lieutenant?'

'Sure. We speak it all the time at home. But I consider myself an American, sir. One hundred per cent.' He paused. 'That's why I'm here.'

'It seems a very long way from New York to King's Thorpe. You must find it very different.'

'It sure is.' He couldn't come up with a bigger contrast.

'Forgive me for asking so many questions, but what made you become a fighter pilot?'

'Well, I saw a movie years ago when I was a kid — all about a barnstormer — you know, someone who goes round doing stunt flying to entertain crowds. I made up my mind then that I'd learn to fly like that one day, if I ever got the chance. So, right after Pearl Harbor I quit college and enlisted as a cadet with the Army Air Corps. Trained in Georgia and Texas and here I am.'

'I rather think you've left out some of the story.'

He'd left out plenty: the whole way he felt about flying. That being in an airplane was the place he really belonged to in the world. That it was as natural to him as being on the ground was to others. That whereas most guys were real nervous when they first soloed, he'd felt like he'd come home. 'I put it in a nutshell for you, sir.'

'And what do you think of our country, now that you're here?'

The Limeys always wanted to know that. He answered truthfully. 'It's straight out of a storybook. I've never seen such beautiful green countryside. Or such great old houses. Or such beautiful old churches.'

'Surely there are a great many of those in Italy?'

'I've never been to Italy, sir. This is my first trip to Europe. First time outside the US. And I sure didn't reckon on my first visit ending up this way.'

When they had finished the bubble and squeak the daughter cleared away the dishes. 'There's baked apple and custard for pudding, if you'd like some.' She said it as though she knew damned well he wouldn't.

'Sounds good to me.'

It *was* good. She'd put some sort of dried fruits in the middle and sweetened them with honey. He skipped the custard, though. His turn to ask some questions, he decided. That way she'd have to talk to him.

'How long've you been teaching at the school, Miss Dawe?'

'Two years.'

He reckoned she must be about twenty. 'You teach the little kids, that's right?' He knew very well that she did and she knew that he knew that she did. She'd seen him looking in through the window. 'What do you teach them?'

She was going pink in the face again. 'The alphabet. Numbers. Counting. Painting and drawing. Reciting and singing.'

'Anything else?'

She hesitated. 'Well, we have a Nature Table.'

'What's that?'

'We collect things on walks — leaves, fir cones, flowers, nuts, feathers, snailshells . . . whatever we can find. They're put on a special table and labelled. The children learn something about nature. They have a rabbit, too, and some guinea pigs that they look after themselves.'

The British were in a class of their own, he thought. Their country had been engaged in total war for four years, bombed to bits, struggling all alone for survival, but these little kids were still busily collecting stuff for their Nature Table.

A telephone started ringing somewhere and the rector headed for the door. 'Excuse me. I must answer that. Agnes, will you take care of Lieutenant Mochetti?'

She didn't look too thrilled about that and he reckoned it was time to leave and said so. He followed her back down the dark passageway to the hall and collected his cap and jacket. She was holding the front door open for him; outside it was still raining cats and dogs. He shrugged on his A2 and zipped it up. 'Say, we're having a dance Saturday at the Officers' Club. We've a pretty good band and we'll lay on the transport. How about you coming?'

'I'm afraid I couldn't.'

'That's a shame.' He twirled his cap round on one finger. 'How about the next one after that? It's going to be a regular thing.'

'I'm sorry.'

'You don't like dancing?'

'Sometimes, yes.'

'Then why not come along?'

'I'd just prefer not to, thank you.'

'Come on, give it a try?'

'No, thank you.'

'You that sure?'

'*Quite* sure.'

She'd got him figured for just another skirt-chasing Yank. No point going on. There were plenty more fish in the sea. He put his cap on. 'OK. Maybe I'll see you around. Thanks for the lunch.' He made a dash through the rain for the jeep, fired up the engine and worked the windshield wipers. As he drove off he could see in the side-view mirror that she'd already shut the door.

* * *

Tom always sat at the very end of the choir stalls nearest the altar. That way, he could read a comic without anyone in the congregation seeing. He didn't mind the singing part but the rest of the service was boring. He'd only joined the choir because Mum had said he needn't go to Sunday school any more if he did, and Sunday school had been even more boring — babyish games and feeble stories, making silly things out of raffia, pretending to be 'little birds that sing' and soppy stuff like that. He'd got into real hot water once when he'd cut off one of Jessie Hardwick's plaits with the raffia-work scissors. Being in the choir was a lot better than Sunday school, even though he hated having to wear the girly clothes and Mum always made a big fuss about starching and ironing his surplice and getting it whiter than anyone else's. They got paid a halfpenny for each service, too, but he thought it was stingy that they didn't get paid so much as a brass farthing for rehearsals.

The church was full. Squinting sideways from his vantage point he could see them all sitting there, always in the same seats and all dressed up in their Sunday best and wearing holy looks on their faces, never mind what they were like the rest of the week. Farmer Dixon, the mean old skinflint, never put more than threepence on the collection plate so he wasn't sorry about the rabbits. Or about the eggs. They were coming to the end of the 'Benedicite' which went on and on about ye Sun and Moon, ye Stars of Heaven, ye Showers and Dew, ye Fire and Heat, ye Whales, ye Fowls of the Air, ye Beasts and Cattle . . . and ye everything else whoever wrote it had been able to think of. A lot of the congregation had given up even pretending to sing. Tom swallowed a yawn before they started on the *Glory be to the Father* bit and then they all sat down for the Second Lesson. Brigadier Mapperton was marching across to the lectern, footsteps ringing out on the flagstones. 'The Second Lesson is taken from the Epistle of Paul the Apostle to the Romans, Chapter Five, beginning at the first verse.' There was a sound like a dog growling as the brigadier cleared his throat. ' 'Therefore being justified by faith, we have peace with God . . . ' '

Tom had already stopped listening. He was thinking about where he'd try next for some eggs for the Yanks. Maybe from one of Mr Barnet's coops behind the bakehouse? With all the chickens they'd got, he'd never notice a few missing. Better not to go back to Farmer Dixon's again. He'd climbed out of the bedroom window one night, so Mum wouldn't know about it, and slid down the washhouse roof below. There'd been a full moon which had made it easy as anything to nip across the fields, though he'd sooner have had it darker so he couldn't be seen. Some bombers had gone by in the distance, droning along. RAF bombers coming back from a raid on Germany, most probably; the Yanks didn't go at night. He'd skirted the farmyard until he came to the henhouses parked in the apple orchard — three of them side by side. The funny thing was there'd been a fox there, too, watching and waiting. He'd seen its eyes shine at him before it turned and trotted off, trailing its brush. He'd waited, too, just like the fox. All quiet. Farmer Dixon and his wife must have been snoring away in their beds. He'd shinned over the orchard gate, made his way without a sound to the back of the nearest henhouse and lifted the lid of the nesting boxes, feeling in the straw for the warm, newlaid eggs. There'd been seven stowed safely away in his pockets when he'd disturbed a hen sitting in one of the boxes and she'd made a real to-do. The farmyard dog had heard it and started barking and growling and leaping about at the end of its chain. By the time Tom had vaulted back over the gate Farmer Dixon had come bursting out of the house with his shotgun, firing it in all directions.

He'd raced back over the fields as fast as he could, afraid that the dog would be set on him, and he hadn't felt safe until he'd scrambled back up onto the roof from the water butt and got in through the bedroom window. One of the eggs had got smashed but the rest were all right. He'd taken them up to the 'drome the next day, together with six loaves from the baker's. Sally had slipped him a dozen rock cakes for free when he'd told her who the loaves were for. 'Don't tell my dad,' she'd warned him. 'He hates the Yanks.' He'd gone straight into the radio shack and they'd paid him a penny each egg and given him a whole lot more toast and peanut butter. He'd kept one penny for himself and put the rest in Mum's Oxo tin on the kitchen shelf. When she asked where he'd got it he'd told her the Yanks had paid him for running errands for them. Well, in a way it was true.

'' . . . in that, while we were yet sinners, Christ died for us.' Here endeth the Second Lesson.'

The brigadier stumped back to his place. Tom heard Miss Hooper kick the side of the organ to give the signal to the verger and then the wheeze of the hand pump starting up. The service dragged on with the Jubilate. He liked the next hymn and sang it his best.

Lift up your hearts! We lift them Lord, to thee;
Here at thy feet none other may we see;
Lift up your hearts! E'en so, with one accord,
We lift them up, we lift them to the Lord.

They'd all woken up now but they'd soon be dozing off again in the sermon. During the final verse Tom watched the rector climbing the stairs slowly to the pulpit, as if he was going to his execution. There was a lot of shuffling and coughing as everybody sat down. 'May the words of my lips and the thoughts of our hearts be now, and always, acceptable in Thy sight, Oh Lord, our strength and our Redeemer. Dear friends, once again we are approaching the celebration of the nativity of our Lord — a time when all Christians try to pay special heed to the doctrine of goodwill towards all men taught to us by Christ himself . . . '

Dick, Robbie and Seth in the choir stall opposite had their heads bent over something — probably teasing the beetle Dick kept in a matchbox. Tom groped under his surplice for the copy of *Boy's Own* that he'd pinched from the shop when nobody was looking. He slid it carefully downwards so he could see part of the front page. There was a colour drawing of a Spitfire shooting down a German seaplane in flames. 'The Secret of Nordstrand', it said (*beginning inside*). He turned the corner of the page to where the story began. The sermon only reached him in bits. Something about being nice to the Yanks. About how everybody in the village ought to ask them into their homes over Christmas as they were so far away from their own homes. There was a lot of fidgeting and muttering and Brigadier Mapperton was making that growling noise in his throat again. He knew Mum would ask the Yanks, only they wouldn't have any food to spare. Tom opened the page a bit more and went on with the story which was about a German secret weapon being built in a cave on a deserted island in the North Sea, off the coast of Denmark. It was a sort of rocket, powerful enough to destroy the whole of London at once and the Germans were going to launch it within a week. An RAF Spitfire pilot, flying alone over the island, had just happened to spot a Jerry seaplane taking off from near the beach . . .

Something stung his cheek. Seth was firing dried peas from a peashooter at him but the rest of them missed and he stuck his tongue out. The rector had got to the end of his sermon at last and everybody was struggling to their feet for the final hymn. Tom shoved the comic back under his surplice and opened his hymn book. The organ had got going again and they were just about to start when he heard the fighter coming. He knew by the sound that it was one of the Yanks' Lightnings. It went roaring low over the church spire, drowning out the first bars of 'All my hope on God is founded'. The stained glass in one of the transept windows shattered into pieces and fell inwards onto the floor.

4

The mobile canteen — converted from an old Skegness charabanc, with the seats taken out and a hatchway cut into one side — chugged up the hill towards the American air base. There had been a light snowfall the day before and a hard frost during the previous night. By mid-afternoon the temperature was still well below freezing. 'I should watch out for ice patches, if I were you, Lady Beauchamp.' Mrs Vernon-Miller, an impressive figure in her WVS overcoat, beret and badges, was riding behind the driver's seat, standing like Queen Boadicea in her chariot and gripping the back with one hand. 'These country roads can be treacherous. Are you sure you wouldn't like me to take over?'

As usual, there had been a polite but prolonged argument between them over who should drive. Mrs Vernon-Miller had, apparently, driven ambulances through thick and thin during the First World War but had never quite mastered the art of changing gear. Whenever she took the wheel, the charabanc leaped along like a kangaroo, the china mugs dancing a wild fandango in the back. This time Erika had moved firmly into the seat and refused to budge. She negotiated the slippery hill successfully and once they'd reached the top it was straight and flat to the aerodrome.

'Roman road,' Mrs Vernon-Miller bellowed

above the engine's faulty rumble. 'Did you know that, Lady Beauchamp?'

She hadn't. It was one of the many things she didn't know about King's Thorpe. What an irony to think that Roman soldiers had once marched where American airmen now drove. A jeep, approaching fast, shot past them with a whisker to spare. The Yank at the wheel grinned and waved and Mrs Vernon-Miller shook her fist after him. 'Some of those young men have no consideration. I've written twice to their commanding officer about the way they drive around here but it doesn't seem to make the slightest difference. No proper discipline, if you ask me. And their flying is just as reckless. It was an absolute disgrace about the church window.'

The row over the transept window — an incident on a par with the three-day electricity power failure — was still smouldering on. The beautiful fifteenth-century stained glass had been judged beyond repair and the Americans' apology and offer to pay for new glass to replace the irreplaceable had by no means smoothed the ruffled feathers in the village. Since there were no materials available for the job and nobody qualified to do it, the window had been boarded up for the duration. Brigadier Mapperton had been specially vociferous and there were plenty of others who agreed with him, including Erika's mother-in-law who was convinced that the pilot had flown low over the church with the express purpose of shattering windows. The fact that the window in question was known to have been in drastic need of leadwork repairs cut no ice and the rector's plea in his sermon for Christmas goodwill towards the Americans had fallen on stone deaf ears. Without consulting Miriam, Erika had sat down and written a letter to the group commander with an invitation to the Manor. Richard, she knew, would have done precisely that.

They were approaching the first entrance to the base and she slowed down to turn in and then stop. The sentry raised the striped pole and waved them through with a sort of casual salute. Mrs Vernon-Miller snorted. 'No idea how to salute properly. Not the faintest. If my husband were alive to see how slack they are he'd have a heart attack.'

They drove past a group of Nissen huts and out onto the concrete perimeter track. Their route would take them all the way round the edge of the aerodrome, stopping at each dispersal point and then at the main congregation of the station buildings and, finally, out by the main gate. The first lot of fighter hardstands were empty and the ground crews emerged from tents and the makeshift shacks that they'd built out of wooden packing cases. Mrs Vernon-Miller peered out. 'It looks just like a native shanty town. The RAF would never allow it.'

'At least it helps to keep them warm. The poor things must get absolutely frozen out here.'

They opened the hatchway and began dispensing hot coffee and doughnuts — Mrs Vernon-Miller with the brisk efficiency of a school matron dealing with delinquent boys. As she frequently remarked, she couldn't see why

Americans couldn't drink tea and eat ordinary buns, like everybody else. Outside the air was arctically bitter, the wind scything brutally across the heathland. The aircraft mechanics, heavy sheepskin coats over their greasy overalls, mud-caked boots on their feet, peaked caps on their heads, some with brims turned up — another bone of contention with Mrs Vernon-Miller — stood by the canteen chewing the doughnuts and warming their hands round the mugs. It must be a ghastly job, Erika thought. Out in all weathers. Miserably cold. Filthy dirty. Long hours, most probably. Vitally important not to make a single mistake because other men's lives depended on the job being well done. And none of the glamour or thrill of actually flying the planes. Normally, there were grins and wisecracks but today there were only grim faces. There was a big combat mission on, the boy that she had come to know as Chester told Erika. A tough one. A real bastard, if she'd excuse the word. Nearly all the Group's fighters had gone and they were waiting for them to return.

'Will they be back soon?'

'They don't tell us guys things like that, ma'am. We never know the target. Just have to sweat it out.'

They were getting ready to drive the charabanc on to the next dispersal point when Erika heard the sound of aircraft in the distance. The men had all turned their heads in the direction, intent as gun dogs. Some of them scrambled up the sloping sides of a blister hangar and balanced on the top for a better view. She bent to look through the windscreen as the fighters came into view from the south-east, gradually descending towards the airfield. Twenty, thirty, forty of them, perhaps more . . . it was impossible to count at that distance. The sound increased and she watched them bank and turn to make a circuit. They swept low overhead, rocking the bus and making the crockery jump and jingle. The circuit completed, they started coming into land in quick succession at the far end of the runway. The leader swung onto the perimeter track and went by close to them, engines roaring. Erika could see the pilot clearly through the perspex dome of the cockpit — his leather-helmeted head, his mask, his gloved hands. She could see, too, that the aircraft had been badly damaged. There were jagged tears along one wing, a big hole in the fuselage above the American star and several more holes towards the tail. Other fighters followed, also with battle damage, and three of them turned off onto the concrete hardstands near the charabanc. Mrs Vernon-Miller was shouting something at her but the ear-splitting din of the engines drowned whatever it was. Propellers windmilled to a stop and the mechanics ran to swarm over the planes.

'They haven't returned all their mugs,' Mrs Vernon-Miller said indignantly. 'There's six missing.'

'I'll go and get them.'

In their eagerness to get to the fighters, some of the ground crews had simply dumped their mugs on the ground. Erika went round collecting them. One was still missing but Mrs Vernon-Miller would have to lump it. As she turned back towards the charabanc, Chester came up with the other mug.

'Sorry, ma'am. I clean forgot it.'

'You've got *much* more important things to think about.'

'Yeah . . . '

'Are they all safely home?'

He shook his head, looking shocked. 'Some of them didn't make it.'

'I'm so sorry.'

'One was the group commander. Got hit by flak. Our guy saw him go down. Looks like he's had it.'

She thought of the tall, tanned, handsome colonel with his flashing smile. 'I'm so sorry,' she said again.

Back at the charabanc, Mrs Vernon-Miller recounted mugs and pronounced herself satisfied. She took up her Boadicea stance behind Erika again and they drove on slowly round the perimeter track. A jeep raced past them ferrying some of the pilots, but none of them waved.

* * *

Miss Cutteridge was in a quandary. Seated at her writing desk, fountain pen in hand, her nerve was failing her. Her conscience, though, spurred her on. The rector, who was such a *kind* man, had preached the need to show goodwill to the Americans. Differences should be put aside, he had told them, first as Christians and second, for the sake of the war effort, and the villagers could begin by inviting Americans into their homes over the Christmas season. They were our allies. They had come from across the seas, a long, long way from their own homes, to help defeat the Nazis. Many of them would never go back again. Miss Cutteridge had been greatly moved by the sermon. She had resolved to do something at once but had found herself making excuses. Her cottage was too small. It was improper for a single lady to invite strange men into her home. With only rations for one it would be very difficult, if not impossible, to provide an adequate meal — especially for Americans who would be accustomed to eating twice as much as any English person. The only one she might manage would be afternoon tea and she had learned that Americans rarely took tea. They didn't care for it as a drink and they didn't seem to like the sort of sandwiches that she could provide. The bloater paste at the Welcome Party had not been a great success; afterwards they had discovered a number of half-eaten sandwiches left by the guests of honour. Christmas had come and gone while she thought of more excuses.

A military lorry was grinding down the street and passed only a few feet from her sitting-room window. She could feel the desk and her chair shaking. Another followed and then another. Americans, of course, on their way to the aerodrome and loaded up with fuel or supplies or men. The peace and quiet of the village had been totally destroyed by an endless stream of American lorries, jeeps, cars, bikes, and by young airmen who monopolized the pubs, the shops, even the pavements so that at times she had had to step into the road to get round them. By now, they must surely outnumber the villagers. And there were so many differences: words used, pronunciation, dress, manners, customs . . . they weren't cousins at all but foreigners who happened to speak a kind of English. Murdering the King's English, Brigadier Mapperton called it and, for once, she was inclined to agree with him.

Miss Skinner, whose opinion she greatly respected, had had grave doubts about their morality from the very beginning and her own first favourable impression, formed from her meeting with the young officer in the church, had not been borne out. Other Americans whom she had encountered around the village had proved rather different and very disconcerting. They chewed gum and smoked in the street, and they left cigarette butts everywhere and chewing gum stuck on gateposts and under windowsills. They talked loudly and boastfully, they used deplorable slang and coarse language. Some of the leather jackets that they wore were painted on the back with pictures of near-naked women and she had observed the way they whistled at girls and how forwardly and familiarly they treated them. She'd heard them calling out things like 'Any time, lady, any time' in a shockingly blatant way, even to the most respectable women, though not, of course, to herself. Not at her age. The village was constantly invaded by the most undesirable kind of girls from other towns. They arrived by train and by bus and hung around outside pubs and on street corners, waiting for the Americans. Certain unmentionable things had, apparently, been found in shop doorways in the mornings. And, apparently, the Americans had now started to hold dances up at the aerodrome. Not tasteful ones, such as she had known in her youth with a small string orchestra playing lovely waltzes and foxtrots, but ones where very modern music was blasted out at top volume by a big American band and something extraordinary called the jitterbug was danced.

Miss Cutteridge put down her pen. Who knew what kind of young men might arrive on her doorstep were she to be rash enough to issue an open invitation? The risk was too great, the prospect too unnerving . . . even for the sake of the dear rector. She rose from her desk, and then sat down again. In addition to all the other talk about the Americans, there had been rumours quite recently of their losses. Several of the American fighter pilots had, apparently, been killed in action, including the group commander. Like so many villagers, she had never quite forgiven him for those unfortunate remarks at the Welcome Party, but he had probably been a perfectly good commanding officer to his men and she had been sorry to hear of his death — and of the others. Young men who, as the rector had so correctly predicted in his sermon, would now never go home again. Miss

Cutteridge sat down and picked up her pen again. She braced herself firmly. It was her clear duty to do something and a duty should never be shirked, however reluctant one might feel. She would address the letter, as the rector had suggested, to the station chaplain. An invitation to tea would be the safest. Four o'clock to five thirty and for no more than three airmen. If she saved one egg she could manage a small sponge cake, but she would have to think of something other than bloater paste for the sandwiches.

* * *

'He was in again today,' Sally said. 'He bought another lot of rock cakes.'

Doris giggled. 'He must be sweet on you, Sal.'

'Pr'aps he just likes rock cakes.' But she knew very well that wasn't the reason. It was easy to tell when a man was interested. You could always sense it and you could see it in their eyes — even the shy ones, like Chester. He'd come into the bakehouse five times in the past fortnight. By the second time she'd learned his name and where he came from; by the third she knew he was something called an assistant crew chief and that he was twenty-one years old; by the fourth he thought he knew how old she was, and today he'd finally asked her out. She'd come straight round to Doris in the evening because she was going to need her help. They'd gone up to Doris's bedroom, where they could talk without her mother overhearing. There was no light or heat up there and they sat on the bed huddled in their coats and with the candle lit. 'He's asked me to the Yanks' New Year's Eve dance up at the 'drome.'

'Oh, Sal . . . Whatever did you say?'

'I said yes, didn't I?'

'But what about your dad? He'll never let you — not the way he is about the Yanks.'

'I'm not going to tell him.'

'He's bound to find out.'

'Not if you help me, Doris. I'm going to say I'm coming round here, just like I often do, and that I'll be late back because I'm helping you make a blouse.' She'd got it all worked out. Dad'd believe that all right because she made all sorts of things for Mum and herself on the Singer, using any old bit of fabric they could lay their hands on. She didn't need any patterns, she'd just got the knack. 'I could bring a special frock with me and change here and then change back again when the dance is over.'

'Just like Cinderella,' Doris said, her eyes gleaming in the candlelight. 'I wish I could come too, Sal. You *are* lucky. I never seem to have any fun.'

'What would your mum say?'

'Don't think she'd mind. She doesn't care about anything much — not since Dad went. What does your Chester look like?'

'Well, he's tall. And he's got broad shoulders and sort of light brown hair.'

'What colour are his eyes?'

'Blue.' She'd noticed his eyes from the first because they were such a lovely deep colour. 'He speaks slowly in a funny accent. He says it's how they talk in Virginia.'

'Where's that?'

'Don't know. Somewhere in the south, I think. He lives in a place called Paradise.'

'That's funny! I expect it's very nice. It all looks wonderful on the films. How old is he?'

'Twenty-one.'

'That's a lot older than you, Sal. Six years older.'

She tossed her head. 'Boys of our age are so stupid . . . I can't be bothered with them. Anyway, I told Chester I was eighteen.'

'You didn't!'

'Yes, I did. He won't find out.'

'No, I suppose he won't. You look much older than fifteen, Sal.' Doris chewed at a fingernail — all her nails were bitten right down. 'I wish I looked like you. All the Yanks'll be after you at the dance.'

'I'm going to dance with lots of them — not just Chester.'

'He won't like it if he's sweet on you.'

'I can't help that. I don't want to be tied to one bloke all evening.'

'Well, I hope your dad doesn't ever find out. He'd be ever so cross.'

'I told you, he won't. If he asks you, just tell him I was with you all the evening.'

'Why does he hate the Yanks so much?'

'Dunno. He's just got a bee in his bonnet about them. I think he's afraid one of them'll go and rape me.'

'*Sal!* You don't think they would?'

She giggled. 'Then I'd find out what it's like,

wouldn't I? And I'd tell you, so's you'd know as well. Like we've always promised each other we would.'

Doris started giggling too and rolling around on the bed. 'I don't think I'd mind, would you? I think they're gorgeous, the Yanks. And I love their voices. Whenever I hear them talking it sends shivers all up and down me.' She giggled some more and then sat up again. 'Old Lady Beauchamp hates the Yanks, you know, just like your dad. I've heard her going on about them. Colonials, she calls them.' Doris put on a la-di-da accent: ' 'Those *frightful* colonials are ruining the village.' Young Lady B.'s gone and invited some of them to the Manor for dinner and she carried on like anything. I listened at the drawingroom door when I was dusting in the hall and heard them arguing. Old Lady B. was saying she wouldn't have Americans over her threshold and then young Lady B. says it isn't actually *her* threshold to say so and she doesn't care, she's going to invite them just the same. 'It's the least we can do,' she says. 'The very least.' '

'I don't know how you can stand working for that old cow.'

'I wouldn't, if it wasn't for young Lady B. She's nice. Not a bit stuck-up. And I like Master Alexander. He's nice too. Anyway, soon as I'm eighteen I'm going to join the ATS, or something. If the war isn't over.'

'Me, too.'

'Bet your dad'll try and stop you.'

'He won't be able to, will he? It's the law.'

Doris giggled again and then suddenly went serious. 'Will you really help me make a blouse, Sal? Another time?'

Sally nodded. Fair was fair. She owed it to Doris. And she felt sorry for her, with her dad killed by the Germans in France and her having to work as a servant and not having much fun. 'Course I will.'

* * *

Colonel Carl Schrader arrived at King's Thorpe to take over as the new group commander three days before the end of 1943. The men had been shaken up by the loss of his predecessor together with four other pilots on the Ruhr mission, but morale, he judged, was good. Major Peters, the group adjutant, summoned to put him in the overall picture, agreed.

'There's no problem operationally, Colonel. The men're up for it, no question. They want to do the best job they can.'

'Living conditions aren't too healthy, I've noticed. Seems like I've been lucky so far. The RAF pre-war bases I've seen are pretty good. Solid buildings, central heating, proper roads. None of that here, though.'

The adjutant said drily, 'You should have been here when we first arrived, sir. This place was knocked together by the RAF in a big hurry in 1940 when they thought they were going to be invaded. They didn't waste any time on frills. We've made some improvements but there's still plenty to be done. Mud's a big problem, too. It rained most of November and everything got bogged down. The cold weather's helped dry the ground out but it's still bad.'

'Hell of a climate.'

'I'm from Minneapolis, sir. It seems rather mild to me.'

Schrader smiled. 'I'm from St Louis, myself. So I guess I shouldn't complain too much either.'

'Speaking of complaints, Colonel, we do have another problem that maybe I should tell you about.'

'Shoot.'

'The folks of King's Thorpe village — with some exceptions — aren't too keen on us being here. There's been a lot of ill feeling and complaints from them.'

'What about exactly?'

'The usual ones — aircraft noise, low-flying exercises, traffic through the village — things we can't do a whole lot about. Then our electricians blew the power out locally for three days while they were trying to figure out the British system. That sure didn't help cement Anglo-American relations. And there've been other things . . . '

'Such as?'

'Public-house brawls. Our boys getting into arguments with the locals at the Black Bull, or the White Horse or any one of the seven pubs in the village. Sometimes it's our guys shooting their mouths off, sometimes it's over a girl, sometimes just nothing much. One of the landlords was overcharging every American that came in before they finally cottoned on that they were being rooked. There was a big row over that. I guess some of the British figure any Yank is an easy mark. And, so far as the folks in the village here are concerned, we're Big Talkers and Little Doers. You can understand it, Colonel. The Group's been here nearly four months and only just gone operational.'

'That's something time should cure soon enough. What else don't they like about us?'

'Drinking all their beer. Taking their women. Being paid better than their servicemen. And, I guess, just being here. We got off on the wrong foot, right from the start, unfortunately.'

'How so?'

'Well, the villagers organized a Welcome Party for us in the village hall when we first arrived — mostly the rector's idea, I gather. He's a real nice guy, incidentally. On our side. They were all pretty much willing to give us a fair try. Only Colonel McLaren made a speech that didn't go down too well. Along the lines of the British wouldn't have to worry any more now we'd come over to win the war for them. He didn't mean to give offence but, frankly, diplomacy was never his strong suit. That was the start of the trouble and things have gone downhill ever since.'

'Fill me in, Major. What else?'

'A while back when one of our P-38s flew low over the church here, a stained-glass window fell in. The locals reckoned the plane had caused it and kicked up a big fuss. We offered to pay for a new one, of course, but that only made things worse. Apparently, the glass was around five hundred years old and irreplaceable. I guess we looked kind of crass.'

'So, did it get sorted out?'

'Not so far. It's tough to get any work like that done right now so they've boarded the window up for the duration. We'll have to sort it out later on, when the war's over.'

'Anything else I ought to know about?'

'Well, lately we've had several letters objecting to the naked women painted on the fighters and on some of the boys' A2s. The village has more than its share of elderly maiden ladies. They see the fighters going low overhead and the backs of the jackets walking along the streets.'

Schrader smiled. 'You figure maybe I should issue an order, telling the guys to paint clothes on their girls? Think that'll do the trick?'

The adjutant smiled as well. 'King's Thorpe is a real backwater, sir. Life goes on pretty much like in the last century. And probably the one before. Maybe the one before that as well. Most of them had never set eyes on an American before we arrived to disturb their peace.'

'The reverse is true for most of us, too, Major. This is my first time in England.'

'Mine, too, sir.'

'So, how many people live in this backwater?'

'Somewhere between eight and nine hundred.'

'Huh. They're outnumbered.'

'About two and a half Yanks to every villager. Like I said, Colonel, we have a public relations problem.'

Schrader thought for a moment. The adjutant was an old hand, around ten years his senior, and he clearly felt the situation needed dealing with. 'The way I see it, Major, is this. Fighting this war comes first because, in the end, that's what counts — not what a bunch of British villagers think of us. If they don't like having us around, then that's just too bad; plenty of our boys'd sooner not be here either. At the same time, there's no sense us having to fight the British as well as the Germans. Our orders from the top are that we're to like them and see to it that they like us because that's the only way this job's going to get done. So, let's try and see if we can do something to mend the fences. How about asking some of them to a party up here?'

'Great idea, Colonel. We could get a list drawn up of the bigger fish in the pond and send out formal invitations.'

'Would they come, do you think?'

'I think they might, sir. If only for the food and the drink.'

Schrader nodded. 'OK, we'll really lay it on for 'em. Thanks, Major.'

The adjutant paused as he was leaving the office. 'A letter came for Colonel McLaren the same day he was KIA. A dinner invitation from Lady Beauchamp. She lives at the Manor in King's Thorpe. One of the big fish.'

'Have you met her?'

'Well, there are two of them. One older and one younger. I'm not sure which one the letter was from but I'd make a guess it was the younger.'

'How come there're two?'

'One's the dowager, I think you'd call it.

The other's her daughter-in-law. They're both widows. The 'Sir' is the son, and he's only a kid.'

'You think it's an olive branch?'

'Very likely, sir. If it's from the younger one. From what I remember, she's very pleasant.'

'How about the older? Is she an old battleaxe?'

'Not a bad description, sir.'

'Well, I guess we should take up the offer. It might do some good. Lady what, did you say?'

'Beauchamp, Colonel. They spell it B-E-A-U-C-H-A-M-P, but they pronounce it Beechum.'

'Sure they do, Major. They would.'

* * *

'And where do you think you're off to, my girl?'

'Round to Doris, Dad. Same as usual. She wants me to help her make a blouse.'

'Why can't she come round here?'

'We've got everything out on the table there and we don't want to have to move it.'

'What's that you're taking, then?'

She glanced innocently at the brown paper package under her arm. 'Magazines. We're going to copy something out of one of them.'

'Hmm. Well, what time will you be back?'

'Depends how long it takes. I promised her we'd get it finished this evening cos she wants to wear it soon.'

'I don't like you being out on a New Year's Eve, Sally. The pubs'll be full of drunks and Yanks.'

She gave an exaggerated sigh. 'I'm not going

near the pubs, Dad. I'm only going round to Doris's.'

'Well, see you're back by ten o'clock.'

'I won't be. That's not near enough time to get it finished. Eleven, more like. Night, Dad.'

She whisked out of the door before he could say another word. He'd be fast asleep long before then, she knew that. He was always in bed and snoring by ten because of having to get up so early to light the furnace and get the dough mixed. Up in Doris's icy bedroom she changed into the frock she'd made out of a pair of old curtains that Mum had got at a jumble sale. The material was soft velvet, the colour of a ripe Victoria plum. She'd used the best bits, where it hadn't faded, and made it with long, tight sleeves and a heart-shaped neckline, like in a picture she'd seen in Mum's *Home Notes*. Doris held the candle up for her while she tried to see herself properly in the small looking glass on the wall, bending down and then standing on tiptoe.

'You look beautiful, Sal. Ever so grown-up. Wherever did you find such thin stockings?'

She stuck a leg out. 'They're not stockings. It's Bisto. I mixed some up and painted it on. Then I drew a line down the back with an eyebrow pencil for the seam.' She twisted her leg round to show Doris. 'I read about doing that in a magazine.'

'You'd never guess. It looks just like stockings.' Doris sniffed hard. 'What's that perfume you've put on?'

'Evening in Paris. A spiv bloke came into the bakehouse the other day and I bought some. He was from up north and he'd got a suitcase full of all sorts of things. Perfume and lipsticks and soap and stockings . . . luckily Dad wasn't about. I'd've bought some stockings but they were five shillings a pair. Mum got some lovely lavender soap but she never told him.' Sally took a last look in the glass, tweaking at the curls on her forehead, and then put on her coat over the velvet frock. 'Wish me luck, Doris.'

'Oh, I do, Sal.'

'Swear you'll never tell.'

'Cross my heart.'

Chester had told her to be outside the Land Girls' hostel by seven and a truck would come by. She hurried down the high street, finding her way easily in the darkness. She knew every bit of the street: every kerb and lamp-post and wall, every dip or bump. The lorry was already parked outside the hostel, the Land Girls, all dressed up in civvies, climbing in at the back. A Yank sergeant in a white helmet shone his torch in her face.

'Any more where you come from?'

'There's only me.'

'Up you go, then, honey. We're leavin'.' He helped her into the lorry and then hoisted himself up after her and swept the torch along the benches on each side, counting heads. 'One, two, three . . . ten . . . thirteen . . . fifteen . . . twenty, two, three, four . . . twenty-nine. OK, girls. When we bring you back, I'm gonna want to count twenty-nine of you again, else I'll be in a whole lot of trouble. An' so will you.'

He dropped back down and went up front to

sit beside the driver. The lorry started off, jolting and swaying down the street.

'Ever been to a Yank dance before?' the girl next to her asked.

'No.'

'They're wonderful. Wait till you hear the band! First one I went to here was in the Aeroclub but this one's going to be in one of the hangars — as it's New Year's Eve. There'll be loads of girls coming from all over this evening, I should think. Know one of the Yanks, do you?'

'Yes.'

'They're so polite, aren't they? Lovely manners and ever such good dancers. Mine's from Milwaukee — not that I've got a clue where that is. I've been invited. We all have. But a lot of girls just go. *Those* sort of girls . . . you know.'

Another one of them said, 'Play your cards right and you'll get some nylon stockings.'

'We're not all like you, Rene,' the one beside her retorted and lowered her voice to a whisper. '*She's* no better than she ought to be.'

'I'm glad it's the fighters,' someone else said. 'They don't get the chop so much as the bombers. When I went to the Yank dances over in Suffolk, you never knew if they'd still be there the next week. Mostly they weren't. You'd meet someone nice and look for him next time and they'd tell you he'd had it.'

'The fighter pilots get the chop too.'

'Yes, but if a fighter goes down it's only one of them. If it's a bomber it's ten. I knew four blokes I really fancied and every one of them got killed, one after the other. It was horrible.'

The lorry ground up the hill and turned in through the main entrance to the aerodrome. It stopped at the guardhouse and then stopped again, further on, to let them clamber out. There were more lorries parked nearby, unloading more girls, and the Yanks started herding them up, like sheepdogs with sheep. They'd decorated the inside of the hangar with American flags, strung all along the walls and hanging down from the roof. A band was playing up on a platform — not just three of them like at the village-hall hops with Miss Hooper at the piano and two old men, but a dozen, at least, all blasting away on brass things with one of them bashing at several drums like he'd gone mad. And there were hundreds of Yanks dancing with girls, like they'd gone crazy too. Spinning them round, lifting them in the air, making the girls' skirts fly up. Chester was nowhere to be seen and Sally stood tapping her foot impatiently. One of the Yanks came up to her. 'Hi, there. I'm Rick. Care to dance?'

Wouldn't she just! She followed him into the crowd of dancers and he started swinging her round. Everything was a blur — the Yank's grinning face, the other couples whirling about — but after a moment or two she started to get the hang of it and it was the best fun she'd ever had. She danced with another Yank and then another and she'd almost forgotten about Chester when he finally turned up in front of her. He'd had to stay late, working on an engine, he told her, and he looked really upset about it. When she danced with him he wasn't so good as the other Yanks she'd danced with, which was a bit of a disappointment.

'That's a real pretty dress,' he told her, his eyes doing a lot of admiring. 'You look just swell.'

'Don't look so bad yourself,' she said. He must have just come out of the shower because his hair was wet and slicked down, and he was all shined up and smart in a dark shirt and light-coloured tie under the Yank jacket. She liked the way they slotted their ties inside the shirt, halfway down, in between the buttons; it looked really swanky. And they all looked so clean. She told Chester so and he laughed.

'Ought to see me out on the flight line, when I'm working. We get *real* dirty. Mud and dirt and grease all over us. It's a hard job getting cleaned up. Made a special effort this evening, though.'

'For me?'

'You've got it,' he said slowly. 'For you. Where did you buy that beautiful dress? London?'

'*London*!' She giggled. 'I've never been to London in my life. I made it myself — out of some old curtains.'

'Well, it suits you just right.'

'It'd be eleven points at least if I'd bought it in a shop.'

'Must be kind of sad for you having clothes rationed.'

'I suppose you don't have any rationing in America.'

'Yes, we do. Since we joined. Sugar, meat . . . and all sorts, and gas — that's petrol. Everyone has ration books. There's lots of shortages.'

'But not as bad as here?'

He shook his head. 'Guess not.'

'You Yanks are lucky. You've had it easy, haven't you?'

'Not any more.'

She thought of what they'd been saying in the lorry and was a bit sorry she'd spoken out like that. There was an interval for refreshments and he brought her something to drink. She wrinkled her nose. 'What's this?'

'Coke. Coca-Cola. Don't tell me you've never drunk that before?'

'We always have lemonade at the village-hall dances. Or ginger pop. But this is all right.' She looked round, seeing plenty of glances coming her way from other Yanks. Rick, the one who'd danced with her first, gave her a big grin and spun his hand round, fingers pointed down, raising his eyebrows in question. 'You don't mind if I dance with some of the other blokes, Chester, do you?'

'That's OK. Go ahead.'

She could tell that he *did* mind but she thought: he doesn't own me, does he? I'm not his girl. I've got a right to dance with anyone I like. The music was starting up again and she could feel her spine tingling. Her head, her heart and her feet were already dancing.

At midnight, when it was 1944, the trumpets played a big fanfare and the Yanks started whistling and yelling and kissing all the girls. One of them picked her right up off her feet and swung her round and round with her red skirts flying out, before he kissed her too. Chester, when she found him again, didn't pick her up or kiss her, or do anything like that. 'Happy New Year, Sally,' he said, looking down at her.

She looked up at him, smiling. 'Happy New Year, Chester.'

Then everything suddenly went quiet and the band started to play the American national anthem. All the Yanks had gone serious and solemn and Chester was standing very straight and still beside her. Same as us with God Save the King, Sally thought to herself, only I like our tune better and we've got a proper King.

The bloke with the white helmet was waiting by the lorry and he counted them as they climbed in. The music was still playing in her ears and her feet were still tapping away. She'd never had such a wonderful time in her whole life.

She changed back into her skirt and jumper at Doris's and let herself quietly into the cottage by the bakehouse, tiptoeing up the stairs. Dad was snoring away just as she'd known he'd be. She got into bed and lay wide awake for a while, smiling to herself in the darkness.

* * *

Brigadier Mapperton had heard the lorry rumble past his house. The Grange was set well back from the road, behind a high stone wall, but the constant racket from American military vehicles infuriated him. He rolled over in bed to look at the luminous alarm clock. Damned Yanks, driving about in the middle of the night! No consideration for anybody. He considered waking Cicily up to tell her so, and then decided against it. No point, really. She never said much. He turned the pillow over, pummelled it hard and lay back again. So far as he could see, the Americans were worse than useless. Their army was sitting around, doing nothing. Their air force was going on those damfool daylight bombing raids and getting shot out of the skies. God only knew what their navy was up to. They might as well have stayed out of the war, for all the good they were doing. Same story in the Pacific. Look what was happening out there. Island-hopping warfare against the Japs who were running rings round them. An island here, an island there . . . too bloody slow, the whole business. The Jap war could go on for ever at this rate. No chance of POWs out there being released for years.

As always, when he was awake at night, he started thinking about John. If only they knew how he was. Where he was. Whether he was alive or dead, for God's sake. Given the choice of being in a German prison camp or a Jap one, he knew which he'd take. The Japs weren't the same at all. Different values. Different code entirely. No respect for life. Sometimes he almost hoped that his son was dead — so that he couldn't suffer. That was the worst of it, the most terrible part: thinking of how he might be suffering. He'd never mentioned that to Cicily, of course. He knew she was as cut-up as himself even though she'd never said so. Never talked about it. Just buried herself in those damned silly library books of hers. He rolled onto his other side and tugged at the eiderdown. He wished now that he'd been a bit more lenient with John when he was a boy. Not quite so keen on all that discipline. He'd brought him up just the way he'd been brought up himself, of course. His own father had never believed in molly-coddling. Pity, though, that he and John hadn't been able to talk more — man to man. Only there'd never been that sort of thing between them, any more than there'd been with his father. Not many opportunities for it, either. The boy had always been coming or going — prep school, Oundle, Oxford, then the army. He regretted it now. Regretted it a hell of a lot.

His turn for Civil Defence duty tomorrow night — not that a damned thing had ever happened. Back in 1940 he'd half-wanted the Huns to invade so he'd get the chance of taking the swine on; of teaching them a thing or two, like he'd done in the last show. They'd given him an MC for it, by God. Now all he was good for was footling around with stirrup pumps and sandbags. He'd had it all worked out if it had ever happened. Kept his old service rifle and ammunition at the ready under the bed. Lock Cicily in the cellar, out of the way, that was what he was going to do, and let them have it from the windows. To the last round. Go down fighting. Not much chance of an invasion now, though. Those days were over.

He remembered suddenly that it was New Year's Eve. They hadn't stayed up for it. Never did now. There was nothing to celebrate. Just another year of war behind and another one ahead. 1944. No hope that it would be over this year either. Or that John would be coming home.

Cicily was making that bloody noise of hers — not snoring exactly but that little click at the end of every breath that was just as maddening. He gave her a prod and his pillow some more pummelling. Another military lorry was passing, making a devil of a noise changing gear. Damned Yanks! No consideration at all.

5

Erika Beauchamp was regretting her invitation to the American group commander. The timing had been unfortunate, to say the least, though that was not her fault; she had only discovered later that she had been writing to a dead man. His successor, a Colonel Schrader, who had eventually replied, accepting, was an unknown quantity. Predictably, Miriam had been against the whole thing from the start and that could easily prove a grave embarrassment. Her mother-in-law was quite capable of playing her *grande dame* act without mercy. Erika had been uncertain who else to ask, with feelings running so high against the Americans, and, in the end, had invited Dr Graham and his wife, both of whom could be relied upon to be friendly, and Miss Skinner who was one of the most fair and level-headed people she knew in the village. The rector, unfortunately, had another commitment that evening. After some more deep thinking, she had invited Brigadier and Mrs Mapperton, but without mentioning the group commander. If she did then the brigadier would certainly refuse but, once under the Manor roof, social obligation would force him to be civil, even to a Yank, and some oil might be poured on the troubled waters. Finally, she had written again to Colonel Schrader, suggesting that he might care to bring another officer with him; it seemed only right that he should have a second in his corner.

The other problem was what to give them all to eat. The cook was firmly under the impression that Americans only ever ate steak, but, steak being out of the question, Erika solved the problem by hardening her heart and sacrificing three old hens at the end of their egg-laying days. Elijah Kerfoot, who came once a week to do battle with the wilderness that had once been a lovely garden, carried out the deed and Mrs Woods concocted a chicken casserole, padded out with root vegetables, to be served with mashed potatoes and Brussels sprouts. They would begin with celery soup and end with Brown Betty, a speciality of Mrs Woods, made from apples and stale breadcrumbs. She hoped the Americans had strong stomachs.

At least she could provide some decent wine. The cellar, laid down by Richard's father, was still reasonably well-stocked with possibilities. She consulted Miriam, who shrugged unhelpfully.

'A complete waste, giving good wine to Americans. They won't know it from vinegar. Don't touch the Chambertin, for heaven's sake, or the Médoc. If you must, then I suppose you might as well give them a Beaujolais.'

On the evening of the dinner, she went to say goodnight to Alexander who was in bed reading another of Richard's old books. He looked up at her.

'What are you all dressed up for, Mummy?'

'We've got guests to dinner this evening, don't you remember?'

'I'd forgotten. Who's coming?'

'Brigadier and Mrs Mapperton, Dr and Mrs Graham, Miss Skinner and the American commander in charge of their air-force base here. He's bringing another officer with him.'

'Can you ask him for some chocolate? And some chewing gum?'

She smiled. 'He won't have any on him this evening.'

'He'll have gum. All the Yanks have gum in their pockets. They're always giving it to us.'

'It's a horrible habit — I really ought to forbid it.'

'They give us chocolate, too, sometimes. Hershey bars. And Baby Ruths — they're sort of chewy. Life Savers are OK, too.'

'I hope you don't bother them, Alex. You mustn't go around begging from the Americans. I absolutely *do* forbid that.'

'We don't. They just give it.'

'Well, it's very generous of them.' She went over to the window to check on the blackout. 'Another half an hour and you must switch out the light.'

'All right.'

'Promise.'

'Promise.'

She kissed him goodnight and left him to his book. Downstairs, all was well in the kitchen. Doris, who had stayed on late, was scurrying about at Mrs Woods's bidding. The chicken casserole was cooking slowly in the bottom oven, the Brown Betty in the top. In the dining room, much to Miriam's disapproval, the Royal

Doulton had been set out, together with the Waterford crystal. Her mother-in-law was sitting in the drawing room in her chair beside the fire. Erika noted that she had put on one of her prewar evening gowns with several of her best pieces of jewellery: definitely her *tenue de grand dame*.

'What is this group commander's name then, Erika?'

'Colonel Schrader.'

'It sounds German to me.'

'It probably is — or was. I believe a lot of Americans are of German descent.'

'Most peculiar, when you think about it.'

'I don't quite see why.'

'Fighting a war against their own people.'

'They're *Americans*, Miriam. Who they're descended from wouldn't have anything to do with it. They fought against *us* once, don't forget.'

'I'm not likely to. And I must say that I think we were well rid of them. Look what they've turned into: a hotch-potch nation made up of all kinds of foreign people. And why *Colonel* when it's supposed to be an air force?'

'It's the United States *Army* Air Force. They have army ranks.'

'Very odd.'

'Actually, the RAF was part of the British army not so long ago, if you remember that too.' The pointless bickering went on for several more minutes before the first guests arrived. Doris showed Dr and Mrs Graham into the drawing room and, soon after them, Miss Skinner. Erika had just seen to their drinks when Brigadier and Mrs Mapperton arrived. She gave the brigadier a large measure from a hoarded bottle of Glenlivet. He sniffed at it approvingly.

'Long time since I've had any of this, Lady Beauchamp. Special occasion, or something?'

'Not really, Brigadier.'

He grunted. 'Well, good of you to ask us. Not often we go out to dinner these days. Quite a novelty.'

'Is your daughter well?'

'Far as I know. They keep her pretty busy in the WRNS but she'll be home on leave at some point, I dare say.'

She had met Anthea Mapperton once: a brusque and unappealing girl in her early thirties. She had never met the son who had been captured by the Japanese, but the village always spoke very well of him. The brigadier himself never mentioned him; the word was that he had been devastated by the news. Imagining how she would feel if it were Alex, she felt desperately sorry for him and his wife. 'I've seated you at one end of the table, this evening, Brigadier. I do hope you don't mind acting host for me, as it were. It's awkward for my mother-in-law and myself — two women on their own.' She could see that he was rather pleased to have been cast in the role — which was just what she'd intended. Cunningly, she had put him even more under an obligation to be civil.

'Glad to oblige, Lady Beauchamp.'

As they conversed about the recent cold spell

and the shocking shortage of fuel, she kept an ear open for the sound of the front-door knocker.

'People have been stealing coal from the station goods yard, apparently,' the brigadier was saying. 'Don't know what the country's coming to when that sort of thing starts happening.'

'Would you excuse me, I think I heard our other guests arriving.'

Doris had opened the door to two American officers, who were standing in the hall. One of them she recognized as Major Peters whom she had met at the Welcome Party. After a slight hesitation, the other said, 'Good evening, ma'am. I'm Colonel Schrader. My apologies for being a little late.'

She smiled at him as she shook his hand. 'I'm Erika Beauchamp. Delighted to meet you, Colonel.' The new group commander was nothing like the old one. This one was shorter, darker and without the filmstar good looks. Much more Humphrey Bogart than Clark Gable. There was a strip of Elastoplast across his right temple and a bruise across his cheekbone.

'I believe you know Major Peters, our group adjutant.'

She shook hands again. 'Good evening, Major. So nice to see you.' She showed them into the drawing room and saw the disgust registering on Brigadier Mapperton's face, and Mrs Mapperton putting a restraining hand on his arm. The introductions were made all round, beginning with Miriam who received the Americans from her fireside throne in the manner of Queen

Elizabeth acknowledging a delegation from some upstart and far-flung land. The brigadier was forced to bark some sort of civil remark. The rest of them, as she had hoped, took great pains to be friendly and Mrs Graham led the conversation at once into the relatively safe realms of the weather. 'Miserable winter we've had so far, Colonel. I hope you're not finding our climate too trying.'

'Not at all,' he replied. 'Where I come from our winters are far more severe. Over here, our only concern is if the weather affects our ability to fly operationally. That's what counts.'

'And has it?'

'If it's possible to go, we go,' he answered obliquely. 'We've got a long way to catch up with what you British have been doing.'

'You rather look as though you've been in the wars yourself, Colonel,' Dr Graham said.

'I ran into some trouble on a mission the other day. Needed a couple of stitches, that's all.'

'I didn't realize until we heard the unfortunate news about Colonel McLaren that your station commanding officers actually went on operational sorties.'

'That's right, doctor. Same as the rest of the pilots. That's the way we do it.'

'You must be a very busy man.'

'Well, it's a real pleasure for me to take the evening off, and to get the chance to meet some of the people of King's Thorpe. It's a privilege for us Americans to be here in this beautiful part of England. I'm only sorry that we've had to disturb the peace.'

He was saying all the right things. Miriam was inclining her head graciously and even Brigadier Mapperton was looking a shade less like a ferocious bulldog.

'You can't help that, Colonel Schrader,' Mrs Graham said. 'You've got a job to do. Whenever one of your planes goes over I say to myself: that's the sound of freedom.'

Miss Skinner, unfamiliar in black silk instead of her tweeds, was talking to Major Peters and, by the look of it, that conversation was going equally well. After a while she came over. 'Colonel Schrader, I've been asking Major Peters if somebody from your Group could come to the village school and give our children an informal talk. Tell us about yourselves and about your country. They've been taught something about the history and geography of the United States, of course, but I'm sure that there are a lot of questions they'd like to ask that have nothing to do with textbooks.'

'That's a good idea, Miss Skinner. We'll fix it for you right away.'

She eyed him shrewdly. 'Thank you, Colonel. It's high time we all understood each other better, don't you agree?'

'I certainly do. And I'd like to hear about anything my men do or say that the people of King's Thorpe don't appreciate.'

Miss Skinner turned to Brigadier Mapperton. 'Did you hear that, Brigadier? Now's your opportunity to speak your mind.'

'Huh. Well, your confounded lorries, for a start . . . the way they go racketing through the village. Damned dangerous for the children and old people, never mind the noise they make and all the mud they leave.'

'I'm sorry to hear that, Colonel. I'll see something's done about it. We'll take a look at whether we can route the trucks round the village instead.'

'While you're about it, you might remind your chaps that we drive on the *left*-hand side of the road here. And stop them hanging about on street corners, making a confounded nuisance of themselves.'

Miss Skinner said briskly, 'Come now, Brigadier, we must be fair. There's nowhere really for them to go — except the pubs and only when they're open.'

'Damned nuisance there, too. Rows and fights all the time. Look at that one at the Black Bull.'

'I heard that was because Fred had been overcharging the Americans disgracefully for months and they finally found out about it. I can't say I blame them for being rather annoyed. It's been happening in other pubs, too.'

The brigadier grunted. 'Huh. Didn't know about that. Can't have that happening, of course. I'll have a word with Harry. Get him to put a stop to it.'

'Our village bobby,' Miss Skinner explained to the group commander. 'Between us, we might manage to make some progress in improving Anglo-American relations, Colonel.'

He smiled at the schoolteacher. 'I sure hope so, ma'am. And I'd appreciate it if I could be kept informed of any other complaints you people have.'

Miss Skinner looked amused. 'Brigadier Mapperton will be more than glad to do that. Won't you, Brigadier?'

The dinner passed off without any incidents. The brigadier, seated at the opposite end of the table to Erika, had Miss Skinner on his left to keep him under control and Mrs Graham on his right, acting as a buffer between him and Major Peters. Erika realized, though, that the silver-haired group adjutant, with his smoothly deferential manner, was capable of handling several Brigadier Mappertons. She had placed the group commander on her right with her mother-in-law on his other side and he, too, seemed to have no trouble in dealing with Miriam's occasional barbs. 'Yes, my grandparents came from Germany,' she heard him saying, in answer to the pointed question. 'I don't have any problem with that, Lady Beauchamp. We're fighting a regime.' He had even pronounced Beauchamp correctly.

The celery soup was rather watery and tasteless but the hens' sacrifice had not been in vain and the Brown Betty pudding was quite eatable. The wine was excellent and she was tickled to hear Colonel Schrader remarking on it appreciatively to her mother-in-law.

Towards the end of the dinner, he said to her, 'I want to thank you for inviting Major Peters and myself here tonight. It's given us a chance to try and smooth things over a little.'

'I think you may have drawn Brigadier

Mapperton's fangs — and that's not easy.'

He smiled. 'I meant what I said. We need to know of any complaints so we have a chance to do something about them.'

He was probably only somewhere in his early thirties, she thought — not much more than her own age. It seemed terribly young to be in charge of all those men; to have all that huge responsibility. And to have to fly in combat as well.

'You must have much more important things to think about than local grumbles, Colonel.'

'We need to get along, Lady Beauchamp. We figure that's important if we're going to do a good job fighting this war together.'

'Miss Skinner pointed out earlier that your men have nowhere to go in the village — except the pubs. The WVS are opening a canteen in the old Methodist chapel — '

'WVS?'

'Women's Voluntary Service. It's made up of women like myself who are not in the Services or doing war work in factories. We try to do our bit in all sorts of other practical ways. Actually, we come round your base with a mobile canteen.'

'Yes, I know about that.'

'This canteen we're opening in the village is for all Service people — whatever nationality or branch. We'll be open every evening and Sunday afternoons, serving snacks — tea and coffee, sandwiches, buns, cakes, that sort of thing. It'll be somewhere for the men to sit out of the weather. Not very exciting but if your men would like to use it, they'd be very welcome.'

'They'd appreciate that. I'll see that word gets around. This is a beautiful house you have here, ma'am.'

'I don't actually have it. It belonged to my husband, Richard, but he was killed in France in 1940 so it's passed to our son, Alexander. Or will do, when he's grown-up.'

'Where is he?'

'Upstairs in bed — asleep, I hope. He's only seven.'

'I have a daughter exactly the same age.'

'And where's she?'

'Back home in St Louis, Missouri. With my wife, Jan. I haven't seen them in months. By the time I get back, I guess Kathy won't even know me.' His eyes were an unusual steel grey, she noticed. German eyes? Miriam's hotch-potch nation. She was a hotch-potch herself with looks that were far more Hungarian than English. Another thing that Miriam had held against her until Alex had been born in the unmistakable image of Richard. The American went on, 'There's something else you could help me with, Lady Beauchamp. If you wouldn't mind.'

'Fire away.'

'We're planning to invite people from King's Thorpe to a kind of get-together party at the Officers' Club. We can't ask everybody — there's just not the room. Would you be able to let Major Peters have a list of all those you think would feel they *ought* to be on it — if you understand me?'

She nodded. 'Yes, I understand you. I haven't lived in the village very long myself, so I'm not the one to advise you, Colonel, but I know just who could. My mother-in-law will know exactly who you should ask.'

When the guests had left, she told Miriam about Colonel Schrader's request.

'I suppose he wants to include all the jumped-up tradespeople who will take offence if they're left out.'

'He wants to smooth feathers, not ruffle them more — that's all.'

'Everybody's somebody in the United States, so I understand. *Anything* goes. Did you notice the extraordinary way they ate? Cutting everything up with the knife and then eating with the fork upside down, like a shovel?'

'That's the way Americans eat. I thought their manners were impeccable.'

A shrug. 'They weren't as bad as I'd feared, I grant you that, but then I don't suppose they're typical.'

'Will you do that list?'

Another shrug. 'I'll see.'

But Erika knew that she would and that, secretly, Miriam was delighted to have been asked.

* * *

'How do you reckon we made out, Major? Think we charmed them enough?'

'I think it went pretty well, sir.'

Schrader leant back against the seat. He wasn't sure that he cared. All he wanted to do was roll into bed and get some sleep. Eight solid, unbroken hours of sleep. He knew there wasn't a chance of it. The evening had been a goddam effort and probably a wasted one. Sure, some of the inhabitants were willing to be friendly, but the rest probably hated Yanks — period. Nothing would change them. His driver swung the car round under the railroad bridge and then turned off to go up the hill towards the base. 'And what a house! You don't get to be in a beautiful old place like that too often. I was frozen to death, but what the hell.'

'I guess they're well used to the cold.'

'Must be. Old Lady B sure was a battleaxe. Glad you warned me about her. She took some charming.'

'I thought you might find her a bit tricky. The brigadier too.'

'He's real unhappy with us. I figure we'll be getting more complaints than ever now that I've opened the floodgates.'

'As a matter of fact, I thought that was kind of smart of you, sir.'

'Think I drew his fangs? That's what the young one said. She was no battleaxe, Major.'

'I told you she was very pleasant, sir.'

'Yeah.' He smiled faintly. 'You sure got that one right.'

* * *

The flowers arrived the next day: a large bouquet of red and white mophead chrysanthemums. Pinned to them was a note of thanks from Colonel Schrader. Where on earth, in the middle of Northamptonshire, in January, in a wartime England of unheated greenhouses, had he managed to get them? Even Miriam's acid tongue was silenced. With the flowers came a box of Whitman's Sampler American chocolates for Miriam and another box addressed to Sir Alexander Beauchamp. Inside it, Hershey chocolate bars, Baby Ruth candy and some things called Life Savers.

* * *

'Hallo, stranger.'

She said it casually as he came into the bakehouse: sort of tossed the remark over her shoulder while she moved some loaves around on the tray, though they didn't need it. Well, he hadn't been near the place for three weeks, not since the New Year's Eve dance, so what was she to make of that after him coming in almost every other day?

'Hi,' Chester said. 'How are you, Sally?'

'Not so bad. Haven't seen you in a long while.'

'They've kept us pretty busy up at the base. Working all hours.'

'We've heard the planes. A real din you've been making. We could hardly hear ourselves speak.'

'Sorry about that.'

'Not your fault.' She turned round from restacking the loaves. 'Dad and Mum have had an invitation from your colonel. He and your officers are giving a big party.'

'They going?'

'Dad's not. Not likely. He makes out he'll be too busy with the baking. Mum's going, though. Nothing's going to stop her, she says. She doesn't want to miss the food.'

'Didn't they invite you?'

She shook her head. 'It's mostly just the old people. Really boring. Do you want anything, then?'

'I'll take six of the rock cakes, please.' He took a brown paper bag out of his pocket and handed it to her. 'I kept this.'

'You're learning.' She picked out the cakes for him. The nicest-looking ones with the most currants.

'Hear you went out with Rick Domingos,' he said.

So that was it. That was what'd been the matter. She'd put his nose right out of joint. 'He took me to the pictures in Peterborough. Nothing wrong with that, is there?'

'No. Just wondered if you'd like to go with me sometime?'

'Maybe.'

'That yes, or no?'

She hesitated. It'd been fun going out with Rick and she liked flirting with all the other Yanks who tried it on. But it was Chester she'd been waiting for to come in again. Every time the bakehouse doorbell'd gone jingle jangle she'd looked up, hoping he'd be standing there. But now that he *was*, she didn't want him to know about it. Stay fancy free: that was her motto, wasn't it? Not just one bloke. That was stupid. But that was what Chester would want, wouldn't he? She could tell he wasn't the sort to play around. He was watching her in that way of his, with his lovely blue eyes, waiting for her to answer him. 'All right,' she said at last. 'If you like. Only I'll have to tell Dad I'm going with a girlfriend. That's what I did with Rick.'

'I'll tell him straight out. Ask his permission.'

'Don't be daft. He'd just say no. Give you a flea in your ear. We'll have to meet somewhere. Say at the bus stop in the village by the Black Bull.'

'I'd sooner there weren't lies told,' he said stubbornly.

'Well, if it worries you so much, I could ask my friend, Doris, to come too, then it'd be the truth, wouldn't it? Have you got another Yank for her?'

'Much better to tell your dad.'

'Then I won't be coming.'

He gave up. 'All right. I'll bring someone. How about this Saturday?'

'OK. We could catch the five o'clock bus in.' The sheep bell jangled loudly as another customer stepped down inside. She passed him the bag of rock cakes. 'That'll be threepence, please, sir.' As she handed him his change, she gave him a wink.

* * *

Miss Cutteridge was putting the finishing touches to the tea trolley. The jam sandwiches, cut into triangles with the crusts off, were arranged neatly on a white doily. She had been saving the jar of strawberry jam in her store cupboard for many months and this had seemed the moment to bring it out. The sponge cake, made with her precious egg, was on another plate. It hadn't risen quite evenly, but she had found a paper frill to put round so that the dip to one side didn't show and she had sprinkled a little sugar over the top. She checked everything again; three cups and saucers, three small plates, three cake forks, three teaspoons, the mother-of-pearl-handled cake knife, jug of milk, sugar basin containing her entire week's ration and the filigree sugar spoon, not forgetting the little basin for the slops. The teapot, ready warmed, was waiting on the side, the kettle simmering on the stove. The Crown Derby tea service, the cake knife, the spoons and the forks had belonged to her late mother and so had the mahogany trolley and the matching lace-edged linen tray cloths. She had clear memories of them all in use, her mother presiding, since her childhood. The napkins! She had forgotten all about them. She hurried to the tallboy where they were kept and took out three, which she folded into neat triangles and placed beside the plates on the lower shelf of the trolley. She consulted her wristwatch. Five minutes to four o'clock. Time to glance in the looking glass over the mantelpiece — just to make sure she was tidy. Then she sat down and waited.

At twenty minutes past four she was still waiting. The sandwiches were beginning to curl at the edges and she had had to turn off the kettle before it simmered dry. It was not until half past that there was a loud knock at the door that made her jump. She went to open it. The young American standing outside in the pouring rain lifted his wet cap to her.

'Afternoon, ma'am. Are you Miss Cutteridge?'

'Yes, indeed.'

'The name's Corporal Bilsky, ma'am. I've been sent to have afternoon tea with you.'

'Sent?'

'Yes, ma'am. They told two of us to come here. Only Gus, the other one, went sick, so he couldn't make it. An' then I couldn't find where you lived. They told me up at the base it was Lilac Cottage in West Street, but I couldn't see that nowhere at first. I've been goin' up and down, and lookin' all over, till I saw that little sign you've got up over the door. I'm real sorry to be late.'

'Please come in.' She retreated as he stepped forward, taking off his cap. 'Would you wipe your feet.' He was wearing some kind of raincoat on top of his uniform and when he hung it on the stand it dripped water all over the lino in the hall. Not a pilot or even an officer. Only a corporal. And only *one* of them, after all the trouble she'd gone to.

'Do sit down, Corporal.'

'Thank you, ma'am.' Ginger, curled up in the best chair, opened his eyes and glared. 'Nice cat you've got there. What sort would that be?'

'Oh, only an ordinary moggy.' Feeling flustered, she jabbed wildly at the fire she'd lit earlier, which was now almost out. 'Excuse me, I'll just bring the tea in.'

She went into the kitchen and put the kettle

back on. It seemed a long time before it came to the boil again and she could rewarm the pot and make the tea. Meanwhile there was silence from the sitting room and she wondered uneasily what he was doing. She measured out the Lyons Green Label. *One spoon each and none for the pot*. That's what Lord Woolton had said on *Kitchen Front* on the wireless and she chanted it to herself every time, from habit. The tea was much weaker, of course, but it went further. Little jingles were rather helpful. *Those who have the will to win, cook potatoes in their skin*. Far more nutritious, of course. She poured in the boiling water, set the teapot on its stand on the trolley and put the cosy over it. When she wheeled the trolley into the sitting room the American was crouching down on his haunches to stroke Ginger. The surprising thing was that Ginger was permitting it. *Most* unusual. He stood up.

'Can I give you a hand with that, ma'am?'

'No . . . thank you. I can manage. Please sit down.' She sat down in her chair behind the trolley. His shoes had left mud on her carpet, she noticed. 'How do you take your tea, Corporal?' She had already forgotten his surname — another peculiar American one. 'With milk?'

'Sure. Thanks.'

'Sugar?'

'Sure.'

He had sat down on the very edge of an armchair and she passed him the tea. He balanced the cup and saucer on his knees while he ladled in the sugar. *Three* heaped spoonfuls, she noted, with dismay. 'Would you care for a jam sandwich?'

She handed him a plate and offered the triangles. He set the plate and the sandwich precariously on one arm of his chair. 'A napkin, Corporal?'

'Oh, thanks.'

She watched him wondering what to do with it; in the end he laid it over the other chair arm. He was a nice-looking young man really. Wiry in build, of medium height and not what she'd call handsome, but the uniform was always a great help. She could see that he was as ill at ease as she felt herself. Conversation was going to be quite a challenge.

'Have you been here long, Corporal?'

'Four months, ma'am.' Half the sandwich triangle had vanished at one go.

'You must be getting quite used to us.'

'Don't know about that,' he said through the other half. 'It's a whole lot different from back home.'

'And where is home?'

'Place called Henryetta in Oklahoma.'

'Really? Where is that exactly?'

'About seventy miles due east of Oklahoma City.'

'I see,' said Miss Cutteridge, who didn't. She really must get out her old atlas sometime. Her knowledge of world geography was disgracefully limited. 'Another sandwich, Corporal?' He demolished three more while she nibbled at hers. Well, at least they weren't going to waste, she thought. 'I expect you find it all rather uncomfortable . . . after America. The rationing and shortages here.'

He shook his head. 'This ain't nothin'. Not to me. It was a darn sight worse when I was a kid, back in the Thirties. The Depression hit us real hard out in Oklahoma. An' we had this big drought an' dust storms blew away all the soil. No crops, no food, no work. People starvin'. We had a smallholdin' then and Dad went out shootin' jack rabbits for us to eat. Me and my brothers didn't wear no shoes in them days.' He shook his head again. 'I know all 'bout things bein' tough.'

She had difficulty in following everything he was saying but she remembered the Depression in America: the photographs in the newspapers of the destitute queuing for soup, the homeless huddled in packing cases, the veterans marching in Washington. America had recovered — just as Britain had recovered from the Slump. Somehow she had never thought of the fit and free-spending young men she had seen strolling about the village as being the children of that dreadful time. 'But, it's not like that any more, is it?'

'No, ma'am. Things got better. Dad gave up the farm an' got work in Henryetta. Me an' my two brothers all volunteered soon as we declared war. We're doin' OK now.'

'The three of you? Your mother must miss you.'

'She passed away when I was four. Don't have no memory of her — not to speak of.'

'How terrible for your father!'

'Sure was, ma'am. But like I say, we came through.'

'Where are your brothers?'

'Jack — he's the oldest — he's with the Marines in the Pacific. Don't know where exactly. Frank — he's the middle one — he's a gunner with the One Hundredth Bomb Group, in Norfolk, England.' He grinned at her. 'An' I'm here.'

'So you're the youngest?'

'Yes, ma'am. An' the dumbest. Least that's what Jack an' Frank always tell me.'

'Another sandwich, Corporal?'

'Thank you, ma'am.' It disappeared in a trice. 'England's sure not the way I pictured. I figured it'd be all lords and sirs, an' folks like that. Everyone talkin' like they was royalty, livin' in castles an' goin' round with their noses in the air. Only mostly it ain't like that at all. An' I hadn't figured on it bein' such a little place. No bigger'n Minnesota, they say. Everthin' so close together an' *real* small.'

'Really?' Miss Cutteridge had only the vaguest idea of what he meant. Americans must have the strangest ideas about England. And where was Minnesota? 'Will you have some sponge cake?'

'Sure thing.'

She undid the paper frill and cut a hefty slice. 'If you would pass your plate, Corporal . . . ' She put the slice onto the plate, together with one of the cake forks, and handed it back to him. He picked up the little silver fork and looked at it, puzzled.

'I'm supposed to use this, ma'am?'

'Well, yes.'

'Wouldn't want to do the wrong thing. Only it ain't like we eat back home.'

She cut herself a small piece and picked up her own fork. He had put the plate back on the chair arm, still balancing the teacup on his knees, and was stabbing at the sponge which kept falling off the prongs; she pretended not to notice. 'What sort of work do you do at the aerodrome, Corporal?'

'I'm with the Signal Company, ma'am. Telephone engineer. You see some guy up a pole, it's me. The RAF left us an underground network but we've had to set up a whole lot more lines. More of our guys arrive, more we need. We've got miles of field wire strung all over the base, an' switchboards connectin' everythin' to everythin'. Works real well now.'

'How interesting.' She put her hand on the handle of the teapot. 'More tea?'

'Sure.' He stood up to pass her his cup and saucer and knocked the plate off the chair arm. It hit the brass fender in front of the fire and broke into three pieces, scattering the remains of the sponge cake. 'Gee ma'am . . . I'm real sorry.' He had flushed scarlet to the roots of his hair and looked stricken with horror and embarrassment.

Miss Cutteridge was equally horrified, but tried not to show it. She said valiantly, 'It doesn't matter, Corporal.'

'Heck, it does, ma'am. That's a real nice china plate. I can see that. Where could I buy another for you?' He picked up the pieces and stared at them miserably.

'I'm afraid you couldn't. Not in wartime, anyway. They don't make things like that now.'

'Maybe I could mend it for you . . . so's it don't show.'

'I don't think that would be possible.' The poor boy seemed even more anguished. 'Please don't worry about it.'

'I'd sure like to try.'

In the end he took the broken pieces away with him, wrapped carefully in newspaper. At the door, she said, 'I'm afraid I've forgotten your name, Corporal.'

'Bilsky, ma'am. Joe Bilsky. Thank you for the tea, ma'am. I sure appreciated it.'

'You're welcome to come again, if you'd care to.'

'That's nice of you, ma'am, only I'd feel real uncomfortable. But I'll do the best I can with your plate an' bring it back.'

She shut the door after him and fetched a brush and dustpan to clear up the crumbs of sponge on the floor. What did the plate matter? It was really of no importance at all. She felt sorry for the young man; he had been quite distraught. Sorry for the father, too, so far away in Henryetta, Oklahoma. The father who had somehow brought up three motherless sons through the Depression. Come through, was the way Corporal Bilsky had put it. They'd come through. It was a good-sounding phrase. Both British and Americans would understand it perfectly, for once. God willing, they were going to come through together.

* * *

Tom hoisted the old wooden yoke across his shoulders and set off down the street, the two empty water buckets dangling and clanking from their chains. Dawn was coming up, the pale sky streaked with dark clouds, and Meg was out on her milk rounds with her horse and cart, filling the jugs left out on doorsteps. She gave him a smile and a wave as she ladled milk from a churn. He waved back. He liked Meg. She always gave Mum a bit extra and didn't charge for it. Some women were already at the water tap and he had to wait his turn, shivering in the cold, while they filled their buckets and gossiped. He never understood why women had to spend so much time talking to each other about nothing.

'Morning, Tom.' Old Mother Becket, who was one of the worst, had spied him. 'How's your mum?'

'She's all right.' He wouldn't have said if she hadn't been. Not if he didn't want the whole village to know about it.

'Doing a lot of washing for those Americans, isn't she? Taking on more than she can manage, I reckon.'

He would have liked to tell her to mind her own business but he said nothing and set his first bucket under the tap.

'How many's she doing for now, then?'

Nosy old cow. 'Don't know.'

'Fifteen, I heard. She'll kill herself, if she's not careful. Though I dare say you need the money.'

The first bucket was full and he started on the second one.

'When's that dad of yours coming home, then?'

'Don't know.'

'Still working on the aerodromes, is he? I'm sorry for your mother with him being away so much and having to cope. Keeps her short, does he?'

He turned off the tap, pretending he hadn't heard, bent his head and shoulders under the yoke and started back down the street. She called after him. 'Kill herself, she will, your mum.'

The full buckets weighed his shoulders down and he walked slowly and carefully down the street so that the water didn't slop over and get wasted. When he reached the cottage he shuffled in sideways through the front door and round the kitchen table into the washhouse at the back, where his mum was laying the firewood under the copper. Alfie was playing with Nell who was crawling around the floor. He let the buckets down and he and Mum hefted one up between them so's they could pour the water into the copper.

'Chop me some more wood, will you, Tom? There'll not be enough.'

He went outside to the shed where the pile was kept that he and Alfie collected when they went out sticking — gathering up all the dead wood they could find. Not that Alfie could carry much and he, himself, couldn't carry as much as Dad could yet, but, between them, they managed to keep the pile in the woodshed going for Mum. He took the axe from its corner and chopped up another lot to go on the copper fire. Alfie came to the shed door.

'Can I do that?'

'Don't be stupid, you'd go and cut your toes off.'

'No, I wouldn't. Go on. Give me a turn.'

He didn't bother to answer Alfie either, same as Mother Becket, but saved his breath for chopping. When Dad was home he sawed up big logs, but he wasn't strong enough to manage the saw himself yet. Maybe next year, when he was ten. 'You can help me take this lot in, then.'

The two of them carried armfuls of sticks into the washhouse. Mum had lit the fire and the water in the copper was beginning to warm up. She was sorting out the Yanks' laundry: the whites to go into the copper to be boiled up with Reckitt's blue, the rest in the dolly tub with warm water drawn off the copper, to be scrubbed on the washboard and worked with the dolly. After that Mum would rinse it all in the tub outside, put it through the mangle and peg it out on the line to dry. It took ages and made her hands go all rough and red and he could tell how tired she was by the end of washdays. Sometimes when she sat down in the evening she could hardly get up again. He thought anxiously of what Mother Becket had said.

'Can I help with anything else, Mum?'

'You could look after Nell a minute. Keep her away from the copper.'

He picked up his baby sister reluctantly. As

usual she stank and she was getting heavier. When he shifted her onto his hip she grabbed a handful of his hair in her fist and pulled it hard so it hurt. He was glad he'd be going off to school in a minute.

'Someone at the door, Tom. Can you answer it?'

Still holding Nell and with Nell still holding his hair, and with Alfie following, the way he always did, he went to the front door and opened it. Lieutenant Mochetti stood there, a jeep parked behind him.

'Hi, Tom. How're you doing?'

'OK, thanks.' He wished he wasn't carrying the baby, like a woman. Nell let go of his hair and started crowing at Ed, who tickled her under her chin. 'Hi there, Nell, sweetheart.'

Alfie stuck his head round. 'I'm Alfie.'

'Hi, Alfie.'

'Got any gum, mister?'

'Sure, kid. Here, catch.'

Alfie went and dropped it, of course. 'Thanks, mister. You a pilot?'

'Yeah, that's right.'

'Thought so. You've got wings on.'

The lieutenant grinned and ruffled Alfie's hair, even though he didn't deserve it for being so cheeky. 'I've brought a couple more bags of laundry for your mom, Tom. Think she can handle it?'

He nodded. Mum never said no to work.

'I'll fetch them in, then.'

Tom went on holding Nell while the pilot swung the bags out of the jeep and carried them into the washhouse. 'Brought something else for you, Mrs Hazlet,' he told Mum. He went outside again and came back with a big cardboard box that he put on the table. He began taking things out of it: packets of Oxydol and Rinso, tins of fruit and spam, a jar of peanut butter, a great big bag of sugar and several bars of soap. Alfie started touching everything while Mum stood there with her hands pressed tight to her cheeks.

'Oh, sir . . . ' She picked up a bar of soap and held it to her nose. 'It smells lovely. Thank you. I've never smelled anything so nice.' Alfie was sniffing away at another bar like a bloodhound.

The Yank pressed something else into her other hand. 'We figured you could do with an advance.'

'But this is much too much, sir.'

'We don't reckon so. Keep it.' He closed her fingers over the pound note. 'And the name's Ed, not sir. Here, kids, this is all for you.' Out of the same box came bars of chocolate and candy and packets of chewing gum. Alfie was grabbing everything he could and stuffing it into his shorts pockets. Ed tossed a Tootsie Roll to Tom who caught it and held it safely out of Nell's reach. 'You going to school today, Tom? Because that's where I'm going too. I'm supposed to tell you kids all about the United States of America. Want a lift?'

Alfie was made to go in the back while he sat up front in the jeep, beside the lieutenant. The bell was ringing out from the belfry as they went roaring down the high street, zipping past old

Mother Becket who flattened herself and her buckets against the wall and shouted something rude. Ed changed gear and spun the wheel with the flat of his hand to take the corner into School Lane. 'Haven't seen you up at the base lately, Tom.'

'Haven't been there for a bit,' he said casually.

He didn't have much chance to see the planes in term-time, with it getting light so late and dark so early, and with all the homework and helping Mum, too, but he'd managed to go up there once or twice at the weekends. Mother Becket would have been even angrier if she'd known it was her eggs he'd taken up to the radio-shack Yanks last time. He'd pinched a dozen of them from her henhouse one night and carried them off in a pocket he'd cut into the lining of his coat. This time, instead of a penny an egg, he'd traded them for cigarettes — two packets of Lucky Strikes worth sixpence each. Then he'd sold those in the village for ninepence. The Oxo tin was getting a lot fuller.

They drove up to the school when everybody else was going in. Dick, Robbie and Seth stood with their mouths open as the jeep came to a halt right outside the gates. Tom jumped out nonchalantly, pretending not to notice them. 'I'll show you the way,' he said to Ed, and he led the American fighter pilot proudly in through the BOYS entrance with Alfie swaggering along behind.

* * *

The schoolroom was straight out of the Charles Dickens novel he'd been made to read in high school. Gas lamps hanging from the ceiling, high-up windows, desks and benches at least a hundred years old, big-faced clock on the wall, a blackboard pegged on an easel, slates and chalks, china inkwells and nibbed pens for dipping in them . . . Ed looked round for the cane and, sure enough, there it was suspended from a hook on the wall behind the teacher's desk. The only thing missing was the dunce cap.

The headmaster who had greeted him was a dead ringer for Mr Squeers. They'd kicked off with prayers and a hymn and then Mr Squeers introduced him.

'Lieutenant Mochetti of the United States Army Air Force has been good enough to spare time to come and tell you something about his country, and to answer any questions you may have. Sensible, intelligent questions only, please. All sit.'

They were somewhere between six years old and eleven, boys and girls, all looking up at him, waiting for him to say something smart and he didn't know where the hell to begin. He laid his cap on the teacher's desk.

'OK kids, hands up who knows anything about America?' Several hands shot up. He picked on the nearest.

'What's your name?'

'Michael, sir.'

'So, what do you know, Michael?'

'There's lots of Red Indians there, sir.'

'Sure, we've got them.'

The boy said eagerly, 'Have you ever killed any, sir?'

He shook his head. 'Sorry, I come from New York City and there aren't any Indians there. And nobody kills them any more. They live in reservations now. That was in the old days when pioneers were settling all over the country and sometimes it was on Indian territory.' He picked up a piece of chalk and drew a rough map of the United States on the blackboard. 'See, you had different tribes living all over. The Cherokees here in the Carolinas and Tennessee. The Apaches down here in Oklahoma and New Mexico — now they were real mean.'

Another hand waved at him urgently. 'Did they scalp people, sir?'

'Sure did. Same as the Sioux further north up here in Montana, Nebraska, the Dakotas . . . ' He filled in some more on the map. 'Those guys were pretty unfriendly too. The Navajo out in Arizona and New Mexico weren't so bad. If you got caught by Indians, you'd want it to be the Navajo.' He picked on another hand. 'What's your question, kid?'

'Have you ever met the Lone Ranger, sir?'

'He's not real. He's just in movies.'

The boy looked crestfallen. 'What about Silver and Tonto?'

'Sure, there's a real horse but Tonto's just an actor, same as the Lone Ranger.'

'Roy Rogers is real, though, isn't he, sir?' somebody called out.

'Yep, he's real all right. Before you ask, though, I've never met him.'

'Are there still lots of cowboys out West?'

'Sure, kid. They're still riding around, herding cattle and lassoing steers. We don't need them near so much because of railroads and refrigeration, but they're still there. Only they don't have shoot-outs any more or fight the Indians. OK. Next question.'

'Can you tell us about the gangsters in Chicago, sir?'

He was going to be a real disappointment to them. 'Never been to Chicago myself, but as far as I know there aren't gangsters there any more. Not like the bad old days, at any rate. Not since they caught guys like Al Capone and John Dillinger.'

A cute little girl with ginger pigtails had her hand up. Her name was Jessie. 'Please sir, do you know any film stars?'

'Well, I met James Cagney once.' It was true, he'd come into the restaurant on 53rd street. Mom had gone into a swoon.

'What was he like, sir?'

'A real nice guy.'

'Have you ever been to Hollywood?'

'Sorry, sweetheart.'

As the questions went on it gradually dawned on him that, to these English kids, America was what they saw in the movies and the things they read in comics or in Wild West books. Sure there was a big map of North America hanging on the wall and they'd learned something about US geography and the climate and the crops, but the rest was dreams. Same as we get it wrong about England, he thought. Just the same.

Tom had his hand up.

'Make it an easy one, Tom.'

'Please, sir, can you tell us about the Lightning. What's it like to fly one?'

He grinned. This was something he could handle. 'It's great, kid. Just great!' They wanted to know all about how fast the P-38 could go, how high it could climb, how many guns it had . . . He had fun telling them.

'Have you killed any Germans, sir?' That was Michael again, who'd wanted to know about the Indians.

'Well, I've shot down one of their fighters. An Me 109. Don't know exactly what happened to the guy in it but he didn't bail out.'

They looked real pleased and impressed, even the girls. Bloodthirsty little monsters, he thought, amused. He looked at his wristwatch. 'OK, kids, I'm winding this up now. Before I go, though, I want to tell you something. America's not like you see it in the movies. It's not all about cowboys and Indians, and gangsters and film stars. Sure, we have rich people with big cars, living in wonderful houses, and we have the bad guys, too. But there's a whole lot of ordinary folk over there, living ordinary lives.' He looked round the classroom; they were all watching him and listening. 'It's a great big country — bigger than you kids can imagine. You could fit the whole of the British Isles into it hundreds of times over. People have gone to live there from other countries because there's a whole lot of space out there for them. Because they want to build new lives. Maybe they go to get rich

— because there's lots of opportunity for everybody to do just that. Maybe to get away from others treating them badly. Maybe to get happy. But I guess, most of all, people go there because it's a free country — just like yours. That's why we've got that great big Statue of Liberty at the entrance to New York harbour. Britain and America both believe in people being free . . . and that's why us Yanks are over here now to give you a hand, fighting the people who want to take that freedom away from us.'

Mr Squeers made a speech of thanks and the kids all clapped hard, so maybe he hadn't done such a bad job. Another teacher, a middle-aged woman dressed in green tweeds, came up to thank him as well. He thought he remembered her from the Welcome Party.

'I know you must be getting back, Lieutenant, but I wonder if you could spare a few moments to say hello to our kindergarten class? They know that you're here and I think they might be feeling a little left out of things.'

'Sure.'

He'd seen the room from the outside before, when he'd been taking a peek at the girl through the window. And there she was with all the little kids gathered round her skirts.

'This is Miss Dawe, our kindergarten teacher, Lieutenant.'

'Yeah, we've already met.'

He nodded to her and to the children. 'Hallo, there. You going to tell me your names?'

They did, with a bit of prompting from teacher. George, Susan, Wilfred, Joan, Peter

. . . all ever-so-English names. He got them to show him their Nature Table and admired the dried leaves and bits of moss, the acorns, the fir cones, the collection of empty snailshells, the nuts, the bird's nest and the magpie's feather. Then they took him to see the rabbit and the guinea pigs in their hutches so he could admire those too. After that, he sat down in teacher's chair and took Joan, one of the smallest, on his knee and set his American officer's cap on her head, at a rakish angle. They all went into fits of giggles and wanted to try it on as well, so it was passed round from kid to kid while they doubled up with laughter.

'You kids know any American songs?'

They shook their heads, fingers in mouths.

'OK. How about trying this one.' He bounced the little girl up and down on one knee while he sang:

Yankee Doodle came to King's Thorpe,
Riding on a pony,
Stuck a feather in his cap
And called it macaroni.

They giggled even louder and he sang it again for them. 'Come on, kids, it's easy. Let's go. All together now. One, two three.' In the end they were shouting it out with him.

'Time for me to leave,' he told them and swung little Joan off his knee. 'Down you get, sweetheart.'

She giggled some more and turned to teacher. 'Please, Miss, is he one of *our* Yanks?'

He got a kick out of that: *our* Yanks.

'Is he, Miss?'

Miss was blushing and avoiding his eye. 'Yes, Joan. He's one of ours.'

* * *

'We're not going, Cicily. Couldn't possibly. Not after what's happened.'

She looked up from her library book. 'Whatever are you talking about, Lionel?'

He brandished the card at her. 'This thing came in the afternoon post. From the Americans. Invitation to some sort of 'do'. We're not going.'

'But I thought . . . after the dinner at the Manor . . .'

He produced the envelope and thrust it under her nose. 'Look at that! Confounded nerve!'

'What's wrong with it?'

He stabbed furiously with his finger. 'Put the stamp on upside down, that's what's wrong with it. Insult to the King.'

'Oh, Lionel, I'm sure they didn't mean anything like that. It wasn't on purpose. It was just a silly mistake.'

'All very well to say that. How would they like it if I stuck their President upside down?'

'Perhaps they don't have Mr Roosevelt on their stamps.'

'No excuse. We're not going.'

'Very well, dear.' She was looking jolly down in the mouth about it, though he couldn't imagine why. 'Only the group commander will be very disappointed. He particularly wanted you to keep him informed, didn't he? To let him know of any complaints. You agreed to do that.'

'Huh.'

'So it would be a bit awkward to refuse the invitation. Rather rude. Still, as you say, perhaps we ought not to go, if you feel so strongly.' She picked up her book again. 'I don't expect they did that with *all* the stamps, so everyone else will be going. I hear they serve wonderful food and drink . . . whisky and all sorts of things.'

The brigadier cleared his throat noisily and walked about the room, pausing to stare out of the window at the early crocuses under the tree at the far end of the lawn. Not as many as there should be. Those damned squirrels ate everything. He'd've shot the buggers long ago if he hadn't had to save the ammunition for shooting the bloody Germans. Cicily had a point. That Yank CO had asked his help. Ought not to let the fellow down. Matter of honour between officers. The chap had his hands full, running the whole show up the road and fighting the war at the same time. Getting in an aeroplane and going out to shoot those damned Jerries down himself, not just sitting around behind some desk. Had to admire that. He cleared his throat again. 'I'll think about it.'

She turned a page. 'Very well, dear.'

6

Coaches had been sent into the village to pick up all the guests. Not ancient, clapped-out old things like the Skegness charabanc, Erika noted, but modern, comfortable, clean, well-sprung, smooth-running vehicles. Miriam, who maintained that she had never been in a bus of any kind before, was grudging about it.

'Well, they wouldn't expect us to walk, I hope. And there's only one taxi in the village.'

'They might have sent a lorry.'

'Don't be ridiculous, Erika.'

'That's what they do for the girls going to their dances.'

'*Hardly* the same situation. I think the way those girls allow themselves to be transported as though they were cattle is scandalous. Have they no pride? No shame?'

'They like the Yanks.'

'I can't think why.'

'I can. They're glamorous and good fun. They've got money to spend and they know how to treat women — from what I've seen.'

'Really, Erika, you'll be getting into one of those dreadful cattle lorries yourself next.'

The American Officers' Club was sited in a wood on the opposite side of the road to the operational part of the airfield. Inside, it looked as though it must have undergone a big transformation from its scruffy RAF days. This was America transported to England, Erika thought, looking at the well-stocked chrome bar, the non-utility furnishings and the Stars and Stripes prominently on display. At least as well as they could manage. And it was warm. Extraordinary to stand in a large room without a shiver; not to feel a single icy draught whistling down one's neck.

And their hosts were taking great pains to be friendly. The drinks were flowing — whisky, gin, vodka, sherry, whatever anybody wanted. Colonel Schrader and his officers circulated diplomatically and everybody was being very polite to everybody else. When he came round to her, she thanked him for the flowers and the chocolates and sweets.

'Wherever did you find such beautiful flowers in the middle of winter?'

He smiled. 'That's a state secret, Lady Beauchamp. I'm not at liberty to reveal it.'

'Well, I loved them. And Alex was thrilled with his sweets. It was so kind of you.'

'It was very kind of you to give that dinner. I wonder where *you* found enough chicken to feed us all.'

'Ah, that's *my* secret.'

He offered her a cigarette and lit it for her. 'How do you think the party's going, so far?'

'Are the natives thawing out, you mean?' She looked round the room. 'Yes, I think so. Definitely. Literally and figuratively. The brigadier is looking almost jovial. How on earth did you achieve that?'

'An unlimited supply of Scotch.'

'A brilliant tactical move.'

'I thought it might help oil the wheels. We've laid on a pretty good supper and then some dancing afterwards to our band.'

She raised her double vodka and tonic to him. 'God bless America, Colonel. I'm sure the evening will be a great success.'

* * *

Agnes saw Lieutenant Mochetti the moment she entered the Club room with her father. He was standing with another officer whom she remembered seeing before at the village hall — the one with the pencil moustache and the leer. She looked away quickly. If Miss Skinner hadn't insisted on it, she would have refused the invitation. But the importance of all three teachers attending had been pointed out to her forcefully by the deputy head. The Americans had taken the trouble to send an officer to the school, therefore there was an obligation to reciprocate the goodwill gesture by going to their reception.

'Something to drink, Miss?' An orderly held a tray of drinks out to her. She grabbed the nearest glass and found, too late, that it was gin. And a strong gin, at that. A group of officers came up and introduced themselves and she found herself surrounded. They were from all over the United States: Maine, Kentucky, Maryland, Illinois, Kansas . . . and they charmed her with their smiles and their easy talking and joking. Another gin later, they escorted her to supper, shepherding her gallantly between them into a room where long, white-clothed tables were laden with kinds of food that she hadn't seen for years, some of them never. And there was wine to go with it all.

After supper she danced with Maine and Maryland and Illinois and Kansas, one after the other, and the band was as good as anything she'd ever heard on the wireless. Actually, it was much better. And the Americans all danced better than anybody she'd ever danced with. She finished a spinning quickstep, expecting Kentucky to be waiting, and found New York instead.

'Hallo, Miss.'

She knew she'd started blushing, but she couldn't help it. He always had that ridiculous effect on her; it was the very reason why she hadn't wanted to come. 'The children enjoyed your visit very much,' she said, mindful of Miss Skinner. 'Especially the song. They've been singing it ever since.' It was true: they had. He'd been a huge success.

'I enjoyed *them*. They're terrific kids. How about a dance?'

She could hardly say no and he took her in his arms, holding her close. Much closer than the others had. It was a beautiful tune they were playing. 'Your band's awfully good.'

'Sure is. I told you so, remember? I guess you didn't believe me.'

Over his shoulder, she could see Kentucky signalling to her hopefully but Lieutenant

Mochetti kept her for the next dance and the one after that. At the end of it he asked her to go out with him.

She shook her head. 'I'm sorry but I can't.'

'There a problem?'

'I'm engaged to be married.'

'Yeah, I know. Is that the only reason?'

'Well, it's quite a good one.'

'It's a lousy one. There's no law against you having dinner with another guy when you're engaged, far as I know. Or maybe there is in old England?'

'No, of course there isn't.'

'And I owe you for the bubble and squeak.'

'You hated it.'

'Matter of fact, I didn't. It was great. Besides, we're under orders.'

'Orders?'

'Direct from Colonel Schrader. The big boss. We've got to be very, very nice to you villagers so we all get along a whole lot better. That's what he says. So, I'm trying to be very, very nice to you and give you dinner, that's all.' He looked her in the eyes. 'Just carrying out my orders, see.'

* * *

In the coach going home, Miriam said, 'Colonel Schrader plays bridge, you know.'

'Does he?'

'Yes, I was quite surprised. I suggested he came over one evening and we could make up a four with Brigadier Mapperton.'

'I'm not sure my bridge is up to it.'

'Nonsense, Erika. It's better than Richard's ever was.'

'I doubt if Colonel Schrader will have much spare time for playing cards.'

'Well, he seemed to think it was an excellent idea. I must admit this evening wasn't nearly as bad as I expected.' For Miriam to admit anything of the kind meant that she had positively relished it. 'Of course, they get all sorts of things wrong, but one mustn't be too critical. They can't help it.'

'I'm sure they'd appreciate your making allowances.'

'I shall write a letter of thanks to Colonel Schrader tomorrow. The Americans really do have some *extraordinary* names.'

* * *

'Make any headway with teacher, Ed?'

'Some.'

'I thought you'd given up on her. It sure is slow. Boy, what a collection they were! Only a couple of women under a hundred — teacher and the Lady of the Manor, and she wasn't playing ball.'

'Don't tell me you tried, Ben?'

'Sure. She's a widow, isn't she? It's always open season on widows. No dice, though. She's a good-looker and I could go for an older woman, specially a genuine live Lady. Tell you what, Ed, let's get down to London, next chance we get. Have ourselves a real wild time.'

'No can do. I'm taking teacher out.'

'Whoa! Hang on a moment. Careful, Ed. You're looking like you're real serious, or something. Easy does it. You want to keep it nice and casual or it's bad news for us guys. Gotta keep a clear head or some Hun's going to bounce you when you're thinking too much about a girl. And you're dead.'

'OK. OK. I know that.'

'Well, just don't you forget it.'

* * *

'This is Hal,' Chester said. 'Hal Hosterman. He's from Pittsburgh, Pennsylvania. He's the armourer on our crew.'

Doris giggled. 'What's an armourer?'

'I take care of the guns, honey.'

Doris was wide-eyed and Sally could see that she thought Hal was all right, though he wasn't anything much to look at — not compared with Chester. She made sure the two Yanks stood behind them in the queue, so nobody could tell they were with them. And on the bus she and Doris sat together with the Yanks further down. You couldn't do a thing in the village without some nosy parker noticing and telling everybody. Saw your Sally at the bus stop, they'd say to Dad. Going with one of those Yanks, is she? On the bus, though, Doris kept turning round and giggling, and Hal kept grinning and waving back, so she might as well not have bothered. When they got to the cinema, Chester and Hal paid for the dearest seats — not the cheap ones that she and Doris usually sat in — and the Yanks sat on each side of them, Hal next to Doris and Chester next to her. She loved going to the pictures. With everything so dreary outside, it was like stepping into another world. The Hollywood films were always the best, especially if they were in Technicolor. Everything looked so bright and clean; nothing was ugly or dirty. Hal was offering Doris a cigarette and lighting it for her with one of their snappy lighters. The Yanks were always quick to do things like that for girls, she'd noticed. Light cigarettes, open doors, offer their arm, carry things . . . they were a lot better at it than the English blokes.

After the B feature film there was a Donald Duck and the British Movietone News with pictures of British soldiers fighting in Italy and then some Yank Marines landing on a beach somewhere, and wading through a lot of surf with their guns at the ready. There was a bit showing the King giving out medals to some RAF pilots and the Queen visiting a hospital and talking to more soldiers — wounded ones in bed, this time. When the lights went up for the interval, she saw that Hal had his arm round Doris and Doris was looking like a cat that'd got the cream. Chester had lit a cigarette.

'Can I have a cigarette, Chester?'

'Sure. Sorry.' He groped for his pack. 'Didn't know you smoked, Sally.' She'd only tried it once when Doris had pinched a Woodbine from her mother. They'd taken turns at puffing it out of the bedroom window. Chester flicked open his lighter and held the flame out to her. She tried to copy how she'd seen the film stars like Bette

Davis and Hedy Lamarr having their cigarettes lit — bending forward to the flame and then leaning back, cigarette held out to one side, while they blew the smoke up into the air. Only when she leaned back and blew, she found the cigarette hadn't lit. Chester started to laugh. 'Try again,' he said. 'Only this time suck in so it catches.' But the next time it went out again and he took it away and put it between his lips and lit it for her. He was smiling as he passed it back.

'I don't see what's so funny,' she said crossly.

'I'll bet that's the first cigarette you've ever had.'

'No, it's not. I've had lots.'

'Oh, sure . . . '

'Your Yank cigarettes are different.'

'Oh, sure.'

When the lights went down for the main feature she was expecting him to put his arm round her, like Hal with Doris, but he didn't, not even when she shifted sideways a little towards him. That made her crosser still. She'd never hear the end of it from Doris.

When they came out of the cinema they found they'd just missed the bus back and had an hour to wait for the next.

'Let's go to a pub, girls,' Hal suggested.

'Sally's not allowed in pubs,' Doris said. 'Are you, Sal? Her dad won't let her.'

'He's not here, is he?' She glared at Doris. 'And I'm not waiting in the cold.'

The pub was beery and smoky and full of Service men — RAF and army and lots of Yanks. Doris asked for a lemonade. 'I'll have a port and lemon, if they've got it,' Sally said. She'd never drunk such a thing but it was Mum's favourite. She kicked Doris on the shin as she opened her mouth. When Chester and Hal had gone off to get the drinks, she hissed at her. 'Don't you dare say a word.'

'But they're not supposed to serve you anything like that until you're eighteen, Sal. It's against the law. You're under age.'

'And who's going to know that? I told you, Chester thinks I'm eighteen. So you just shut up.'

Doris looked offended. 'Anyway, I thought he was supposed to be sweet on you. He doesn't act like he is.'

The port and lemon tasted horrible but she pretended it was lovely, and when Chester gave her another cigarette she managed it better. Hal was talking away to Doris and Doris's face was all flushed and her eyes shining; she didn't look nearly so plain as usual.

'We're having a dance in the Aeroclub Wednesday next,' Chester said. 'Think you could come?'

She shrugged. 'Maybe.'

'I've been learning some new steps. One of the Red Cross girls has been teaching me.'

'Has she?'

'Yeah. There's a couple of them on the base now. American girls. They run the Club and they've been teaching some of us guys. They're pretty good.'

'Then you'll be able to dance with them, won't you?' Sally puffed at her cigarette and blew the smoke up in the air, just like Bette Davis. Then she took another gulp of the port and lemon. A Yank standing over by the bar gave her a wave and she saw it was one of the ones she'd danced with at the hangar dance. She smiled and waved back and he came over with three more of them. After that she didn't take any notice of Chester.

In the bus going back to King's Thorpe, Doris and Hal sat together in the dark at the back and she plonked herself down next to some old woman so Chester couldn't sit beside her. When they got to the village, Hal said he'd see Doris home.

'Don't bother,' she said to Chester when he started walking along beside her. 'I can see myself back, thanks very much.' But he carried on, shining his torch ahead on the pavement. 'How about that dance? Like to come?'

'You've got your Red Cross girls to dance with. Doesn't seem you'd care if I came or not.'

'I care a heck of a lot.'

'Well, you don't act like it.'

He stopped walking. 'You mean because I'm not all over you, straight off, like some of the other guys? Like Hal with Doris? That's not my way, Sally. I reckon it takes time. You need time to figure out what you really think about me. You don't know yet, do you? All the while you're still looking round at other guys, talking with them, dancing with them, to see if maybe you'd like them better.'

'Well, how about you with your Red Cross girls?'

'You've got that all wrong.' He sounded angry. 'They're like sisters. And I sure as hell don't think about you like a sister.'

She tossed her head. 'Oh *really*? Seems to me you do.'

'Want me to prove it? OK.' He switched out the torch and the next thing she knew he'd pulled her to him and started kissing her. Nobody had ever kissed her like that before — only village boys who didn't know what they were doing, fumbling and slobbering. Chester knew how to do it properly. She put her arms up round his neck, like she'd seen in the films, and kissed him back. When he let her go, she could hear him breathing fast as if he'd been running. He switched on the torch again. 'Guess I'd better get you home.'

* * *

Sam Barnet had fallen fast asleep in his armchair but he woke up the minute he heard his daughter come in. He took his watch out of his waistcoat pocket and looked at it. 'Where've you been, Sally?'

'The pictures. Like I said.'

He tapped the watch face. 'Half past eleven! You ought to have been back an hour ago or more.'

'We missed the bus.'

'Who's we?'

'Doris and me. Who else?'

He lurched to his feet. 'Have you been smoking?'

'Course I haven't.'

'That's not drink I can smell, is it?'

'Don't be silly, Dad.'

She looked flushed and sounded out of breath. 'Somebody been chasing you?'

'I ran the last bit, that's all. I was cold.'

She slipped past him like an eel and fled up the stairs. He called after her.

'You'd better not have been with any of those Americans.'

He heard her bedroom door slam shut and trudged slowly up after her. Freda was in bed, the eiderdown pulled up so he could only see her hair, all rolled up in curlers. 'Sal back, Sam?'

'Yes. Half past eleven it is. She should have been home an hour or more ago. Says she and Doris missed the bus, but I didn't believe her. I'd like to know what she's been up to.'

'Waiting in the cold for the next one, I should think. You were silly to stay up for her, Sam. You need your sleep.'

'I could smell cigarette smoke on her.'

'It gets on you in the cinema, with everybody smoking.'

'I thought I could smell drink, too.'

The eiderdown heaved as she sat up. 'Now, Sam, you're getting yourself in a state about nothing.'

'If she's been in a pub . . . '

'I'm sure she hasn't. And even if she had, it's legal, so long as she's over fourteen.'

'It's not legal to drink before you're eighteen, though. I'm not having a daughter of ours arrested and bringing disgrace on our name.'

'It's the landlord'd be arrested if that happened.'

'It'd be all over the *Mercury*. We couldn't hold our heads up.'

'Honestly, Sam, all you ever think about is your name.'

'Well it's important,' he said. 'It is to me, anyway. Once you lose your good name, you can't ever get it back. I've a business to run in the village. A reputation to keep up. Barnets have been bakers here for four generations. I've got Roger to think of and him taking over.' He sat down heavily on the edge of the bed. His back was aching like fury and he felt tired to death. In another four hours he'd have to get up again and start work, never mind the tiredness or the pain. He bent down to untie his bootlaces. 'I think she's been with some American, that's what I think. They come into the bakehouse and talk to her.'

'Of course they do. Our Sal's a pretty girl. Of course they talk to her and flirt with her.'

'I've seen her flirting back.'

'That's only natural at her age. They're good-looking boys.'

'They've no morals, Freda. Look at what's going on in the village. That Mrs Fitt, with her husband away in the Forces, carrying on with one of them, brazen as anything, and she's not the only one, not by a long chalk.'

'You can't blame the Yanks for that. If it's offered they're going to take it, aren't they?'

Sometimes Freda shocked him. 'Well, I think it's disgusting behaviour.'

'It's nature's way, that's what it is. When people fancy each other, it happens. Don't you remember how it was with us, Sam? Have you forgotten that time in the hayfield, that summer?'

He reddened, remembering it. He'd courted Freda in the proper way for over a year. Calling to see her regularly and sitting for hours in the hovel of a place she'd lived in, with the five brothers and sisters hanging round and sniggering. He'd asked permission of her drunken old father to address her before he'd bought the ring in Stamford and gone down on one knee to propose. Everything done as it should be. All right and proper.

'We were engaged, Freda.'

'Weren't married, though, were we?' She smiled at him and wagged a forefinger playfully. 'Jumped the gun, didn't we?' For a second, in spite of the curlers and the years in between, he saw the girl she'd once been with the long, nut-brown hair. 'Now Sam, stop fretting and fussing so. Sally works hard for you. She's a good girl and she does well, so don't be too strict with her. It's only fair to let her have a bit of fun. The Yanks are here and there's nothing you can do about it. Besides, you've been making money out of them, haven't you? You can't grumble. Not when they're spending so much in the bakehouse and with all the orders you're delivering up there.'

It was true enough. He'd got a regular twice-weekly order and the Officers' Mess were always asking for special cakes. Tuesdays and Fridays he took the horse and van up to the

American base to deliver it. It had gone against the grain with him but in his book you didn't turn down honest work, not if you could help it. He placed his boots neatly together by the bed and slid his braces down over his shoulders. 'Business is business. That's a different thing from what I'm talking about, Freda.'

She yawned and lay down, tugging at the eiderdown. 'Come to bed, Sam, and get some rest before you have to be up again.'

He undressed and clambered in beside her. She was asleep almost at once but he lay awake for a while, thinking of that hayfield and that summer long ago.

* * *

'I've brought your plate back, ma'am.'

Corporal Bilsky was standing on the doorstep, holding a brown paper package out to her. Miss Cutteridge, who had never expected to see him or the plate again, was taken completely by surprise. 'Good gracious me. Bless my soul!'

There was a bitter wind blowing down the street and she felt obliged to invite him inside and then into the sitting room, as the hallway was so narrow. He waited, cap in hand, while she undid the brown paper. The Crown Derby plate had been beautifully mended. So well that she couldn't see the joins.

'However did you manage this, Corporal?'

'Well, I can fix most things pretty good. Are you satisfied, ma'am?'

'Of course I am. It's wonderful — the breaks

are quite invisible. Thank you, Corporal.'

'I'm real sorry it got broke.' He felt in his left pocket and then his right. 'These are for you, ma'am.'

'For me?'

'Yes, ma'am.'

'Oh, my goodness . . .' He was holding out a bar of chocolate and a tin of spam. She stared at them in dismay. 'Oh, dear.'

He looked deflated. 'I guess you don't like them. Tried to get some ham but there weren't none this time.'

'No, no . . . it isn't that. But I really can't accept them, Corporal. I hardly know you. It wouldn't be correct, you understand.'

It was obvious that he didn't understand at all. Perhaps they had different rules in America? Different customs?

'Gee, we're givin' this stuff away all the time, ma'am. Just tryin' to help you folks, seein' as you're so short of things. I'd be obliged if you'd take it.'

How could she refuse when he put it like that? It would be most ungracious. And the spam would be very nice. It was on points and not always available and it made delicious fritters. As for the chocolate, well, she'd always had rather a sweet tooth.

'It's very kind of you, Corporal. Thank you so much.' She accepted the tin and the chocolate bar and put them on the table.

'My pleasure, ma'am. Anythin' else I can do for you, while I'm here? Like I said, I'm pretty handy at fixin' things.'

Miss Cutteridge hesitated. She could think of several things that needed repairing and it was almost impossible to get anybody in. 'Well, if it's not too much trouble, one of the handles on a kitchen cupboard has broken.' She showed him the faulty handle that she had tried hard to mend without success, and fetched the tin box where she kept a few tools. He put it right in a matter of minutes.

'Anythin' else, ma'am?'

'Well, this drawer has stuck. I don't know why.' Her string and brown paper drawer had jammed halfway. He crouched down to take a look and whistled. 'My, you've sure got a whole lot in there, ma'am.'

'I save it, you see. Every bit. String is very scarce and so is paper. Almost everything is. We have to save every single thing we can.'

He rocked the drawer carefully. 'Uh-huh. Looks like there might be somethin' gone and got itself caught up some way.' He pulled some of the string and paper out of the drawer, reached inside with his arm and felt around. 'Yep, that's your trouble, ma'am.'

The drawer was soon freed and, after that, he mended a dripping tap, the part-blocked sink waste pipe, and a collapsing shelf. Ginger appeared and wound himself lovingly round the corporal's ankles. So unlike him, Miss Cutteridge thought.

'Would you like a cup of tea, Corporal?'

He grinned at her wryly. 'Better not. Wouldn't trust myself with the cup. Anythin' else need fixin'?'

'No, really. Thank you.'

'Well, I'll come by another time, case you think of somethin'. Or somethin' else gets broke.'

'Thank you so much for the chocolate and the spam.'

'Weren't nothin'. I'll see what else I can bring.'

When he'd gone she put the spam away in the back of her store cupboard, together with her other special treasures: the Tate & Lyle's golden syrup, the gasproof Mazawattee tea, the Prince's salmon, the Nestlé's condensed milk, and the Oxford marmalade. She picked up the chocolate bar, examining it more closely. Hershey's Milk Chocolate, it said, in silver letters on a brown background. 5c. The c would stand for cents. They had dollars and cents — not pounds, shillings and pence — which must be so much simpler. She unpeeled the wrapping, just to see what American chocolate looked like. It seemed very like Fry's or Cadbury's, but of course she wouldn't know that until she had tasted it. Miss Cutteridge nibbled cautiously at one corner of the bar. It tasted delicious.

* * *

Lieutenant Mochetti shone his torch on the jeep. 'I'll give you a hand getting in.' There was no running board and no step of any kind. He put his arm under Agnes's elbow as she climbed up awkwardly into the passenger seat. There were no doors either; instead he clipped a webbing strap across. 'Sorry, it's going to be kind of draughty.' He shone the torch again. 'There's a grab handle just here on the outside if you need it, but don't worry, I'll take it real easy in the dark.'

He swung himself in on the driver's side, as though there was nothing to it. They drove out of the village, under the railway bridge and up the hill in the direction of the aerodrome. She soon discovered how right he'd been about the draughts.

'We're going to a place called the Haycock. Know it?'

'Yes, I know it.' She knew the Haycock because Clive had taken her there often and it had been there that he'd proposed to her on one of his leaves. Well, not exactly proposed. He'd produced the ring at the end of the dinner, picked up her left hand and slid it straight onto her fourth finger. 'I'm not taking no for an answer, Agnes.' It hadn't come as any surprise. She had always supposed that she and Clive would get married one day and it meant that she would never have to worry about Father.

The American pilot changed gear. 'Been there to the bar a couple of times. One of the guys said the food's OK. He'd better be right.' He changed gear again at the top of the hill. 'Let's get one thing straight,' he said. 'I'm not Lieutenant, whichever way you pronounce it. My name's Ed. And in case you're wondering, that's short for Edoardo. The Italian version of Edward. But nobody calls me that, except my family. You speak any Italian?'

She shook her head. 'Just French.'

'I know some French, but not too much.

Italian's real easy to learn. Seems so to me, anyway. A darn sight easier than English, I reckon. I can switch, no problem. Makes no difference to me which one I'm talking. And that can come in handy. There's a whole lot of Italians in New York and everywhere in the States. And a whole lot of other immigrants from all over, speaking all kinds of languages. Of course, when you get a generation or two down the line, some kids don't learn their own lingo and that's a pity. My family, they made sure I did.' He slowed to avoid a rabbit caught, frozen in fright, in the jeep's masked headlights. It skittered on across the road and vanished. They roared on. 'I forgot to mention back there that you're not Miss Dawe. You're Agnes. OK?'

'OK.'

'Now we're getting somewhere.' In the dark, she could tell that he was smiling. 'You lived round here long, Agnes?'

'About fifteen years. We lived in Norfolk before that.'

'I know where Norfolk is all right. Always a country girl, huh? I guess you'd have a real problem picturing a place like New York. I'm sure looking forward to seeing it again myself, when I get to the end of my tour. If I make it.'

'How long is a tour?'

'Three hundred hours combat mission time.'

According to the King's Thorpe grapevine, the Americans had been losing a lot of fighter pilots. The village always got to know about it . . . who hadn't come back; what had happened to them; all the gory details. She said, 'That sounds an awful lot.'

'Yeah . . . it can go real slowly on some missions. Boy, is it cold, sitting up there for four or five hours with no heat. Flying icewagons, we call the P-38s. You get so you're so damn cold you don't care about anything else. We've had some bad problems over here. Too cold and too wet for them. Engines quitting on us all the time. But we're getting different kites. Brand new ones that can go a whole lot further. That's good news for our bomber guys and real bad news for Hitler and Goering. The good news for us fighter pilots is they've got heating.'

'But you'll be flying longer missions?'

'Yeah, but what the hell. We'll be warmer.' He flipped the wheel for a sharp turn. 'Ben and me have been thinking what to call our new planes,' he went on. 'We figured something from Walt Disney. Thought we'd pick out a couple of the Seven Dwarfs and have them painted on. Ben's going to be Grumpy because he's forever complaining about things. Mine's going to be Bashful.'

She smiled, too, in the dark. 'For a joke?'

'Hell, no. I'm dead serious. I'm a very shy sort of guy.'

At the Haycock he helped her off with her coat and held her chair for her to sit down at the table in the dining room — by coincidence at exactly the same table where she had sat with Clive. The other diners were mostly Service men — a good number of them Americans. Nobody from King's Thorpe that she could see, thank heavens.

She looked at the menu. They'd done their

best to make it all sound *haute cuisine*, dressing the dishes up with fancy French words, but it was still corned beef, sausagemeat, smoked haddock, tripe and onions . . . He was frowning. 'What in the world are *les tripes*?' She explained. 'Good grief, you British eat that sort of stuff?'

'It's food. We eat anything: sheeps' hearts, pigs' trotters, intestines, turnip tops, nettles . . . The fillets of pork will be sausagemeat, by the way. And the *rissoles de boeuf salé* will be corned beef.'

'Thanks for telling me. Well, I guess I'll settle for the corned beef. Least I know what *that* is. Now, what're you having?'

She chose the corned-beef dish as well and watched him ordering from the elderly waitress and then some wine from an even older wine waiter. When the wine waiter had shuffled away he said, 'I can see you're trying to figure me out, Agnes. You're saying to yourself, I've never met anybody like this guy. I don't know what to make of him. That's the trouble with us Yanks. We don't behave the way you British are used to. We talk different, too.'

'We can understand you — mostly.'

'Easier than the other way round, I reckon. When we first got here most of us could only get three words out of ten.'

'Well, we've heard Americans speaking before. In films.'

'Hadn't thought of that. There aren't too many British films or British actors in the US. Guys like Leslie Howard, Charles Laughton, Ronald Colman . . . but most people over here don't talk too much like them.'

'People speak differently all over the British Isles.'

'Same thing in the States. You'd have a problem with some of our accents.'

'I expect we would.'

'Matter of fact, I've never met anybody like you either, Agnes, so I reckon that makes us quits. This guy you're engaged to — he's in the army, that's right?'

'Since the very beginning of the war. He was in France with the BEF and then evacuated at Dunkirk.'

'You been engaged to him for long?'

'Two years.'

'That's a pretty long engagement.'

'There's been a war on,' she pointed out. 'Clive's been away most of the time. A lot of people have had to wait.'

'Your father told me his family's from King's Thorpe.'

She nodded. 'His family have farmed here for over a hundred years. It's the biggest farm in the parish.'

'Is that why you're marrying him?'

'Of course it isn't.'

'Then I guess you must be in love with him?'

'We've known each other for a long time. Since we were children.'

'That's no answer.'

'Well, it's all I'm giving.'

'OK. Sorry. I was just curious. Where is he now?'

'Somewhere in England.'

'Somewhere in England . . . that's where all of us guys are. Somewhere in England. That's all they let you tell them back home. And pretty soon we're going to be somewhere in France, beating the hell out of the Germans.'

'You sound confident.'

'Sure am. This war's not going to last that much longer. Maybe another year. You reckon you'll get married, soon as it's over?'

'I expect so.' There was no point in telling him about the big wedding that the Hobbses had planned when Clive finally came home from the war. People from all over the county were going to be invited. It was going to be the biggest wedding King's Thorpe had ever seen, according to them. 'There's no rush about it. I've got my teaching job and my father needs me to help in the parish.' She hesitated. 'My mother left us six years ago. She hated being a rector's wife. She couldn't stand how everyone in the parish behaved as though they owned her — at least that was how she saw it. The way she was expected to do so much and be at everyone's beck and call all the time.'

'I guess I can sympathize with that,' he said, 'but it must have been real tough on you and your father when she went.'

'She was twenty years younger than him. I think that was part of the trouble.'

'Yeah, that's a big gap. She remarried?'

She shook her head. 'They're not divorced. Father would never divorce her — not unless she asked him to and so far she hasn't.'

'I guess he doesn't believe in it, anyway. So, she dumped the workload on you? That was kind of a raw deal.'

'People in the village help, so it's really not so bad.'

The wine and the rissoles appeared and there was a pause in the conversation while the waitress served them. Now was the moment to ask the favour she needed of him.

'I was wondering . . . '

'I'm wondering too — what's in these rissoles besides the corned beef?'

'It's mashed vegetables. Carrots and turnips and potatoes, and that's wheatmeal breadcrumbs on the outside. It's one of our wartime recipes — to make things go further.'

'You don't say. So, what were *you* wondering?'

'About your station band.'

'What about them?'

'Do you think they'd play for one of our village dances?'

'They're kind of different from your band.'

'Yes, that's rather the point, you see . . . we need to raise some money. Some of the church roof timbers have got dry rot. I don't know if you know about dry rot, but if you don't get it treated quickly it spreads everywhere and costs a fortune to get rid of.'

'That sure would be a pity with a beautiful old place like that. You figure our band could help in some way?'

'Well, they're awfully good, aren't they? People have heard about them in the village. If they played at one of the Saturday night dances we could charge extra for the entrance fee — say one and sixpence instead of a shilling. Perhaps even two shillings. People wouldn't mind paying that for something special. It wouldn't make enough but it would go quite a way towards the roof repairs.'

'Well, I figure it's up to our group commander. Want me to find out what the score is?'

'The score?'

'What he thinks about it.'

'If you would, please. We'd be very grateful . . . Ed.'

'With him so keen on being very nice to you villagers, then I'd say you wouldn't have a problem . . . Agnes.'

Driving back in the jeep he said, 'Now if we were in New York I'd've taken you to my parents' restaurant on 53rd Street. They'd've made a great big fuss of you and my mother would have cooked something pretty special. Maybe *Pollo alla Bolognese*. That's a great dish: chicken cooked with onions and tomatoes, and white wine. You serve it over spaghetti with grated cheese on top. Or maybe *Pasta con Gamberetti* — that one's with prawns and cream. I reckon you'd like that too.'

She tried to picture it: the crowded Italian restaurant, plates piled with exotic, foreign food; outside, the brightly lit New York Street. A million miles away.

It had started to rain, spattering the jeep's wind-screen.

'Say, do you mind working the windshield wipers?'

'What do I do?'

'There's a handle your side as well — just up in front of you.' She found it and worked it to and fro every now and then, keeping the screen clear for him. 'Thanks, that's a real help.'

At the rectory he got out and came round to unclip the webbing strap. The only easy way out was to jump down into his arms.

'I'll let you know about the band — soon as I can.'

'Thank you. And thank you for the dinner.'

'Just carrying out orders.' He let go of her. 'Goodnight, Agnes.'

'Goodnight.'

Her father was still up, writing at his desk in the study.

'I asked Lieutenant Mochetti about their band,' she told him. 'He thinks they might be able to play at the village hall. He's going to find out.'

He smiled at her. 'It was a very good idea of yours, my dear. Quite inspired.'

'Of course they may not let them.'

'Oh, I have a feeling that the lieutenant will succeed in arranging it for you.'

'I hope so. That's the only reason I went.'

'Just so. But he seems a very pleasant young man.'

'Yes. He is.'

'Did you have a nice evening?'

'Yes, thank you. His name's Ed, by the way.'

'Ah . . . I must remember that.'

'Don't work too late, Father.'

'I'm just finishing my sermon, my dear.'

She climbed the stairs slowly and thoughtfully to bed.

7

The otter's sleek, dark head broke the surface of the brook. Tom instantly froze where he was on the bank, motioning to Alfie to keep still. He held his breath, watching the wet muzzle and whiskers and the bright little eyes. Then, as suddenly as it had appeared, the otter vanished beneath the water, leaving a long trail of bubbles.

'You went and scared him, Alfie.'

'No, I didn't.'

'Yes, you did. You moved.'

'Only a bit. I couldn't help it.'

It was hopeless taking Alfie along; he always ruined everything. Otters were mostly only around at night and Tom had hardly ever seen one, but he knew they were there in that stretch of the water because he often saw their spraints on the old elder tree that had fallen down over the brook. 'Come on, then.'

They crossed the brook by the fallen tree, balancing along its narrow trunk with their arms outstretched like tightrope walkers. He waited for the splash of Alfie falling in behind him, like he'd done last time, but he did it all right, for once. On the other side, Tom cut across Fitt's meadow, over the stile, past the old claypits and on round Spinney field where the blackthorn hedge was already blossoming. Alfie panted along after him.

'Where're we going, Tom?'

'You'll see.'

He heard the sound of fighters starting up at the airfield in the distance, and stopped to watch two planes soaring up into the sky, followed by another pair and then another and another. Leader and wingman taking off together, one beside but a little bit behind the other. A whole squadron of them.

'What're they doing?' Alfie asked — another of his stupid questions.

'Going to meet up with Yank bombers, of course. They'll be going on a raid with them. Berlin p'raps . . . somewhere like that. Those are the new planes they've got. P-51s. Mustangs, they call them. They can go all the way to Berlin and back with the bombers, so's they can stop the Jerry fighters from shooting them down.'

'But those've only got one engine, so how can they? The others had two.'

'It's a special engine. A Rolls-Royce Merlin. Same as the Hurricane and Spitfire. And they have extra fuel tanks under the wings that they can drop when they're used up.'

'Is our Ed in one of those planes?'

'How should I know? Can't see the markings from here, can I?' Tom stood watching the fighters until they had all disappeared into the clouds. 'Come on, then.'

He kept going at a steady pace without looking behind him. Alfie would follow wherever he went. They crossed more fields, jumped ditches, wriggled under wire, scrambled over gates and presently they came towards the forest. Tom stopped again.

Alfie stopped too. 'We're not going in there, are we?'

He fingered the rabbit's foot in his pocket. '*I* am. You needn't come if you don't want to. You can stay here.' He knew Alfie was afraid of the forest. Afraid of the stoats and the weasels and the snakes and of the noise the great trees made in the wind. It was different from the woods where they gathered the sticks and branches for the fires. Tinker's Wood and Gipping Wood and Bonny Wood were small, sunny places where there were rabbits and nightingales and badgers and where bluebells grew in the spring, but the forest was so big and overgrown in parts that you could get lost in it easily and not be able to find your way out. King John had hunted deer and wild pigs there, hundreds of years ago, and there were strange tales told about it. Stories of wolves and robbers and outlaws, of elves and goblins, of mysterious things happening. And there was the witch.

Mum said she wasn't really a witch, just a mad old woman who lived in a hut in the forest, but other people in the village believed she could cast spells and blamed her for anything bad that happened: a poor harvest, a child dying, an accident. She brewed things up in a big black pot, they said. Newts and toads and snakes and poisonous plants: deadly nightshade, hemlock, stinking hellebore, devil's eye . . . She could make magic — for evil, or sometimes, if she'd a mind to, for good. The tiler's wife who'd never had a baby had gone to see her and soon after she'd found she was expecting, though he'd heard some people, Mother Becket for one, saying that it was more likely one of the Yanks who'd made that happen.

'What d'you want to go in there for?'

'I'm going to see the witch.'

'The *witch*!' Alfie's mouth fell open. He looked scared stiff. 'Don't go, Tom. She'll put a bad spell on you, that's what she'll do. Or she'll cook you in her oven, like Hansel.'

'Course she won't,' he said airily. He took the rabbit's foot out of his pocket. 'I'm going to ask her to make this lucky. Then I'm going to give it to Ed. So's he won't get shot down by a German. You don't want him to get killed, like all those other Yank pilots, do you?'

'No, I don't. He's nice, Ed. And we wouldn't get so much chocolate and gum any more, neither.'

Trust Alfie to think of that. 'Well then, we've got to do something about it. You'd better wait here.' He was more scared himself than he'd let on but he had to do it, for Ed's sake. 'I won't be long.'

He walked into the forest as bravely as he could. It wasn't too dark or difficult because the leaves were only in bud and the undergrowth wasn't thick yet. He could see deer slots clearly in the soft ground. Dad poached deer sometimes when he was home. He'd trap them with a noose strung between two trees, then he'd slit their throats and hold them up by the hind legs to bleed. After that he'd cut off the head and bury it far away. Once Tom had gone with him and it had made him feel a bit sick with all the blood and the deer struggling.

The witch's hut was in a clearing — a tumbledown wooden hovel with one window and a stovepipe sticking out of the roof. Even the packing-case huts that the Yank ground crews built up at the base looked better. He saw a curl of smoke rising from the pipe. The witch would be in there, brewing her potions. Tom took a deep breath, walked up to the door and knocked on it.

The door opened with a jerk and he almost turned tail and fled. She was the ugliest old woman he'd ever seen — even uglier than Mother Becket — dressed in black with straggly grey hair, a great long chin and a nose as sharp as a knife. And she stank even worse than Nell.

'What do you want, boy?'

He swallowed and held out the rabbit's foot. 'Please, missus, can you make this lucky?'

Her dark eyes snapped at him. 'Lucky? How could I do that?'

He gulped again. 'They say you can. They say you can do magic spells.'

She looked angry and uglier than ever. 'Who says, pray?'

'In the village.'

'Gossiping fools.' She nodded at the rabbit's foot. 'What's that for?'

'It's for someone. To keep him safe. One of the American pilots. I want to give it to him so's he doesn't get shot down by the Germans and killed.'

She stared at him for a moment and he wanted more than anything to run away as fast as he could. But he stood his ground.

'You must like him a lot, this American.'

He nodded.

'How much will you pay me?'

The tiler's wife had paid three shillings, he knew that. He'd been saving up from selling the radioshack Yanks' cigarettes but he hadn't got anything near that.

'I'll pay you ninepence.'

'And where would a boy like you get ninepence?'

He took the three threepenny bits from his other pocket and held them out. She bent to peer at them closely and picked them out of his palm. Her fingernails were blacker than Alfie's ever got. 'Come inside, boy.'

His mouth was dry with terror. If he went inside, he might never be seen again. She'd go and cast a spell on him, like Alfie had said; turn him into a frog or a newt, or bake him in her oven. Then he thought of Ed and what might happen to *him* if he didn't go in.

The hut was dark and dirty and smelled of her. He could see a truckle bed with a patchwork blanket in one corner, a rocking chair, a big pot cooking on the iron stove. Something squeaked and scuttled away in a corner. He stood close to the door, ready to run.

'Shut the door, boy. And give me that.'

He did both, with trembling hands.

'What's your pilot called?'

'Ed Mochetti.'

She didn't put the rabbit's foot into the pot or do anything like he'd expected. Instead, she cradled it in her hand for a while and stroked the fur gently, crooning words that he couldn't understand. He waited, his heart thudding.

'There you are.'

He grabbed at the foot. 'Will it keep him safe now?'

'It might and it mightn't.' The witch leaned closer. 'What's your name, boy?'

'Tom, missus.'

Her mouth gaped suddenly, showing blackened stumps for teeth. 'You're a nice-looking boy, Tom. A brave boy.' She took a step towards him and reached out a claw. He fled. Wrenched open the door behind him and ran for his life through the forest; tripped and fell flat over a root and ran on with bleeding knees. He burst out of the trees, going full tilt, and found Alfie waiting fearfully.

'Did you see the witch?'

He nodded, gasping for breath, still terrified.

'Cor . . . ' Alfie looked impressed. 'What was she like?'

'Horrible.' Tom shuddered.

'Did she do a lucky spell for you, like you wanted?'

'I think she did. Sort of. Come on, let's get away from here.'

As they trailed back across the fields towards the village, he wondered, shamefacedly, if perhaps the witch had only been trying to smile and be friendly.

* * *

'There's an American gentleman to see you, milady.'

Erika stopped typing. 'Who is he, Doris?'

'The one with all the brass bits and the silver wings and the medals.'

'Colonel Schrader, you mean?'

'Yes, milady. I went and forgot his name. Shall I show him into the drawing room?'

'No, in here, thank you, Doris.'

He came into the study, carrying his cap, and she got up from the desk to greet him. 'How nice to see you again, Colonel. How are you?'

'Fine, thanks.' He gestured at the typewriter and the pile of papers. 'I hope I'm not interrupting you.'

'Not at all. I'm just doing some WVS admin work.'

'You look pretty busy.'

'We do anything and everything.' She smiled drily. 'Our motto is if it should be done, the WVS will do it. Luckily, I did a secretarial course years ago and it's come in very handy.'

He was looking round at the panelled walls and the collection of books. 'This is a great room.'

'It was Richard's study and his father's before him. Actually, it's one of the nicest in the house — certainly one of the warmest. Would you like some coffee or tea or anything?'

He shook his head. 'No thank you.'

'I'm afraid my mother-in-law is having her afternoon rest. She sets great store by it. Every day from two until four and nothing is allowed to disturb it; not even the war.'

'I enjoyed the bridge.'

'So did she. She was delighted to find you were such a good player, by the way.'

He smiled. 'I guess she didn't expect us colonials to play that much.'

'If at all.'

The bridge evening had been a success. Miriam had partnered Colonel Schrader and found him worthy of her, while her own partner, Brigadier Mapperton, once he had got his latest complaints off his chest to the group commander (far too much noise outside the pubs at closing time, bicycles left lying around on the pavements and something else that he'd taken the American into a corner to talk about out of their hearing) had gallantly borne their defeat.

'I'm sorry I haven't had the chance to get back since. There's been no time.' He looked completely exhausted, she thought. The village gossip had been that things hadn't been going at all well lately for the Yanks. One couldn't ask, of course.

'Is there anything I can do for you, Colonel?'

'As a matter of fact, there is. I've sneaked off for a couple of hours. Playing truant. It's a beautiful sunny day and I've got a car outside. Would you have time to give me a conducted tour of the local countryside? Just about all I've seen of England so far is either out on an airfield or from ten thousand feet up. Seems to me that's a great pity.'

'I don't know how good a conductor I'd be — I don't know this part of England very well — but I'll do my best.'

'I'd appreciate it.'

The car was an American Ford saloon, painted dark olive with the white star on the side. 'First time I've ever driven on the left,' he told her. 'There's usually somebody driving me. Tell me if I do anything stupid.'

She directed him west out of King's Thorpe into some of the loveliest parts of the county. It was mid-April: fresh young grass growing in the meadows, some of the blossom already out, primroses and cowslips flowering along the banks, buds breaking into leaf.

'Your green and pleasant land,' he said.

'This is nothing. Give it another month and you'll really see what Blake meant.'

'I'll look forward to it. How am I doing with the driving?'

'Extremely well.'

They drove slowly through a small and very ancient village, past church and schoolhouse, pub and pond. Children were playing on the green, old men with pipes were sitting on benches in the sun, women filling water buckets at a spring. 'A trip back in time,' he said. 'Boy, it's wonderful.'

'It's also very feudal. This village, for instance, is owned entirely by one family who live in the big house. The villagers are all tenants, working for them. A lot of forelock-tugging still goes on. It's the same in most of the villages round here. Northamptonshire is known for its spires and squires. King's Thorpe's rather different, thank goodness.'

'How so?'

'Well, the Beauchamps used to own most of it

but over the past few hundred years the family ne'er-do-wells have been steadily selling off land so the Manor's down to less than a hundred and fifty acres now, and it's all rented out.'

'That's a shame.'

'Personally, I'm rather glad for Alex. I'd hate him to be a feudal overlord. The King's Thorpe villagers are free spirits and that's a good thing. Apparently a lot of them came to settle here from other places for that very reason, so Richard told me. Now, if we had a real squire who owned everything and everybody, and if he wasn't on your side, you'd have had a much harder job winning people over.'

'Do you reckon we've done that?'

'You're getting there. There're a few old diehards who'll probably never come round but I wouldn't let that worry you. Most of them are realizing how hard you're fighting. Mind you, does it matter to you very much what they think? Does it make any difference to winning the war?'

He glanced at her. 'Frankly, that's the way I saw it to start with — but those at the top of our tree believe it does. We can't win together if we're at odds with each other, that's their perception. It's militarily stupid to fall out with your allies. And I guess they're right.'

'Together we stand, divided we fall?'

'That's about the size of it. And the morale factor's pretty important for us, you know. A soldier away from home who feels good about things is going to fight a whole lot better. And he's not going to feel good if he's getting spat on by the locals and into fist-fights.'

She took him into Stamford to show him the old market town and suggested they stop for tea at The Olde Spinning Wheel. 'Another bit of quaint Olde Englande that you might enjoy, Colonel.'

The tea room was a low-beamed, copper-kettled, lace-clothed parlour with a genuine old spinning wheel beside the inglenook and elderly, be-hatted ladies sipping from dainty teacups. Conversation and sipping ceased instantly as they entered. All eyes were trained on the American commanding officer in his impressive uniform with the gilt buttons and badges, the row of medals and the silver wings on his breast. The proprietress hurried forward. 'Tea for two? Will this table suit?'

Erika poured the tea and passed the home-made scones and jam. He looked so incongruous in those surroundings that she wanted to laugh. She said in a low voice, 'You're the centre of attention, do you realize?'

'Am I? Heck . . .'

'They're admiring you, don't worry. By the way, what does the blue patch under the wings signify?'

'It means you're doing a flying-combat tour in England.'

'That's rather nice — a special badge.'

'It's a special place.'

'You're very diplomatic.'

'I'm trying to make up for my predecessor.'

She smiled. 'You heard about the village-hall speech?'

'Yeah.'

'Poor man. I'm sure the last thing he wanted was to give offence.'

'I guess he just chose the wrong words.'

'And I'm afraid they were waiting for him to say something like that.'

'It's been said before, so I hear. Us Yanks telling you British we've come over to win the war for you.'

'We're rather sensitive on the subject.'

'I don't blame you.'

'More tea, Colonel?'

'Yes, thanks.'

She changed the subject. 'The village canteen seems to be going well. Your men come in quite a bit.' It had taken some time for them to appear — in ones and twos, hesitantly, as though not too sure of their welcome, and then, gradually, more and more of them as time had passed and, presumably, word had got around. They were unfailingly polite and well-behaved.

'No trouble with them, I hope?'

'None at all. They're very appreciative.'

'So they should be. It's run by your volunteer workers, isn't that so? The WVS. This country has women to be real proud of. They don't care what they turn their hands to. All kinds of jobs. If it helps win the war, they'll do it. Every one of them. All ages. We've got some of your WAAFs on the base and they're respected a hell of a lot.'

All ears in the room were tuned in to their conversation: she could tell that by the general frisson of gratification; by the patting of hair and rearranging of fox furs. And the colonel was a very attractive man. Not in an obvious film-starry way but something much more indefinable and interesting. It was no wonder that he'd created such a stir among the teacups.

Going back in the car, he said, 'I want to thank you, Lady Beauchamp, for this afternoon. It's been a wonderful break for me.'

'Please call me Erika.'

'I'd like to, if you don't mind.'

'It's Erika with a k, by the way.'

'My name's Carl, with a c. I've never met an Erika with a k before.'

'It's the Hungarian version. My father was Hungarian, my mother English.'

'That so? You don't look at all typically English, if that's not too personal a remark to make, but you sure sound it.'

'I was born and brought up over here. I hardly speak any Hungarian.'

'By descent, I should be speaking German, but I'm a couple of generations down the immigrant line. So I'm Carl with a c and I speak American. I *am* American. And that's the way I like it. Your parents both in England now?'

'My father died sixteen years ago. My mother remarried — a Scottish landowner up in the wilds of the north. I hardly ever see her.'

'That's too bad. Same as me. Haven't seen my parents in three years. I don't even get to see my wife and daughter any more. It's been a heck of a time since we got into the war. Trying to catch up. Get things up and running as fast as we can.'

'Have you been in the Air Force long?'

'It seems like forever. I went straight to West Point from high school — that's our equivalent of your Sandhurst — and I'm thirty-three now, so that's about fifteen years.'

She'd been right about his age. He was only two years older than herself. She wouldn't have cared to carry his burden.

He dropped her at the Manor and thanked her again. 'In return, I'd like to take you out to dinner, Erika. If you've no objection.'

'None at all.'

'I'll call you,' he said. 'As soon as I can.'

Miriam came out of the drawing room. 'I gather Colonel Schrader was here.'

She took off her coat. 'Yes, we went out for a drive. He had some time free and wanted to be shown the local scenery.'

'What a pity I was resting, I could have given him a proper tour. There's a great deal of interest to be seen.'

'I'm sure he'd like that another time.'

She went and sat down at the typewriter again. Miriam had looked quite put out; it had been wiser not to mention the dinner.

* * *

The lucky rabbit's foot was in his pocket, a tin loaf under each arm and a dozen eggs — pinched from Mr Barnet, the baker — stowed carefully in the lining of his coat. He felt a bit guilty about the eggs because of Sally but they kept lots of chickens so they wouldn't really be missed. He didn't think she'd have minded too much, anyway. Her dad would have done, though. Tom took his usual short cut across the fields, downhill to the stream at the bottom, across by the two stepping stones and then up towards the aerodrome. A Mustang was taking off just as he reached the perimeter fence and he stopped to watch it, as he always did. It was the only one, so they weren't going off on a mission — just a test flight most probably. He ducked under the pole at the main gate and the sentry gave him a wave. They all knew him. In the radio shack the Yanks stopped work while he handed over the loaves of bread and the eggs. This time he swopped the eggs for torch batteries. Four eggs for one battery that he could sell in the village for sixpence each. More for Mum's Oxo tin.

'What else've you got, Tom?'

'That's all.'

'What about those rock cakes?'

'Sorry, there weren't any spare this time. Oh, Mrs Honeybun in the village says have you got any Silvertex she could have? She said she'll give you fresh eggs in exchange.'

They all started laughing, though he didn't know why.

'Tell her she can have some for free, Tom, long as it's us guys using it. How about that name? Mrs Honeybun. Oh, boy . . . '

He didn't understand why it was so funny. He'd thought it was some kind of silver cleaner. 'What is it? Silvertex?'

The one called Mitch patted his head. 'You'll find out when you're older, kid. Want some toast?'

They still had the stove going, even though it

was April, and he sat on a wooden crate, eating the peanut-butter toast and watching them at work. They'd tuned one of the radios into some Yank band music and Mitch, cap peak flipped up, started dancing round the shack with a broom, making them all laugh some more. As he watched, laughing too, he heard another fighter taking off and listened to the sound of it climbing, over the sound of the dance music, and then to a different noise as something went wrong. There was a booming thud in the distance and all the Yanks rushed to the windows. Tom dropped his toast and ran outside. He could see black smoke billowing up into the air from the end of the main runway and orange flames flickering. A fire engine was careering across the grass. *Ed.* He was sure it was Ed. Tom started to run round the peri track. He ran and ran until his breath came in great gasping gulps and his heart felt as though it would burst. If only he'd given him the rabbit's foot sooner it wouldn't have happened. It was all his fault.

There was a gap on the hardstand where Ed's Mustang usually stood and a group of Yanks there, looking over towards the fire. He stopped to catch his breath and then ran towards them. As he reached the group one of them turned round and he saw that it was Ed.

'Hi there, Tom . . . what're you doing here?'

He couldn't answer; just stood there, his chest heaving. Beyond the group he could see Ed's Mustang standing in a different place. He could see the big letter A near the tail, the dwarf,

Bashful, painted on the nose and the three black swastikas underneath for the Germans Ed had shot down now. He wiped a tear quickly away from his cheek.

The pilot rested a hand on his shoulder. 'Hey, you don't want to worry about that guy . . . They got him out real quick. He'll be OK.'

'I thought it might be you.'

'*Me*? Sure hope I take off better than he did. The guy's a rookie. He got it wrong. He'll learn. Here, have some gum.'

Tom put the gum in his pocket and took out the rabbit's foot. 'I brought this for you.'

'What the hell's that?'

'It's a rabbit's foot. It's lucky. You can take it with you on missions.'

Ed grinned. 'Well now, that's real nice of you, Tom. I'll certainly do that. Gee, the other guys have got all sorts of good-luck things, but I'll sure be the only one with a rabbit's foot.' He stuck it in the pocket of his leather jacket. 'Say, like to sit in the Mustang for a moment?'

He took him over to Bashful and showed him how to get up onto the wing so that he could climb into the cockpit. 'You put your right foot here, see, where it says STEP and grab a hold of this handle in the side and up you go.' Ed always made it look easy; the same as he made everything look easy. Tom couldn't manage it anything like that, but he got up onto the wing somehow, with a bit of help. The canopy was pushed back and he climbed into the cockpit and sat there, heart beating fast, breathing in the fighter smell of fuel and oil and leather. He looked at all the dials and gauges in front of him and at the gunsight above. The stick was between his legs, and he put out his hand and held it reverently. The shiny black button on top would be for the gun. He felt it with his thumb. 'Don't touch anything, Tom,' Ed called up. 'Wouldn't want you taking off.' He took his hand away quickly. One day, though, he would. One day, when he was grown-up, he'd be a fighter pilot.

He climbed out again and jumped down off the wing, trying to do it just the way he'd seen Ed and the others do it.

Ed ruffled his hair. 'Better cut along, kid. We're kind of busy right now.'

He wandered back slowly along the peri track, chewing the gum that the pilot had given him. A skylark was warbling away somewhere high up in the sky and the sun was shining. Ed was all right. And now he'd got the rabbit's foot he'd always be safe.

* * *

'Please, Miss, there's a Yank at the window.'

'Yes, I did notice him, Charlie.'

'It's *our* Yank, Miss.'

'Thank you, Joan. I can see it is.'

A moment later the Yank appeared at the classroom door. The children all ran and gathered round him, jumping up and down with excitement. He put his cap on Charlie's head where it fell down over his nose and little Joan took hold of his hand and dragged him over to the Nature Table to show him the catkins and the primroses they'd picked on their last walk. He admired everything and talked to the rabbit and guinea pigs. Joan tugged at his sleeve.

'Sing us that song again, please.'

'You'll have to ask Miss if that's OK with her.'

'Please, Miss, can we sing it?'

So he sat down, with a child on each knee, and they all sang 'Yankee Doodle' several times. After that he taught them 'Camptown Races' and soon they were all shouting out: '*Doo-da, doo-da.*' And then another one: '*Oh, Susannah, don't you cry for me, cos I come from Alabama with a banjo on my knee*,' while he strummed an imaginary banjo.

Joan was tugging at his sleeve once more. 'Will you tell us a story?'

'You'll have to ask Miss again.'

'Please, Miss,' they all chorused. 'Can he?'

They sat down cross-legged in a circle round him, watching him expectantly. Charlie was wearing his cap back to front, the peak down his back.

'Gee, let's see . . . There's an Uncle Remus one I know about Mr Rabbit and Mr Fox.' He told it with actions and different voices, making them laugh and clap. 'More, more,' they pleaded. 'Tell us another one.'

He shook his head. 'Sorry, kids, I've got to go. I only called by to tell Miss something.' He came over to her. 'Hope you didn't mind all that.'

'Of course not. They loved it. You're very good with them.'

'Well, I've got a bunch of little nephews and

nieces back home. We're a big family. Besides, I like kids.'

'I can see you do.'

'Same as you,' he said. 'Listen, I came to tell you that it's OK about the band. The group commander's all for it and they'll play at the village hall whatever Saturday you want — you just let me know.'

'That's wonderful. Thank you, Ed. What will they charge?'

'Zero. They'll do it for nothing. And maybe you'd like us to get some posters done, so you could stick them around and get a whole lot of people coming from all over. The more people, the more money.'

She thanked him again, embarrassed by such generosity.

'Forget it,' he said. 'Glad to help. Gotta get that dry rot fixed.' The children were clustering round him again, faces lifted to his. 'So long, kids. Be good and do what Miss tells you.' He whisked his cap off Charlie's head. 'See you around.'

They crowded to the window and waved as he went by. Agnes picked up little Joan so she could see better and waved too.

* * *

Chester was waiting for her at the bridge over the brook. As she coasted down the hill on her bike, Sally could see him leaning over the wall in the sunlight, smoking a cigarette, his bike propped beside him. She pedalled for the last bit and braked to a stop. He turned round and smiled his slow smile. 'Hi there. I've been watching the fish while I was waiting and wishing I'd got a line. What kind are they?'

'Nothing special. There are otters in the brook too, but you hardly ever see them.' She pointed to the wicker basket strapped onto the handlebars. 'I've brought a picnic tea for us.'

'Great.' He ground his cigarette under his foot. 'So, where're we going?'

'Anywhere you like.'

'OK. Let's just take off and see what happens. Never can figure out all these lanes, anyway.'

They rode along side by side, the American weaving a little to keep to her slower pace. Her cotton skirt kept creeping up above her bare knees and she knew he was looking. After a while she didn't bother tugging it down any more and pretty soon it was right up round her thighs. Well, it wasn't as though he was a stranger exactly. He'd kissed her several more times since that evening when they'd come back from the pictures and each time he'd gone on longer. She'd told Doris about it because Doris was forever telling her about Hal and how the last time they'd gone out he'd kept putting his hands where he shouldn't. 'I wouldn't let him, though, Sal,' she'd said, looking smug. 'I said no.'

'I thought you said you wouldn't mind it with a Yank.'

'Well . . . not just yet.'

Doris had lost her nerve, she could tell that.

They biked up the hill along by Squirrel Wood and stopped when they got to the top.

'Sure is a beautiful place, England,' he said quietly, looking down at the countryside below with everything coming out into leaf and the blossom starting along the hedgerows. It didn't seem all that marvellous to her; lots of other countries in the world must look much better. She'd seen pictures in magazines of wonderful foreign places: palm trees, white sands, really blue skies. She leaned her bike against a tree and picked some of the wild flowers growing at the side of the lane and showed them to him.

'Real pretty,' he said, looking at her more than the flowers. 'Don't think we've anything like that back home.' She could tell he wanted to kiss her and skipped out of reach. 'Race you to the bottom,' she called, and tore off down the hill on her bike, the wind in her hair, her skirt blown right up. Of course he got there first — not that she minded. She'd known he would. Meant him to. He was bigger and stronger and faster. She liked that. She let him kiss her then, for a bit.

They found a place for the picnic in a meadow, in the shade of the willows beside a stream. She unpacked the basket and brought out the little sponge cakes she'd made, and the ginger pop. He sat with his back leaning against a willow trunk.

'What's it like where you live, Chester?' she asked him. 'What did you say it was called?'

'Paradise.'

She giggled. 'Funny name.'

He smiled. 'Yeah. Nothing very like paradise about it, I guess, but we've got some nice old buildings — not as old as yours here, of course, but they're painted up real pretty. It's a good place to live. Decent town, decent people. We've got a couple of movie theatres, plenty of stores, a beauty shop, a great soda fountain, good places to eat out . . . '

'Whatever's a soda fountain?'

'You don't have them over here?'

She shook her head. 'I don't think so. What are they?'

'Gee. Well, it's a place where you can get all kinds of ice-cream sodas, and milkshakes and malts and splits, things like that. Most times they're in a drugstore — I guess you'd call that a chemist. There's a long bar and you sit up on high stools. You'd like it.'

'Ice cream — ' she said wistfully. 'That sounds lovely. I can't remember what it tastes like. Mum said she had it at your Officers' Club when she went there. How do they make them — all those things you said.'

'Well, for the sodas they put a couple of scoops of ice cream in a tall glass, then some syrup — maybe strawberry or chocolate — then they stir it up and squirt soda water into it. Then they put whipped cream over it and a cherry on the top. They're twenty cents. A Coke soda's only a nickel, but it's not so good.'

She closed her eyes. 'Mmmmmm. I'd love those. What about the other things?'

'For malts they whizz up malt powder and milk in a mixer so it goes all frothy, and milkshakes are milk and whatever flavour you want — vanilla, strawberry, chocolate . . . '

'Banana?'

'Guess they could do that, if you wanted it.'

'I used to love bananas. We haven't had any since the war.'

'Oh boy, you'd like the splits, then. See, there's a banana cut in half on a dish with three scoops of ice cream on top, then some syrup, then whipped cream and nuts — '

'Don't,' she begged. 'I don't want to hear any more, Chester. Tell me about something else. What sort of house do you live in?'

'I guess it's about twenty years old. Wood-framed with a front porch. It can get real hot and humid in Virginia in the summer. I often sleep out there then.'

'Hotter than here?'

'Well, I don't know anything about English summers, but I'd say so. Much hotter than today.'

'This is only spring.'

'Yeah, and it's real pleasant. Just right.'

'It isn't always like this,' she said truthfully. 'It changes.'

He grinned. 'Sure does. I've noticed that. Never the same weather two days running — unless it's rain.'

'Don't you get rain?'

'Sure. But not like you. That's why England's so green. Greenest place I've ever seen.'

She passed him another cake. 'What does your father do?'

'He runs a garage downtown — doing auto repairs and selling gas. He makes a good living. I was working there before I joined the army and some day I'll take over, I guess. That's the idea, anyway. I'd like to open another one somewhere else, maybe several of them one day. I keep thinking about what I'll do when the war's over.'

'Have you got brothers and sisters?'

'Two sisters, still in school. Betty and Rose. Fifteen and thirteen. I'm the oldest by a long way. Mom lost another one in between us.'

'Did your parents mind you going away?'

'Sure, but there wasn't much choice. I got drafted. I didn't mind, though. I was glad I was. I got to come to England and be part of the war. And I met you. I wish you'd let me tell your dad about us, Sally.'

'Nothing to tell, is there?'

'Well, we're dating, aren't we? That's the way it seems to me. Unless you're seeing a whole lot of other guys I don't know about.'

'Course I'm not.'

He'd gone all serious. 'I'd like to tell him, face to face, that I'm seeing his daughter. He's got a right to know.'

She sighed. 'I've told you, Chester, he'd go mad if he found out.'

'Why? I don't get it.'

'You're a Yank.'

'Anything special he doesn't like about us?'

'He doesn't trust Yanks. I don't know why. Anyway, he thinks I'm too young to go out with anybody.'

'You're eighteen. That's not too young. What did you tell him for this time?'

'Didn't need to say anything. After church and lunch, Dad sleeps all day Sundays.'

'I guess he's tired.'

'Well, he always has to get up in the night to get the dough done in time for baking and get the oven hot.'

'Never really known how bread's made. What does he do?'

'He mixes up a sack of flour and yeast and water in a big trough. Then he has to wait for it to rise up in a great sort of mound. Then he knocks it back and kneads it all again. And waits some more. It takes ages and it's a lot of hard work. His back's always killing him and he's got arthritis in his hands and his chest gets wheezy from the flour.'

'Poor guy.'

'My brother, Roger, used to help him, before he got called up in the army.'

'I didn't know you had a brother. Where's he?'

'He was in Africa. We're not sure where he is now. Somewhere in the Mediterranean. He's the apple of Dad's eye. He's going to take over the bakery business one day, like with you and your dad. Dad's got it all planned. He took over from his dad and his dad took over from *his* dad, and his dad's dad took over from *his* dad. He's lucky Roger doesn't mind the idea.'

'How about you? What's he got planned for you, then?'

She shrugged. 'Dunno really. I think he'd like me to go on working in the bakehouse so's I'm under his eye, and then marry somebody posh and settle down.'

'Posh? What's that mean?'

'Well-to-do. You know . . . '

'Swanky, I guess. Is that what you want?'

'I don't want to go on working in the bakehouse for ever.'

'No reason why you should.'

'I don't want to settle down either,' she said. 'Not yet. I'd like to do something else first. Work in a dress shop in Peterborough, maybe. With nice things. Pretty things. Not always bread and cakes.'

He said slowly, 'Think you'd ever like to come to America? When the war's over.'

'Maybe. Not over yet, though, is it? Not by a long chalk. Want another cake?'

He shook his head. 'Cigarette?'

'Yes, please.'

He lit it for her. She'd got used to handling cigarettes now; she could do all the Bette Davis bits, blowing the smoke up in the air and flicking the ash away.

'What's an assistant crew chief, Chester? You've never told me exactly.'

'Well, each aircraft has a three-man crew to look after it. Service and maintain it. Make sure everything's working properly and get it ready for the pilot before he takes off. There's a crew chief, then his assistant — that's me — and an armourer — that's Hal. We've got our names painted on the aircraft, up in front just below the cockpit. Kind of gives me a kick to think of my name going into combat even if the rest of me's stuck back at the base, down on the ground.'

'Who's the pilot?'

'Lieutenant Mochetti. He's got his name painted on, too. He's a real nice guy and a heck of a good pilot. Three kills. Real tough. We take care of his aircraft for all his tour. Unless he goes missing.'

'If he's killed, you mean?'

'Not necessarily. Sometimes they're shot down but they're OK and get taken prisoner-of-war. We've had a lot in the Group get killed, though.'

She shivered. 'Don't they get scared?'

'Guess they must be. Sometimes there'll be a pilot who'll make some excuse and turn back — he'll say the engine's rough or something like that — but mostly they go. Lieutenant Mochetti, our guy, always flys the mission. He never turns back.'

'He must be brave.'

'Sure is. So are most of the pilots. They're a great bunch.'

'So are the RAF.'

'Sure they are. We know that. And they've been fighting and dying a lot longer.'

She took another puff and blew the smoke away. 'Remember when you first came into the bakehouse, Chester? And you bought all those rock buns? It was ever so funny really.'

'I'd never seen a girl like you, Sally. You knocked me out.'

She giggled. 'Did I?'

'Sure did.' He looked at her from where he was sitting, leaning against the willow, cigarette dangling between his fingers. 'Never felt about a girl the way I feel about you.'

'Go on . . . There must be lots of pretty girls in Paradise.'

'None like you.'

'I don't believe you. I bet you Yanks say that to

all the girls. Bet you've got a girl back home.'

'You know darned well I haven't.'

She pursed her lips in an O to blow some more smoke upwards. 'How do I know?'

'Thought I'd shown you.'

'Oh, *that* . . . that doesn't mean anything.'

'Does to me.'

She shrugged. 'Does it?'

He stubbed out his cigarette and came over and took hers away from her. 'Guess I'll have to show you some more.' He took hold of her by the shoulders. She could see he was quite upset. After a bit, he said, 'Believe me now?'

She shook her head, teasing him again. 'Not really.'

He pushed her down onto the grass and kissed her some more; lifted his head and looked at her with his deep blue eyes. 'How about now?'

'That all?'

'Jesus, Sally . . . '

Next thing, she was flat on her back and he was kissing her all over her face and neck, and soon he started undoing all the buttons down the front of her blouse, one by one. She could hear him breathing ever so fast and feel the grass tickling her, and his hands touching her all over. Then his mouth, too, warm on her bare skin. She didn't try to stop him. She felt as though she was melting away inside. She wasn't going to lose her nerve like Doris. She wanted Chester to do it. She wanted to know what it was like. She thought: I do like him. I like him a lot. He's gorgeous. And then she thought: just wait till I tell Doris.

8

In Miss Cutteridge's opinion, the month of May was the loveliest of the year. Trees loaded with blossom, spring flowers in the gardens, the hedgerows a foaming mass of hawthorn and elderflower, the banks and verges dotted with primroses, celandine, cowslips, lady's smock, jack-in-the-pulpit, cow parsley. Bluebells carpeting the woods, the mallards hatching their young by the brook, birds singing, the evenings drawing out: a joy to the eye, the ear, the nose and the heart after the long, grey winter.

It was also the month when she turned her attention to the garden. Before the war she had employed a man on one day a week to do the heavy work and to cut the lawn, but he had been called up long ago, back in 1940. Since then she had struggled along on her own and every year the garden had become more and more like a jungle. She could manage cutting the grass with the lawnmower, and the rose-pruning and most of the weeding but the shrubs had got away from her, growing so tall and so wild that she could no longer reach to keep them in any order, and wild brambles had grown from the other side of the garden wall, smothering everything in their path. And then there was the vegetable plot. The weekly gardener had always looked after the plot: dug, raked, planted and hoed, leaving Miss Cutteridge with only the pleasure of picking the fresh vegetables. At first she had tried to cope on her own, though her arthritis made the work painful and difficult, but the results had been so disappointing — everything had either failed to grow or been eaten by pests — that she had finally given up and left the plot to grow over. But this spring she had decided that she ought to give it another try. Dig for Victory. Grow More Food. Is Your Garden on War Service? There were advertisements and posters everywhere exhorting people to grow their own vegetables, talks on the wireless, articles in magazines and newspapers, leaflets distributed. They'd even had a colour film shown at the village hall entitled *A Garden Goes to War* which she had unfortunately missed owing to a heavy cold. It was her patriotic duty, not to mention how much it would help her limited budget.

She fetched the fork and rake from the toolshed and made a start on clearing the patch. After an hour her back and her hands were aching and she had only managed to clear and dig a very small area. She wiped her forehead and leaned on the fork handle, head bowed, afraid that the task was going to be beyond her strength, and yet unwilling to give up.

'Hey there, ma'am. You OK?'

Startled, she turned her head to see Corporal Bilsky standing on the path. Miss Cutteridge straightened up quickly. 'I'm quite all right, thank you.' She went pink with embarrassment. He had caught her at a great disadvantage: all dishevelled and perspiring, wearing her oldest skirt and the jumper with the hole in the elbow and with a ladder in her lisle stocking.

'Couldn't get no answer at the door, so I came round the side gate,' he said. 'Hope you don't mind.' He stared at the plot. 'Gee, that looks like a lot of hard work. Here, let me give you a hand.'

He took off his uniform jacket, rolled up his shirtsleeves and removed the fork from her grasp. 'Want me to do the whole patch?'

She hesitated for a moment, but the temptation to take advantage of the offer was overwhelming. 'If it's really not too much trouble.'

He grinned. 'No trouble at all. You goin' to grow things here?'

'Vegetables, I hope.'

He lifted the fork. 'Well, you go indoors an' take a bit of a rest, ma'am. A lady like you shouldn't be doin' this sort of work.'

Miss Cutteridge retreated and watched discreetly from the kitchen window. He was digging away deep and fast and making it look so easy, but then he was a strong young man and she was a feeble old woman. She went upstairs to comb her hair and change her jumper and her laddered stocking and then came down again and sank into her armchair, feeling quite worn out. She wondered how much she should pay him — another awkwardness. The Americans were paid very well, she'd heard — overpaid, some people said — and she had no idea what to offer. If she asked him he might say a sum that she simply couldn't afford. She sat wondering and worrying about it. After a while, when she had recovered her strength, she went to look out of the kitchen window again and averted her gaze hurriedly when she saw that the corporal had taken off his tie, shirt and vest and was working bare-chested. Her former gardener had never taken off so much as his hat, except to raise it to her, but then Americans were so much less formal and, of course, he must be feeling quite warm from all the digging. He was probably thirsty, too. She searched anxiously in cupboards and found a bottle of Robinson's barley water with just enough left in the bottom to make one glassful. It was out of the question to take it out to him, given his state of undress, but she mixed it up ready in the glass and went and sat down again and picked up her knitting to keep herself calm and usefully occupied while she waited.

Another hour and a half passed before there was a knock on the back door and she hurried to open it. To her relief his shirt and tie were back on again, both neatly tucked in. He carried his uniform tunic over his arm.

'All done, ma'am. I've dug it over and raked it real good, an' I put all the weeds 'n' stuff on that trash heap at the end of the garden.'

He looked dreadfully hot. 'Thank you so much, Corporal. I'm very grateful to you. Will you have a glass of barley water?'

'Long as it's not in a teacup . . . thank you, ma'am. I'm real thirsty.'

She watched as he gulped the barley water down in one go. The poor boy must have been absolutely parched. 'I'm so sorry, there isn't any more.'

'Plain water'll do nicely,' he said. He filled the glass from the kitchen tap and drank it down.

She steeled herself. 'I was wondering how much I owed you for all your hard work, Corporal. I'm not quite sure what would be acceptable — '

He interrupted her, shaking his head. 'Not a cent, ma'am. I don't want nothin'.'

'Oh but I couldn't possibly allow that . . . '

He smiled. 'Reckon you'll just have to, ma'am, seein' as I'm not takin' nothin' from you.'

She really ought to point out his double negatives but that would be very impolite, especially in the circumstances. 'It's very good of you, Corporal. But I really think I owe you something.'

'You already paid me with the afternoon tea, ma'am, and invitin' me here in the first place. So that's an end to it. What vegetables're you thinkin' of plantin'?'

'Potatoes, I think. Some broad beans. Runner beans and carrots and cabbage. Perhaps some beetroot. It rather depends on what seeds I can find.'

'Sounds good,' he said. 'Don't know nothin' 'bout growin' those things but I'll be glad to help in any way I can. Seems a good idea to grow your own, everythin' bein' in such short supply over here. I've noticed most folks have a patch in their yard. Lot of folks have a pig, too. How about you keepin' a pig?'

'There's nowhere to keep it.'

'There's that tin hut near the dump.'

'The Anderson, you mean?'

'That what you call it? Well, that'd do just right.'

'But it's an air-raid shelter.' The gardener had erected it for her in the early days of the war. So far she hadn't used it once.

'Reckon you're not goin' to need it no more, ma'am. Those German bombers ain't goin' to come over this way, not with all us guys around. If you could get a piglet from some place, I could bring you stuff from the kitchens up at the base to feed it up — peelin's and scraps and such. One of my pals is a cook, see. Wouldn't cost you nothin' and when the pig's growed enough you'd have some nice pork to eat. You can salt the rest so's it keeps.'

'I don't think I could cope with a pig, Corporal. I've never kept any animals. Not even hens. Only the one cat.'

'Just an idea, ma'am.' He delved in the pocket of his tunic. 'I brought some photos to show you.' He fanned them like a hand of cards and held them out to her, pointing with his forefinger. 'There's my dad right there in the middle, with my two brothers. That's Jack standing next to Dad on this side. He was all-state third base in '38. Got picked up by the Brooklyn Dodgers and played for one of their minor league teams.'

'Really? How interesting.' She had no idea what he was talking about.

'Yes, siree. Could've made the big time if he hadn't got drafted. And that's Frank on the other side. He was All-America — left guard from Henryetta High.'

'Goodness me.'

'Yeah. No kiddin'. And this next photo here's of me and Jack on the front porch — that's our house in Henryetta. Frank took that one. This one's us all on the Fourth in '42 — my Aunt Sara took that. Last time we were all together: Dad, Jack, Frank and me.'

They were a smiling and happy family. In spite of the hardships and difficulties, Miss Cutteridge could see that the father, who looked a very nice man, had done a good job. Three fine sons who were a credit to him. If she and William had ever had a son, what might he have been like? Perhaps a little like Corporal Bilsky. An absurd fancy, of course. What was she doing even thinking of such a thing? He was nothing like William in looks or manners or speech, nothing at all. But there was something about him — a concern for and consideration of others, a decency, that reminded her very much of William.

The corporal was putting on his jacket. 'Well, if there's nothing else I can do, ma'am, I'd best be getting back. I'll be by sometime, soon as I can, an' give you a hand with the vegetables, if you need it.' He put his hand in another pocket. 'Oh, I darn near forgot. This is for you. Might come in handy.'

He was gone before she could protest, bicycling away down the street. She picked up the tin he had left on the kitchen table and saw that it contained American ham. Best quality, it said on the label. She put it away in her store cupboard carefully. Next time he came she would open it and give him a proper meal with potatoes and vegetables. She had bought a tin of Smedley's select garden peas on her last visit to the grocer and they were always very nice. From what he had said about a pig, the corporal would probably prefer fresh pork but it was a long time since she'd been able to get any, other than in sausages and she often wondered what parts of the pig those contained. It was almost certainly far better not to know. Occasionally, the butcher sold her some streaky bacon under the counter because he had a soft spot for the elderly, and that made quite a good meal. But a joint of pork, roasted so that the crackling was brown and crisp, and served with apple sauce . . . her mouth watered. Miss Cutteridge put on her hat and coat and picked up her shopping basket. It was time to sally forth in search of vegetable seeds. There was not a moment to lose. As she set off, she wondered where on earth one might buy a piglet.

* * *

'I recommend the fish.'

'Any particular reason?' he asked.

'Well, it's one of the very few things not rationed. The sea's not far away so it should be fresh, and sole is rather good, if they cook it well.'

'I've heard about your fish and chips. Haven't tried any yet.'

'There's nothing better. Unfortunately we don't have a fish-and-chip shop in King's

Thorpe, or I'd be down there all the time. It must be eaten straight out of the newspaper it's wrapped in, though, to be properly appreciated — preferably the *Daily Mirror*. I'm not sure I could persuade my mother-in-law to do that.'

Carl Schrader smiled. 'Somehow I don't see it . . . Sole it is, then. The same for you?'

'Yes, I think so, thank you.'

Miriam had been very huffy about this dinner outing. 'Not a wise thing to do, I should have thought, Erika. It's one thing to invite an American to bridge, but quite another to associate with him.'

'I'm not associating with him. I'm having dinner with him. It's a thank-you for the Cook's Tour the other day, that's all.'

'He's still an American. They have an appalling reputation.'

'He's a group commander, not some randy GI, Miriam.'

'There's no need to be coarse, Erika.'

'Anyway, I thought you liked him.'

'He may be a good bridge-player but that's irrelevant where this situation is concerned.'

'There *is* no situation.'

'People will gossip. I assume you have some regard for the Beauchamp name, if only for Alexander's sake. Colonel Schrader is a married man.'

'I am perfectly aware of that.'

Sitting opposite him in the panelled grandeur of the George restaurant, she was not only perfectly, but painfully, aware of it. I'm falling in love with him, she thought. I hardly know him, but that's what's happening. Already happened, in fact. I don't know exactly how, when or where, or even why. Miriam was right, blast her. This wasn't a wise thing at all.

'This is a famous old coaching inn,' she said, briskly continuing the Cook's Tour. 'The stagecoaches used to stop here to change horses and for the passengers to stay overnight. Stamford is only a mile from the Great North Road — the main route between London and York. King Charles the First stayed here and William the Fourth. It's full of history.'

'I can tell that.' He looked round the room. 'It's a very fine old place. I wish we had something like this in St Louis. We just don't go back that far.'

'I've forgotten what state St Louis is in.'

'Missouri. It's right on the border of Illinois. Very hot summers, very cold winters.'

'Were you born there?'

'Born and raised there. Lived there until I left high school to go to West Point. Since then, I haven't been back too much.'

'But your wife and daughter are there?'

He nodded. 'It's Jan's home town too. We met at high school and then got married when I was through West Point. After that she moved around with me whenever it was possible. Then Kathy came along and then the war. It got so I was never around, so they went back to St Louis to be near her family. It was the only thing to do. Same as with lots of people.'

'The war's hard for everybody.'

'Sure is.'

'You must find your job extremely demanding, Carl.'

'I've got a deputy and squadron commanders and a whole lot of other officers dealing with different things. I don't handle it all. It would be impossible.'

'But you're in overall command and you fly combat missions as well.'

'Sure. The guys wouldn't be too impressed if I stayed home hiding under the desk.'

'Leaders have to lead?'

'That's it.'

To her relief the Sole Véronique was all right. Why is it, she wondered, that one feels so apologetic to foreigners about everything in England? We shouldn't be. We should be proud of not being occupied by Germans. Of never, never, never being slaves.

He said, 'You haven't told me much about yourself, Erika. You said your father was Hungarian and your mother English and that you were born in England. That's as far as we went. How did your father come to be over here?'

'He was a musician. A violinist. He found life in Hungary fairly impossible so he went to Paris and then came to England afterwards and met my mother in London. He was extremely handsome and he swept her off her feet and married her, much to my grandparents' disapproval.'

'Was he a good violinist?'

'Yes, he was rather. Concert standard. A very nomadic life, though. I didn't see a great deal of him and I was sent away to boarding school, as well. He died when I was fifteen, but all the memories of him are good. Very good.'

'I guess that's what counts. And your mother's remarried?'

'To a very rich man with a lot of land in Scotland. She's made a new life up there.'

'Did you meet your husband in London too?'

'We met on Waterloo Station. We bumped into each other — literally. I was running for a train and he was going the other way and we collided. My suitcase came open and everything fell out. He helped me gather it all up.' She smiled at the memory of Richard dashing about retrieving undies and solemnly handing them over. 'It was an odd way to meet one's husband.'

He smiled too, 'Yeah, but there are no rules. Did you live in London when you were married?'

'Yes. Richard had a job in the City and we lived in a flat in Kensington. I still have the flat, as a matter of fact. Do you know London?'

'I've been there a couple of times, that's all. What I've seen I liked.'

'I've always adored London. I'm not a countrylover, to be honest, but I appreciate lots of things about it. Richard loved King's Thorpe, though. We used to come up here at weekends, until the war broke out and he was called up. He was killed in France, during the retreat to Dunkirk. I didn't hear for nearly three months. Everything must have been pretty chaotic over there. Nobody knew whether men were dead or taken prisoner, or what had happened to them. Some of them were never even found. One keeps hoping, you know. While there's hope, there may be life. Then eventually, I was told that there wasn't.'

'I'm sorry,' he said. 'It must have been tough.'

'It was. They sent me the usual letter.' She remembered how she had felt when the envelope had landed on the mat; how long it had taken her to steel herself to open it, to look at the first words. *It is with great regret that we have to inform you . . .* 'Alex was only four and we stayed on in the flat in London at first. Then the Blitz happened and we came up to King's Thorpe. My mother-in-law and I have what you might call an armed truce. If it weren't for Alex I'd be back in London like a shot, bombs or no bombs.'

He smiled. 'Let's hope the war's over soon, so you can escape.'

'Well, there seem to be enough Americans over here now to deal with any number of Germans.'

'Yeah, I guess you've been invaded by Yanks, instead of Huns. The British sure have had a lot to put up with.'

When they'd finished dinner he drove her back to the Manor. Miriam, she guessed, would be waiting up past her usual bedtime to deliver a late-night lecture. He stopped the car and turned the engine off.

'I'd like to see you again, Erika. Whenever that's possible.'

'Yes, of course. You're welcome at the Manor any time.'

'That wasn't exactly what I meant . . . but thanks, anyway.' He got out and came round to open the door for her.

'Thank you for the dinner, Carl.'

'The pleasure was all mine. Goodnight.'

The drawing-room door was half open, the lights still on. As she had expected, her mother-in-law appeared, looking pointedly at her watch.

'Oh, there you are at last. I was very worried. Alexander woke up and got into quite a state, wondering where you were.'

'He knew perfectly well where I was, Miriam. I told him at bedtime.'

'Well, he was very upset.'

'I'll go up and see him.'

Her son was sound asleep in his bed, his book fallen to the floor beside him. There was no tear-stained face, no evidence of any upset state, just a child sleeping peacefully. She tucked the blanket round him, straightened the eiderdown and picked up the book. To hell with Miriam, she thought, suddenly furious. To hell with what she thinks. To hell with everything.

* * *

'I think we should donate part of the proceeds to the Red Cross, Agnes. It seems only right to me. I shall raise it at the next Parochial Church Council and I'm sure there will be full agreement. How many people do you expect to come to the dance?'

'I'm not sure. We've put posters in all the neighbouring villages.'

'There will probably be a big turnout. People

seem to like the American band music very much, especially the young. I can quite understand it, though I do find it a little loud sometimes and rather difficult to dance to.' Her father drank his tea and got up from the breakfast table. 'Well, I must get about my business. I have some early visits to make.' He touched her shoulder as he passed. 'We shall see each other at lunchtime, as usual, my dear.'

She cleared the breakfast table and washed up in the kitchen. It was Mrs Halliwell's morning to oblige but her bunions were playing her up again and she was at home keeping her substantial weight off them. As Agnes finished the drying, she heard somebody knocking at the front door. When she opened it Clive was standing there. Unsmiling.

'Big surprise, eh? I got home late last night. They've given me forty-eight hours.'

'That's wonderful, Clive.'

'You don't look that thrilled, Agnes. Sorry, more like.' He came into the hallway and grabbed her by the shoulders. 'I want to sort things out with you. Here and now.'

'What on earth are you talking about?'

'I'm talking about you running around with some Yank. That's what.'

'I've been doing nothing of the kind.'

'That's not what I've heard. You were seen having dinner with one of the bastards at the Haycock. Mother wrote and said it was all round the village. It's true, isn't it?'

'I had dinner once with one of them.'

He shook her. 'What's his name? Tell me and

I'll break his bloody neck.'

'Let go of me please, Clive,' she said coldly. 'You're hurting. There was a reason for it, if you'll give me a chance to explain.'

He dropped his hands. 'Well, it'd better be good.'

'I wanted to ask him about getting their band to play at one of the village-hall dances. The church has got dry rot in the roof and we have to raise money, a lot of money, to get rid of it. They're playing this Saturday. You must have seen the posters.'

'Come off it, Agnes. You don't expect me to swallow that? Why him? And why go to dinner? Why didn't you just write to whichever Yank's in charge?'

'I'd met him and I thought he'd be able to arrange it.'

'Because he's been after you, that's why. He'd do anything for you, wouldn't he? You damn well knew that. And you fancied him. Has he been coming here? To this house?'

'Father invited him to lunch once, that's all.'

'Christ almighty! I'd have thought at least you'd be safe here. But your father's been the one who's been so keen on the bloody Yanks all along, hasn't he? I've heard about that, too. What the hell did the old fool think he was doing, encouraging them? This is all his fault.'

'How dare you speak of my father like that! How *dare* you!'

He took a deep breath. 'OK, OK. I'm sorry. Listen to me, Agnes. Everyone's talking and I'm not having you making me a laughing-stock in the village. Or my family. I want you to promise me here and now that you won't see or speak to that Yank again. Or any other Yank.'

'No, I won't promise you that.' She stared at him, seeing him very clearly for the first time and wondering how she could ever have imagined that she loved him.

'Why the hell not? You're engaged to me.'

She dragged the ring off her finger and held it out. 'Not any more, Clive. I should never have agreed to marry you. It was a big mistake — for both of us — and I'm sorry.'

He looked stunned and then snatched the ring out of her hand. 'You know, my parents always said I could have done much better than you. All that funny business with your mother, and your pathetic old father . . . It seems they were quite right about it in the end, doesn't it? You're no better than any of the other tarts in the village who've been playing around while their men were away fighting.'

'Get out, Clive. *Get out*!'

'Don't worry, I'm going. I don't want any Yank-soiled goods.'

He slammed the front door behind him. She stood quite still in the hallway, her hands clenched at her sides. In the distance the school bell started ringing.

* * *

The rector could feel the whole village hall shaking. He had retreated to a corner to watch the wild cavortings that were, apparently, the modern American way of dancing, and hoped to heaven that the floor would stand up to it. By comparison, the party at the Officers' Club had been a sedate affair; this was very different. He stared, flabbergasted, as the Americans threw their partners around. He'd never seen anything like it in all his life. And the girls didn't seem to mind. On the contrary, they had picked up the dance steps and were enjoying themselves enormously. The band was at the other end of the room, up on the stage, but the players might as well have been within inches as far as his ears were concerned. The noise was deafening — trumpets and saxophones blasting away, drums and cymbals thudding and clashing. Conversation would have been impossible, though, clearly, the dancers wanted only to dance. He watched their faces as they spun by and, just for a moment, he envied them their youth and their capacity for sheer joy.

More than four hundred had turned up and paid their two-shilling entrance fee — King's Thorpe villagers, people from neighbouring villages and even further afield, and a lot of Americans from the air base. The evening was undoubtedly a great success. Sylvia, he thought, would have found it all wonderful fun, for once. He searched among the maelstrom for Agnes but couldn't see her. She was probably helping with the refreshments in the kitchen, which was a pity; he would have liked to see her dancing with one of the Americans and enjoying herself. With Lieutenant Mochetti, perhaps. Her broken engagement had upset her a lot, he could tell that. Personally, he had been hugely relieved, though he had not actually said so, of course, or shown it. He had tried hard but never succeeded in liking Clive Hobbs, and he had never believed that he would make Agnes happy. Unhappiness in marriage was the last thing on earth that he would have wished for her. He looked round for the lieutenant but couldn't see him, either, which was odd, since it was he who had helped to make the whole evening possible.

At last the music finished and he stopped a passing American officer. 'Do you happen to know if Lieutenant Mochetti will be here tonight?'

'He couldn't make it, sir. Overdue from a mission.'

'I hope that doesn't mean bad news?'

'Couldn't say exactly, sir. That's all I know.'

'I see. Well, thank you.'

He made his way towards the kitchen. Through the hatchway he could see Agnes busy pouring out the Coca-Cola provided by the Americans. He hesitated. It would be better not to tell her about Ed Mochetti now; it could wait until later. Instead, he went outside the hall for a breath of air and stood for a while looking up at the few stars showing in a cloudy night sky. It was cold for late May: the weather very unsettled and unseasonable, not that that was so unusual. He could hear the drone of RAF heavy bombers to the east. There had been a great deal of activity lately, from both the RAF and the American Air Force. They must be bombing Germany relentlessly, by night and by day.

Preparing the ground, he supposed, for the Allied invasion that was rumoured to be happening within weeks — but surely not until the weather had improved?

The band had started up again but this time the music was much quieter: rather a pleasant tune that one could slow-foxtrot to. He listened to it, remembering how he and Sylvia had sometimes danced together when they were first married — not that he had ever been very accomplished. One of the many ways in which he must have disappointed her and let her down.

The moon appeared for a moment before vanishing again behind a dark cloud. He wondered what had happened to Lieutenant Mochetti and offered up a silent prayer for his safe return.

* * *

'Can we talk, Sally?'

'What about?'

'Things. We can't talk in here. Come outside with me.'

'I promised Rick I'd dance with him next.'

'Tough luck on him.' Chester put his hand on her arm firmly. 'Just for a moment.'

She shrugged. 'Oh, all right then.'

The night air was cold after the stuffy heat of the village hall and she shivered. Chester took off his jacket and put it round her shoulders.

'There's someone standing over there,' she said warily.

'Just some old guy. He's gone in now. It's OK.'

'Well, what did you want, then?'
'I want to talk about us, Sal. You know how I feel about you and I want to know how you feel about me.'
'I like you a lot, Chester.'
'Is that all?'
'An awful lot, then.'
He could hardly see her in the dark, let alone her expression; her voice told him nothing. He said steadily, 'After what happened, I thought things had got kind of serious between us.'
'Well, it just happened, didn't it?'
'Like I said before, I'm real sorry about it.'
'I don't know why you're sorry.'
'You know what I mean. I sure didn't plan to go that far. It's only ever happened once with me before — some girl I met after I'd gotten drafted. She was nothing to me, but you are, Sally. And I want to know how things stand.'
'I told you, I like you an awful lot.'
'Yeah, but you still look at other guys, and you still dance with them.'
'I love dancing, that's why. There's no harm in it.'
'I want for us to get married one day.'
'*Married*?'
'Sure. Why not? Wouldn't you like that?'
'I don't know . . . not yet, anyway. I don't know you well enough.'
'I'd say you knew me pretty damn well. And I know you.'
She giggled suddenly and he took a hold of her and kissed her and she kissed him back, sweet as anything. 'So, what about it, Sally?'

'What about what?' She shivered again. 'It's freezing out here, Chester.'

She was playing games with him, he realized that, and he was getting nowhere. 'OK, I guess we'd better go in.'

He leaned against the wall in the village hall, smoking a cigarette and watching her dancing with Rick and then a string of other guys. Trouble was, he liked her a heck of a lot more than an awful lot: he loved her.

9

Brigadier Mapperton had taken refuge in the garden. Cicily had another of those damned knitting circles going on in the drawing room and the house was full of women. The only place he could get any peace was outside, as far away from them as possible, which meant at the bottom of the garden. He stumped down to the far end and looked at the vegetable plot. Cooper was an idle old bugger if he didn't keep him up to the mark, always complaining about his rheumatism and the make-do-and-mend tools. All excuses, of course. Gardeners were always finding them. If it wasn't the weather it was the pests or the birds, or anything they could think of. He went up and down the rows, inspecting potatoes, carrots and peas as though they were troops on parade, stopping to glare ferociously at the broad beans. Damn things had got some sort of blackfly. Why hadn't that idiot Cooper sprayed them? He'd probably give him some cock-and-bull story about not being able to get the insecticide stuff when the truth was he was too damned lazy to bother. He strode on to the runner beans, the leeks, the onions and the marrows. All well there, and the peaches were coming along on the wall though they could do with some decent weather. Bloody awful June so far.

He looked at his watch. The knitting circle

wouldn't be over for another hour or more. They'd be sitting there like those women at the French guillotine, needles clicking like castanets. If he showed his face anywhere near the place they'd catch sight of him and he'd have to go in and be polite. He unbolted the door in the garden wall and went down to the brook. After all the rain, it was running deep and muddy, making a rushing sound instead of the usual quiet babbling over the stones. He walked along the banks by the willows towards the old water mill. When he was a boy he'd seen it working and villagers taking their gleaning to be ground at harvest time. He could remember the thunder of the machinery, the thrash and splash of the great wheel, the clouds of dust, the sacks of corn and the sacks of flour, tied at the corners like pigs' ears.

Things weren't what they used to be in the village, he thought morosely. It was all vanishing. There'd been a windmill, too, at the top of East Street until it had burned down, and in the old days there had been a thriving wood-turning industry with the turners making bowls and eggcups and spoons and rolling pins and butter pats in their cottages and back gardens. All gone now. Before the war, in the Twenties and Thirties, there'd been a damn good cricket team and a drama club. They'd put on plays and concerts in the village hall: good, sound, old-fashioned things like Gilbert and Sullivan and *The Quaker Girl*. None of this modern rubbish. He'd taken the odd chorus part himself. The Great War had started the rot, of course:

things were never the same by the time that was over and now this war was going to change it all a whole lot more. Bloody Huns! They'd got a lot to answer for. Thrashed them in 1918. Rubbed their faces in it. And twenty years later, he was damned if they hadn't gone and done it again. Infernal cheek!

He skirted the old millpond, now part silted up, and the decaying mill house, rejoining the bank further along the brook. His temper wasn't all it used to be either, he had to admit that. He got a bit shirty sometimes, and often he regretted it. The Huns were partly to blame for that too. His frustration gnawed at him like a rat. Drove him mad. D-Day plus six and here he was stuck with knitting circles and the ARP while other men were in Normandy fighting the enemy: getting to real grips with them at last. Damned tough situation over there. Machine-gun fire rattling away, snipers everywhere, juggernaut tanks, entrenched artillery, bombardment overhead . . . He knew something of the Normandy terrain. High hedges and deep, narrow lanes. Good defensive cover for the enemy and damned difficult for the Allies. They'd need officers capable of resolute leadership. Chaps like he'd been himself, once. You had to throw caution to the winds. Advance boldly; lead your men into the attack; knock out the enemy at all costs.

The brigadier stopped and stood staring fixedly at the brook, yet not seeing it. Instead he was somewhere in Normandy, leading his men on, storming into a French village, routing Huns who fled before him. The lines from *Henry V* came into his head: *And gentlemen in England now a-bed Shall think themselves accursed they were not here*. He shook his head and walked on. That's what he was: accursed. Dammit, even the *Yanks* were there. Last time he'd gone into Peterborough, there wasn't one to be seen. He'd known their air force could do their stuff but he wouldn't have given a thank-you for any of the army of GIs he'd seen slouching and slopping around the towns for months on end. Useless lot of no-good buggers, he'd reckoned. If *The Times* was to be believed though, and he rarely doubted it, they were doing a pretty decent job over there. Fighting and dying like real soldiers. He had to take back some of the things he'd thought and said about them. Give credit where credit was due; that was only right.

Fighters were taking off from the American base yet again. He could see them climbing fast in the distance. Still covering the D-Day convoys and the landings, of course. They would have been right up there with the first assault wave, fending off the Luftwaffe, escorting the Yank bombers while they pounded the enemy fortifications behind the beaches, going for the shore batteries, protecting Allied bridgeheads, shooting up enemy convoys. And the RAF night-fighters took over after dark. Damned useful to have those chaps around when you were down on the ground in the thick of it. Pity they hadn't had them like that in the first show.

He looked at his watch again and sighed. Give it another half-hour and it would be safe to go back. He squared his shoulders and strode on.

* * *

'You can come if you don't ask stupid questions all the time.'

'Course I won't, Tom. Cross my heart.'

Of course he would: Alfie always did. But it was his birthday and, much as he'd like to have left him behind, Tom relented.

'All right, then.'

'Where are we going?'

That was the first one already. 'Up to the airfield. To a special place I've found where you can watch the fighters taking off. They go right over your head, close as anything.'

'Will we see Ed?'

'Dunno.'

'He's all right, though, isn't he?'

'Far as I know.'

'Bound to be, with the rabbit's foot.'

The rabbit's foot had looked after Ed when he'd come down in the sea. He'd been floating about in the dinghy for hours and then a lifeboat had found him and brought him back safely. Tom was glad he'd only heard about it afterwards on one of his visits to the radio shack. The Yanks wouldn't let him go out to the flight line any more. It was too busy and too dangerous now, they said. Ever since the Invasion the squadrons were going on missions to France all the time and he hadn't seen Ed for nearly two weeks, or any of the other pilots. That was when he'd found this special secret place — a deep hollow in the ground several yards inside the perimeter fence at the very far end of the main runway. Nobody could see him when he lay down in it but he could see the pilots in their cockpits as they took off and climbed right over his head, and he could see the markings so he knew exactly whose plane it was: Ed's or Ben's or Chuck's or Randy's or Zell's or Don's . . .

Alfie followed him across the fields. Tom didn't bother to turn round as he knew he'd be there panting at his heels, like a dog. After they'd watched the fighters he might take him to the radio shack, if he wasn't being too stupid. They never minded him going there, but they wouldn't let Dick or Robbie or Seth or any of their gang on the base at all any more. Not since they'd caught them siphoning petrol out of trucks. Tom thought doing that was wicked. It was one thing to pinch eggs for the Yanks, but taking their petrol was different. You couldn't fight the Germans with eggs — not unless they were rotten and you threw them at them — but the Yanks needed petrol to win the war.

They reached the stream at the bottom of the hill and Tom crossed by the two stepping stones, jumping from one to the next. Behind him, he heard the splash as Alfie missed and fell in. The water was only shallow but the inside of his boots and his socks'd be all wet and probably his shorts, too, and Mum would be cross and he'd get the blame.

At the perimeter fence by the end of the main runway there was a spot where he'd scraped out enough earth to wriggle underneath the wire. He stopped and waited for Alfie to catch him up, feet squelching in his wet boots.

'We've got to crawl the last bit.'

'What for?'

'So's nobody can see us, idiot. The Yanks wouldn't let us stay there when the fighters are taking off.'

'Why not?'

'Cos it's dangerous, of course. If they see us, they'll come and throw us out. Then they might not let us on the base ever again.'

'But they can't see us all this way away.'

'They've got binoculars in the control tower, stupid. You'll have to keep down low all the time, especially when the planes are coming.'

'Why?'

He rolled his eyes. 'Cos they're ever so low, that's why. You'll see. Follow me and just do what I do.'

They wriggled under the wire and did a Red Indian crawl on their elbows and stomachs over to the secret place and slithered down into it. Of course Alfie went and tore his jumper on the wire so Mum would be upset about that as well. It was all quiet in the hollow except for the skylarks overhead.

'When are they going, Tom?'

'Not yet. We have to wait. You've got to be patient.'

Alfie was patient for about five more minutes. 'Are they going yet?'

Tom lifted his head and peered over the rim of the hollow. In the very far distance, on the other side of the airfield he could see the ground crews climbing over the fighters and some jeeps loaded with pilots coming along the peri track. 'Won't be much longer now. That's Ed's squadron over there, getting ready to go. The other two squadrons may be going too. But they're on different parts of the airfield and we can't see them from here.' He tore up some bits of grass and tossed them into the air.

'What're you doing that for, Tom?'

'Making sure which way the wind's blowing. I can't see the windsock properly.' He watched how the grass fell. 'It's OK. They'll be using this runway.'

'Have they got another one, then?'

'They've got two more going across different ways. They use them sometimes if the wind's changed. They always have to take off into the wind, see.'

'Why?'

'It's too long to tell you. You wouldn't understand.' He wasn't very sure why himself but he wasn't going to admit it.

'Will Ed go?'

' 'Spect so. He's a captain now, you know.'

'What's a captain?'

'One higher than a lieutenant. He's Captain Mochetti. They told me in the radio shack. That means he wears two bars on his shoulder, instead of just one. And they've given him a medal. The DFC.'

'What's that?'

Tom rolled his eyes again. 'The Distinguished Flying Cross. You get that for being a very good pilot and doing very brave things. If Ed flies over us you'll see the swastikas painted on his Mustang up by the cockpit. That shows how many Germans he's shot down.'

'How will you know if it's his aeroplane?'

'They've all got markings,' he explained patiently. 'Big white letters painted on the side, before and after the Yank star. Two letters to say which squadron it belongs to and then another letter after the star to show which plane it is. Ed's is A. We'll see it easily. We'll probably be able to see Bashful painted on it, too, but sometimes it's too fast to see everything.'

'Bashful?'

He sighed. 'You know, one of the Seven Dwarfs in *Snow White*. Doc, Sneezy, Happy, and all that lot. Ed's called his Mustang Bashful and it's got a picture of him on the nose. Ben's is Grumpy. Ben who comes with the washing sometimes.'

'He's nice, too,' Alfie said. 'He gave me some Baby Ruths last time. I like those.'

Mum always said that the way to Alfie's heart was through his stomach.

Tom rolled over onto his back and looked up at the blue sky and the big white puffy clouds. He tried to imagine what it must be like to climb up there so fast, up and up and up, and then go straight through the clouds. He'd asked Ed once what flying through a cloud was like and he'd laughed and said darned bumpy. He pictured himself up there in the cockpit, holding the stick, like that time he'd sat in Ed's Mustang, and checking all the dials in front of him — Ed had said you must never stop doing that — and keeping a lookout for Jerries. Ed said you had to do that all the time, too, or else they could come up on you and shoot you down before you even saw them.

'I can hear engines, Tom.'

He rolled over onto his stomach again and peeked out of the hollow. One of the Mustangs was already taxiing off the hardstand.

'Can I look, Tom?'

'All right, but keep your head down.'

They watched the fighters coming out onto the peri track, one behind the other, weaving.

'They do that so's they can see properly,' he told Alfie kindly. 'The nose is in the way.' He counted up the fighters. 'Seventeen. They always take a spare, case one of them has to drop out, then the spare goes instead.'

'Why've they got black and white stripes over them?'

'That's since the Invasion happened, else when they fly to France our side over there might shoot them down by mistake. They can see they're friendly easily with those big stripes. They paint them underneath as well as on top.'

'There's a lot more of them coming along now, Tom.'

He turned his head and saw the other fighters taxiing along the track. Two squadrons going. Maybe even the third as well. Must be a big mission. His insides tingled with excitement. 'We can stay like this now, so we can see them coming straight at us. That's the best bit. Two of them'll take off together, leader and wingman, then two more.'

'What's a wingman?'

He'd known that one was coming. 'He stays a

bit behind his leader and watches his tail to make sure no Jerry gets him.'

'What if a Jerry gets the wingman?'

He didn't know the answer to that one but he was spared having to admit it because the first two fighters had reached the far end of the main runway and turned. He could hear the spluttering growl of the Merlins. His stomach lurched and his heart thudded. 'Any minute now.'

He watched the two Mustangs starting their takeoff run: racing flat out towards them, engines at full power. Closer and closer, faster and faster. He kept his eyes fixed steadily on them, saw them lift into the air together and their wheels fold up inwards into the fuselage. They flew straight over him and Alfie, with a mighty roar that went through his whole body. He turned his head to watch them zooming up into the sky, and then back again quickly as another pair came. This leader was Ed. He saw the big white A and Bashful and the swastikas, and he saw Ed in the cockpit, clear as anything. The Mustang screamed over, so low and so close he felt he could have reached up to touch it. He waved with one hand and crossed the fingers on the other as he watched it climbing away, hoping Ed hadn't forgotten to take the rabbit's foot. The next pair were already hurtling towards them and that leader was Ben's plane, Grumpy. And then the next, and the next, and the next . . . He counted thirty-four fighters altogether. Two squadrons. After the last pair had taken off and disappeared he was still trembling with the thrill of it. He looked round for Alfie. His brother was lying with his face buried in the grass and his hands clapped over his ears.

'You missed it all,' he said in disgust.

'No, I didn't. I saw most of it. Did Ed go?'

'Yes. He was the second leader. Didn't you see him?'

'I think I did.'

Alfie was fibbing, as usual; Tom could always tell. 'He's got another swastika painted on. That's five Germans he's shot down now. That makes him an ace.'

'What's an ace?'

'A pilot who's shot down five enemy planes, of course. Come on, then. We'd better go.'

'When will they be back?'

'Depends. Usually it's about four hours. It might be a lot more. We can't wait here that long.'

'Can we go to the radio shack now? You promised.'

'Oh, all right.' It was his birthday, after all.

They crawled back under the perimeter wire and trotted round to the main gate. 'This is my brother,' he told the guard on duty. 'We're just going to the radio shack, that's all.'

'OK, kid.'

They were all in there, working at the benches. 'Hi, Tom. How ya doin'? What've you got this time?'

'Nothing, sorry. I'll bring some more eggs soon.' He pulled Alfie forward by one ear. 'This is my brother, Alfie.'

They all grinned. 'Hi there, Alfie. Good to meet you, kid.'

'It's my birthday,' Alfie said. 'I'm seven.'

They whistled and whooped, and Mitch started them singing Happy Birthday. They yelled it out while Alfie stood there, beaming all over his face. Then they whistled and whooped some more and clapped Alfie on the back so he almost fell over. After that, they showed him what they were working on and let him fiddle with knobs and twiddle dials. Mitch tuned into some loud Yank music again and did one of his funny dances round the hut with the broom and Alfie laughed and laughed. Then they all searched their pockets and gave him Hershey bars and Baby Ruths and Butterfingers and Tootsie Rolls and Wrigley's. One of them found an old cloth cap and put it on Alfie's head, flipping the peak up like they did.

'Here Tom,' Mitch said, coming over to him. 'Chester gave me a letter for you to deliver, next time you came by. It's for Sally — that girl at the bakery. Can you take it to her for him?' Mitch winked. 'Must be sweet on her, I reckon.'

'Yes, course I will.' He hadn't known Sally had ever met Chester.

'Thanks, kid. Guess we'd better get back to work. See you soon and bring your brother again. He's real cute.'

'I liked them all a lot. They were nice,' Alfie mumbled happily through a mouthful of chocolate as they trailed back across the fields. His pockets were crammed with the sweets and the chewing gum. They'd let him keep the cap and he was still wearing it on the back of his head, the peak pointing to the sky. 'Can I come again, Tom?'

'I'll see,' he said. The Yanks in the radio shack were sort of his Yanks; he didn't really want to share them with anybody. Not even Alfie.

* * *

Doris had opened the attic window as wide as it would go but the room was still stuffy; as hot in summer as it was cold in winter.

'When I get married I'm going to have a house with fans in the ceiling to keep it nice and cool in summer. Hal says houses in America have those. He says they have proper central heating too and everything's much better than here. They have all sorts of wonderful things to do the housework for you: labour-saving devices, he calls them. I wish they had them at the Manor. His mother's got everything like that and they've got a great big refrigerator to keep food cold in and a machine that washes the clothes. Washes them and rinses them all by itself. You just switch it on and go away and when you come back they're all done. Can you imagine that, Sal?'

'No, I can't.'

'It must be wonderful living in America. I'd like that.'

'Maybe Hal will ask you to marry him, then you can.'

Doris giggled. 'I wouldn't say no. He's ever such good fun. What would you say if Chester asked you?'

'He already has.'

'*Sal*! When?'

'A while ago.'

Doris looked hurt. 'And you didn't tell me about it. Whatever did you say to him?'

'I said I didn't want to get married yet.'

'Well, you couldn't, could you? Not till next month when you're sixteen and even then your dad'd have to give permission. He'd never do that, would he? Not to a Yank.'

'He might change his mind if he knew what's happened.'

'What do you mean?'

'I think I'm expecting.'

Doris's jaw dropped. 'A *baby*?'

'Well, it's not an elephant.'

'But how could you be?'

'Because I let Chester do it, that's why. How else could I be?'

'You never told me.'

'I don't have to tell you every single thing, Doris.'

'But we always said we would — about that. We always promised each other. Whoever was the first.'

'Well, I was going to, but then I didn't want to. I didn't feel like it. You can't tell anyone about it, really. You have to do it yourself. And I think it must be different for different people.'

Doris was still staring at her with a shocked expression. Sally could see she was going to be no help. No help at all. She wished she hadn't said anything.

'Are you *sure*, Sal? About the baby?'

'Well, I'm six weeks late and I keep being sick in the mornings.'

'You must be, then. What are you going to do? Whatever will your dad and mum say?'

'I'm not going to tell them,' she said. 'Or Chester. He doesn't know either. I'm not going to say a word and don't you dare, Doris.'

'Of course I won't, but they'll have to know sooner or later. I mean, it'll show, won't it? You won't be able to hide it for ever.'

'I'm going to try and get rid of it. There's some woman in Peterborough does that — I heard a girl talking about it at a Yank dance.'

'Don't go, Sal. It might be dangerous for you. They say girls can get poisoned and die. Why don't you try jumping off a chair?'

'I've already done that. Lots of times.'

'You could try with a table; that's higher. Mum's out so we could go downstairs and you jump off the kitchen table.'

'In a minute. I'm feeling a bit funny.' She sat down on Doris's bed. When she wasn't feeling sick, she felt faint and the smell of the yeast in the bakehouse made her retch.

Doris sat down too, still staring at her. 'What if it doesn't work, Sal? You'll have to marry Chester as soon as you're old enough.'

She said fiercely, 'No I won't. I'm not going to get married yet. Not for years and years. I want to have some fun first. Enjoy myself. Get away from this place — to London, perhaps. Get a job doing something different.'

'If you married Chester, you could go and live in America. That'd be different.'

'I don't want to marry *anyone* yet, can't you understand? I haven't had any sort of life.' She could feel tears coming into her eyes and blinked them back quickly. 'I don't want this baby. I hate it. I *hate* it.'

Doris looked even more shocked. 'It's not its fault.'

'I know, but I can't help feeling like that. If I don't get rid of it, then as soon as it's born, I'm going to give it away.'

'What would Chester say? It's his baby too, isn't it?'

'I'm not telling him.'

'You'll have to. He's going to notice, isn't he?'

'I won't see him any more. I haven't seen him since the Invasion, anyway. He gave Tom Hazlet a letter for me. Says they've been working all hours with the fighters . . . he doesn't know when he'll get away next. I'm going to write him back and tell him I don't want to see him any more. Get Tom to deliver it for me. That's what I'm going to do.'

'But I thought you liked him, Sal. He's so nice.'

'I do. But I don't want to marry him, or anybody else. Not yet.'

'He'll be so upset when he gets the letter.'

'I can't help that either.'

'Of course, it's his fault that it happened, isn't it? I mean he shouldn't have taken advantage of you.'

'He didn't. It wasn't his fault at all. I led him on. On purpose. You know how we've always wanted to know what it was like.'

Doris leaned forward. 'Do tell me, Sal. Please. What *was* it like?'

She shook her head. 'No, Doris. That's between me and Chester. It's private.'

* * *

'How good to see you again, Ed.'

'Thank you, sir.'

'It's Captain now, isn't it? Congratulations.'

'Thank you, sir.'

'And a medal. Well done.'

'How did you know about all that?'

'Oh, news travels fast in a village. We were quite anxious a while ago — when we heard you were overdue on that mission.'

'Yeah, I had some trouble but it worked out.'

'I prayed for you.'

'Thank you, sir. I reckon that must have helped.'

'Lately, of course, the thoughts and prayers of everyone in King's Thorpe have been with you American fliers. We had a special service in the church after the Invasion.'

'Sure appreciate that, sir.'

'You're our Yanks, you see. You belong to us.' The guy gave him a real nice smile. 'Agnes is in the kitchen garden, if you wanted to see her.'

What the hell was a kitchen garden? Indoors, or out? 'If that's all right, sir.'

'She's digging up potatoes for supper. You'll stay, I hope.' The rector came out of the front doorway onto the steps and pointed to the side of the house. 'If you go round that way, you'll come to a lawn. Go straight across and you'll find the kitchen garden at the far end, behind the row of apple trees.'

The lawn was one of those English things that you never saw anywhere else in the world. England green, flat as a billiard table and with the early evening sun lighting it in gold. Sometimes he couldn't get over the contrast: the war and the peace. One moment you were up flying in a kind of hell, the next back down here in a sort of heaven. Ed walked down the length of a border of plants which didn't happen anywhere else in the world either: flowers of all kinds and colours, growing together in a haphazard glory, except that he figured it was all arranged artfully on purpose. He came to the apple trees and the kitchen garden beyond turned out to be a large vegetable patch with rows of different sorts growing — this time in an entirely orderly fashion. Agnes was digging with a fork at the far side, turning over the dirt and picking things out of it. He stood watching her for a while before he walked round the edge of the patch towards her. He was within feet of her before she looked up. She was already flushed from the digging but she coloured some more.

'Hi, there.'

'Hallo, Ed.' He didn't say anything else for a moment: just went on looking at her. She was still holding the garden fork up in the air, like she'd frozen stiff. 'Thank you for the note you sent. Tom delivered it safely.'

'I thought you'd wonder why I didn't show up

for that dance, I was real sorry to miss it. I hear it went pretty well.'

'It was a wonderful success. We raised nearly fifty pounds. Part of that's going to the Red Cross — Father thought that was the right thing to do. The rest will be towards the dry rot. They've already started work at the church.'

'I'm real glad. Can't have that nice old place falling down. I'd have called by sooner, but this is the first chance of getting off base. We've been pretty active.' He nodded at the row of plants. 'Potatoes, right? You know, I've never seen them growing before, or anybody digging them up. Can I take a turn?'

'Yes, of course,' she handed him the fork. 'It's a bit like lucky dip.'

'Lucky dip? Never heard of that.'

'It's a game where you try to unearth a prize.'

She showed him how to dig the fork down under the plant to bring up the potatoes and then turn the dirt over to find the ones that had got away. He added his to her basketful. 'They look good.'

' 'Eat-More-Potatoes,' ' she quoted with a smile. 'That's what the Ministry of Food have been telling us to do since the war started. Potatoes feed without fattening and give you energy — that's the general idea.'

'I guess that's right.'

'And carrots help you to see in the dark — useful for the blackout.'

'You don't say. Do you grow those too?'

'Carrots, onions, beans . . . anything and everything. Everybody grows what they can.

Congratulations on your promotion. And on the medal.'

'I can't figure out how you heard about that.'

'Everyone in the school knows. I think it was Tom who told them. They look on you as their special property, you see. Ever since you gave that talk.'

He grinned. 'You don't say. Tom's a real nice kid.'

'He's one of the brightest in the school. We're hoping he'll get a scholarship next year. That means a free place at the grammar school.'

'Sure hope he does, then. He hangs around up at the base quite a bit and all the guys like him. He gave me a rabbit's foot for luck. I guess I'm not sure I really believe in good-luck charms but I always take it with me, just the same. He's got a pretty cute brother, too.'

'Alfie?' She smiled. 'I taught him in the kindergarten. He's lovely.' She stuck the fork into the ground. 'I've got to pick some peas now.'

'I'll give you a hand. Never picked peas either.'

She handed him another basket and they went up and down the rows of peas.

'How's Ben?'

'Fine. Never happier than when shooting up the enemy. Ammo trains are his favourite target. I keep telling him he's never grown up. He's got a puppy now. A Scottie. He saw her in a pet-shop window.'

'They let you keep dogs?'

'Sure. A lot of the guys at the base have them.' He picked away, snapping off the pods at their stalks. It was peaceful, pleasant sort of work, and, boy, was it a contrast to what he'd gotten used to doing in the past months. 'Mrs Hazlet does laundry for some of us guys. We feel bad, the way she has to work. No running water, no electricity in that place, but everything done real well. We can't see how she manages it.'

'There are a lot of women like that in the village. They manage everything somehow.'

'Not exactly a lazybones yourself, are you? Teaching those kids, running the house, helping your father, growing all these vegetables.' He showed her the basket. 'How am I doing?'

'That's plenty, thank you. I expect you have to get back.'

'In a couple of hours or so.'

She hesitated. Then: 'Would you like to stay for supper?'

'Thought you'd never ask me.'

They walked back across that sunlit, very English lawn. With double summer time it would be light until around eleven o'clock. He liked that: the long, long evenings, the golden light fading very slowly into purple dusk before darkness finally fell.

'The supper won't be very exciting, I'm afraid.'

'Bubble and squeak?'

She laughed. 'No, a bit better than that. The hens have been laying well, so I'm doing a soufflé. We've saved up some cheese.'

'I can't eat your cheese ration.'

'We'd be very offended if you didn't.'

'Guess I've got no choice then. Anything I can do to help? I'm pretty useful in the kitchen.'

'You can shell the peas, if you like.'

He sat at the kitchen table, popping the pods and thumbing the peas into a colander; and watching her as she scraped the potatoes and whisked the eggs and grated up the minuscule cheese ration.

'What happened to the ring?' He'd noticed it was missing when she was showing him how to pod the peas.

'I gave it back.'

'End of engagement?'

She was busy looking inside one of the cupboards. 'Yes.'

He picked up another pod. 'None of my business, I guess, but was that him or you ended it?'

She still had her head in the cupboard, moving things around. 'Me. I realized it was a mistake. That's all.'

He wondered what else lay behind it and whether there was any chance it had anything to do with him. She sure wasn't giving much away. He said easily, 'Well, it's a whole lot less trouble to figure that out now than later.'

She came out of the cupboard and went back to stirring things. He didn't ask any more questions and he was careful not to look too damned pleased.

The rector came into the kitchen after a while and they had supper at the big table. The cheese soufflé was terrific and the fresh potatoes and peas tasted great. He almost felt sorry for the guy she'd dumped. Afterwards, he helped do the dishes, putting them to drain in a big wooden rack over the sink. Her father had gone off back to his study.

'How about taking a walk?' he suggested. 'There's still plenty of daylight.'

She nodded. 'We could go along by the brook, if you like.'

He liked anywhere with her. Anywhere at all. There was a door in the old stone wall at the bottom of the garden and the creek that she called a brook was only a stone's throw away. The trees growing along the banks trailed pointed leaves in clear running water, the grass was long and lush and the late evening sun glowed like firelight. They followed the creek as it wound through fields shaded by great spreading trees and the incredible peace and beauty of it knocked him sideways. So did the girl he was with. She'd done that when he'd first seen her in the church, standing there with the light coming down on her from the high window, and every time he saw her, it was just the same.

She was keeping a safe distance from him, though. Same as she'd always done. Fending him off. He walked along, hands in pockets, and he thought soberly to himself: this isn't one of those tough cookies like Ben and I picked up in London. This is Miss. All right, she's fancy-free now, but I've got no right to get something started. Not now. Low-level strafing's sure as hell no picnic and enemy ground fire's knocking down us guys over there like clay pigeons. One truck, train, barge, loco, airfield too many and I could run out of luck, rabbit's foot or no rabbit's foot. Ben's right — for the wrong reasons. It's not me I need to think of, it's her. Get something serious going — and I mean serious because that's what it'd be — and the next thing she hears I'm a smoking hole in the ground. I can't do that to her. I've got no goddam right at all.

He said, 'We'd call this a creek back home, and this one sure is pretty. Any fish in it?'

'Grayling and perch, not many trout. The village boys, like Tom, catch them when they can. There are otters too.'

'Never seen one of those.'

'We hardly ever see them either. They're really nocturnal and they're very wary.'

He glanced at her, walking along, keeping at a safe distance. 'I'd say you're kind of wary, too, Agnes. Of me. I guess us Yanks can be real hard to figure out and you and I come from two different worlds. You've never seen skyscrapers and I've never seen countryside like you've got here. When I get home this is going to seem dreamland.'

'When will you be going back?'

Did she sound sorry about that, or was it just him hearing things? 'Hard to say. Haven't finished my tour yet. Maybe a month or so more to go. But we don't count chickens; not in our game.'

'Will you be given leave then?'

'Yeah. A good long one. Guess I'll go back home to New York. Spend some time there with my family. See what comes next.'

They followed the brook for another half-mile before they turned back. The daylight was going and by the time they reached the house it was that purple English dusk. He said goodnight on the doorstep like a good boy, got in the jeep and drove away. He'd passed up a hell of a chance out there alone with her. Maybe he was wrong. Maybe he was right. Time would sure as hell tell.

* * *

'It's called a weaner.' Miss Cutteridge peered anxiously at the small pig snuffling round inside the Anderson shelter. She had barricaded it in with some old chicken wire tied up with garden twine. Corporal Bilsky crouched down to see better. 'Looks a real fine one to me. Where did you get him, ma'am?'

'From one of the local farmers. Our butcher suggested it.' She'd bought him from old Mr Quince with his smallholding, rather than someone like Mr Hobbs who would have been far too busy and important to sell one piglet. She had never much cared for the Hobbs and had been quite delighted to hear that dear Agnes had broken off her engagement to Clive. An arrogant sort of boy in her private opinion. Rather a bully. Like father, like son: it so often happened.

The piglet had come to take a look at them now, its flat pink snout pressed against the wire. She said delicately, not quite knowing how to put it, 'The farmer said he's been seen to.' Castrated was the actual word that Mr Quince had used, quite baldly, but she didn't feel able to say it to the corporal.

'Yeah, you couldn't keep a boar, ma'am. He'd

be a heck of a handful when he got bigger. This one'll stay nice and docile. It's the ladies often give the trouble; they can be real mean sometimes. I remember some of the sows Dad kept when we had our farm. How old's this little guy?'

'Eight weeks. I've been feeding him on vegetable peelings and scraps.' She saved everything she could in a pail and boiled it up in her jam-making pan and then mixed it with a few handfuls of barley meal from the sack Mr Quince had sold her with the piglet. He'd also sold her some bales of straw to use for bedding. 'He seems to be doing all right.'

'Like I told you, ma'am, I'll bring you stuff from our kitchens. You won't have no problem fattenin' him up.'

'The farmer said he'd be ready at six months.' That was the part she preferred not to think about but Mr Ford, the butcher, had promised to deal with it all for her.

Corporal Bilsky was scratching his head. 'Seems to me that wire's not goin' to hold him, ma'am. Not once he gets bigger. I could get fencin' wire from the base and some wood posts an' fix somethin' a whole lot stronger. We could make a bit of a run for him, so's he could get outside and root about. He'll like that. He won't want to foul his beddin', see. Pigs are clean animals, though most people don't know that. He'll have a corner out in the run, see, an' I'll clean it out for you an' put it all on a heap, an' keep it turned till it's well rotted, then we can use it on the vegetables.

How're they doin', by the way?'

She showed him the rows of potatoes, cabbages, carrots, broad beans and beetroot plants and the runner beans climbing the poles he'd put up for her. 'As soon as they're ready you must come and help me eat them,' she told him. 'I'm going to open your tin of ham then.'

'Gee, that's for you.'

'Oh, I couldn't possibly eat it all.'

He'd brought her another tin of something called Sloppy Joe Sauce. Ground beef he'd called it. From the picture on the label, it looked like some kind of mince that you apparently put inside a bun. She had put it to one side of the store cupboard.

'Had a letter from my brother, Frank, the other day,' he told her as they went back into the cottage. 'The one that's with the heavies over here.'

Heavies, she knew, were the big bombers: Flying Fortresses and Liberators. She'd seen and heard them in the distance and occasionally one would pass low over the village. It was easy to tell that they were American because of the big white star. 'How is he?'

'Doin' OK, far as I could tell. They censor the mail so he can't say much. I reckon he won't have too much longer before he's finished his tour. Then they'll send him home. Boy, is he lucky. I figure they won't be sendin' me back till the war's over. Got a feelin' they might send us Signal guys over to France, though. Must be plenty needs doin' there.'

His words worried her. Here in England he

was quite safe; in France it would be another story. According to the newspaper reports, the fighting was very fierce indeed over there. Thousands of men had died in the Normandy landings — ten thousand Americans, she'd read somewhere, let alone the rest. And since then the Allies had been battling away for weeks to gain ground in Northern France. 'Have you heard from your other brother? The one in the Pacific?'

He shook his head. 'No, ma'am. Not in a real long while. I guess the mail's not too good from the sort of places Jack'd be fightin' in.'

She said encouragingly, 'The newspapers say that the American marines have been making great progress against the Japanese.' She didn't mention the price in lives that had also been reported.

'Yeah, that's what I heard, too.'

She'd cooked him some fairy cakes with a glacé cherry on top of each one, and he sat at the small table in the kitchen eating them in two bites and drinking tea out of a china mug. 'Real good, these are, ma'am. Thank you.'

'You mustn't bring me any more tins,' she told him firmly. 'It's very kind of you, but I really don't need them. I manage quite well.'

'If that's the way you want it, ma'am.'

'Yes, it is, Corporal.'

'Joe's the name, ma'am, if you felt easy with that.'

Putting on his cap at the door, he said, 'I'll bring the pig food though. And I'll come by and fix that run, soon as I can.'

Miss Cutteridge went to look at the piglet again. He had gone back inside the shelter and was lying dolefully in a corner with his snout on his trotters. Missing his mother and his brothers and sisters, she thought, conscience-stricken. Oh dear, oh dear.

⋆ ⋆ ⋆

Instead of the maid in the white apron, it was Erika herself who opened the front door to him. He said, without preamble, 'I'm playing truant again. Will you come out for another drive?'

'Another guided tour?'

'Let's just go anywhere. If you don't mind.'

She got in the car straight off. No questions asked, no going off to get dolled up. No hat, no coat, no gloves, not even a purse. What a woman! Carl drove out of the village and took the first turning he came to. It turned out to be one of those one-track, winding lanes that wandered all over the countryside in no particular direction to fetch up God knew where. There were no signposts, quixotically removed to confuse the enemy, but even with them the result would have been the same. They would have pointed to lost-in-time places that only figured on big-scale maps. Places with names like Little Buggins, Nether Wallop, Big Snoring.

She didn't talk; just sat quietly beside him as though she'd judged his mood right on. He drove uphill and down dale, following other lanes at random between cornfields dotted with bright red poppies like drops of blood. Finally, they came to a high point overlooking a valley. He stopped the car on the grass verge, switched off the engine and wound down the window. 'Cigarette?' She took one and he lit it for her and then his own. 'Thanks for coming out. You're the one person I wanted for company.'

'Anything in particular wrong, Carl? Or is it just the war?'

'I guess it's just the war. We've lost some good kids lately. Twenty-six pilots killed in action in just the last couple of months.'

'I'm so sorry. That's dreadful for you.'

'They were all great guys. After a while it gets so you start to feel responsible, even when you know you're not. And it's not only *our* kids. When you're doing our escort job you see what happens to the bomber boys if we foul up and some Luftwaffe shark gets to them. Or maybe it's enemy flak that you can't do a damn thing about and you're in a ringside seat, watching. Either way, it's not pretty.' He drew on the cigarette. 'After the war, when they get around to building some kind of memorial to all those guys, it's sure going to have a hell of a lot of names on it. Same with the RAF. I guess we just have to hope it's going to be worth it.'

'It has to be, Carl. There's no alternative, except to give up.' No cosy platitudes trotted out for his benefit, but he knew she understood what he was talking about.

'Yeah . . . and we sure can't do that.' He smoked some more in silence. 'How do you figure we're doing with the villagers these days?'

'They give you ten out of ten.'

'We got a zero last week from some farmer guy. One of the Mustangs lost a full belly-tank bang in the middle of one of his fields, taking off. It bust wide open and ruined the crop. He was one real angry farmer, I can tell you. Name of Hobbs. Do you know him?'

'Everybody knows everybody in King's Thorpe. He's a big wheel round here.'

'Well, we had to pay big compensation.'

'He'd make sure of it. He's that sort of man. Some people are probably doing very well out of the war.'

'Same thing back in the US too, I guess. War's a great money-spinner for the lucky ones, while the other guys pay up with their lives.' He drew on the cigarette again and flicked the ash out of the window. 'I've got three days' leave coming up in a while. Not sure when yet. There's a hell of a lot on right now. When it comes round, I thought maybe I'd go down to London. I'd like you to come with me, Erika, if you would. What do you say?'

'I say yes.'

No shocked protest. No maidenly blushes. Just a plain and simple yes. No wonder he felt as he did about her.

'I don't know where we'd stay. Some hotel . . . '

'I still have the flat in Kensington. We could stay there, if you like.'

He nodded. 'That would be great. If it's OK with you.'

'It is.'

He looked at his wristwatch and started up the engine. 'Think you can navigate us back to King's Thorpe?'

'We'll have to steer by the sun.'

He smiled. 'Well, I guess I can manage that.'

10

Chester leant his bike against the bakehouse wall. As he opened the door the sheep's bell jangled and Sally looked up from serving a customer. She went on picking out buns from one of the trays and then a loaf of bread from the stack on the other table, putting them all in the woman's basket. He waited while she took the money and gave the change and then he held the door open for the woman, who thanked him with a smile. Sally wasn't smiling but he thought she looked prettier than ever.

'Didn't you get my letter, Chester?'

'Sure,' he said. 'Tom delivered it.'

'I told you I didn't want to see you any more.'

'Yeah, I know.'

'I meant what I said.'

'Well, I've been thinking about that for a good long while. In the end, I figured I'd come down here, just the same. Didn't make a lot of sense to me. What's gone so wrong, Sally? We got along just fine.'

'Did we?'

'You know we did.' He looked hard at her, searching her face. 'So what's suddenly changed things?'

She wouldn't meet his eyes; turned her back on him and started moving the bread around even though it didn't need it. 'I decided I didn't want to see you any more, that's all.'

‘Is it because I wanted us to get married? Because I won’t bother you with that again, if that’s what the trouble is.’

‘No, it’s not that.’

‘Something else I’ve done? Or maybe said?’

‘Nothing. I just don’t want to go out with you again.’

He said slowly, ‘Well, I guess that’s that, then.’

She turned round and he could see she was real upset: it looked like there were some tears in her eyes. ‘I’m sorry, Chester. Very sorry. I never wanted to hurt you. But I can’t help it.’

‘That’s OK. It happens.’ He made himself smile at her. ‘Don’t worry about it. Any objection to me still coming in sometimes to buy your rock cakes? Wouldn’t want to have to do without those as well.’

‘Please don’t. I’d much sooner you didn’t.’

‘Guess I’d better take some now, then. My last chance.’

‘How many would you like?’

‘I’ll have a dozen. Share ’em around.’

‘Have you got a bag?’

‘Shucks, I forgot.’

‘I’ll go and find one.’

While she was gone her father put his head round the door for a moment and gave him a black look. The guy sure hadn’t gotten any friendlier. When Sally came back, he said, ‘Just as well I never said anything to your dad.’

‘You never would, would you Chester? Swear you won’t.’

‘No need now, is there?’ He paid for the rock cakes and pocketed the change. He tried to think of an excuse to linger, just to be able to see her for longer and talk some more, but the sheep's bell went and another customer came in. He biked slowly back with the paper bag of rock buns resting on the handlebars. At the base he gave them all away to the other guys; he sure didn't feel like eating.

* * *

'Gin,' Ben fanned out his hand. 'Tough luck, Ed. That makes three pounds you owe me.'

'Bloodsucker.' Ed tossed down his cards and passed the notes over.

'Your mind wasn't on the game, pal. You still thinking about that schoolteacher? That's mighty bad. I told you, you don't want to think about anything but surviving this tour and winning at cards. Ain't that right, Jessie?' He leant to pat the Scottie dog lying beside him. 'Just as well we're nearly through.'

'I never think about anything but flying when we're up, you know that, Ben.'

'Sure hope not. No girl's worth it. Drop her, Ed. Or put her on ice till the lousy war's over.'

'I'd already figured that out for myself — not from the same angle, though.'

'Whatever way, it adds up the same.' Ben wagged a finger. 'Serious is prohibited. Always kiss the girls goodbye. Heck, there'll be plenty more back home. Gorgeous American girls, not these English ones: they're either loose as a goose or tight as my maiden aunt. Soon as you get back Stateside you'll forget Miss like she never existed. Boy, I can't wait to get back to California. Sun, golden gals, steaks, no Brussels sprouts . . . '

'I'm putting in to do another tour.'

'*What*? Did I hear right? You gone crazy, or something?'

'No. I mean it. I don't figure on spending the rest of the war teaching other guys to fly.'

'I don't buy it. Got a death wish, Ed? Another three hundred hours of it? Another sixty-two missions — maybe more? And those sons of bitches could send you anywhere. Aw, come on . . . you're kidding.'

'I don't want to quit yet.'

'You're loony. Don't push your luck, Ed. You've done your share. There's plenty more where we came from.'

'Yeah, I've thought about that.' He chewed on his gum. 'But we've got the experience, Ben. We've learned the hard way. Been through the fire. I figure we're a hell of a lot more useful now than when we started. Half the guys never hit a darned thing. You know that. It's only a few do the real work. Like us.' He tapped the ribbon on his chest. 'That's why we got given these, right? The Germans aren't going to give up without a real hard fight and I want to be in there at the finish. See it all the way through.'

Ben scooped up the cards and shuffled them fast. 'I don't want to hear any more — you'll have me in tears. You're crazy.' He slapped the pack down on the table. 'Your deal, pal.'

* * *

'Haven't they noticed yet, Sal?'

'Dad hasn't. I'm not sure about Mum. She keeps giving me funny looks.'

Doris put her head on one side. 'You can't really tell. Not in that frock.'

'I've let it out, see. And when I've got my apron on it doesn't show at all.'

'But they'll notice in the end, Sal.'

'I know that, Doris. You don't have to keep on telling me.'

'What about the woman in Peterborough?'

'When I went there, she'd gone. Got arrested by the police, or something.'

'Well, I'm glad she didn't do anything to you. You might have got poisoned. How about that old witch in the forest? The one that did the spell for the tiler's wife? If she can do one to get a baby, she might be able to do another to take one away.'

'Don't be daft, Doris. It wasn't a spell, it was some Yank. Everyone knew that except him.'

'Well, I didn't know it. Fancy that. I'd never have thought it of her.'

'Lucky for her the tiler didn't either.'

'Have you tried jumping off things any more?'

'It doesn't work. For God's sake, don't smoke, Doris, it makes me sick.' Sally went to the window, stuck her head out and took some breaths of fresh air.

'Sorry.' Doris stubbed the cigarette out quickly. 'What does it feel like? Having a baby growing inside you?'

'I don't want to talk about it.'

'Sorry. I was just wondering. Well, what'll you do now?'

'Dunno. There's a place I heard about for unmarried mothers. I might go there — just to have it. Then I'm going to give it away — soon as I can. And I'll go to London, or somewhere.'

'All on your own? That'd be horrible.'

'No, it won't. I'll be all right. Dad wouldn't have me at home, anyway. He's going to go mad when he finds out. Throw me out on my ear.'

'Poor Sal . . . Have you thought of marrying Chester? You could, now you're sixteen, if your dad gives permission. And he'd do that, wouldn't he, to make things proper. So the baby wasn't illegitimate.'

She turned on Doris. 'I've *told* you. I'm not marrying Chester. I don't want a husband and I don't want a baby. Not yet. I don't want to be tied down for the rest of my life, like you see happen to girls in the village. All worn out like old hags before they're thirty. I don't want that. I want a life of my own first. You don't understand, do you?'

'Not really. I'd like to get married, soon as I can.'

'We're different, Doris, that's all.' Sally took some more breaths of fresh air. She felt all dizzy, and ever so tired.

'Have you seen Chester lately?'

'I told him to stay away.'

'I feel sorry for him.'

'Be quiet, Doris. All you do is make me feel worse. Can't you think of something helpful to say?'

She breathed in deeply again and the baby moved with a sudden twitching. She loathed the thought of it growing inside her. Oh, God, she thought despairingly, what am I going to do?

⋆ ⋆ ⋆

Brigadier Mapperton poured himself a brandy. It was almost the last of the last bottle of Hennessy from the cellar, but he needed it. Anthea had left an hour earlier, the King's Thorpe's taxi bearing her and her suitcase to the railway station, and Cicily had gone to bed early with one of her trashy novels. For once, he couldn't blame her.

Anthea's leave, it had to be said, had been more a pain than a pleasure. Always more bossy than was attractive in a woman — in his view — she had grown even more so since her recent promotion and, to his considerable irritation and annoyance, she had spent the time trying to reorganize them as though they were a bunch of bloody WRNS. They'd been bombarded with a whole lot of damfool suggestions and advice, none of which they had asked for: how to run the house, the garden, their lives. And she had talked about John. He and Cicily had had a tacit understanding between them ever since the news of his capture that it was better not to speak of him. Not even to mention his name, let alone discuss what might have happened or be happening to him. In his firm view, it was the only sane way to deal with the situation, unless they wanted to go demented. Or, at least, it was *their* way. Anthea had had the nerve to tell them that they should face up to it and talk about John all the time; that it would do them good. Cicily had begun to weep and he had lost his temper and shouted at his daughter to mind her own damned business. Inexcusable of her to go upsetting her mother like that. He was damned if he'd allow it.

He tossed back a good quarter of the glassful. The fact was that Anthea and John had nothing in common. Different sex, different everything. Poles apart. She reminded him unfortunately sometimes of his late mother-in-law, who had had the sensitivity of an ox. He wondered whether, if it had been his daughter who had been captured by the Japs, he would have felt such terrible anguish; and realized, guiltily, that he would not. He might not speak of John but his only son had occupied his mind every day of every week of every month since he had gone away.

Lately, he had allowed himself a small ray of hope — though he had said nothing to Cicily. He kept a large map of the world pinned to the wall in his study — a sanctum that she never entered — and periodically marked up the Allies' setbacks or progress with pencilled jottings and appropriate paper flags. He had followed all campaigns in Europe, North Africa and the Far East, but it was the Americans' grim and bloody struggle in the Pacific that concerned him the most. Every newspaper and wireless report of military activity in that theatre of war was meticulously entered onto his map and its significance considered. It had taken almost a month for the American marines to capture the island of Saipan, a key base in Japan's defence system, and nine days to take Tinian. Guam had been retaken around the same time. The Stars and Stripes was making slow but vital progress across the Pacific and he pinned his hopes with each flag. It was clear to him, studying his wall map, that the capture of Saipan had brought the Japanese home islands, only fifteen hundred miles away, within the range of the heavy bombers and long-range escort fighters of the American Air Force for the first time. There was a long way to go but the tide was at last beginning to turn. The eventual defeat of Japan would mean John's release. If he was still alive.

He carried his glass through into his study and stood studying the wall map yet again and the wide scatter of islands throughout the Pacific Ocean. Fighting the Japs entrenched in those places must have been hellishly tricky. You knew where you were with the Huns but those oriental chaps didn't play by the rules: they had their own peculiarly nasty ones. They fought to the death and life was cheap. Cruel, inhuman, barbaric, were adjectives that came to mind. He went on staring at the map for a long while before he drained the last of the brandy. It helped to dull his mental pain, in the same way as it could dull the pain of a nagging tooth.

* * *

Friday nights were bath nights. Once a week Mum took down the tin bath from its hook on the wash-house wall and ladled steaming hot water from the copper into it before she poured on cold water from a bucket to cool it down. She bathed Nell first, as usual, then scrubbed Alfie who always made a big fuss. By the time it came to Tom's turn to bath himself the water was tepid and looked like cabbage soup.

He soaped himself all over with the Yank soap. It smelled a bit cissy to him compared with the carbolic, but if Ed and all the others used it, then it must be all right. As he scrubbed away at his fingernails he thought about whose eggs he'd pinch next. What with Dad being home last week and going down to the Black Bull every evening, the Oxo tin was almost empty by the time he'd gone off again. Something had to be done about it for Mum. He went through the possibilities and thought of Mr Hobbs. He only ever took them from people who had plenty of eggs and wouldn't miss a few, and Mr Hobbs had more than anybody. He'd never been there before because the farmer kept fierce dogs and let them roam about the yard at night, and because he was almost as scared of him as of his dogs. But he knew there were a lot of hens and there'd be a lot of eggs.

He got out and dried himself on the towel that was sopping wet after Nell and Alfie and put his clothes back on. Then he dragged the bath outside and tipped the soupy water away. Mum was doing the ironing on the kitchen table, on top of a blanket and sheet. There was a big pile of Yanks' shirts waiting to be done on the chair beside her. The room was hot with the heat from the range and from the irons, and flies were buzzing about. The flypaper hanging from the oil lamp was all black with the dead ones stuck to it, some of them still alive and struggling by the legs.

'Time you were in bed, Tom. And be quiet about it so you don't wake Nell.'

He hated going to bed while it was still daylight. 'Can't I stay up a bit? It's the holidays.'

'No, you can't. It's past nine. And it's potato-picking tomorrow, don't forget.'

That was another thing he hated: being made to go and pick up potatoes from the fields all day long. Sixpence a sack was all the farmer paid and a shilling for the women. It took Alfie the whole day to pick up enough to fill one sack, not that he tried very hard. 'Do we have to, Mum?'

'The money'll be handy, Tom. We're very short. And it'll keep you both out of mischief.' Mum took another hot iron from the range and spat on it so it sizzled. She wiped her brow with the back of her hand. 'Off you go now.'

She was always tired, it seemed to him. Always working at something because Dad never sent enough money when he was away. He'd long ago made up his mind that when he was grown-up he'd earn lots so's she didn't have to go on working any more.

He climbed the stairs slowly. Nell had gone to sleep in her cot in Mum's room but Alfie was still wide awake, wriggling around in the bed. He took off his outer clothes and his boots and socks and climbed in beside his brother. If Mum needed the money that badly he'd have to get the eggs tonight. He'd hide them and sell them to the Yanks soon as he got the chance, the day after tomorrow. And he'd tell Mum they'd paid him for running errands, the same as he always did. With any luck, Alfie would go to sleep by the time it was dark and he'd be able to slip off without him knowing. He always made sure Alfie didn't know when he went out at night because he'd want to come too, which he couldn't, and he might give him away by mistake because he could never keep quiet about things.

'What's Mum doing, Tom?'

The thing to do was not to talk to him, or he'd go on for hours. 'Still ironing.'

'The Yanks' things?'

'Mmmm.'

'Ed hasn't been down himself lately, has he?'

'They've been busy. Him and Ben, and the pilots. They've been shooting up German trains and engines, and stuff. That's what they told me in the radio shack.'

'They are lucky. I'd like to do that. Shoot up trains.' Alfie stuck both arms out and made what he thought was a machine-gun noise: 'Da-da-da-da-da-da.'

Tom rolled his eyes. 'They don't shoot like that or they couldn't fly the plane, could they? They've got a gun button on the top of the control stick so they don't have to let go.'

'How do you know?'

'I saw it when Ed let me sit in the cockpit of his Mustang.'

'Do you think he'd let me do that?'

'Shouldn't think so. He couldn't trust you not

to touch everything.'

'I wouldn't.'

'Yes, you would.' Tom yawned. 'I'm going to sleep.'

'I'm not a bit tired yet.'

'You have to go to sleep anyway. We've got to get up early.'

'I don't want to go potato-picking tomorrow. It's horrible.'

'Well, you've got to. We've got to earn some money for Mum.'

Alfie was quiet for a bit. 'We won't be here when Mr Aller comes in the morning. That's good.'

Alfie was afraid of Mr Aller. When he came round the village with his soil cart to empty the closet buckets once a week, he'd stomp through the kitchen in his great big black boots and out of the washhouse door, down the cinder path to the closet. Then he'd come back again, swinging a full bucket in each hand and shouting 'out of my way' at anyone who got in it. In summer flies buzzed all round him like a black cloud. Alfie always hid in a corner, holding his nose because of the stink.

Tom gave another great big yawn. 'Shut up and go to sleep. And stop kicking me.'

'I can't help it.'

'Yes, you can. You do it on purpose.' He turned over and pretended to go to sleep himself but it was a long time before Alfie stopped squirming around and he heard him breathing steadily. He listened to Mum coming upstairs to bed and waited until it grew dark outside. The coast was clear. He didn't feel much like going out now — he'd sooner have gone to sleep too — but it had to be done. The bed creaked as he slid out and Alfie stirred and squirmed around but he didn't wake up. He pulled on his clothes and his coat with the special pocket in the lining, picked up his boots, and lowered himself out of the bedroom window onto the tin roof, sliding down it backwards until he could jump to the ground. The stars were out and there was a quarter-moon so he could see his way easily.

Mr Hobbs's farm lay to the north of the village. Tom took the shortest route — down the high street, up Pig Lane and over the railway track near the station. He slithered down the embankment on the other side and under a wire fence. The land from there onwards all belonged to Mr Hobbs — acres of it in every direction. The corn had been cut and he was able to go straight across the field, keeping between the rows of sharp stubble. Two more fields, sloping downhill, and he came towards the big farm-house in the valley. He stopped and listened hard; an owl was hooting somewhere but that was all. It was very still and quiet: no sound or sign of anyone about. He'd never dared trespass there before but there was a public footpath that passed close to the house and not even Mr Hobbs could stop people using it if they wanted. Tom had gone by enough times to know exactly where the hens were kept — not in henhouses with nesting boxes that he could get at from outside, but in a long outbuilding that backed straight onto an orchard. The hens were let out there during the day; he'd seen them pecking and scratching about in the long grass. At night they'd be shut up because of the foxes. All he had to do was get in through the door by the orchard and find the nesting boxes inside.

He made his way stealthily, being careful to keep a good distance from the yard because of the dogs; with no wind they wouldn't scent him but they'd hear any sound he made. He crept between the apple trees until he reached the door, groping with his fingers for the iron bolt. It was well-oiled and slid back noiselessly. Inside it was so dark he couldn't see anything but he could smell the hens and hear one of them flutter its feathers and cluck softly. He felt his way round the walls until he found the wooden nesting boxes ranged all along the far side. The first few were empty but the next one had three eggs in it; they were still warm and as smooth as pebbles from the brook. He put them away carefully in his coat lining and worked his way silently along the boxes. One of them had a hen sitting and as he slid his hand under her she started squawking and flapping about. A dog barked from the yard and Tom froze, his heart racing. If he got caught, he'd be in real hot water. Mr Hobbs had once had a man sent to prison for poaching pheasants. He waited motionless while the dog barked a few more times and then stopped. There were thirteen eggs in his pocket but he'd set himself a target of twenty at least; he took three more eggs, his heart still beating fast, and then decided to leave. Sixteen wasn't a bad haul: one shilling and fourpence for the Oxo tin.

As he opened the door the dog sprang at him.

* * *

Erika was surprised to see Agnes Dawe on the Manor doorstep. Alex had been with her predecessor in the kindergarten and their paths seldom crossed. The whole village had been astounded when she had broken off her engagement to Clive Hobbs. Nobody, it seemed, rejected a Hobbs lightly. There had been rumours that it was over one of the Americans and Miriam had seized the chance of another dig. 'I told you, it's folly to be seen with any of them, Erika. She's ruined her reputation and her chances.'

'That's nonsense, Miriam. I should think she's well rid of the man. You've never had a good word to say of any of that family.'

'They may not have breeding, it's true, but they have money. It would have been a good match for Agnes Dawe, considering her situation.'

'What situation?'

'The daughter of an impoverished country parson. No dowry to her name. Only her looks.'

'Which happen to be lovely and very English. I'm not a bit surprised that some Yank muscled in.'

'She's a very foolish girl if she takes any of those Americans seriously; his intentions are most unlikely to be honourable.'

‘We don’t know who he is, or anything about him.’

Miriam said darkly, ‘I heard he was of Italian extraction.’

‘How on earth do you learn these things?’

‘I’ve warned you before: in a small village people talk. You would be well advised to remember that.’

Erika shepherded Agnes into the study, out of range of Miriam’s inquisitive ear.

‘It’s about Tom Hazlet,’ the girl said at once. ‘You’ll have seen him around in the village. He lives at number fourteen in the high street. Ten years old. Brown hair, freckles, rather small for his age . . . ’

‘Yes, I know him. His brother, Alfie, is a chum of my son, Alex. What’s the trouble?’

‘He was caught stealing eggs from Mr Hobbs’s farm last night and Mr Hobbs is insisting on bringing charges against him.’

‘A ten-year-old? Over some eggs? Surely not?’

‘I’m afraid so. Tom’s father is away on airfield-building work most of the time, and his mother has a hard job making ends meet. He was stealing the eggs to sell to the Americans up at the base to help her.’

‘How resourceful of him.’

‘Unfortunately, this could ruin his chance of a scholarship next year which would be such a pity. He really deserves to get it. I wonder, Lady Beauchamp, would you speak to Mr Hobbs on his behalf? I’d go myself but it wouldn’t do any good. In fact, it might make things worse.’

'Since you broke off your engagement to Clive, you mean?'

She nodded. 'But he might listen to you.'

'Why me?'

'Because of who you are in the village. Your position.'

She had met Ronald Hobbs on several occasions, including at PCC meetings, and none of them had been enjoyable. This one was unlikely to be any improvement. It was much more in Miriam's line to pull rank, but she doubted if she could be persuaded to go pleading to Mr Hobbs for anything. 'Well, I'll do my best but I'm not sure he'll listen.'

'Thank you. Tom's worth it, or I would never have asked you.'

At the door, as she showed Agnes out, she said, 'It's none of my business, I know, but I think you did exactly the right thing breaking off your engagement.'

'A lot of people don't seem to agree.'

'I shouldn't let that worry you. I'm sure you had a very good reason.'

The girl nodded and blushed.

Good luck to the American, whoever he is, Erika thought, noting the blush. She's obviously in love with him.

She wasted no time in calling that evening at the Hobbs farm. Iris Hobbs was out visiting her mother, but Ronald Hobbs was at home and she chatted pleasantly about parish matters before she raised the subject of Tom Hazlet.

'Of course, there's no excuse for stealing those eggs, Mr Hobbs, but I understand he was only trying to help his mother. I wonder if you would reconsider your decision to bring charges against him?'

'The boy trespassed on my land, and he's a thief, plain and simple. He should be punished for it.'

'He's never been in any trouble before and his teachers think a great deal of him. Apparently he could well win a scholarship next year. But of course this episode will probably spoil any chance of that.'

'He should've thought of that before, shouldn't he? It's too late now.'

What a really unpleasant man he was. Unpleasant to look upon with his beetroot face and his gooseberry eyes, and unpleasant to listen to. 'He's only ten years old. Still very young.'

'Time he learned a lesson.'

'It was a few eggs, Mr Hobbs. Nothing of any value.'

'It was sixteen eggs, Lady Beauchamp. And it's the principle of the thing. If you let these village lads get away with it, they'll be pinching and poaching everything they can lay their hands on. You don't know them like I do.'

She tried a different tack. 'You own the cottage that the Hazlets live in, don't you?'

'It's one of my properties, yes. I own the whole row of cottages along there.'

And all of them rundown, insanitary places, without electricity or running water, as she well knew but refrained from saying. 'So I understand. Since they're your tenants, I expect you know something of the family. How Tom's father's work keeps him away so much of the time and how his mother has to take in washing to get by. About his small brother and baby sister?'

'I can't know everything about all my tenants. Haven't the time. I'm a very busy man. All I know is the boy's a thief. And you can't tell me otherwise, Lady Beauchamp, no matter how you try.' He stared at her. 'What's it to you, anyway? You've only been living here five minutes. Why should you care?'

'I think my late husband would have cared, Mr Hobbs. He always took a great interest in the villagers' problems and tried to help if he could.'

He looked contemptuous. 'The Beauchamps don't have any say here any longer. Your mother-in-law may think herself above the rest of us, but she's living in the past. And I have to tell you, Lady Beauchamp, that I don't take too kindly to your coming here, telling me what I ought and ought not to do. Least of all a newcomer like yourself.'

Agnes Dawe had been quite wrong about any hope of her talking him round. Erika suspected that Miriam, in her imperious, tactless way, had given offence to the Hobbses once too often and a grudge was borne. But thinking of her mother-in-law reminded her of something that Miriam had once remarked about Ronald Hobbs. Something quite unfounded, based only on a suspicion and on her long nose and sharp eyes. The chance comment had somehow lodged in Erika's mind — forgotten, but now suddenly remembered. It was a long shot but it was worth a try. She stood up to leave. 'I'm sorry to have taken up your time, Mr Hobbs. You must do just as you think fit.' He saw her to the door and she paused there for a moment, drawing on her gloves. 'By the way, how is Alice Reeves these days?'

His ruddy face turned a shade darker. 'No idea. How would I know?'

'But surely you must, Mr Hobbs. I've happened to notice you calling on her. With her husband away on active service in the Navy, it must get very lonely for her sometimes. It's good of you to keep her company. I must tell your wife what a considerate husband she has. I'm sure she has no idea. Or Commander Reeves either. Or anybody in the village, as yet. It's a shame that your kindness is not more widely appreciated.'

'I don't know what the hell you're talking about.'

She went on smoothly, 'You see, that was why I felt so sure you would change your mind about Tom Hazlet — knowing what a generous-spirited man you were. Do tell Mrs Hobbs that I'll look forward to seeing her tomorrow. She's coming to help at the canteen.'

She walked away and before she had gone more than a few yards, he shouted angrily after her, 'All right, damn it, I'll drop the charges.'

Sometimes, she thought, smiling to herself, Miriam had her uses.

* * *

The jeep was parked outside the rectory front door and he was sitting at the wheel, smoking a cigarette. He swung himself out as she pedalled up the drive on her bike. 'Hi, there. I've been waiting for you.'

She dismounted and stood holding the bike by its handlebars. 'Will you come in?'

He shook his head. 'Guess not. I've come to say goodbye. Just been to pick up my laundry from Tom's mom. I'm off today. Finished the tour. Packing up. Going home on leave.'

Her heart skipped a beat. 'Back to New York?'

'Yeah. It's going to seem kind of strange.'

She smiled at him. 'Well, thank you for coming to say goodbye, Ed. Father isn't here, or I know he'd want to wish you all the best.'

'I'm sure sorry to miss him.'

Something moved inside the jeep and she turned to see a Scottie dog hanging out over the side, wagging its tail.

'Meet Jessie,' he said. 'Ben's dog. She came along for the ride.'

'Is Ben going home too?'

'He didn't make the end of the tour.'

'You don't mean . . . ?'

'Yeah. That's what I mean.'

She was shocked. 'What happened?'

'Well, he got shot up on a mission so he was in real bad shape. Almost made it back, then he crashed on landing.'

She could see that was all he wanted to say. 'I'm so sorry.'

'Yeah. Me too. We'd been together since training. He was a great pal. Pain in the neck sometimes, but we got along just fine. And he'd got real guts. More than almost any other guy I know. Still, that's the way it goes.' He ground the cigarette under his heel. 'I've put in for another tour, as a matter of fact.'

'But I thought you only did one.'

'If you're a big enough sucker you can volunteer for a second. No idea where they'll send me. Back here, maybe, but you never know.'

'What about Jessie?'

'One of the other guys'll look after her. There's nothing else I can do with her. Can't take her to New York.'

The Scottie was watching them from the jeep, wagging her tail. 'We'll have her, if you want.'

'I can't let you do that. She'd be another mouth to feed.'

'We'll manage.'

'You sure?'

'Yes. Honestly. We had a Scottie once, years ago. They're lovely dogs. I know Father would like her.'

'Well, I guess that's settled, then. Tell you what, I'll get one of the guys to bring down leftovers from the Mess hall for her — that way you won't have to worry too much about her food. And I'll come back and get her as soon as I can. Is that a deal?'

'Yes,' she said. 'It's a deal.'

He whistled to the dog and she jumped down and trotted over on her short, stumpy legs. 'You're in luck, Jessie. Miss here's going to take you in. You be a good girl.' Agnes bent to pat the Scottie. He watched them for a moment. 'I can see you two are going to hit it off.'

'She's sweet.'

'Yeah. Ben was real fond of her. She'd always be out there, sitting waiting for him to come back from a mission.' He looked at his watch and then at her. 'Well, I reckon I'd better get going. I've got transport all set up.'

'Goodbye, Ed.' The bike stood between him and her and she kept it there. 'Good luck.'

The jeep roared away down the drive. When he turned out of the gateway she caught one last glimpse of his hand raised in farewell.

* * *

Ben would have been real proud of him. Serious is prohibited. Always kiss the girls goodbye. Only he hadn't even gotten to do that with the goddam bike in the way.

Ed changed down to go under the railroad arch and swung the jeep round to the right and fast up the hill back towards the base. No more Ben lounging around up there. No more Ben at all. He'd been there with him, both of them screaming across that Luftwaffe airfield, when Ben had got caught by ground fire, wounded in the chest and Grumpy all shot up. God knows how he'd made it back. He'd flown alongside him all the way, talking to him, nagging at him to keep going somehow. Talked him down at the base, coming in right beside him, done everything he could to save him; then the guy had gone and fucked up at the last moment. Grumpy a ball of fire. End of Ben. Two other guys lost that day, too. Kind of a reminder of the odds stacked against getting through another tour.

He turned in at the airfield entrance, past the guard and his salute. Goodbye, Miss. New York here we come! He'd look up some of the girls there. Get her out of his mind. Get cured.

11

The piglet had grown into a large pig. It seemed to Miss Cutteridge that every day she went down to the Anderson shelter he was bigger than the day before.

'Puts me in mind of Porky Pig,' Joe told her on one of his visits with a bucketload of cookhouse scraps.

'Porky Pig?'

'Gee, you never heard of him? He's in the cartoons. Wears a blue coat and a red bow tie.'

'I'm afraid I've never seen him but then I very seldom go the cinema. I know Mickey Mouse, of course. At least, I've seen pictures of him. And Minnie Mouse. And Donald Duck.'

She looked over the wire fence at the pig, who was certainly porky. He ate anything and everything and, at that moment, was gobbling up some windfall apples with a lot of appreciative snuffling and grunting.

'Gettin' some good meat on him,' Joe observed. 'He'll make a nice roast for you. And a real nice side of bacon. Time to think about gettin' him slaughtered soon. You don't want to leave it much longer. Older he gets the more fat there'll be on him and he'll start to get tough. You want him porker size.'

Miss Cutteridge closed her eyes. She preferred not to think about it at all. In fact, she wasn't sure she was ever going to be able to bring herself to send him to slaughter, let alone cook and eat him. Growing vegetables was one thing — the potatoes and beans and cabbages and carrots had all been a wonderful success — but growing a pig was quite another. They were friendly creatures — or at least hers was. Whenever she went down to the Anderson he would come trotting over, grunting a hello.

Joe brought the scraps regularly and she had taken to cooking meals for him whenever he had some time off. She had never bothered much with cooking for herself but now she began searching through recipe books and reading hints in newspapers and magazines and leaflets. She'd pored over everything she could find: *Making the Most of Meat, Seven Appetizing Meals Without Using the Meat Ration, A Hundred Cheese Recipes, Thrifty Wartime Recipes, A Kitchen Goes to War, Gert and Daisy's Wartime Cookery Book*. She'd cooked him vegetable marrow with liver stuffing, national roly-poly with mince and potato and vegetables, rabbit stew with dumplings, cabbage stuffed with sausage meat, beef hash, devilled cod, savoury onions, tomato macaroni au gratin, and all manner of English puddings.

They always ate at the kitchen table off her cheap Woolworth's china because he was still afraid of breaking her best set. Afterwards, though, they sat in the sitting room with Ginger curled up companionably on the best chair. Sometimes they listened to the wireless and Joe would twiddle the tuner until he found American dance music. It wasn't all as loud and terrible as she had feared — in fact, some of it was rather pleasant. Other times they played cards or ludo or snakes and ladders, and occasionally Joe read out letters from his father about what was going on in Henryetta. She'd heard all about the Fourth of July celebrations — the flags and the picnics and the fireworks, and she'd learned a lot about baseball: about pitching and hitting and fielding; about home runs and curve balls and fast balls and screwballs and knuckleballs; about singles and doubles and triples and exactly where Jack, who had got picked up by the Brooklyn Dodgers, stood at third base. And when the football season had started she'd learned about touchdowns and conversions, about coin-flips and snaps and huddles and Frank's quarter-back position on the field at kick-off, behind the centre. 'I've written to my dad all about you, ma'am,' Joe had said, 'and how you've invited me into your home.' And he'd read out the bit where his father had sent his thanks. *Please say hello to Miss Cutteridge for me and let her know how much I appreciate her kindness to you. I hope she comes to Henryetta, one day, so I can repay some of her British hospitality.*

She had told Joe a little of her earlier life, growing up as an only child in the house in Oundle where she was expected to be seen but not heard. She had showed him the old sepia photographs of her parents — sombre, upright, Victorian figures, stiffly posed against a velvet curtain beside a potted palm. And she had told him about her father dying before his time and how she had taken a course in shorthand and typing and held a post in a solicitor's office for many years until she had been obliged to give it up to look after Mother until she died. That was when she had sold the Oundle house and bought Lilac Cottage. Left on her own, the idea of being part of a small village community had appealed to her.

Once, she had shown him the photograph of William — something she had never shown anyone before. She had taken it out of her bureau drawer where it was kept out of sight, partly because it saddened her too much to look at it and partly to shield it from the prying eyes of visitors. William was her private grief: an agony she had not shared with anyone — until Joe.

'He was my fiancé,' she had explained. 'But he was killed in the second Boer War. At Ladysmith.'

'Gee, that must have been sad for you, ma'am. He's a fine-lookin' gentleman. Real handsome.'

'He was. And a very fine person. And a brave soldier. I have his medals here.' She had taken them out of the same bureau drawer and Joe had held and admired them respectfully. 'Don't know nothin' about that war, ma'am, but he sure must've been a great guy. I guess you never met anybody else you wanted to marry, after that, then?'

'No,' she said. 'I didn't.' William had come into the office one day and into her life and when he was gone from it she had never even wanted to meet another.

'Never had a girl of my own,' Joe had told her. 'Not yet, leastways. Met a few English girls since I've been over here an' they're mostly real nice, but none I've taken a real shine to, if you know what I mean.'

'I'm sure you will, one day.'

'Yeah, maybe when I get back home. Maybe I'll get myself married an' settle down an' raise a whole lot of kids. Maybe in Henryetta. Maybe somewhere else. It's a big country, America. Lots of places to go.'

He had become like a son to her — the son she had never had — and her heart was heavy at the realization that, like William, she would lose him. One day, when the war was over, he would return to America to live his life and, of course, she would never go there. He might write to her sometimes, perhaps even over a few years, and always send a card at Christmas, but she would never see him again.

* * *

'You've been eating them again, Alfie.'

'No, I haven't.'

'Yes, you have. I can tell by your face. If you go on eating them we'll never get enough.' Alfie's mouth was stained purple and the level in the wicker basket had gone down, not up. Tom moved the basket to where he could keep an eye on it while he picked. It was a good patch of brambles he'd found along the hedge, full of juicy big blackberries, but a lot of them were high up, out of reach, and Alfie ate more than he picked. 'We've got to fill the basket up before we take it to the Yanks.'

'How much'll they pay us?'

'Dunno yet. Get on with it, Alfie, and mind your Sunday best. We've got to get some money for Mum.'

They'd gone off straight after church. He couldn't pinch eggs any more, not since he'd got caught. He still shuddered to think of the dog with its teeth sunk in the sleeve of his coat, snarling like a wild beast as it dragged him to the ground, and of Mr Hobbs jerking him up again. Mum had burst into tears when he'd been marched home with the police constable, then Nell had started up and so had Alfie. There'd been a real to-do. All of them upset. Then all of a sudden he'd been let off the hook with a warning: next time he was caught nicking anything he'd be up before the magistrate. So, now he had to think of something else. The hedges and woods were full of good things: elderberries and wild crab apples, rosehips, haws and sloes, but they were no good to the Yanks. Blackberries was all he could think of.

He went on picking and, of course, Alfie went on eating though he swore he wasn't. When the basket was full at last they set out for the airfield. Tom didn't see why Alfie should come too but he couldn't be bothered to argue about it. Shaking him off was like getting rid of a burr. The sun was quite warm, even though it was almost October, and the grass full of silvery spiders' webs. Alfie was kicking his boots through them and lagging behind because he kept stopping to pick and eat more blackberries along the hedgerows. 'Come *on*. I'm not waiting for you.'

He plunged on downhill to the stream at the bottom and crossed by the two stepping stones, balancing himself and the basket carefully to jump. Sure enough, there was a loud splash behind him as Alfie missed one of the stones again but he took no notice. He toiled on up the hill towards the airfield. A Mustang was taking off and he watched it climb and circle.

'What's it doing, Tom?'

He didn't know but Alfie would expect him to. 'Test flight.'

'Whose is it?'

He shielded his eyes. 'Can't see from here.'

A whole lot of new pilots had come and he hadn't learned their letters yet. It wasn't as much fun as it had been with Ed and before Ben had been killed. Some of the new Yanks brought their washing down for Mum to do and they gave her washing powder and soap and sugar and things, just like the others had done, but it wasn't really the same. He missed Ed a lot. So did Mum. Alfie kept saying he did, too, but that was probably only for the candy and the chewing gum.

'When's Ed going to come back, Tom?'

'He may not ever. Not if they send him somewhere else.'

'I hope he does. I liked Ed.'

They walked in by the main gate, ducking under the pole. 'What're you eating now, Alfie?'

'A crab apple.'

'It'll give you a bellyache, stupid. You're

supposed to cook them. Throw it away.'

They went round to the radio shack. His Yanks were still there: Mitch and Wally and Russ and Dan . . . all of them sitting at the workbenches in their overalls and their flipped-up caps.

'Hi there, kids! What've you brought us?' They crowded round the basket.

'Blackberries,' he told them. 'I thought you might like to buy some.'

They each tried one and pretended to be poisoned, clutching their throats and rolling their eyes up and falling about. Alfie roared with laughter but somehow Tom couldn't. Mitch clapped him on the shoulder. 'Just kiddin', Tom. They're real good. How much do you want for the lot?'

He wasn't sure what to ask. It'd been a lot of work picking the blackberries but they weren't as valuable as fresh eggs. A shilling seemed too little but two shillings seemed too much. 'One and six,' he said in the end.

'OK. Pay up, you guys.'

He put the money away in his shorts pocket and they passed the basket round between them, taking handfuls of the berries. Somehow Alfie got his hand in too as it went by.

'How's that little sister of yours, Tom? She growed up any? How old's she now?'

'She's two.'

They all grinned. 'Tell her to hurry up else the war'll be over 'fore any of us can take her out.'

'What's that Sally of yours done to our Chester?' Mitch said. 'He's been goin' round with a face long as a fiddle. She gone and dumped him?'

He didn't know the answer to that. All he knew was that Sally didn't smile nearly so much and she didn't always give free cakes with the bread, like she used to. He hadn't seen Chester around the village for a long while.

Wally turned round from his bench. 'Hey, Mitch, how about we take the kids over to eat with us? Reckon anybody'd mind?'

'Wouldn't think so. Everybody knows Tom. Like to come and get some lunch, guys?'

'Yes, please,' Alfie said quickly.

They queued up at the airmen's Mess and held out tin plates for great dollops of fried chicken, sweet-corn and mashed potatoes and, after that, vanilla ice cream. Alfie had three helpings of the ice cream.

'You'll be sick.'

'No, I won't. I could go on eating it for ever.'

Afterwards, they walked back across the fields, Tom lugging the blackberry basket that was heavy with tins of meat and fruit, chocolate bars and candy. Alfie sighed. 'I wish I was a Yank. They have lovely food.'

'That's all you ever think about. Food.'

'No, it isn't. I think about other things too.'

'Such as?'

'Lots of things.'

'Name one.'

'I will in a minute when I've thought.'

He couldn't, of course.

* * *

Sam Barnet pulled the hessian sacks off the dough trough. Underneath the dough had risen up into a yeasty mountain. He punched both fists hard down through its crust so that it collapsed like a pricked balloon and then he started to knead. The sweat formed on his brow and his back began to ache but he forced himself on, working away steadily, his arms deep in the dough. Work was pain but it was also a blessing: it helped him not to think about Roger. He could concentrate on the mixture forming and re-forming rather than on his only son fighting his way across France with the Allies. He kneaded on, pounding his fists into the troughful of dough, turning and pummelling, turning and pummelling until it was ready. The sweat was rolling down his face and he wiped it away with his handkerchief and brushed the flecks of dough from his bare arms before he lined up the baking tins on the table.

When the dough had risen up again he cut great slabs off with his knife, as much as he could lift at a time, and heaved it up onto the table to weigh it out on the scales and mould it into the tins. Bloomers and coburgs were shaped in his hands and cottage loaves fashioned from two dough balls, smallest on top. He set them all on trays to prove in the warm space under the oven before he slid the tin loaves into the hot oven on the peel. The bloomers were slashed across their tops and he punched the cottage loaves in the centre with his fist, nicking them round the edges with his knife. In they went as well, together with the coburgs, balanced in a line on the long wooden slip to be tipped off neatly sideways onto the brick floor.

He heaved the oven door shut, wiped his forehead again and sank down on a stool. His left eye felt sore in one corner — probably another ulcer starting like he'd had before — and he could hear himself wheezing. The flour always got to him. What he needed was a bit of a rest; for him and Freda to take a holiday somewhere. Skegness or Cleethorpes or somewhere like that. Breathe some good clean sea air. If Roger was home they might have managed it, but as things were it was hopeless. He sat there wearily until it was time to get up and turn the tins halfway through. Towards the end he got up again to check to see how close they were to being ready. He put on his sacking mitts and hauled one of the tins out on the peel, tipping it upside down quickly to see the bread underneath.

The loaves were all cooked and he was stacking them on end to cool when Mrs Trimwell arrived to start on the cakes. Sally was late again and when she did turn up, after nearly half an hour, there was no good morning and no smile. He didn't know what was the matter with her. She'd been a cheerful, hard worker once and very good at the cakes, now she couldn't seem to care less and the customers were complaining. He watched her put on her white overall and start the sponge mix in the bowl. She looked pale to him. Quite peaky. Perhaps she needed a holiday too?

He wiped the tins out with a cloth and stacked

them away before he went off to get a cup of tea. Freda was in the kitchen, making a pot, and he sat down at the table and waited while it brewed.

'What's up with Sally? She's been out of sorts for weeks. She got the sulks about something?'

Freda poured the tea: it was good and strong, the way he liked it. None of that 'none for the pot' nonsense. 'You haven't noticed, Sam?'

'Noticed what?' He sipped the tea and felt better. 'All I've noticed is she's not doing her work properly. Late down every morning, making a mess of the cakes . . . it's not like her at all.'

Freda sat down opposite him. 'You may as well know, since you'll find out soon enough. She's expecting.'

His cup stopped halfway. 'What did you say?'

'She's going to have a baby.'

The shock hit him like a blow in the chest. He felt his heart leap violently, the breath knocked out of him, and for a moment he couldn't speak and felt quite faint. The feeling subsided but his heart was still pounding. 'It's not true. It can't be. She *can't* be.'

'She can and she is,' Freda said calmly. 'Nearly six months gone. I don't know how you haven't seen, to tell the truth, though she's been clever with hiding it and she's not big.'

He stared at her. 'You've known about this — all along?'

'Not for a while, I didn't, but I've got eyes in my head. I asked her straight out in the end.'

'And you didn't tell me? You kept it a secret from me?'

He was bitterly enraged, as well as badly shocked. 'It's one of those bloody Yanks, isn't it? I'll kill whoever's done this to us. The disgrace'll finish us. We'll never be able to hold up our heads, it'll ruin us — '

'It won't do anything of the kind, Sam. It won't be the first child in the village born the wrong side of the blanket, not by a long chalk. I could name half a dozen or more. Ellen Turner's little Ned, for instance. That was never her husband's: it was a Pole from the army camp down the road, but it's never made a difference. Nice-looking boy, he is.'

He said furiously, 'She happens to be married. Sally'll have to marry the man, whoever he is. That's for a start.'

'She doesn't want to. She's told me that.'

'Doesn't *want* to? I don't give a damn what she wants. She'll bloody well marry him. I'm not having a bastard in this house, under my roof.'

'Don't swear, Sam. And do try to keep calm. You'll go and have a heart attack or something at this rate.'

He clenched his fists and took a deep, slow breath. 'Six months, you say? That means she was fifteen when this happened. Under age. That's *rape*. I'll have him in prison.'

'You were going to kill him a moment ago.'

'It's that Yank's been hanging around the bakehouse all these months. I've seen him. I'll know him. I'll make sure he's court-martialled.'

'Make up your mind, Sam. No point in doing that if you want her to marry him, unless you'd like a jail-bird for a son-in-law. And do you really want to put Sally through giving evidence in court — lawyers saying things about her, him denying it and all that. What will that do to your precious family name, let alone Sally's? Besides, we don't know it was that one you're talking about at all. She won't say who it was.'

'She must know. And by God, she's going to tell us.' He stood up and blundered towards the door leading into the bakehouse, shouting his daughter's name.

She came into the kitchen and stood by the door. He saw at once what he should have seen long before — the telltale swelling under the white overall — and he wondered how he could have missed it and how many other people had noticed it. He said harshly, 'Your mother's told me about your condition. I want to know who the father is.'

She lifted her chin. 'I'm not telling you, Dad. So that's that.'

'That's that?' His voice crescendoed to a roar. 'That isn't that, my girl. You tell me this minute or I'll, I'll . . . '

'What'll you do, Dad? Turn me out of the house? Don't worry, I'm going anyway. I'm going now. Soon as I've packed. I've found a place to have the baby and soon as it's born I'm going to give it away. I don't want it any more than you do.' She rushed from the room and he heard her running up the stairs and her bedroom door slam. In the silence, he said lamely, 'Well, she can't stay here, Freda, can she?'

'Of course she can, Sam. And she's going to. She's our daughter and we'll look after our own.

Stand by her, the way we should.'

'She'll have to marry him.'

'We'll see about that. We can't force her to. And if she really wants the baby adopted, then maybe that's best all round. We'll have to see how she feels when the time comes.' Freda stood up. 'You stay here and drink your tea. I'll go up and have a talk with her.'

He collapsed onto the chair and sat with his head in his hands. All his plans and hopes lay in ruins. The Barnets would be a laughing stock in the village. He could hear the whispers, see the pointing fingers. The gossips would have a field day — if they weren't having it already. Nothing like it had happened to the family before. They'd been God-fearing, church-going, hardworking, respectable, decent people, their reputation handed unblemished from father to son over more than a hundred years. All wrecked now. And all because of some lecherous bloody Yank.

The tea was cold and he left it. He dragged himself up and went through into the bakehouse. Sally's sponge mix was still in the bowl and he carried on doggedly with it, ignoring Mrs Trimwell's curious glances. The customers would be at the door before long and they'd want their cakes as usual. Barnets had never let them down and he didn't intend to start now.

⋆ ⋆ ⋆

'I'll only be away for three days, Alex. Do you mind?'

He looked up from his book. 'Granny will

make me go to bed early.'

'I'll ask her not to.'

'She'll make me eat spinach.'

'No, she won't. I'll tell Mrs Woods not to cook it. What would you like best?'

'Sausages and baked beans and chips.'

'All right. What about pudding?'

'I like spotted dick, with lots of custard. And that coconut pudding she makes.'

'I'll ask, but just this once.'

'Why do you have to go to London, Mummy?'

'There are some things that I need from the flat.'

'Can't I come too? I like London.'

'Not in term-time. You mustn't miss school.'

He pulled a face.

'I'll bring you back something,' she said, knowing she was indulging him from sheer guilt. 'Something nice.' Three days, she thought. That's all. Three days with another woman's husband. Guilt. Betrayal. Lying to her son. Lying to Miriam, who wasn't nearly so easy to placate.

'*London*, Erika? What on earth for?'

'I want to get some things from the flat and to make sure everything's all right.'

'There's a porter, isn't there? He would have let you know if it wasn't.'

'I'd still like to see for myself. And, as I said, there are some things I'd like to get.'

'What things?' Miriam looked suspicious and probably was.

'Books, clothes, photographs.' It was no business of hers, for God's sake. I don't have to explain a thing to her.

‘What about the risk?’
‘What risk?’
‘Flying bombs. And now those V2s. It’s utter madness to go anywhere near the place.’
‘People are going about their ordinary daily lives in London. They don’t let the Germans dictate to them and I don’t intend to either.’
‘Well, you might at least consider your responsibility to Alexander, if nothing else.’
Her Achilles heel, and Miriam invariably aimed at it in the end. ‘I always consider it.’
‘No you don’t, or you wouldn’t be going. If anything happened to you, he’d be orphaned.’
‘Nothing will happen to me. I shall be back in three days.’
Her mother-in-law was right, though. For the first time she was putting herself before Alexander: her own selfish desires before his welfare. For the first time something else was too strong, too longed-for, too overwhelming to resist. She was ashamed of it, but she couldn’t help it.
She packed a small suitcase; a lot of her London clothes, including evening dresses, were still hanging in the wardrobe at the flat. ‘We’ll go out on the town,’ he’d said. ‘Dine and dance.’ It was a very long time since she’d done anything of the kind.
She took King’s Thorpe’s only taxi to the railway station, fending off friendly enquiries from Mr Stoke, the Daimler’s owner — a dear old man who liked to know exactly where everyone was going and why. He shared Miriam’s view that her trip to London was

nothing short of madness. 'Wouldn't go near the place if it was me, your ladyship. You'll be dodging the bombs all the time.'

The booking hall was a mob of American air force men going on leave, dressed up in their best, shaved and shined and hell-bent on getting to London. There were no army Yanks. Since D-Day they had become rare birds. Carl had bought the tickets and they found seats in a first-class carriage with five other American officers and a middle-aged British major. As bad luck would have it, she had met him before in connection with the WVS. He leaned across eagerly. 'Lady Beauchamp, Major Winthrop. I don't suppose you'll remember me.'

'Of course I do, Major.'

He looked pleased. 'You're going to London?'

'Just a brief visit.'

'Pleasure, I hope.'

'I have some business there.'

More subterfuge but she could hardly say, 'Actually, I'm going for an illicit three days with the American colonel sitting opposite me by the window, on your left. Only we're pretending we hardly know each other, because we're not married and he's married to somebody else.'

The major talked nearly all the way to London. Tedious trivia about the trials and tribulations of his desk-bound job and, lowering his voice only slightly in spite of the strong American presence in the compartment, how tricky the Yanks were to deal with. At King's Cross, she managed to shake him off and they joined the long queue for a taxi. In the fading light of early evening she could see fresh ruins where the monstrous new German weapons had found their mark, and everywhere the old scars from earlier bombing raids. A few doors away from the block of flats in Kensington a house had been hit, only its elegant facade left standing while the remainder behind had collapsed into a pile of rubble. They took the lift up to the top floor and she opened the front door to the flat hallway.

'The drawing room's through here.' She led the way for Carl. 'I'll do the blackout.' She pulled the blinds down by their acorns before she turned on the lamps. A thick film of dust lay over everything but otherwise there was no damage. It was like stepping back into the past — a past she had shared with Richard. He had lived here, sat on that sofa, eaten off the table in the dining room, slept in the bed. She switched on the electric bar fire. 'I'm sorry, it's freezing.'

'I don't feel it.'

'You must have got acclimatized.' She peeled off her gloves and took off her hat and fur coat. 'Would you like a drink? That's if there is anything.'

He was still standing over by the door, looking so very American in his so very fine American uniform, with what Doris called all the brass bits and the silver wings and the medals. And she was so very much in love with him.

'Sure. Can I help?'

'You can pour out whatever I can find. I'm sorry, but there won't be any ice. The fridge is turned off.' She opened the drinks cupboard and discovered a near-empty bottle of Tio Pepe, a near-full bottle of Martini and a half-full one of brandy. She held it up. 'With luck there'll be some soda in the siphon to go with this.'

'Exactly what the doctor ordered.'

'And here are the glasses. Very dusty, I'm afraid. I'd better give them a wipe.'

He poured the brandy for them and squirted the soda. He handed her one glass and raised his own. 'To you, Lady Beauchamp.'

'And to you, Colonel Schrader.'

They smiled at each other.

'So, where shall we dine and dance, Lady Beauchamp? I'm not too familiar with London.'

'Well, the Savoy's rather nice. They've danced all through the war, so to speak. Blitz and all. Carroll Gibbons's band. He's a compatriot of yours.'

'Sounds great. Will they let me in dressed like this?'

'Certainly. Uniforms are fine. Almost *de rigueur*. I'll need to change, though, if you don't mind waiting.'

'I'll wait as long as it takes.'

'There are some records in the gramophone cupboard, if you'd like to put one on.'

In the bedroom she went through the wardrobe and decided on a pre-war Chanel of coffee-coloured tulle. She hadn't worn it for years. She redid her face and her hair and went back into the drawing room. A record was playing quietly. *East of the sun and West of the moon*. 'One of my favourites,' she said from the doorway.

He turned and stood up. 'Mine too. You look very beautiful.'

'Thank you.'

He went on looking at her and the record played on and finished. He drained his glass and put it down. 'Shall we go?'

They took another taxi across wartime, blacked-out London: traffic crawling along on dimmed headlights, buses and trams with blinds down, traffic lights thin crosses of red, amber and green, the white glimmer of S for shelter, the orange blink of Belisha beacons, torches wielded by unseen pedestrians. Apart from helping her on with her coat he hadn't touched her.

Inside the hotel there was light and warmth and music. If it hadn't been for the predominance of men in uniform it would have been possible to forget that there was a war on at all. Looking round, she saw that many of them were American.

'This is a wonderful place,' he said.

'Richard and I used to come here quite a bit. It's a good dance floor, as well as a good band.'

'I'd like to try it out.'

He danced very well. Miriam would probably have been surprised at that too, as well as at the bridge-playing. They danced and they dined and they talked and they laughed. She watched him shed years before her eyes. Felt herself doing the same.

It was after midnight when they returned to the flat. 'Another brandy?' she asked him.

'No, thanks. Another dance, instead.' He put the same record on again and took her in his arms. She closed her eyes, longing for him. As it finished, he started to kiss her.

* * *

He saw her through the window and drew back. He'd kept away for weeks, like she'd wanted, but the need to see her, just to look at her, was too great and, in the end, he'd ridden the bike down the hill to the village, like he always used to, and leaned it against the wall beside the bakehouse. He waited until the sheep's bell sounded as a customer came out, and then went in. She hadn't seen him, he realized that by the look on her face when she did. It was something like fear but he must have been mistaken. She had nothing to fear from him, she'd know that.

'Half a dozen of the rock cakes, please,' he said. 'I've brought a bag.'

'You mustn't come here, Chester. I asked you not to. You mustn't.' She kept tugging at her overall, real nervous. What the heck was the matter with her?

'No harm in it, surely. I missed those cakes.'

'If Dad sees you . . . '

'He's seen me before.'

'That's just it.'

'He still on about Yanks?'

She nodded. 'Worse than ever. You've got to stay away, Chester. Please. For my sake.'

'OK,' he shrugged. 'If that's what you want.'

'I've told you before it is.' She put the rock cakes into the brown paper bag he'd given her. 'Just go.'

'Haven't paid for them yet.'

'Oh . . . it's threepence.'

He was handing over a threepenny bit when her father came into the bakehouse, stopped dead and then rushed at him like an angry bull.

'By God, it's *you*! Showing your face here! I'm going to see you court-martialled for what you've done.'

He backed away from the onslaught. 'I'm sorry, sir. I don't know what you mean.'

'You took advantage of my daughter. You raped her!'

'*Dad*, please . . . '

'Hold your tongue, Sally. That's what he did. Let him deny it, if he dares. Fifteen years old you were. That's against the law in this country. *Fifteen*.'

'He didn't know, Dad. I told him I was eighteen. He didn't know.'

The father snorted in fury. 'You'll be telling me next he doesn't know you're carrying his child.'

Chester saw now why she'd been tugging at the overall and wondered how he could have been so blind. So dumb.

'He doesn't.' She moved between her father and himself and crossed her arms over her swollen stomach. 'And I don't know whose child it is. That's a fact.'

'What do you mean you don't know? You know very well.'

'No, I don't, Dad. I've gone with several Yanks — four of them — and I don't know which one it was. I can't tell, can I?'

Her father raised his hand as though to strike her, and then let it drop. He shook his head, bewildered. 'I don't believe it — a daughter of mine, acting like a whore. I don't believe it.'

She tossed her head at him. 'Well, it's true, Dad. And you can't make me marry all of them.' Over her shoulder, she said to Chester, 'It was never just you, see. You ought to've known that.'

He stared at her and he thought about the way she'd always looked at other guys. He said steadily, 'I still want to marry you, Sally, like I asked you before.'

'I told you, I don't want to get married.'

'What about the baby? You've got to think of the kid.'

'I'm giving it away. Aren't I, Dad? He doesn't want it. I don't want it. Nobody wants it.'

'Well, I sure do.'

'It's not yours to have, Chester. It's mine. And I don't know who the father is. Tell him to go, Dad. Go away and not come back. Ever.'

All the anger had gone out of the poor guy; his shoulders were sagging, his face grey and defeated. He felt real sorry for him.

'You'd better go. Go away, like she said, and don't come back. Go *on*. Before I throw you out.'

'Sally?'

She turned her back on him.

The sheep's bell jangled loudly as he wrenched the door open. In his acute distress, he almost knocked down an old woman with his bike as she was hurrying across the road.

* * *

Miss Cutteridge collected herself and her fallen shopping basket. The young American had ridden past so close that she had had to leap for the pavement. She'd seen him come bursting out of Mr Barnet's, jump on the bike and tear off as though the hounds of hell were after him. From the brief glimpse she'd had of his face, he'd looked very upset and he had scarcely seemed to see her.

She straightened her hat and went to the bakehouse to collect the small tin loaf that Sally always put by for her on a Friday. The young man had left the door open and the bell was still jiggling on its leather strap as she stepped inside. Sally wasn't there, which was unusual, and it was Mr Barnet himself who served her. He looked upset, she thought, just like the young man, and seemed quite distracted too.

'Is Sally well?' she enquired.

He almost snapped at her. 'Perfectly, thank you.'

'I just wondered . . . she's normally here.'

'Well, she's not at the moment. Will there be anything else?'

She didn't like to ask for the stale bread that Sally sometimes put by for her for Porky Pig. 'No, thank you, Mr Barnet.'

She paid for the small tin loaf and walked back to her cottage. It seemed to her that the rumours about Sally must be true, after all. For a time she had persisted in believing that the girl was simply putting on rather a lot of weight, perhaps eating too many of those delicious cakes she made, but the encounter with Mr Barnet had signified some serious trouble. He was always politeness itself with customers; always so anxious to please and give the best service. And then there was the young American rushing off like that. She could remember having seen him before, calling at the bakehouse. If Sally was expecting, as half the village said she was, then, most probably, he was the father. Perhaps he had refused to marry her? That seemed unlikely as he looked a very nice young man, even if he had nearly knocked her down. It was all very shocking, of course, but somehow she seemed to have become quite used to being shocked these days.

She let herself into her cottage and put the fresh loaf away in the bread bin. There was only a little stale bread left which she would mash up for Porky with the last of the potato peelings. Fortunately, Joe would be bringing another bucket of scraps later on, or she would have had nothing else left to give the pig who seemed to have an insatiable appetite. He had grown and grown until he almost filled the shelter, and he had become even more sociable, knowing exactly when to expect her visits. He would trot over to the wire to grunt his welcome and wait for her to scratch his back with a stick. She had never imagined that it would be possible to grow so fond of a pig, just the way she was fond of Ginger, and the time had long passed when he should have ceased to exist. She had put it off again and again. 'You've got to do it, ma'am,' Joe kept telling her. 'You can't keep him for ever.'

'I'll do it next week,' she always said, but when the next week came she couldn't bring herself to send for Mr Ford, the butcher.

She went down to the bottom of the garden and Porky came out of the Anderson and ambled over, grunting. On the way she had found him a windfall apple in the grass and she dropped it over the wire in front of his snout. He crunched it up noisily in a flash and looked up at her with his little eyes, hoping for more. 'You'll have to wait till Joe gets here,' she said. 'He won't be long.'

By late afternoon Joe had still not arrived and it was getting dark and had started to rain. Miss Cutteridge watched the street anxiously from the sitting-room window, waiting for him to come riding along on his old bike with the bucket hooked over the handlebars. She put on her mackintosh and went to feed Porky the last of the stale bread and the few potato peelings. Then she went back indoors, drew the blackout blinds and the curtains, switched on a lamp and sat waiting. It was very unlike Joe to let her down. He always came when he said he would, so something must have happened to him. Her imagination started to paint horror pictures of him lying badly injured in a fall. He was always climbing up telegraph poles — she remembered him telling her so in the very beginning, when he'd first come to tea that day. *You see some guy up a pole, it's me*. Perhaps he'd fallen and nobody knew. He was lying there in the dark, badly injured, all alone and suffering. Perhaps nobody would miss him until it was too late

. . . She stood up and began pacing up and down, wringing her hands.

When she heard the knocker she rushed to the front door and flung it open. Joe stood there in the rain without any waterproof coat, carrying the pig bucket, and she could see at once that something was terribly wrong. She took the bucket from him and set it down on her polished lino floor, and then she grasped his hand and drew him into the sitting room. Made him sit down, not caring about the water dripping all over the sofa or the thick mud that his shoes left on the carpet. 'Joe, dear, what is it? What's happened?'

At first he couldn't answer and she went on holding his cold hand, waiting for him to speak. 'Jack and Frank,' he said at last. 'Both my brothers. Both killed. On the same day. Both gone. They told me earlier.'

He began to sob. Miss Cutteridge put her arms around him and cradled him against her, like a child.

12

'Honoria Vernon-Miller here, Lady Beauchamp.' The romantic Christian name seemed wildly at odds with the stentorian bellow coming down the telephone wire. 'Just been given a piece of news I thought I ought to pass on.'

Erika held the receiver a little further away. 'Yes?'

'Seems we won't be needed up at the King's Thorpe fighter base any more. The American Red Cross have taken that over. Got some brand new mobile canteens, apparently — all fitted out with the latest equipment. No expense spared. They don't need us and our old charabanc any more.'

'I see.'

'The point is, what do we do with the thing? The Americans paid for it but they say we can use it for what we like.'

'That's very nice of them.'

'Huh! Well, you know how fussy they are. Nothing but the best for their boys. Personally, I think we should offer our services to the RAF. Take it round one of our own bomber bases in the area. Tea and buns, not all that coffee and doughnuts nonsense. What do you think, Lady Beauchamp?'

'Yes, I agree, if the RAF do.'

'I'll get on to them at once. See if we can help. I'll come back to you.'

As Erika hung the receiver back on its hook, Miriam came into the study.

'Who was that?'

'Mrs Vernon-Miller.'

'Oh, *her*. Interfering creature. She's always meddling in everything.'

'She actually works very hard.'

'At being a busybody.'

'No, for the WVS. The country needs people like her. She gets on with things and gets things done.'

'So do others but they don't make such a noise about it.'

Here we are arguing again, Erika thought. It won't do. She mustered patience. 'Did you want something, Miriam?'

'Only to talk about Alexander.'

'What about him?'

'The child spends far too much time on his own. Always with his nose in a book. I noticed that most particularly when you were away in London.'

'He loves reading. So did his father.'

'Richard also did other things. Played sports. Mixed with other boys of his own background. Lots of activities.' Erika could see what was coming and it came. 'I really think, Erika, that you should reconsider the whole question of preparatory school. It's not fair to keep the child here for much longer. He should be given the advantages that are his birthright.'

She wanted to say, 'I don't know how you have the nerve to criticize Mrs Vernon-Miller for meddling.' Instead, she said, 'I'll talk to Alex about it, Miriam, and see what he thinks.'

'What he thinks shouldn't be the consideration. He's too young to know what's good for him.'

'He's also too young to be sent away and he's very happy as things are at the moment.'

'He should be making other friends, not among village boys.'

'He has some extremely good friends here. Alfie Hazlet, for example.'

Miriam gave an exaggerated shudder. 'That merely makes my point. Preparatory-school friendships can last a lifetime and be of great benefit. I cannot conceivably imagine a boy like Alfie Hazlet being of any benefit to anyone.'

'Can't you? I can. His brother Tom, too. They're both fine boys.'

'I understand Tom Hazlet was caught stealing eggs recently. Is that really the sort of fine boy you want Alexander associating with? A young criminal?'

'For heaven's sake, Miriam — '

The telephone rang again and Mrs Vernon-Miller barked in her ear. 'Just had a word with one of the chaps at RAF Boxhall. They'd be delighted if we could do them. Tea and buns, like I said. I suggest we tackle it this way.'

The conversation went on, mainly at Mrs Vernon-Miller's end, and by the time it was finished her mother-in-law had given up waiting and left the study. Erika sat for a moment at her desk, wondering about Alex. Miriam's constant dripping was wearing away her defences. Was it really wrong and selfish of her to keep him here?

Was he truly content being at a school with boys who saw his home as 'too different'? The thing to do was to talk it all over with him again. He had a right to be consulted.

The phone rang again and this time it was a soft, deep American voice that was sweet music to her ears.

'Sorry I couldn't call sooner. I've been away down at HQ and there's been no chance. How are you?'

'I'm fine.' She was anything but fine but one didn't say so. Nobody was fine in wartime. Not when you were worried sick about someone; not when you could only be with them for such a cruelly short while.

'I might be able to grab a couple of hours this evening. Can I take you to dinner?'

She could have wept. 'It's my turn in the village canteen. I can't let them down.'

'Sure. Then we'll make it another time. Soon as I can.'

She wanted to ask if he'd been flying combat missions and where, but of course she couldn't do that either. Careless talk costs lives. Be like Dad, keep Mum. Talk Kills. 'Are you all right, Carl?'

'Sure. Everything's OK. I'll call you again soon.'

She hung up the receiver slowly.

* * *

The big Conker Battle always took place around Halloween in Rush Meadow. Not the feeble playground game with the conkers threaded on the end of bits of string but a real war. Dick and Robbie and Seth and their gang against everyone who wasn't in it — each side lined up at opposite ends of the meadow and hurling conkers as hard as they could at each other. The first ones to get all the way across the meadow to the hedge on the other side were the winners. The conkers were collected for weeks beforehand, as soon as they started to fall.

'Where're you going, Tom?'

'To get some more conkers. We haven't got nearly enough.'

'Can I come too?'

'S'pose so.' At least Alfie couldn't eat them. 'I'm taking a stick to knock them down.'

'If I help, can I fight in the Battle too?'

'No, you can't. You have to be over nine. That's the rules.'

When they got to the wood, Tom set about picking up any fallen conkers on the ground and putting them in a sack. Alfie walked around, kicking his boots through the drifts of fallen leaves, making a loud rustling noise; he was wearing his Yank cap with the peak stuck up.

'I thought you were going to help, Alfie.'

'I'm just looking for them.'

'Well, there're none over there.'

'Why not?'

'Because that's an oak you're under. Conkers come from horse chestnuts. You've got to look under the right tree, stupid.'

Alfie kicked his way over and rummaged around. 'I've found one.'

'Put it in the sack, then, and keep looking. We've got to get hundreds of them, 'less you want Dick and his side to win again, like they did last year.' The memory of that shameful defeat still rankled. They'd been driven backwards by the enemy under a nonstop hail of conkers; some of their side had even turned tail and fled, though he'd stood his ground to the last until he'd gone down under a combined assault by Dick, Robbie and Seth and at least ten others. The black eye and bruises had upset Mum no end. He went on searching and the sack grew fuller, but not full enough. Then he started bashing at the branches he could reach with his stick until some more fell down.

'There aren't any left now,' said Alfie, who'd hardly got any.

Tom looked upwards into the tree. 'Yes, there are. There're a whole lot still up there. I'll have to climb up and shake them down.' He hauled himself up onto a lower branch.

'Can I come up, too, Tom?'

'You won't be able to.'

'Yes I will.'

Sometimes Alfie surprised him. Mostly he was hopeless and then he'd suddenly go and do something all right. He jumped up and caught hold of the branch and swung up like a monkey. 'Here I am, see. I told you I could do it.'

'Well be careful. Mum'll kill me if you go and fall off and break something.' Tom climbed up to the next branch and reached out to shake it so that the conkers in their spiky cases rattled to the ground. Then he climbed on up to the next branch, Alfie scrambling behind him. He was shaking away as hard as he could when they suddenly heard voices.

'Who's that, Tom?'

'How should I know?' He waited and watched as a Yank came along with his arm round a woman, stopped right under the horse chestnut tree and started kissing. Just his luck! He flapped his hand to Alfie to tell him to keep quiet. Maybe they'd go away soon. But they didn't. After a bit more kissing the Yank spread his coat on the ground and they lay down. Tom groaned. They'd be there for ages, being soppy and doing things. He'd seen them all over the place in the summer — under the hedges, in cornfields, orchards, haystacks, barns . . . It was mostly the women's fault, he reckoned, the way they chased the Yanks.

'Why're they taking their clothes off?' Alfie whispered.

He didn't feel like trying to explain any of it. 'They're hot.'

'They can't be.' Alfie peered down. 'What're they doing now?'

'He likes her, that's all.' He looked away.

'That's Mrs Honeybun under there, isn't it?'

'Shut up.'

'He's *squashing* her.'

Before he could stop him, Alfie had pulled a prickly conker off a branch and taken aim. It hit the Yank hard on his bare bottom and he yelped and looked up. The woman screamed and started grabbing at her skirt and things.

'Hallo, Mrs Honeybun,' Alfie said, leaning

down. 'I thought it was you.'

'You oughtn't to have done that,' Tom said later on as they were going home dragging a sackful of conkers between them.

'I thought she'd be glad.'

'Well, she wasn't, was she? Nor was the Yank. They thought we were spying on purpose, like Dick and Robbie and the others do. We ought to have waited till they'd gone.'

'But he was squashing her.'

'She didn't mind, stupid.'

Alfie kicked his boots all along a deep gulley of beech leaves, sending them sailing high up into the air in front of him. 'Anyway, we got the conkers, didn't we?'

★ ★ ★

'When's our Yank coming back, Miss?'

'I don't know, Charlie. Get on with your painting.'

'Billy says he's never coming back. He told Joan and made her cry.'

'Billy doesn't know anything about it.'

'He's got to come back for Jessie, hasn't he?'

'Yes, that's what he said he'd do.'

'Then he'll sing some more songs with us, won't he? Yank ones.'

'Yes, I expect so, Charlie.'

'I hope he does. I liked him. Joan says she's going to marry him when she grows up.'

'Get on with your painting now.'

'If he doesn't come, can we keep Jessie?'

'I should think so.'

The Scottie came to school with her every day and the children loved her. They took her out into the playground and with them on Nature Walks, and Jessie let them pat her and hug her and squeeze her. Father had been delighted with her, too. 'I shall be quite sorry when Ed comes back for her, Agnes. Quite sorry.'

If he ever does, she thought. He may never come back again. He could be posted somewhere else, miles away, perhaps not even in Europe. Three hundred hours to a fighter pilot's combat tour. What chance of survival was that? For all she knew he might be dead already. There had been one letter from New York, that was all. It had said very little and it had taken weeks to reach her.

'Please, Miss, I've finished.'

She went over to admire the painting. 'That's very good, Joan. What lovely flowers you've done. We must pin that up on the wall.'

'Can we do 'Yankee-Doodle' later, Miss?'

'If you like.'

They sang it all together, gathered round her.

Yankee-Doodle came to King's Thorpe
Riding on a pony.
Stuck a feather in his cap
And called it macaroni.

Then they did 'Oh, Susannah don't you cry for me' and 'Camptown Races', shouting out the *Doo-da! Doo-da*! bit as loud as they could.

But it wasn't the same without a Yank to sing it with them and to bounce little Joan on his knee.

* * *

'Rang up that fellow in charge up the road,' Brigadier Mapperton said to his wife from behind *The Times* newspaper.

'Who dear?'

'You know, Colonel Whatsisname. The American chap.'

'Schrader.'

'Yes, that's it. Keep forgetting. The memory box isn't what it used to be. Damned odd name for someone on our side, if you ask me, but then they've all got odd names.'

'Not all of them.'

'Well, most of them. They all come from somewhere else, I suppose.'

'What did you want to telephone him for?'

'Couple of complaints, you know. Minor stuff but it's only right to keep him in the picture. Saves any ill feeling.'

'Yes, of course.'

'We've got to fight this war together, so we may as well get on together — that's what I say. I think I've always said that.'

'Oh yes, dear.'

'I asked him over for bridge one evening, as a matter of fact. Thought I'd make up a four: Miss Skinner and Lady Beauchamp — the young one. Don't much care for the old one. Damned fine bridge-player, though. Pity you don't play, Cicily.'

The brigadier turned over a page of the newspaper. He'd tried to teach her years ago, when they were first married, but it had been hopeless. She simply hadn't got a head for cards. 'Anyway, the chap couldn't make it. Apologized and all that, but he's got too much on his plate. Quite understandable, of course. Pity, though. He was quite a reasonable player.'

'Isn't there anybody else you could ask instead?'

'Huh. The rector, I suppose, but he's not much good. No point, really, unless you can have a decent game.'

'I meant one of the Americans. Don't they rather like playing cards? They always seem to in films.'

'You're thinking of those damn Westerns, Cicily. Gambling saloons . . . that sort of thing. That's hardly what I meant.'

'Well, I'm sure some of them must play bridge, besides the colonel. Major Peters, the adjutant, for instance. He was a very nice man and just the type who would.'

'Huh. I'll think about it.' He thought about it as he looked through the newspaper. Perhaps he'd give that adjutant fellow a ring and sound him out. There might be some others up there who played too. Ground officers, not the chaps who had to go off flying. Might be able to make up three or four tables and get a regular evening going. Make it a penny a hundred, say, just to liven things up. Not a bad idea of his at all.

He turned over another page and his eye fell on a piece about the American and Australian attack on the Huon Peninsula. Looked like they were making headway at last. Got a stronghold established there. He'd pinned several Allied flags on his wall map lately, a good many of them the Stars and Stripes. That chap MacArthur wasn't everyone's cup of tea but he'd got the right idea with the Japs. Give it to them with no quarter. Straight for the jugular. No pussyfooting around. And, by God, those American Marines sounded as though they were a pretty hard-bitten bunch. They'd go for Rabaul next, he reckoned. Bomb the port to hell. Then land and take New Britain eventually. He wouldn't say anything to Cicily, of course. No point raising her hopes. He cleared his throat. 'The colonel told me they've got some band coming to play up there next week in one of the hangars. Wanted to know if I thought any of the village would like to go. A chap called Miller, or something. Plays dance music, I gather. Confounded racket, if you ask me, still I said I'd put a notice up about it at the hall. If anyone wants to go, that's their lookout.'

He turned another page.

⋆ ⋆ ⋆

Sam Barnet gave the horse a flick of the whip, not that it made much difference. The old roan was getting on for seventeen and not to be rushed up steep hills. In her young days, when he'd first got her, she'd been in the habit of bolting and he could remember times when he'd had a hard job stopping her and there'd been loaves and cakes scattered all over the road. But, finally, she'd settled down. He ought to have got rid of her by now because she'd become a slow old thing, but she'd served him well over the years, pulling the van on his rounds in all weathers. People knew her as well as they knew the green van with its black lettering on the side: *S. Barnet. High class bakers and confectioners*. It needed repainting now and when the war was over it was one of the first things he was going to have done — soon as there was the paint. Roger would be demobbed and formally joining the business, as planned, and he'd change it to *S. Barnet & Son*.

He'd been the *Son* painted on the side once himself, when the van had belonged to his father. It must be close on sixty years old but, like the horse, it had served him well and he'd seen no good reason to change it for a newer one. He liked the traditional, old-fashioned look of it and the quality of the craftsmanship — the way the trays in the back slid in and out so easily and the doors fitted so well that no rain ever found its way inside. In winter, when it was dark, he'd light candles in the brass lamps on each side to see his way, same as on the coaches in the old days. Sometimes it was so cold on his round that his hands would all but freeze to the reins and the roan's hooves would slip and slide on the ice. There'd been no frosts yet but November was the month of fogs and, sure enough, there'd been one this morning. Not a real thick peasouper, like they sometimes got, but damp, grey, swirling patches of it and enough to have grounded the planes. None of them had come over and as he drew near the top of the hill and the horse clip-clopped along the old Roman road, he could see the shrouded outline of a Mustang out on the airfield, covered by a tarpaulin and pegged down close to a revetment.

He'd left the Americans until last. Delivering to them had always galled him, but, as he'd said to Freda, business was business and they put in regular orders for extra bread and fancy cakes for the Officers' Mess. Paid well for them, too. One thing about them, they didn't quibble about any bill. He drove on past the main gates to the woods on the other side of the road where the Messes were located. In the RAF days they'd been nothing more than shabby tin huts, but the Yanks had smartened them up and built onto them so that they were scarcely recognizable. He took the van round to the back of the Officers' Mess, unloaded the delivery into baskets and carried it in through the stores entrance. When he came out again he found a Yank waiting by the van with his bike.

'Can I speak with you please, sir?'

He slung the baskets into the back and shut the doors. 'I've nothing to say to you.'

'I know that, sir. But I wanted to tell you something.'

He turned round to face the young man. A sergeant: he noticed that for the first time. Not a badlooking sort. A lot tidier than most of them and respectful.

'What is it, then?'

'I wanted you to know that I love Sally and I want to marry her. If you'll let me.'

Sam stared at him. There was no doubt that

the lad was serious and meant it. He could tell that from his face.

'She won't marry you. Or anyone. Refuses to, point-blank. There's nothing I, or you, or anybody else can do to make her. That's all.'

'You sure about that, sir?'

'Quite sure.' The lad looked miserable and Sam, who'd felt such rage and bitterness against him, couldn't find it in his heart to feel it any more. He'd liked the way the boy looked at him, straight in the eye. Man to man. Facing up to things. And he liked the way he'd sought him out, never mind the consequences. He'd failed the same way himself when he'd been young, after all — let temptation get the better of him with Sally's mother. He knew all about how hard it was to resist a lovely young girl. And who could ever know if this one was the father? If what Sally had said was true, there were three other possibilities. Nobody would ever know whose it was, and yet this one still wanted to marry her. He went round to the front, climbed up on the box and took hold of the reins. The lad went on standing there forlornly, beside his bike. Sam said in a gentler tone, 'I'd forget all about her, if I was you, son. Just forget all about her.'

He flicked the whip and drove the van away. The old horse, knowing that it was the end of the round, picked up speed almost to a trot. He steadied her down the hill, the van jolting and rattling over all the potholes and rough patches made by the endless procession of American trucks and jeeps. The encounter had upset him all over again. He felt worn out by the whole business and by keeping up the pretence that everything was normal. It had made him careless with the baking, short with customers, sensitive to every look and every word. Tongues would have wagged and the whole village must know by now of their disgrace, though nobody had said so to him outright. Another month and Mother Becket and the rest like her would be tut-tutting openly and turning down their vinegary mouths at him, while others sniggered behind their hands. The name of Barnet, painted so proudly on his van, would be pointed at and mocked. What would Roger think about it when he came home? He was like his mother in so many ways — never fussed too much about things. Easy-going. He could hear him saying, 'What does it matter, Dad? There's more important things to worry about these days.' To him, it did matter, though. Families still counted. The unbroken, legitimate line was still worth something. Pride. Decency. Standards. Service. He clung to all that in a world where everything seemed to have gone topsy-turvy.

They reached the bottom of the hill and the horse clattered round the bend under the railway bridge, faster still as she sensed the closeness of home, the stable and her hay-net. She turned into the yard beside the bakehouse without him telling her and stood still for him to unhitch the van and to take off the harness. Then she walked straight into her stable and started snatching at the hay with her long yellow teeth. He closed and bolted the door and went into the house through the back door.

Freda and Sally were standing in the kitchen, side by side and facing him. He saw that they'd both been weeping and that Sally had an arm round her mother's shoulders, and he wondered wearily what on earth had happened now. Then he saw the yellow telegram in Freda's hand.

* * *

'That American gentleman's here again, milady. Shall I show him in here?'

'No, thank you, Doris. I'll come out.'

That American gentleman was standing in the hall, cap in hand, and when he turned and smiled at her she had to stop herself from walking straight into his arms. Doris was still hovering.

'Hallo, Carl. How nice to see you.'

'Any time spare to take another country tour?' he asked. 'The car's outside.'

'Yes, of course. I shan't be long, Doris.'

She grabbed her coat from the hall chair. He opened the front door for her and then the car passenger door. She sat at a careful distance from him. Doris would almost certainly be spying on them from a window.

'Where shall we go?'

'Anywhere,' she said. 'Anywhere.' All that mattered was being with him.

'I think I said that last time.'

'I remember.'

He took the same turning he'd taken on that other drive and they ended up at the same spot as before, overlooking the wooded valley. He switched off the engine and reached for her.

Later, he said quietly, 'Do you have any idea how much I love you, Erika?'

'Yes, I do.' She smiled at him. 'As much as I love you.'

'I want to talk about us and what we're going to do about it.'

'No, don't let's talk about the future, Carl.'

'But we ought to, sweetheart. Because I'm not going to give you up.'

'Let's leave it for now, though. It's better. Please.' She clung to him, burying her face in his chest; the metal wings were cold against her cheek. He held her close, stroking her hair.

'I guess I'll have to get back. I'm sorry.'

'Not your fault.'

On the way, she stared out of the window and thought of his wife, Jan, and the little girl, Kathy, waiting patiently for him to come home, and how hard a man like Carl would find it to let them down; and how she could never ask it of him.

She could see Miriam peering out of her bedroom window as they drove up to the Manor. Another confrontation. Another argument.

'Don't come in,' she said. 'Don't even get out. Just drive off straight away.'

'I can't do that.'

'Please, Carl.'

He hesitated. 'OK, if that's the way you want it.'

Her throat had tightened up and she had to

swallow hard before she could speak again. 'Yes, that's the way.' She laid her hand on his sleeve — only for a second — and got out of the car. At the front door she turned for just one more look at him, and then went inside.

13

There had been so much rain lately and the ground was so wet and boggy that instead of cutting across the fields, Tom took the road up to the base. It had great tracks of mud all along it from the Yanks' comings and goings and he had to keep hopping from one side to the other. If Alfie had been with him he'd've trodden straight in it, but this time he'd given him the slip and left him behind. As well as the four loaves in the sack over his shoulder, there were half a dozen letters for Yanks from people in the village stuffed into his pockets. He charged a farthing a time to deliver them, each way, and an extra farthing to the Yanks if it was one where he had to hang about so he wasn't seen handing it over — to someone like Mrs Honeybun who'd been under the conker tree.

He gave a wave to the sentry, and went straight round to the radio shack. More mud everywhere on the concrete pathways and great oozing lakes of it where it'd been grass before. He jumped over a big puddle and opened the door to the shack.

They looked up from the workbenches, grinning at him. 'Hi, there, Tom. How'ya doin'?'

'Great.' He'd learned quite a lot of the lingo now and he could speak more or less the way they spoke.

'What've you got for us, kiddo?'

He unhooked the sack from over his shoulder and brought out the tin loaves. 'Here's the bread, like you asked for, and some letters. There's one for Dan and one for Russ. The rest're for other guys.'

Dan and Russ got a lot of whistling and leg-pulling about girls, though he knew the letters were only asking them down to a Sunday roast. Most houses in the village had a Yank they asked to things. It was a lot different from the beginning when nobody'd wanted them.

'Have some toast, kid.'

'Gee, thanks.'

They got the stove stoked up and the bread toasting away. There was a nice warm fug in the shack and Tom sat on the crate near the stove and ate toast and peanut butter, just like the first time he'd been there.

'How's that kid brother of yours?'

'He's OK.'

'Bring him with you next time, he's real cute. Bring your little sister too, if she's growed any.'

They always laughed about Nell but he didn't mind.

'Captain Mochetti's back, you hear that, Tom?' Mitch said. 'Saw him this morning.'

His heart lifted. 'Are you sure?'

'Yeah, saw him with my own eyes. Back doin' another tour here. The guy's plumb crazy.'

Mum'd be pleased, and not just for the washing. She'd always liked Ed. Alfie'd be pleased, too, but probably just for the candy and the gum. He didn't mind about the candy and the gum, himself. He just minded about Ed

— that he'd come back.

He finished the toast.

'You want some more, kid?'

He had one more slice before he went on his way. They chucked him over two Hershey bars at the door. 'One for you and one for your brother. You come back soon, kiddo.'

He took the letters for the other guys round to the Yank post office and left them there. They knew him there now and one of them gave him a packet of Wrigleys. As he was coming out, Chester came up on his bike and stopped.

'Hey, Tom, you still taking letters to the village?'

'Sure.'

'Can you take this for me? It's for Sally.'

'Sure.'

'What's the charge?'

He hesitated. Everybody was gossiping about Sally. 'Do I just give it to her, or is it a secret?'

'You can just give it to her straight.'

'It costs a farthing, then.'

Chester paid him. 'Well, I guess I won't be seeing you any more, Tom. I'm being transferred out of here.'

He was very sorry about that. 'I hope you come back.'

'Yeah, maybe one day — after the war.' He got back on the bike. 'Well, so long, kid. It's been swell knowing you. Good luck.'

'Good luck, Chester.'

He stood and waved as he rode away.

'Ed's back, Mum,' he said when he got home. 'They told me up at the base.' She was scrubbing shirts on the washboard in the dolly tub and he saw by the way her face lit up that she was as pleased about the news as he was. 'That's nice, Tom. I didn't think we'd ever see him again.'

He told Alfie and he was pleased too.

'He'll come and see us, won't he, Tom? Bring some more washing?'

' 'spect so.'

'I hope he brings some more sweets.'

Just as he'd thought. 'The Yanks in the radio shack gave me a Hershey bar for you.' He handed it over. 'I don't know why they did, though.'

Alfie looked smug. 'Cos they liked me.'

* * *

'How's your dad now, Sal?'

'He's better.'

'Been really poorly, hasn't he? Must have been if you had to close the bakehouse for all that time.'

It had been a big mistake to let Doris in. She was as nosy as the rest. They'd shut the door against the lot of them while Dad had been ill, except for the rector and Dr Graham who'd both been ever so kind. They'd been kind about the baby, too — not a bit like the cow of a district nurse who'd told her she should be thoroughly ashamed of herself. 'Your father will be all right,' Dr Graham had said. 'He just needs time to get over things and get his strength back.' She wasn't sure if Dad would ever get over Roger being killed in action, though. Mum wasn't sure, either. She didn't think any of them would. He'd been the best brother anyone could have and she knew he wouldn't have minded about the baby.

'He's all right now,' she told Doris firmly. 'And I don't want to talk about it.'

'I was ever so sorry about Roger, Sal. Everybody was.'

'I don't want to talk about that either.' She could see by Doris's disappointed face that both those things were exactly what she'd come to talk about. 'What've you been up to, then?'

'Nothing much. Just working at the Manor, same as usual.' Doris brightened up. 'You know what, one of the Yanks is after young Lady B.'

'Well, they would be, wouldn't they? She's beautiful.'

'He's a colonel. I think he's the one who's head of it all up there, so he must be very important. He's not exactly handsome, but he's ever so attractive, if you know what I mean. Sort of like Humphrey Bogart. He makes me go wobbly at the knees when I open the door to him. And he's got a lovely smile.'

'How do you know he's sweet on her?'

'Well, he's been round to the Manor and taken her out in a car. I've watched them go off alone together and I've seen the way he looks at her, and how she looks at him. You can tell, can't you? They don't have to say anything. Only trouble is, I think he might be married because he's got a ring on his left hand. Still, I expect it happens a lot with the Yanks when their wives are so far away.'

'How's Hal?'

'Well, *he's* not married, if that's what you're wondering.'

'Has he asked you yet?'

Doris pulled a face. 'No. I'd say yes, quick as anything. I've been going to the dances at the Aeroclub and we do a lot of snogging outside, but that's all. I don't think he wants to settle down, that's the trouble.'

'Maybe the trouble is he doesn't love you.'

Doris looked hurt. 'Well, I've been very nice to him.'

'That's got nothing to do with it. I wasn't very nice to Chester.'

'No, you weren't, were you? Poor Chester, I used to feel really sorry for him. He thought the world of you. I expect he still does. Did he ever find out about the baby?'

'He came to the bakehouse and Dad went for him about it.'

'*Sal*! That must have been awful. And he'd've known straight away it'd be his.'

'He thought it was for a bit. Then I said I'd been with some other Yanks, too. Four of them, I said, and it could be any of them. I didn't know which one.'

Doris gasped. 'What did you go and say such a dreadful thing for? It's not true.'

'So Chester couldn't be sure it was his and so Dad couldn't try to make me marry him, like they both wanted.'

'Whatever did your dad think about it?'

'He thinks I'm a whore. That's what he said.'

'No wonder he got ill. What with that and then

Roger getting killed. Do you know what happened?'

'I told you, I don't want to talk about Roger.'

'Sorry. Have you seen Chester since?'

'Not since then. He's stayed away, like I told him to do. Tom Hazlet brought me a letter from him the other day. He said he'd asked to be transferred and they were sending him away somewhere else.'

'So that's that, then. You'll never see him again. That's so sad, Sal. He was ever so nice. And he'll never see his baby. I think he'd've been a lovely father.'

'Be quiet, Doris. I don't want to talk about it.'

'You don't want to talk about anything.' Doris looked resentful. 'It's not the same any more.'

'No, it isn't,' she said. 'I'm sorry but it never will be.'

* * *

It was kind of weird to be back. A trip through time again to Merry Olde Englande. Not so merry these days and now that he took a long, hard look after spending time in the US he could see how badly battle-scarred the old country was and how weary. On her knees after five years of war. From the train window he saw people in the back streets of bomb-scarred towns looking like ragged scarecrows, thin kids staring up with pale, unhealthy faces. He wondered what would have happened if the Yanks hadn't joined the party. OK, they'd been late, but they'd got there in the end.

But, boy, was he glad to be back. That was the other weird part of it. Any guy in his senses would have thanked his lucky stars to have been home, stateside, away from it all, but, as Ben had told him, he was nuts. His family had thought he was nuts, as well, and there'd been a whole lot of weeping and wailing and hand-wringing about it, Italian style, with most of the folks in the neighbourhood joining in. They'd all made a real big fuss of him, as though he'd been winning the war single-handed, and he'd eaten like a king, and drunk like one. Must've put on pounds. When he'd had a moment to himself, he'd called Ben's family in LA and spoken to his mother. He'd tried to say something that might help but she could hardly speak for crying.

At the end of his leave, he'd got roped in by the Air Force to do some talks to people who wanted to hear the US was winning the war in Europe and to see some guy who'd just been over there, doing it. He'd spoken at bond drives and scrap drives and to kids in school saving defense stamps and he'd done visits to aircraft factories and told the workers there what a great job they were doing.

And, all the time, he'd thought of Agnes: kept on seeing her face and hearing her voice, even when he was with other girls.

When he'd finally arrived back he'd almost gone straight round to the rectory before he'd stopped himself. No change in the rules that he could see. His second tour hadn't even begun and the war wasn't over by a long shot. He could still hear the sound of Ben's mother sobbing.

He took a bag of laundry down to Mrs Hazlet, driving the jeep fast down the hill, skidding round under the railroad bridge and on into the village. The high street was just as he'd left it. Still the same beautiful old stone houses, the butcher's, the baker's, the grocer's, the candy store. Still some old woman tottering slowly across the street, getting in his way. One or two people waved at him and he waved back. They hadn't done that at the beginning — or not those sort of waves. Goddamit, he thought, grinning to himself, it's like coming home.

Tom's mother looked real pleased to see him too, so pleased she gave him a hug and a kiss on the cheek. Nell had grown big and was running around. He picked her up and gave her a kiss and some candy.

'Tom and Alfie are at school, Ed, but they'll be out in the playground just now.'

'I'll swing by there. See if I can see them.'

He drove down the high street and turned into School Lane. The kids were out in the playground — girls in one half, boys in the other, separated by a mesh fence. The girls were playing nice quiet games like skipping and hopscotch; the boys running around yelling and fighting. He stopped the jeep and got out and looked through the railings. Alfie saw him first and came tearing over, beaming all over his face.

'Hallo, Ed. We heard you were back.'

'Hi there, kid.' He tossed him a pack of Wrigleys through the bars. Some of the others started crowding round. 'Got any more gum, mister?' 'Sorry, guys. Next time.'

‘We won the Conker Battle,’ Alfie said, chewing away. ‘Tom and me and our side.’

‘That’s great.’ He’d no idea what a Conker Battle was, but it sounded important.

‘Robbie and Dick and Seth and all their gang ran away.’

‘Good for you, kid. I’d take you on my side any day.’

He looked round for Tom and saw him coming over, kind of shy and dragging his feet. ‘Hi, Tom. Good to see you.’

‘Hi, Ed.’

‘You OK?’

‘Sure.’

He was tickled to hear the way the kid could speak American now. ‘Got a brand new P-51 Tom. A new Bashful. You coming up to the base to take a look soon?’

‘Gee, thanks . . . that’d be great.’

‘You do that. Don’t forget.’ He searched the playground. ‘Are the kindergarten kids out here?’

Tom shook his head. ‘They don’t let them out the same time as us, case we knock them down. They’re indoors.’

‘Well, I’ll just go by there and say hello. See you guys later.’

He went in through the gateway and walked round to peek through the window. They were all in there, sitting at the little tables, busy painting pictures, and Agnes was leaning over helping one of them. He saw Jessie lying nearby, her head on her paws. Charlie, who was fooling about painting his fingers blue, caught sight of him. He watched him run up to Agnes and she turned around. By the time he'd got to the classroom door and opened it they were all there, waiting. They gathered round him, jumping up and down and squealing like a litter of piglets while Jessie bounded about, barking. Little Joan tugged at the sleeve of his A2 and he bent down and swung her up high into the air so that she squealed louder still.

Agnes had stayed standing just where she was. He looked at her over Joan's chubby arms which were wound tightly round his neck.

'Hallo, Miss,' he said.

* * *

The smell of pork roasting was delicious. Miss Cutteridge sniffed the air appreciatively and her mouth watered. Roast leg of pork with crisp crackling, roast potatoes, apple sauce and winter cabbage, steamed the quick way advised in the *Kitchen Front* recipe book, rather than Brussels sprouts because she knew Joe hated those.

She had laid the table in the dining room in honour of this very special Sunday lunch: a celebration of Joe's twentieth birthday. The best dinner service — and she didn't care if any of it got broken — the solid silver knives and forks, all polished up, and the double damask table napkins. She had put her present for him beside his place and dressed in her best day dress, with her pearls and her mother's cameo brooch.

She opened the oven door again to baste the joint. If it had been Porky Pig, she would never have been able to cook, much less eat, any part of him. But this wasn't him. This was some unknown pig that she had never met in her life and so it was quite a different matter. Joe had found the solution to the terrible dilemma. 'See here, ma'am,' he'd said on one of his visits. 'You can't keep Porky here for ever. Sooner or later he's got to go and the way I figure's best is for you to give him over to the butcher and ask him to give you another one, already slaughtered in his place. Get him to come round when you're out and that way you won't have to see Porky go, or anything like that.'

She'd had a word with Mr Ford and he'd been most understanding. 'Don't you worry, Miss Cutteridge, you just leave it to me and don't think about it any more. I'll bring you a nice joint of pork and some for you to keep. As much as you can manage.' He was such a nice man that she felt that all the poor animals who passed through his hands would be kindly dealt with. He had come round on the day she had taken the train into Peterborough to visit the dentist and when she had come back, there had been a leg of pork in the larder and a side all salted down in the scullery. She had walked down the garden to the empty Anderson shelter and wept for Porky Pig but it had been for the best.

She checked the oven again and turned the potatoes. The cabbage would only take ten minutes with the *Kitchen Front* method and everything would be ready on time. Back in the sitting room, she glanced at her reflection in the glass above the mantelpiece. She saw the face of an old woman, to be sure, but one who looked lively. Happy, one could say.

But something was missing — she could feel that in her bones. Something she had not done that she should have. She searched her mind and then, suddenly, knew what it was. William's photograph should be present at this celebration. She took it out of the drawer and set it on top of the bureau. 'You would have liked Joe, William,' she said. 'You would have approved of him very much.' It looked rather dusty and so she went to fetch a cloth and was just giving the frame an extra polish when there was a knock at the door. Joe was a little early but that didn't matter. She was quite ready.

It wasn't Joe; it was Tom Hazlet, holding out a letter. She thanked him and went and sat down to read it. She had a little difficulty with the writing.

Dear Miss Cutteridge,

I'm real sorry I can't come to lunch today for my birthday. They're sending some of us from the Signal Company overseas to help fix things up for the guys fighting over there. They never told us nothing till today so I couldn't let you know before or get down to say goodbye, like I wanted. I'm real sad about that.

I hope you enjoy the roast pork, now it's not Porky Pig.

Thank you for everything you've done for me. I won't ever forget it. It was like another home for me. Maybe I'll get back one day when the war's ended to see you again.

love from,

Joe

Miss Cutteridge put her hand up to her eyes.

14

Christmas Eve wasn't a Friday but Mum had got the tin bath down from its hook, dragged it in front of the range where it was warmer and filled it up from the copper and the buckets. The water was steaming away and she was giving Alfie an extra scrubbing and he was making a really silly fuss about it. Mum wasn't taking any notice, though. 'I'm not having you going all dirty, Alfie, so you may as well keep still.' More howls and splashes and scrubbing noises. When it came to his turn the water'd be worse than soup. Mum had washed and starched their surplices and ironed them so there wasn't a single crease. She put Alfie's on over his cassock and brushed his hair flat. His face was all clean and shining. Mum said he looked like an angel, which made Tom retch.

He didn't know why they'd let Alfie in the choir in the first place. He never sat still in church and kept blowing dried peas across at Seth and Robbie and Dick with the pea-shooter Tom had stupidly made him out of a bit of elderwood. He never ought to have done that. Miss Hooper was always saying his voice was one of the best she'd ever heard which was just the sort of thing that nobody ought ever to say to Alfie either.

Tom got into the lukewarm soup, washed himself quickly with the Yank soap and got out again. It was going to be a special Christmas; he could feel it. For a start the church choir were singing at the Yanks' carol service. The whole village had been invited and afterwards there was going to be a big party for everyone: a real feast. Only, Dad wasn't home because he was too busy with another airfield. As Mum said, the war didn't stop just because it was Christmas. She couldn't afford to buy them presents, but that hadn't mattered because the radio-shack Yanks had given him and Alfie a great big box all wrapped up in red paper and when they'd opened it they'd found bars of chocolate and candy and two oranges and two bananas. Of course, Alfie had eaten his banana straight away and he'd had to hide the box from him or he'd've scoffed the lot before Christmas had even started.

Best of all, Ed had come down in the jeep — not with washing but with presents he'd brought back from America. Very special thin stockings for Mum and a lipstick which had made her so pleased she'd cried. Nell had been given a soppy doll but Alfie had got a toy Cadillac car in a cardboard box with a picture of it on the outside. It was made of shiny green metal with rubber wheels that went round, doors that opened and shut and a steering wheel that moved. He'd been really envious until Ed had given him *his* present in another box: a wooden model kit for a Mustang, just like Ed's, and he'd promised he'd help him make it. They were going to paint it with Ed's letters on it and the name Bashful.

There was a thick fog outside and the trucks they'd sent down to collect people went grinding very slowly back up the hill in a long convoy to the base cinema where the service was being held. The choir were all together in one truck and when they got there the Yank padre took them into a room at the back where they formed up for the procession. Of course Alfie had got his surplice creased already and there was a dirty mark down the front, and his hair had curled up again. *And* he'd got something in his mouth.

'What're you chewing?'

'Black Jack,' Alfie mumbled.

'Let's see. Open your mouth.'

Alfie did, but shut it again so fast that Tom couldn't see inside properly to know by the colour if he was telling the truth. More likely he'd found the box the radio-shack Yanks had given them and pinched something out of it.

'Well, hurry up and finish it. You're starting in a minute.'

Alfie had been chosen to do the solo at the beginning of the service and he sang the first verse of the first carol from the doorway.

Once in royal David's city
Stood a lowly cattle shed,
Where a Mother laid her baby
In a manger for his bed . . .

He was holding a lighted candle and looking all goody-goody, like he never ever did a single thing bad or wrong, and everyone had gone very quiet while they were listening to him. Then the organ joined in and so did everybody else for the rest of the carol. The choir walked slowly down the middle aisle between the rows and rows of Yanks and the villagers, and up onto the stage where there was the biggest and brightest Christmas tree that Tom had ever seen in all his life. There were so many people squashed into the hall that when they were supposed to sit down there weren't enough chairs. The padre said the prayers and the Yanks read the lessons, except for the final one which they'd let Brigadier Mapperton do, and the rector gave the blessing at the end. The very last carol was 'O come all ye faithful' and everyone roared it out so loud, Yanks and villagers together, that Tom couldn't hear himself singing. Some people were smiling and some people were crying. He could see the tears trickling down their faces. Women were always crying but he'd never seen men cry before.

* * *

Carl could see Erika across the packed room, but he couldn't get to her. A woman with a voice like a foghorn off Nantucket had him pinned in a corner while she went on about mobile canteens. He could vaguely remember meeting her before.

'That's very interesting, Mrs . . . ?'

She gave another blast in his ear. 'Vernon-Miller. We've met twice before, Colonel.'

'Of course, I'm so sorry.'

'As I was saying — '

He interrupted her firmly. 'I wonder if you'd

excuse me for a moment, I rather wanted a word with Lady Beauchamp over there.'

'That's a coincidence, so do I. I'll come with you.'

It was near the end of the evening before he had the chance to speak to Erika alone.

'It's been wonderful, Carl,' she said. 'The carol service and then the party. The children are having the Christmas of their lives. You Yanks are incredibly generous. All that marvellous food . . . I expect Alex will be sick as a dog when we get home.'

'I sure hope not. That wasn't exactly the idea.' He met her eyes. 'You know, I thought I was never going to get to talk to you. How are you?'

'All the better for seeing you. How are you?'

'The same applies. I've missed you like hell.'

'Ditto. Don't look at me like that, or people will wonder why.'

'Don't smile at me like that either, or they won't wonder for long. Erika, I've got to see you again soon — '

'Careful,' she warned. 'Brigadier Mapperton is coming up fast on your port side.'

'Oh, Christ . . . ' With an effort, he turned round politely. 'Hallo there, Brigadier. Good to see you.'

* * *

Agnes watched Father Christmas giving out presents to the village children after the feast, sitting them on his knee and making them laugh. Santa Claus, the Americans called him, but it was all the same to the English children. She knew perfectly well who it was under the snow-white locks and bushy eyebrows and long beard, dressed up in the bright red costume; knew it easily by the way he was with them and by the way they clustered round him. He delved once more into the sack and came out with yet another present. 'Ho, ho, ho. This says Miss on it, kids. Who's Miss? I don't know any Miss.' 'She's there,' they chorused, pointing. 'That's Miss.' 'Where? I don't see her.' '*Over there*!' they yelled, dragging him across to where she was standing, and jumping up and down with excitement.

He put the present into her hands. 'Merry Christmas, Miss.' His false whiskers tickled her face and the children shrieked in delight as he kissed her.

* * *

Alfie felt sick on the way back in the truck.

'Serves you right,' Tom said. 'You shouldn't've eaten so much.'

'I couldn't help it.'

'Yes, you could. You had three helpings of everything.'

'I was hungry. Anyway, I sang all right for them, didn't I? A Red Cross lady said I sounded like something from heaven. She said I made her cry.'

'I'll be sick as well in a minute.'

Luckily they were sitting at the back of the truck so if Alfie *was* sick he could do it over the tailgate and not over everyone else. Tom thought about the carol service and all the singing, and the great Christmas tree with its hundreds of coloured electric lights and the grown-ups smiling and crying. And the big feast they'd had after with the roast turkey and the jelly and ice cream. And the presents. Of course, he'd known all along that Father Christmas was Ed, who'd given him a huge wink, but he hadn't said anything, specially not to Alfie or he'd've told everyone.

He'd known it was going to be special and it was being the best Christmas he'd ever had. So special he felt like crying too. He wondered if he'd ever have one like it again.

* * *

Sam Barnet was raking out the ashes from the bottom of the bakehouse furnace and shovelling them into the bucket. He wouldn't be baking in the morning but the furnace would have to be lit just the same so the oven was ready to roast the Christmas dinners. Threepence a time he charged people, and sometimes he wondered if it was worth it for all the work. He carried the ashes out into the yard and groped around in the fog for some coal and wood. The Yank lorries were making a din, bringing everyone back from the carol service and the Christmas party. He'd never wanted to go but Freda would have done if Sally's labour pains hadn't started. They'd come a lot earlier than expected and they'd been going on for nearly four hours. He could hear Sally groaning and shrieking out, even from the bakehouse. Freda was up there with her, and the district nurse, and Dr Graham had been sent for. Supposing there was something wrong and Sally was in danger? He'd been hard on her, he knew that. She'd behaved like a trollop and brought shame on the family, but the thought of losing his daughter as well as his son was unbearable.

He laid the furnace fire, ready to put a match to, swept the floor clean, and put things tidy. Then, when there was nothing left to be done, he went through into the kitchen and put the kettle on. Freda had been boiling hot water for the doctor and he might as well get some more ready in case it was needed. He sat down at the table and, just as he did so, there was another shriek from Sally: more than a shriek, a loud and terrible scream of agony that horrified him. And it went on and on until he clapped his hands over his ears in distress. He couldn't remember Freda going through anything like that when Roger and Sally had been born. When, at last, he took his hands away there was silence and in the silence he could hear the church clock striking midnight. As the twelfth note faded away there was another sound — the full-lunged, furious yell of a baby protesting at being thrust into the world.

Sam ran to the foot of the stairs and stood waiting, his heart thumping hard. After what seemed to him a very long time, Dr Graham came down the stairs and put a hand on his shoulder.

'Congratulations, Sam. You've got a fine healthy grandson.'

His voice was croaky: 'Is Sally all right?'

'Yes, don't worry. It wasn't an easy birth and she's very tired, but she'll recover quickly. The nurse will take care of things and I'll be back again in the morning.'

'Thank you, doctor.'

The doctor paused at the door. He said with a smile: 'A pretty good Christmas present, Sam, I'd say. Just what I'd order for you. You're a lucky fellow.'

He went back to the foot of the stairs and presently Freda came down, carrying a bundle in her arms. 'I thought you'd like to see him.'

He stared down at the tiny face, nestled in the lumpy woollen shawl that Freda had knitted. 'He's got blue eyes, just like that Yank.'

'All babies have blue eyes to start with. They might turn brown later, like yours. I think he looks a bit like you, Sam.'

He couldn't see any resemblance to himself at all. Freda held out the bundle. 'Would you like to hold him?'

He backed off instantly, shaking his head. 'When's Sally going to have him adopted, then?'

'She's got to look after him herself for a bit, hasn't she, poor little mite? She can't give him away just yet.'

'The sooner the better, I reckon,' he said. 'Best all round.'

* * *

'What is it, Doris?'

'If you please, there's an American officer at the door.'

Miriam said sharply, 'What does he want?'

'He didn't say, milady. He just asked to speak to Lady Beauchamp.'

'Well, which one of us did he mean?'

Doris looked at Erika. 'I think he must have meant your ladyship. But it's not the colonel. It's a major.'

'You'd better show him in here, Doris.'

'Very well, milady.'

'Another of your American admirers, I suppose, Erika. You seem to attract them like flies.'

She ignored her mother-in-law and waited, her eyes fixed on the drawing-room door. When Major Peters walked in she rose to her feet. He looked directly, and only, at her and she knew by his face what he had come to tell her. She listened without flinching to his words. Deep regret . . . Colonel Schrader . . . leading the Group in a vital attack . . . flying at low level . . . enemy ground fire . . . too low to parachute . . . no chance . . . no hope. So very, very sorry.

'Thank you for coming to tell me, Major.'

'He asked me to do so, Lady Beauchamp. If it ever happened.'

'Thank you.'

'I suppose they'll have to get a replacement,' Miriam said when Major Peters had left. 'I wonder if he'll play bridge.'

* * *

Alex put his head round her bedroom door. 'I heard you crying, Mummy. What's the matter?'

'I'm sad because Colonel Schrader has been killed.'

He came into the room over to the window seat where she was sitting. 'He was a nice man, wasn't he?'

'Yes, he was very nice.'

'Did you like him a lot?'

'Yes, I did.'

'More than Daddy?'

'No, not more than Daddy. In a different way.'

'I've got a clean handkerchief, if you want it.'

She took it and wiped her face and blew her nose. 'Thanks, darling.'

'Are you OK now, Mummy?'

'Yes, of course. Perfectly.'

'I've been thinking about what you asked me — whether I wanted to go away to boarding school.'

'And what did you think?'

'Well, I think I'd quite like to next year. Would that be all right?'

'If that's what you really want to do. You won't get homesick?'

'I might at first, but I think I'll be OK. Daddy liked it there, didn't he?'

'Yes, he did. He loved his schooldays.'

'Then I expect I would, because I'm rather like him, aren't I?'

'Yes, you are, darling. Very like him. I shouldn't say anything to Granny about this just yet. We'll keep it a secret between ourselves for the moment, shall we?'

'I wasn't going to anyway. Are you sure you're all right?'

'Quite sure. You run along now.'

At the door he said, 'I'm very sorry about Colonel Schrader. I expect you'll miss him a lot, won't you?'

She tried to speak normally in answer, but luckily he had gone.

15

It snowed hard early in January. The rector, arriving for the first Parochial Church Council meeting of the New Year, found the temperature of the parish room barely above freezing. There were radiators, of course, but no coal to run them and only one paraffin stove to provide any warmth. He lit it, but without much hope of it having any real effect other than to create an unpleasant smell.

The meeting was timed, as usual, for six o'clock in the evening. The blackout blinds were already drawn and so he had been able to switch on the lights immediately and prepare things. He had dragged a trestle table into the centre of the room and was flapping at the dust on it with his handkerchief when the outside door opened and Sam Barnet came in, muffled up in overcoat, scarf, cap and gloves. Invariably early and invariably the first.

'Evening, Rector. I'll give you a hand with the chairs.'

'Thank you so much, Mr Barnet.'

He was looking better, the rector thought. He had been very concerned for him during his illness. Overwork, together with the tragic loss of his only son and the unfortunate business with Sally had taken a great toll, but he appeared to have rallied; to have recovered his strength and his customary dignity. The rector would have liked to raise the question of the baby's baptism, but thought it best not. Sally seemed determined to have him adopted and the matter would soon be out of his hands. The baker helped him move the chairs into position and no sooner was that done than the other Council members began to arrive: Miss Cutteridge, Miss Skinner, Mr Wells, Mr and Mrs Dakin, Miss Hooper, Mr Rate, Brigadier Mapperton, Lady Beauchamp. They were all clad in heavy winter clothing and nobody, except for Miss Cutteridge who removed her gloves to hold her shorthand pencil, took off a single garment.

The rector bowed his head and began with the prayer: his customary appeal for peace and harmony. 'Oh Lord, we ask Thy blessing upon this meeting. Give us Thy guidance in all our deliberations and grant us the wisdom and understanding to work together so that we may serve Thee faithfully and truly here on Earth. Through Jesus Christ our Lord. Amen.' As he spoke he could see his breath clouding the icy air.

He read out the apology for absence from Mr Hobbs who was in bed with influenza. Nobody seemed very sorry either about the absence or the influenza, unless he was imagining it. The minutes of the previous meeting were read and approved after Brigadier Mapperton had pointed out one or two small inaccuracies and they had been corrected. The first items on the agenda were plain sailing. The King's Thorpe Brownies had raised one pound three shillings and fourpence carol-singing at Christmas and this was to be spent on comforts for the elderly poor in the parish. Miss Cutteridge and Lady Beauchamp undertook to buy and distribute suitable gifts. The rector noticed how wan both those ladies looked and wondered if they, too, were going down with influenza. There was a great deal of it about. The second and third items passed without difficulty but the fourth — repairs to the organ bellows — was more tricky. The estimate was for twenty-six pounds ten shillings, and the organ fund stood at fourteen pounds eleven shillings and fivepence. 'Either the work's done, or I can't play,' Miss Hooper announced. 'Can't we use some of the other money?'

'Unfortunately, there is still the question of the dry rot.'

'Dry rot? What dry rot, Rector? I thought that was all done and finished with.'

Mr Rate leaned forward. 'We've found some more, Miss Hooper. I was about to report that officially to the Council in the next item.'

Brigadier Mapperton shifted ominously. 'Keeping yourself in business, eh?'

'I find that remark very offensive, Brigadier. If you will recall, I was asked at the last meeting to check the overall condition of the church fabric and timbers. In doing so, I discovered another area in a corner of the chancel roof where there are clear signs of some dry rot. As you are all aware, this should be dealt with at the first possible opportunity, before it spreads.'

The rector said quickly, 'Yes, indeed, Mr Rate. We're very grateful to you for your vigilance.

Have you an estimate of the cost?'

The builder laid a sheet of paper on the table. 'Forty-five pounds. And I've cut that to the bone.'

'Are there sufficient funds to meet that, Mr Wells?'

'Fortunately, yes. Just. The credit balance stands at a little over fifty pounds, at present.'

Brigadier Mapperton raised a hand. 'Just a moment. We should get another estimate. Ask Prescott's what they'd charge. Got to do the thing properly. All above board.'

'I don't know what you mean by above board, Brigadier. I can assure you that there has never been anything below board about my firm in all the fifty years we've been in business. On the last occasion when you insisted on an alternative estimate from Prescott's it was considerably higher than mine. I'm confident that the same would apply in this case. Any work I do for the parish is always carried out at the lowest possible rate — at some financial sacrifice to myself, I might add.'

'You mean you overcharge everyone else?'

Mercifully, Miss Hooper interrupted. 'Blow the dry rot! What about my organ, that's what I want to know.'

The rector said soothingly, 'It looks as though the balance needed for that will have to be raised by other means. Has anyone any suggestions, please.'

They discussed jumble sales and bring-and-buys and concerts at the village hall with Miss Hooper at the piano. Brigadier Mapperton's suggestion of rattling tins round the village was given consideration. 'Nothing wrong with a straightforward approach, in my view. I'll start the ball rolling myself: give them something to rattle. No good having a church without an organ.'

Item five concerned the damaged transept window. 'You will remember the Americans' offer to pay for its replacement.'

'I should damn well think so. They broke it.'

'Quite so, Brigadier. Though it was never actually proved, of course, and may have been sheer coincidence.'

'Stuff and nonsense, Rector. The fellow was flying far too low.'

He cleared his throat. 'The original stained glass is irreplaceable, of course, and, in any case, so far we have been unable to find a craftsman to carry out the work of creating a new window.'

'You can't find anybody to do anything these days,' Miss Skinner said. 'Hopeless.'

'Indeed. However, since our last meeting I have received a very substantial cheque donated by all the Americans who have attended some of our church services, taken part in our various village activities and come into our homes over the past year. They have particularly requested that it should be spent on the damaged window. We now have a chance to create something rather special in our old church. Not, I would think, until the war is over and such peacetime work can be undertaken once again. But, if you have any suggestions as to what would be appropriate, perhaps we could discuss this now so that I can give our benefactors some idea of what will, eventually, be done with their generous donation.'

Thea Dakin lifted her hand. 'If I may speak, Rector?'

'Yes, of course, Mrs Dakin.'

'I heard about this gift — Mr Wells just happened to mention it when I met him at the post-office counter — and in my prayers I have been asking God exactly what sort of new window should we create? It seems to me that this is a great responsibility. It should be something special, as you rightly say, Rector. Something uplifting. Something commemorative of this time for those that come after us to see and appreciate.' The rector waited anxiously. God had a habit of answering Mrs Dakin's prayers with controversial edicts; the argument over the Lady chapel had continued for three more meetings before it had finally died a death. She went on, with her eyes shining. 'My prayers were answered. God spoke to me quite clearly.' The brigadier muttered something but she took no notice. 'He told me that we should create a window for our American airmen here at King's Thorpe. A memorial stained-glass window to give thanks for their valour and their sacrifice in our common fight against evil. That's what He told me. And that's what I believe we should do.'

The rector held his breath for the broadside that would surely come from Brigadier Mapperton. To his complete astonishment the brigadier held his fire. 'Humph. Maybe not such a bad idea, especially since they're paying for it.

They've been doing a pretty fine job. Credit where credit's due. I've always said that.'

They all agreed: not a single voice was raised against Mrs Dakin. The rector, who had already thought of the same idea himself, rather than direct from God, but had hardly dared suggest it, gave an inward sigh of relief.

* * *

She was crossing the rectory hall when she heard a vehicle crunching through the snow up the drive. By the sound of its engine, she knew it was an American jeep. And she knew who it was before she opened the front door. He stamped the snow off his feet onto the mat and brushed it off the sleeves of his sheepskin jacket. 'Jeez . . . it's kind of cool out. Real icy. Thought I was going in the ditch on the way down, once or twice. I brought your father a New Year's present.' He handed over a brown paper bag.

'It feels like a bottle of something.'

'Sure is. Sherry. I thought he'd like it.'

'Thank you, Ed. He'll like it a lot. We ran out months ago. How on earth do you get hold of such things?'

'Ways and means.'

'I'm sorry he's not here at the moment. He's in the Parochial Church Council meeting.'

'It wasn't just him I came to see.'

'Oh.' She put the bottle on the hall table. 'Well, would you like to come into the kitchen? It's the warmest place in the house. The *only* warm place, in fact.'

He shed his jacket and cap and followed her down the passageway. 'There's something good cooking.'

'Sausage casserole. Will you stay to supper with us?'

'I can't eat your food.'

'There's plenty.'

'Well, if you're sure.'

'I am. How's Jessie?'

'Just fine. She usually goes everywhere with me, but I left her behind this time.'

'Thank you for the chocolates, Ed.'

'What chocolates?'

'From Father Christmas.'

'He gave you chocolates? What a guy!'

'The box is beautiful and the chocolates look much too good to eat.'

'Hey, listen, you've got to eat them. That's what they're for.'

'Anyway, thank you.'

'Don't thank me. Thank Santa Claus.'

'I knew perfectly well it was you.'

'You quite sure? I bet all us Yanks sound the same to you.'

She shook her head. 'No, you don't. Not a bit. And I'd know you anywhere.'

'That so?' He put his hands on her shoulders and looked down at her. 'I'm crazy about you, Miss, do you know that? Have been all along.'

'Oh, Ed . . . ' She was half-laughing, half-crying. 'I've been crazy about you all along as well.'

He smiled slowly. 'I kind of hoped you had. Do you reckon you could take a chance on my making it through the war OK?'

'I'd take any chance with you.'

He pulled her into his arms. 'Those goddam whiskers sure got in the way.'

* * *

At the end of the meeting, the rector bowed his head in prayer. 'Oh Lord, we thank Thee for Thy heavenly guidance. As we stand at the gate of a new year, we ask that we may be given strength in all our endeavours. We thank Thee for the year that has passed: for the victories achieved by the Allies against our enemies. We pray for all soldiers, sailors and airmen, and especially the American airmen of King's Thorpe, that they may be given courage to continue the fight until the world is free once more. And we ask that the souls of all those who have sacrificed their lives for us may rest in eternal peace.'

It was far too cold to linger for long in the hall. The brigadier paused briefly for a word. 'Not the usual damfool idea Mrs Dakin comes up with, Rector. Military theme. Honouring the fallen. All that sort of thing. Perfectly sound tradition. Better than a lot of angels or that Mary woman. I thought she was going to bring her up again.'

Miss Cutteridge was the last to leave. He thought, again, that she looked rather unwell. 'Are you feeling all right, Miss Cutteridge? Not going down with this nasty influenza, I hope.'

'I'm quite all right, thank you.'

He persisted a little, out of concern for her. 'You don't quite seem your usual self.'

'I've been a little down in the mouth lately but I'm much better now.'

'Is it anything I can help with?'

'Oh, no. It's nothing. Really nothing.' She smiled brightly at him as she tugged on her gloves. 'We must all soldier on, mustn't we, Rector? Life has to go on, come what may.'

'Yes, indeed. God will give us the courage.' He held the blackout curtain aside for her as she slipped out into the snowy night. When he had turned off the oil heater and switched off the lights, he went through into the house. Agnes would be in the kitchen, cooking supper. He went down the passageway, opened the door and stopped dead when he saw his daughter locked in the arms of a Yank. He shut it quietly again, smiling to himself, and tiptoed away.

In the hall he caught sight of the paper bag on the table beside Ed's battered cap and peered inside. Tio Pepe! What a treat! He carried the bottle into his study, found a glass and poured out a generous measure. The fire was out and the room damp and chill but he scarcely noticed. Two good happenings in one day: the memorial window and now Agnes and Ed. Cause for real celebration. Of course, it meant that he would lose her, after all, but he couldn't do so to a better man. He had decided that when the war was over it would be time for him to retire and give way to somebody younger and stronger with new ideas for the parish. A new broom. Life, as Miss Cutteridge had so accurately said, had to go on. He would find a small cottage in the village and settle down to do some of the things he'd never had time for — leisurely reading, some writing, water-colour painting, gardening — while still helping in the parish if his help was needed. And perhaps even paying visits to America.

He sat down in his chair, raised his glass to the future and drank.

* * *

'How did the meeting go, Erika?'

She sat down opposite her mother-in-law beside the drawing-room fire. 'Rather more smoothly than usual. The brigadier and Mr Rate had their usual spat, but otherwise everyone agreed on most things.'

'That's a change. In Geoffrey's day they used to fight like dogs over bones.'

She held out her hands to the flames, thawing them. 'The Americans sent a huge cheque to replace the transept window as soon as we can, after the war. They collected money from almost everyone at the base.'

'They think that money solves everything.'

She ignored the remark. 'It's been decided to make the new window a memorial to the American fighter group here.'

'In our church! I suppose they insisted on it.'

'As a matter of fact, they didn't. They didn't ask for anything. Thea Dakin suggested it.'

'She would. She has some extraordinary ideas. I think she's definitely loopy.'

'We all agreed on the proposal. Unanimously.'

'Surely Brigadier Mapperton opposed it?'

'No, he was all in favour.'

'Quite extraordinary. I should have expected *you* to agree, Erika, knowing your predilection for Americans, but scarcely him.'

'He's changed his views considerably. Did you know that he holds a regular bridge evening at his house for a number of officers from the base? Mrs Mapperton was telling me about it the other day.'

Miriam sat up very straight. 'No, I did not. He might have had the courtesy to invite us.'

'It's men only, I understand. Not a social occasion. They play for money.'

'I must say, I'm surprised at the brigadier. I didn't know he was a gambling man.'

'Hardly. A penny a hundred.'

'It's still gambling. Look what happened to the Beauchamp fortunes as a result of it. I hope you'll bring Alexander up to avoid making any kind of wager.'

'I don't think we need to worry about Alex; he's got his head screwed on all right. By the way, he's told me that he'd like to go away to boarding school in September. It was his own choice entirely.'

'Thank heavens for that! I'm delighted to hear it.'

'I knew you would be. And when he goes, I'll go back to London.'

'Whatever for?'

'With any luck the war will be over by then. I'd like to find something that I can do in life other than making sandwiches and pouring teas — useful though that has been. I can't find it here in King's Thorpe.' She drew back from the fire. 'And besides, let's both face it, Miriam, you and I have never exactly seen eye to eye. You'll be glad to see the back of me.'

There was a moment's silence before her mother-in-law spoke again and she was astounded to hear a break in her voice. 'As a matter of fact, I won't, Erika. It will be extremely lonely without you.'

'I'll try to come back when I can, and Alex can spend at least part of his holidays here with you. If you'd like that.'

Miriam had collected herself rapidly. 'That would be appreciated.' She cleared her throat and looked at her wristwatch. 'It's high time dinner was ready.'

Erika stood up. 'I'll go and chase Mrs Woods.'

'Erika . . . '

'Yes?'

Another pause. 'I was actually very sorry about Colonel Schrader. I want you to know that. He was a fine man and I believe he meant a great deal to you. You have my sympathy.'

She went over to her mother-in-law and bent to kiss her cheek. Something she had very seldom done. 'Thank you, Miriam.'

* * *

Sam Barnet trudged home through the snow, his overcoat collar turned up about his ears, his knitted scarf — another of Freda's attempts — wound round his neck. He'd given his vote to the memorial window when the last thing he wanted was to be reminded of any of the Yanks. But he prided himself on being a fair man. The Americans had earned it, so far as he could see, and the war wasn't finished yet. There'd be a lot more of them dying before that happened, on all fronts.

Instead of going straight into the house, he turned into the yard to check on the horse. The narrow torch beam showed her contentedly munching hay in her stable. He bolted the top half of the door shut again and swung the torch over the van safely under cover in its shed beside the stable; and stiffened. Someone had scrawled in white chalk on the side. *S. Barnet & Bastard*, it now read. He found a rag and rubbed out the addition furiously. At the back door he knocked the snow from his boots and dragged them off before he padded in his socks into the sitting room. Freda wasn't there but he heard a sound from the corner and saw that she'd brought the rocker down. He went over quietly and stood looking down at his bastard grandson who was stirring in his sleep, waving his small fists around. He bent a little closer. He still couldn't see any likeness to himself, though Freda kept saying there was. As far as he was concerned, the child looked just like that Yank.

Freda whispered behind him, 'Sally's gone to the pictures with Doris. I brought him downstairs so I could keep a good eye on him.'

He grunted. 'She oughtn't to have gone off and left him.'

'She's very young, Sam. It's good for her to

have a bit of time to herself.'

'Well, she'll have plenty of time soon enough, when he's gone.' He went on staring at the child who was peacefully asleep again. 'What's she going to call him? He's got to have a name.'

'She doesn't know. I thought of Robert — your father's name. Robert Samuel. After you both.'

'Not much point in that, is there?'

She touched his arm. 'We can't let him go, can we, Sam? Our own flesh and blood?'

'He's the flesh and blood of some Yank too. Whichever of the four it was.'

'There were never four of them. Sally told me that. She just made them up. There weren't any others at all. Just that nice young Chester. He's the father and he was a good lad.'

'Supposing he gets to know about it? Supposing he comes back?'

'I don't think he ever will. They've transferred him somewhere else, Sally says. He'll go back to America when the war's finished and he'll marry some other girl and forget all about what happened here. That's the best way.'

'What about Sally? She never wanted to keep it.'

'We'll look after him, Sam. You and I. We'll let Sally go off and do what she wants and we'll take care of him. I've talked to her about it and she doesn't mind. I think she's glad. Relieved. She felt bad about giving him away.'

The baby must have heard them talking because he stirred again and opened his eyes. Sam bent for another look. They looked a bit darker, he thought. As though they might be changing colour, after all.

Freda said, 'You can pick him up, if you like. I'll need to change him and give him a bottle.'

He lifted the child very gingerly and held him awkwardly in his arms, wrapped in Freda's shawl. Robert Samuel. The sixth generation of Barnets. The baby waved a fist at him and he could have sworn it smiled.

'We'll keep him, won't we, Sam?'

He nodded.

* * *

'Stop wriggling, Alfie.'

'I'm cold.'

'Put your socks on.'

'They are. I've got all my clothes on and I'm still cold. It's freezing.'

'Well, keep still, I'm trying to think.'

'What about?'

'How to make some money for Mum. The tin's almost empty again.'

'Steal some more eggs.'

'I can't do that any more. I promised her. Don't know what I can do.' Tom blew out the candle and lay back in the darkness. He was cold, too, even though they'd got Dad's old topcoat spread over the blanket.

'I've thought of something, Tom.'

Alfie's ideas were always useless. 'What, then?'

'Lucky rabbits' feet. Like you did for Ed. Get that old witch in the forest to do her spell over them and then sell them to the Yank pilots. They like having lucky things.'

He considered it carefully, and honestly. 'I don't know that she does proper spells. She might have been pretending.'

'She must do. Ed's all right, isn't he? And I'll bet he always will be. Ben didn't have one and look what happened to him — and all those others. It's a brilliant idea of mine.'

'Mmm.' It never did to let Alfie get above himself. Tom debated the possibility some more. Getting the rabbits' feet was no problem. He'd just set three snares in the snow by the big warren at Gipping Wood that dusk. There could be three rabbits caught in them when he went over first thing in the morning. Three times four was twelve. Twelve feet in one day. The witch had charged ninepence to do one, but maybe he could make some sort of deal with her: say sixpence each — six shillings for a job lot of twelve rabbits' feet and he'd have to pay her later. Then he could sell them for a shilling and make a big profit. Six shillings out of three rabbits. There were at least a hundred and fifty pilots up at the base and Alfie was quite right about them liking lucky charms. Of course, it would mean going back to the witch again, several times over, but he'd do it for Mum — like he'd done it for Ed.

He said offhandedly, 'It might work. I'll think about it.' And the more he did think, the better he liked it. 'I'm going over to see if I've caught any, soon as it's light in the morning.' He paused and added generously, and against all his better instincts, 'You can come too, if you like.'

But there was no answer. Alfie was sound asleep.

THE END